ANNABEL ABBS

FRIEDA

THE ORIGINAL
LADY
CHATTERLEY

TWO
ROADS

First published in Great Britain in 2018 by Two Roads
An imprint of John Murray Press
An Hachette UK company

This paperback edition first published in 2019

1

Copyright © Annabel Abbs 2018

A CIP catalogue record for this title is available from the British Library

Paperback ISBN 978 1 473 68102 6
eBook ISBN 978 1 473 68103 3
Audio Digital Download ISBN 978 1 529 31955 2

Printed and bound in Great Britain by Clays Ltd, Elcograf S.p.A.

Hodder & Stoughton policy is to use papers that are natural, renewable
and recyclable products and made from wood grown in sustainable
forests. The logging and manufacturing processes are expected to
conform to the environmental regulations of the country of origin.

Hodder & Stoughton Ltd
Carmelite House
50 Victoria Embankment
London EC4Y 0DZ

www.tworoadsbooks.com

To my daughter, Imogen
Who is, and always has been,
utterly and wholly herself

'You know I would have died for you.'

Ernest Weekley, Letter to Frieda Weekley, 1912

'My love for you will live as before, and more strongly than before, and should you return, even after many years – and should my hope be alive or dead – you know, I am yours.'

Otto Gross, Letter to Frieda Weekley, 1907

'If she left me I do not think I would be alive six months hence . . . God, how I love her and the agony of it.'

D.H. Lawrence, Letter to Edward Garnett, 1912

PART ONE

Nottingham 1907

'Nothing is so bad for a woman as she
gets on in life as the feeling that she's
missed something: perhaps the most
important thing . . . It is a dreadful
feeling, to feel you're going to die without
having had what you were born for.'

D.H. Lawrence, *The First Lady Chatterley*

ONE

Frieda

Later, after the scandal had broken and the newspapers had turned her into a pariah, she traced it all back to a particular day. A particular moment. Sometimes the moment spun dizzyingly before her, everything coming into focus in a single frame. Thirteen years of marriage and three perfect children condensed into a single image. And she wondered how something so vast could spring from such an uneventful moment.

The day had started with such excitement. A sky flushed pink, the silver birches bursting into leaf, the grass and leaves spangled with heavy dew, a glimmer of yellow where the first celandines were thrusting through the black earth. The children had torn round the house shrieking 'Aunt Nusch is coming all the way from Berlin.' Monty had jumped up and down on the sofa, Elsa had draped strings of purple beads over her shoulders, and even Barby had banged her spoon on the breakfast table, shouting 'Nusch comin'.'

Mrs Babbit spent the morning scrubbing, polishing, dusting. Monty and Barby picked primroses and bluebells which Elsa arranged in jam jars. Frieda baked *Apfelkuchen*, lavishly dusting its cratered surface with cinnamon and icing sugar. Even Ernest, who rarely left his study, roamed the house dabbing at the coal dust settling on the sills, and prodding at the paint flaking from the skirting boards.

By early afternoon, as Nusch was due to arrive, the weather changed. Rain began slicing at the window with a spitting sound and the sky seemed to split in two, one half sagging with cloud and the other a pale milky blue. Ernest went to meet Nusch at the station, waving his tightly rolled umbrella as he left and calling out 'Prepare to be dazzled by her jewels!' And he'd shaded his eyes with his hand in a theatrical gesture, making everyone laugh and giving Frieda a dim feeling of pride.

The image that etched itself on Frieda's mind forever came an hour later. Nusch dismounted from the trap, holding her skirts high enough to display the fine lace hem of her petticoat and her costly leather boots with their carved heels and pearl buttons. After brushing the dust and grit from her travel suit, she looked up at the narrow house with its plain brickwork, its pinched front door, its cramped little garden and said, 'Oh, you poor, poor dear!' Frieda opened her mouth to protest, but then decided against it and led the way into the hall, talking cheerfully about their plans for Nusch's visit: a ramble in Sherwood Forest, a tour of Newstead Abbey, a peek at Wollaton Hall.

As she held herself tight against the wall, so that Ernest could pass with Nusch's trunk, she heard something that made her pause. It was Nusch, nose tilted, sniffing extravagantly at the air. As if she had a cold or a touch of influenza. Then she made a faint gagging sound in her throat and plunged her gloved hand into her reticule, pulling out a handkerchief and pressing it hard against her mouth.

'The children have picked wildflowers for you,' Frieda said. Even as she spoke she knew her home had disgusted Nusch, that all the primroses of Nottingham couldn't disguise the dogged reek of boiled bones and kitchen gas. She gestured to the drawing room, but in that split second she saw it through Nusch's eyes: cotton curtains eked out with a mismatched border, paint blistering on the walls, the frosted light-shade stippled with grime. Even her embroidered cushion covers – roses and lilies in vermilion and ivory – looked amateur and crude.

Nusch surveyed the room, her upper lip twitching, her brows arched. She lifted her skirts as she swayed across the room, as if rodents or fleas might scramble from the balding rug. Then she scrutinised the sofa and wiped at it with her handkerchief before perching, carefully, on its edge. Her gaze flickered round the room again, pausing at the slouch of rising damp, the meagre fireplace, Ernest's framed certificates hanging in proud lines on the wall.

'You should never have married so far beneath us. The impudence of that man . . .'

Frieda was about to defend Ernest when she caught a glimpse of herself in the mirror that hung above the hearth: her hair caught in a straggled bun, a streak of cinnamon on her forehead, rouge-less cheeks that had lost their youthful contours, a tight smile stuck to her mouth. Why hadn't she wiped her face? Why hadn't she pinned her hair elegantly, with the little painted combs Ernest bought her when they married? And the plaid dress with the collar that griped her neck like a noose – too tight after three children, old-fashioned, the shapeless skirt without any drop left in the fabric. She should have spent less time baking and more time on her appearance.

She turned to the door with relief as the children tumbled in, flinging raindrops from their hats and from the sodden hems of their clothes.

'Take your coats off and dry your hair. Aunt Nusch doesn't want to be soaked by you.' She spoke brightly, shooing them out with a too-careless flap of her wrists. 'They are so excited that you have finally come to see us, dearest Nusch. They have hundreds of questions about their little cousin. If only you could have brought her.'

5

Nusch gave a short laugh. 'One should never mix travel and children, a fatal combination.' She leaned forward and dropped her voice a fraction. 'I have not had a single appreciative look since I stepped off the boat. What is wrong with English men?'

'They are reserved and you are too used to military men. But I have something much nicer for you: a cake I baked myself.' Frieda wished Mrs Babbit would hurry up with the tea. A generous slice of cake would give her the strength to ignore her sister's jibes, she thought, the insides of her mouth moistening in anticipation.

'The children look charming, even with all that wet hair. Far too charming to be the spawn of Ernest.' Nusch stood up and smoothed at her skirts, and it struck Frieda that her sister's clothes flounced too much and fitted too well; the immaculate travelling suit was too new, the buttons too shiny, the egret feathers too lustrous. None of it looked right in her tawdry little home.

Later, after Ida had taken the children away and Mrs Babbit had served tea and left the room, Nusch cleared her throat. 'All the most modern ladies in Berlin and Munich are having affairs.' She lowered her eyes and peered coyly into her teacup. 'I know we are baronesses but we must be seductive or we are nothing at all. And I have no intention of being nothing.'

'But you aren't nothing. And you have everything,' said Frieda, bewildered.

'Oh, I'm not thinking of myself. Anyway, we von Richthofens are not made for boring lives. It simply doesn't suit us.'

Frieda felt a pain inside, as if a metal belt had tightened sharply round her chest. 'My life's not boring,' she said, gesturing at the window with an arm that seemed suddenly stiff and heavy. The children were playing in the garden and she wanted to tell Nusch how happy they made her. But a thin small voice had crept into her head and its impatient drone was distracting her: Boring, boring, boring. Nothing, nothing, nothing.

'You should go and visit Elisabeth in Munich. The cafés are full of anarchists and artists discussing free love, and she is at the very heart of it. I prefer military men but I think you would like it. You always were a little radical.' Nusch paused, staring narrowly at the rings scuffling on her fingers. 'Do you remember how you used to pee against the pear trees in Father's orchard? You used to cock your leg like a dog. Shameless!'

Frieda put a large forkful of cake into her mouth and tried to think of an appropriate retort. But Nusch had settled herself against the cushions and was talking of the past again. 'I never understood why you didn't die when Father hurled you into that lake. Do you remember? He used to leap off that wobbly bridge with you clinging to him like a monkey . . . And all those naked soldiers bathing there!' Her pencilled brows waggled up and down. 'Mother kept forbidding him from doing it. But he took no notice. Did you actually like it? Or were you just placating the old rogue?'

'Hush! I was just a child.'

'He was so desperate for you to be a boy. I do believe he thought he could turn you into one, the old fool!' Nusch plucked the napkin from her lap and tossed it onto the table. 'And now here you are. A happy little wife in England!'

She stretched and yawned. Frieda pushed her *Apfelkuchen* round the plate, watching it collapse into a mass of yellow crumbs and apple chunks. When the door clicked sharply in the silence and Ernest appeared – stooped and bowed with a thin strand of pale hair over his eyes – she felt an unexpected relief.

'Nusch wants me to visit Elisabeth in Munich.'

'Before motherhood turns her into a complete bore.' Nusch gave a coquettish wiggle of her shoulders and the diamond drops at her ears shot a flurry of light across the table.

Ernest nodded placidly. 'Why not? Mrs Babbit and I can manage and Ida can look after the children.'

'But won't you come with me, my dear?' Frieda reached for Ernest's hand. It felt cold and papery and she wished he would let Mrs Babbit light the fire in his study. He was so frugal, so hard on himself. 'We could attend one of Elisabeth's salons and see some Munich theatre. You've not had a holiday since I met you.'

He shook his head vigorously. 'I'm far too busy. Go on your own.'

'On my own?' She felt a prick of anxious excitement. She hadn't left the children before but Monty was seven now, Elsa was five and Barby was three. Could she? She glanced at her sister. Nusch was staring coolly at her, head cocked neatly, like a cat observing a mouse.

'Yes, Frieda. Come back to us, before it is too late.'

'The etymological properties of lateness . . . yes, most intriguing.' Ernest paused and stroked his moustache with his thumb. 'Debatable whether the word comes originally from the Latin, *lassus*, meaning weary or exhausted, or from the Germanic or even the Middle Dutch, *laat*, meaning lazy and sluggish. And then of course there is the Greek word, *ledein*.'

'I think lazy and sluggish will do for now.' Nusch gave a snort of laughter, her fingers prodding at the ivory combs pinning up her sleek golden hair.

'It is not so easy when you have three children. You only have one, so you wouldn't know.' Frieda turned away, stung. The window panes had started their nervy rattling as darts of rain splintered against the glass. 'But perhaps I will go to Munich alone.' As she spoke she felt a tiny flare of defiance, infinitesimal but unmistakable. 'Yes, perhaps I will . . .'

TWO

Frieda

The following day, Nusch announced her intention to return early to Berlin. She and Frieda were walking home across the fields, a favourite route of Frieda's because of the amethyst orchids that appeared every spring. Nusch disliked the mud, fretting over her kid boots and her silk stockings. And instead of admiring the orchids, she kept her eyes fixed on the horizon, a dark sullen line of smoke and steam and pit fumes.

'You've only just arrived,' Frieda said, hurt and confused. 'I had trips planned. England is so beautiful in the spring, the blossom and the new leaves and the lambs.'

'Yes, yes, but my lover wants me back. We can hardly bear to be parted at the moment.' Nusch smirked, one hand fluttering demurely at her throat. It struck Frieda that this was the real reason for Nusch's visit. Not to see her. Or the children. But to crow about her lover.

'We meet every afternoon, in his curtained carriage, and we drive up and down Unter den Linden, until we're quite exhausted. He's so passionate, so in love with me. I'm sure all of Berlin have heard our cries of pleasure.' Nusch gave a quick trim shake of her head, then lowered her voice and added, 'He likes me on top.'

Frieda thought of Ernest in the spare bedroom, lying rigid in the narrow guest bed with its scanty mattress and the Bible he kept beneath the pillow. How easily, how softly he'd slipped away. She wriggled too much, she breathed too noisily, her weight made the mattress dip. And now that he had so many mouths to feed, he needed his sleep. And so he'd slunk off to sleep alone. But she wouldn't tell Nusch that. Nor would she tell Nusch that she had never been *on top*. No, she wouldn't give her little sister that satisfaction.

Besides, she loved the early mornings when the children poured into her room, bouncing on the bed, burrowing beneath the covers, begging for a story or a pillow fight. That wouldn't have happened with Ernest in the bed.

A vicarious curiosity gripped her. 'Surely Elisabeth doesn't have a lover?'

'Of course she does! Oh you poor dear. You have no idea, do you? She has the most extraordinary lover, renowned in Munich, apparently. They practise free love. No curtained carriage for them!'

'W-what?' Frieda felt her jaw fall open. Elisabeth, one of the first women in Germany to go to university, to get a doctorate, to have a man's job, now married to the sober, bespectacled Edgar. No – this was too much. Nusch was lying.

'Munich is a hotbed of free love. Elisabeth is quite a convert.'

'So what do these *converts* do?' Frieda felt her face flush with shock, a flush that travelled down her throat and into her dress until every inch of her body felt hot and rosy.

'They share lovers. Nothing furtive. All out in the open, with anyone they want! Personally I like the frisson of something a little more illicit.' Nusch looked at Frieda from beneath her lashes. 'Doesn't it tempt you? Ernest is such a dry old stick.'

'I thought Elisabeth was busy with her suffragettes and her two houses and her salons and spending Edgar's mountains of money,' said Frieda, indignantly. All of a sudden she didn't want to hear any more about *free love* or her sisters' paramours.

'Yes, she's busy with the Bund Deutscher Frauenvereine but she still has time for pleasure. You'll meet her lover if you go to Munich. It's worth going just to see him.' She stopped and sniffed, in the same exaggerated way she'd sniffed at Frieda's hall. 'What is that ghastly smell?'

'The wind is blowing from the factories today. It could be ammonia or sulphur or the ash pits or perhaps the cattle market. But look at the trees,' Frieda pitched her head upwards, at the dusty catkins and the tiny leaves unfurling like miniature green parasols. 'Aren't they marvellous?'

Nusch put her handkerchief to her nose and fanned at the air with her fingers. 'Elisabeth doesn't understand why you don't hold a salon. She holds one every week, either in Munich or Heidelberg. I attended one last month, Max and Albert Weber spoke and afterwards the room erupted into such a buzz of excitement I could barely hear my own thoughts. You would have loved it.' She lowered her handkerchief and sniffed cautiously. 'Has she written to you about the Weber brothers? Max is a genius and has quite a following now. Elisabeth says his ideas will change the world. She says all the most exciting ideas are coming from Munich or Heidelberg now. England is quite finished, apparently.'

Frieda tried to still her mind by looking at the violets and dandelions bursting through the verges, at the crunchy white blossom on the blackthorn thickets, at the birds cutting and twisting in the sky. It was the only way to *endure*: focus solely on the beauty around her and let her sister's voice fall away to nothing. But all she could see was Nusch in her curtained carriage, her velvet skirts hitched to her waist. Or Elisabeth in the swirl of her salon, presiding over the animated discussion of great men.

'Yes, she writes often of Max Weber and his books and essays,' she said flatly. But never of free love, she thought.

11

'He and his brother, Albert, kept me up all night, talking about mixing the intellectual and the erotic. I didn't understand a word but they defer to Elisabeth on everything. She says her salons are creating a new age of freedom.' Nusch coughed loudly and batted at the grainy air. 'Couldn't you try a salon?'

'There is no one I could invite – we don't have philosophers or poets in Nottingham,' Frieda replied. 'We live quietly here.' Too quietly, she thought. And her sister's words of the previous day tolled in her head: *boring . . . nothing . . . before it is too late.*

'Elisabeth and Edgar discuss the works of Tolstoy, every night that she's not with her lover. Apparently they are working through his entire oeuvre. Couldn't you and Ernest do the same? He must discuss books with his students, so why can't he discuss them with you?'

Frieda sighed. She had tried, of course. She had tried to discuss Shakespeare and Stendhal and all the other writers she read during her solitary evenings. She had tried to share her fascination with the characters, their feelings and dilemmas. But Ernest either began lecturing her on the *forms* of literature or correcting her grammar. Eventually he'd stopped bothering, disappearing to his study instead, and she'd felt a sense of relief.

'He is too busy preparing his seminal book on etymology,' she replied, her eyes on the ground.

'Your life gives me the creeps, you poor dear.' Nusch gave a visible shudder, then a relieved laugh. 'Thank goodness I'll be back in Berlin for the weekend!'

Later that night Frieda slid into Monty's bed, wrapping her arms around him and breathing in his smell of wet buds and soap. She stared into the darkness and wondered what it was like to be an admired salon hostess in Munich. She closed her eyes, pictured herself there. The crush of voices and laughter. The press of bodies. The clink and clatter of glasses. The crystal bowls of fruit punch. The bright flames of sundry lamps burning long into the night. And herself, clothed in dazzling silks with scarlet poppies in her hair, at the epicentre of an impassioned debate on the future of literature. A tingle swept up her spine.

The morning after Nusch's departure Frieda flung open all the doors and windows, pushing back the curtains as far as they would go and holding doors in place with stacks of books. The light poured in and the sharp April air gusted through the house, blowing hats from the hatstand and sending Ernest's papers billowing down the hall. When Elsa asked what she was doing, Frieda replied, 'I want to feel spring rushing through the house. I had forgotten how it feels.'

'But it's dirty!' protested Elsa.

And as Frieda chased after Ernest's papers, she called back 'So do not tell Papa!'

THREE

Monty

'Mutti, what's a Hun?' Monty spoke in a whisper. He didn't want anyone to hear and the Mikado Café was very busy with ladies and gentlemen at every table, and waiters and waitresses running to and fro with cake stands and silver trays of tea and coffee.

'A what, my love?' His mother lifted her head from her book. She'd been reading a lot recently, ever since his Aunt Nusch left, a week ago.

'A Hun. Is it like a nun?' Monty reached for another scone and then began picking out the lumps of strawberry from a pot of jam and arranging them in neat circles on his scone.

'The Huns were a tribe of warriors. Very fierce and very ugly.'

'Is Barby called Barby because she's a Bar-barbarian?' He rearranged the strawberry lumps into a tight whorl and reached for the bowl of cream.

'Barby is short for Barbara and it is nothing to do with barbarian. Is someone teasing you at school?'

Monty shook his head quickly. He didn't want to tell her about the big boys who called him a Hun, how they'd jostled him and taken his satchel and thrown it so high it had burst open and all his books and papers had come fluttering from the sky like dying leaves.

'You should be proud to be half-German. We have produced some of the best minds in the world, like this.' She showed him the cover of her book. It was a story about a man called Zarathustra. But it had no pictures and looked very dull.

'Why do people stare at us when we speak German?'

'Oh my dear.' She put her book down and poured herself another cup of coffee from the silver coffee pot with the twirly lid. 'Germany wants an empire now. But the English think only they should have an empire. They think we Germans are getting too big, too important. English people only like themselves.' She dropped a cube of sugar into her coffee and stirred it slowly.

Monty chewed and frowned and tried to make sense of his mother's words. 'Is that why you have no friends?'

She looked at him but said nothing. Monty wished she would laugh. He liked it when she laughed so hard the curls tumbled from her hairpins and the gold flecks in her green eyes sparkled.

Instead she tapped the cover of her book and said, 'Mr Nietzsche is my friend, Monty.'

'Is he coming for tea soon?'

His mother didn't answer for a long time so Monty noisily swallowed the crumbs that had stuck to his gums and the insides of his cheeks. He wondered if her words had stuck to her mouth like crumbs of scone had stuck to his. He swallowed again, encouragingly.

But then she blurted out her reply in a single breath. 'Now you are seven, I can tell you, Monty. But you are not to tell anyone else. It is to be our secret.'

Monty nodded and wiped the cream from his mouth with the back of his hand.

'I have realised there is something inside me struggling to come out. I call it the what-I-could-be. It is difficult to explain, *mein Liebling*.'

Monty's eyes fell to her stomach. He nodded very slowly. He didn't want another sister, but a brother would be all right.

15

'It feels like a secret fire.' She paused and placed her hand first on her chest and then on her stomach. 'I am scared to die before I have lived.'

Monty nodded sympathetically. He knew some ladies died when they had babies. 'I'll pray for you,' he said, taking another scone and smearing it with butter.

'My friend, Mr Nietzsche, is helping me.' She picked up her book again. 'And you, Monty. You and Elsa and Barby.'

He reached across and lightly patted her hand, like his father did sometimes. He was worried that her only friend was in a book. How could someone in a book help her have a baby? 'Does Papa know?'

'About what, my love?' She lifted her eyes from her book and looked distractedly at him, as though she was reading something very difficult and he had broken her concentration.

'The thing growing inside you.' He jerked his head in the direction of her stomach. It was definitely larger, he thought. And floppier.

'That is to be our secret, Monty. I should not have said anything, but I have no one else to talk to.'

'When will your friend come to tea?'

She smiled and stroked his cheek with her thumb. 'Mr Nietzsche is dead, my love.'

Monty blinked hard and chewed at his scone. She wasn't reading any more. She was staring at the ceiling with a faraway look on her face. Monty thought there must be something up there, on the ceiling, because she sat gazing for a very long time. But when he looked up, there was nothing – not even a cobweb.

FOUR

Ernest

Ernest decided to walk home from the University. There was a biting wind and a thin drizzle had made the cobbles dark and slippery. But he needed time to think. Nusch's aborted visit seemed to have unsettled Frieda and he wanted to make amends. If he walked via the marketplace perhaps he could buy her some flowers. Perhaps the florist's stall would have a few tulips left. Or some early carnations, in cream and pale pink. He wanted her to know they could afford proper flowers now, cultivated flowers, grown and picked by other people. Frieda insisted on collecting cow-parsley and honeysuckle from the hedgerows. She even picked ragwort from the fields, in spite of his abhorrence of a weed known – by any English peasant – to poison cattle. 'But we are not cattle, my dear,' she had laughed, 'and they are so bright and jolly.'

And now the children were doing the same thing. Filling the house with limp, drooping stems. Jars of scummed water placed haphazardly on their best mahogany tables. Dead petals littering the floor. Pollen all over his newspaper. At least they had Mrs Babbit to sweep it up.

His thoughts swerved to all the new staff swarming in and out of his house: the housekeeper, the nanny, the man who came to mow the lawn. He'd tried, unsuccessfully, to emulate his wife's combination of disdain and sympathy. She had an aristocratic ease with them that he envied and admired. His clumsy attempts to appear equally at ease had made him feel curiously diminished. Now he left dealing with the servants to her.

He liked thinking about his wife. Her vitality, the abundance of her. The way she seemed to occupy every corner of the house at the same time. The way she dashed up and down the stairs like a human earthquake. Of course, it was enormously provoking when he was trying to work, but he enjoyed thinking about her when she wasn't around.

The vitality seemed to have leached out of her since Nusch left. He wondered, just briefly, if Nusch's flaunting of her sumptuous suits and opulent hats had made Frieda feel lowly in some way. Nusch had made a better match, he supposed. A husband as old as he was, but rich and aristocratic, with a distinguished duelling scar across his left cheek. The sort of military husband Baron von Richthofen had wanted for each of his three daughters.

He'd have to work harder, Ernest told himself. Do some extra marking for the Examination Board or teach another evening class for labourers. And he'd let her order a new hat from London . . . with a fine plume in the brim. Egret feathers perhaps . . .

Her eyes still shone when she played with the children. Only yesterday he'd come home to find her on the floor, her skirts splayed, her sturdy stockinged legs circling in the air. Monty had explained that she was pretending to be a bicycle. Inappropriate and undignified, of course. But he'd been so relieved to hear her laughing, he decided not to comment.

The depth of her motherliness never ceased to surprise him. She seemed to love the children with a fierce energy that he couldn't quite comprehend. It had made him aware of a weakness within him, buried beneath the layers and layers of sophistication he'd acquired in his slow, steady path to respectability, to the position of gentleman. A weakness he could neither articulate nor locate, rather like a mosquito bite trapped beneath tight clothing.

A crimson tram rattled past, breaking his stream of thought. He hurried on towards the marketplace, momentarily distracted by the image of his wife's generous thighs. He shook his head. It was Nusch he needed to think about. What had she said to make Frieda so dispirited? He'd never much liked Nusch's combination of rapacious spite and flirtatious superiority. He knew she looked down on him – even as she flirted with him. There was something ungodly about her, he thought. Something vaguely immoral. Words from the Bible swam into his consciousness . . . *Yea, in my house have I found their wickedness, saith the Lord* . . . At least Frieda had the moral fibre of her mother, not the shameless laxity of her father or her sister.

A gritty breeze swept through the market, stirring the brim of his homburg hat and plucking at the handkerchief protruding from his breast pocket. He gripped the handle of his umbrella and looked round at the straggle of remaining stalls. No tulips or carnations. A basket of limp sorrel leaves. Another of green rhubarb stalks. A tabletop of rabbit carcasses. He paused and looked at them. Slivers of translucent flesh still clung to their spines.

'Carcass,' he murmured. 'Carcase, *carcosium* . . . perhaps from *carchesium* originally, or even from the Persian, *tarkash*. Carcase in Australia, I believe.'

He caught the grim eye of the stall holder and quickly turned away. The drizzle was getting heavier, he needed to get home. He was about to leave when he spotted a woman packing crocheted lace into a basket.

'I'd like some lace,' he said, careful to make his voice sound both decisive *and* disinterested.

The woman thrust a square of mouse-coloured lace at him. 'These are all the rage in London.'

Ernest cleared his throat. They looked like handkerchiefs, but something told him they weren't handkerchiefs. And yet they were too big to be mats or doilies.

'For the backs of chairs. Where greasy little heads go,' explained the woman.

'I'll take four.' Ernest drew back and let his mind dwell on the word 'four'. From the old English, *feower*, and before that quite possibly from the Germanic, *fedwor*. And before that? His mind drifted back through the linguistic litter of time gone by – to the Latin, to the Greek, to Old Norse, to Old Frisian.

He was still thinking about the origins of the word 'four', when he found himself home, inside the hall, handing his damp parcel of lace to Frieda.

She tore off the paper, her smile stiffening very slightly as she looked at the lace squares.

'Nottingham lace is still the best in the world,' he said, feeling a small swell of pride. It was a pride – of England, of her empire, of himself as an English gentleman – that he'd fostered over the years of their marriage, and that he dated dimly, obscurely, from the morning of his wedding when he'd seen the regret in Baron von Richthofen's eyes.

Frieda dropped the paper into the waste basket. 'Yes, my dear,' she said. 'I suppose it is.'

As she moved away, he noticed a weariness in the turn of her shoulders. As if she was overcome with fatigue. Yes, he would buy her a ticket to Munich. She needed a holiday, some time to herself. Munich was the answer.

FIVE

Frieda

After Nusch's visit, Frieda found herself thinking back, over and over, to the day she met Ernest. As she brushed his hat or arranged his umbrellas or polished the little mirror he kept in his study, she would close her eyes and picture the fountain where they first met. She could remember, so clearly, the sensation of sun-seared stone and springy moss beneath her fingertips. And Ernest, leaning nonchalantly on his cane and examining the carved water spout. She'd liked the way his pipe sat jauntily in the corner of his mouth, the silk bow tie at his neck, the boater angled rakishly on his head. He'd spoken to her in German, then French, then English. She had liked that too – his talent and sophistication.

She'd rushed home to her sisters and told them about his years of studying, the four universities he'd been to, the many scholarly books he was working on, and his new job as a Professor of Modern Languages in an exotic-sounding English town. 'He is even cleverer than you,' she'd said to Elisabeth. She didn't mention his age, or the blue veins that throbbed at his temples, or the way he draped his thinning hair over the shiny plates of his skull.

When her mother said Mr Weekley wanted to marry her and take her to England, Frieda had looked up from her volume of poetry and smiled, already imagining herself as an inspirational wife, bringing levity and joy to a great scholar. Even then, at the age of eighteen, she had believed in greatness. She'd pictured them walking over the rolling English hills deep in discussion – philosophy, poetry, politics – their tongues slipping effortlessly from one language into another. Only afterwards had Frieda felt the thrill of sibling victory, whispering into the pages of her book 'I shall be the first to marry, the first to shed the burden of virginity!'

'Of course, he's not our sort,' said the Baroness. 'But he doesn't mind that you have no dowry. And beggars cannot be choosers.'

Frieda hadn't cared about money. It was life she wanted. Adventure. Discussion. Love. Ernest had offered them all. And then there was the promise of England: the very word seemed imbued with mystery, glory, passion. She felt the land of Shakespeare, Wordsworth and Byron calling to her. A land of kings and queens. An empire that stretched to the very ends of the earth. *A sceptred isle . . . a demi-paradise . . . a precious stone set in the silver sea.* She repeated the word 'England', over and over, and felt it reverberate on her tongue.

Later, after a cringing meeting with Ernest's parents at Dover – his pious little mother scuttling and scraping in her darned gloves, his hunched father bobbing and stooping in a shirt leaf-thin from washing – the Baroness had flounced furiously back to Metz. When Frieda returned, her parents made it clear they no longer approved of Ernest. His obvious virginity had become a family joke, his pauper parents were a disgrace, his lack of class a crime.

But Frieda had seen something in Mr and Mrs Weekley's modest marriage that filled her with hope: the small gestures of affection and familiarity that passed between them, the devotion with which Ernest's father blacked the stove for his wife, the way she combed his beard every morning, and smoothed the creases from his trousers when he stood up. Little gestures of loyalty and love she'd never seen before.

In the early days of marriage she'd tried to do the same, brushing the crumbs from Ernest's moustache and straightening his tie. She picked buttercups and forget-me-nots, arranged them with a little foliage and placed them in egg cups on his desk. At breakfast, she laid his paperknife beside his post and cut the crusts from his toast. Things had changed after the children were born. Something had happened to Ernest, she wasn't sure how or why, but she'd felt slowly pushed to the very periphery of his life. Confused, she'd wondered if he no longer loved her, if he'd ever loved her. Her confusion had turned briefly to anger. After a few weeks, the anger settled and dulled into a fond acceptance of him, of their separate lives, and she'd thrown herself with great gusto into motherhood.

But on occasion her acceptance would spill over into a mute sadness. And always she sensed that a role had been thrust upon her. A role not quite of her own choosing. It was something she felt rather than knew, something she couldn't articulate. Until Nusch arrived, with all her talk of affairs and salons. Implying that she and Elisabeth – neither of whom had an ounce of Frieda's courage – had somehow made their own lives and chosen their own roles. Lives that were unfettered and joyful. Lives in which they were loved with the sort of passion Frieda had always dreamt of.

I'll go to Munich, she thought, and see how they've exaggerated the fullness of their lives. Perhaps they were punishing her for marrying so far beneath them. She arranged Ernest's pipe and tobacco pouch, exactly as he liked them in the far corner of his desk with the brass ashtray and a fresh box of matches. Then she straightened the drab little squares of lace he'd bought her which now sat, one on top of the other, on the back of his wing chair. And as she did so another thought struck her. What if Nusch hadn't lied or exaggerated? She shook her head. The scholarly, serious Elisabeth cavorting with a handsome lover in the open air? A ridiculous notion!

SIX

Monty

It was a week after his mother had imparted her big secret and Monty was finding it more and more difficult to stop thinking about his brother-to-be or the possibility of his mother dying. When she'd talked of a fire inside her, she must have meant she had a fever. He remembered his last fever. He had felt as though he was burning up, as though his blood was boiling in his veins, and flames were licking at his insides.

That evening, when his father came to tuck him up, the question that had been gnawing away at Monty came rushing out. 'Papa, where does a baby come from?'

His father sat on the edge of his bed, frozen and silent. Eventually he said, 'It's a gift from God.' And then he coughed as though he had something stuck in his throat.

'If it's a gift, why do so many ladies die?'

'That only happens sometimes. If – when . . . when . . .' His father's voice tailed off and he stood up quickly, moving towards the door as if he was in a hurry to get somewhere. Back to his study, no doubt. Back to his books.

'Would a lady die if she had a baby and a fever at the same time, Papa?'

His father's hand gripped the door handle. 'It's time you went to sleep. Goodnight.'

'But how does something so big get into a lady's tummy?' Monty heard the click of his door closing and the hurried tread of his father on the stairs. Pictures of babies and flames bursting through his mother's skin, popping out of her mouth, erupting from her head, her nostrils, her tummy, churned through his mind. And then pictures of her dead, with her eyes closed, nothing moving – just lying there in her best Sunday dress with the velvet-covered buttons. How was that a gift from God?

The next day at breakfast, he asked his mother how she felt. 'How is . . . your fever?' He nodded at her stomach and then concentrated on spreading marmalade over his toast, making sure the shreds of orange peel were evenly spaced.

'Fever?' She sounded surprised.

'The fire.' Monty lowered his voice. Ida had taken Barby and Elsa to the farm to buy some eggs and his father was at work, but Mrs Babbit was in the kitchen and could come through at any moment.

'Fire?' His mother turned to the grate where a couple of logs were burning half-heartedly. 'You are always so observant, Monty.' She pushed back her chair, went to the hearth and flung a small log onto the fire so that a shower of sparks flew into the air.

'Does a baby come from God?'

'In a way, yes.' She looked curiously at him. 'But it is really a man who puts it there. Then it grows and grows and out it comes.' She picked up the butter knife and began gouging at the butter, dropping yellow clods haphazardly over her toast.

Monty chewed pensively. 'What man puts it there?'

'Why, the father of course. You remember that bull we saw last week? The one who was climbing on the cow, by the oak tree with the rope swing?'

Monty nodded.

'He was putting his baby in the cow. Now the cow will get fatter and fatter and then she will have a calf. Like magic!'

'Oh,' said Monty, perplexed. And he remembered the bull and its enormous red penis and the way it had grunted and heaved – and he felt a flush of heat spread over his face. He still wasn't sure how God fitted in but he didn't want to think about his little brother any more, or angry bulls, or his father climbing over his mother. 'Can we go to Sherwood Forest today? Just you and me, without Elsa or Barby. Can we take some plum cake with us?'

'You have only just finished your breakfast!' She reached across the table and squeezed his hand. 'I like it when you eat lots, Monty.'

She put the last corner of toast in her mouth and stood up. Monty looked at her stomach. Was it getting bigger? It looked the same as before. He decided to look at her stomach every day. And then he would tell his father. Someone had to tell. Even if it meant snitching.

SEVEN

Frieda

As Frieda prepared for Munich – getting her hats repaired and her shoes resoled, oiling the hinges on her travelling trunk – letters continued to come from her sisters: Nusch writing regretfully that she would not be able to get to Munich, such were the daily demands of her lover and her seamstress; Elisabeth instructing her to stop immediately at the Café Stefanie *whatever time of day or night you arrive*, and hinting at the *intellectual and artistic oasis* that Munich had become. Frieda tossed their letters into the waste basket but couldn't help feeling oddly excited. She seemed to veer between flippant disbelief and nervous anticipation. She had tried, again, to persuade Ernest to join her. But he'd insisted that a holiday was quite out of the question.

One night she awoke parched and gasping for water. As she reached for the glass beside her bed, the dream she had awoken so violently from came flooding back. She frowned, blinked, gulped at the water. Not a dream, she thought. A perfectly recalled memory. A memory she had packed away ten years ago. She wondered if her imminent trip home had, in some oblique way, unlocked a small door to her past. Lifting her from her cramped sunless house and returning her, momentarily, to the military garrison of Metz. She lay down and closed her eyes.

The memory spun back, as vivid as her dream. She was in the drawing room, her mother's pacing footsteps and ruptured voice filling the air. The Baroness sending Nusch to beg for money from the commanding officer, rouging her girlish cheeks so that he would be made pliant by her beauty. The news unfolding bit by bit. The servants had been dismissed. The house was to be sold. No money for dowries. No chance of marriage to an army captain now. Money must be borrowed, secured against their few remaining possessions. The Baron's gambling debts had become too large, too unwieldy.

She put her fingers in her ears and gave herself a shake beneath the eiderdown. She didn't want to be reminded of what had followed. But the memory forced itself upon her, like water from a dam that has found a fissure and must tear its way through. The Baroness's skirts swishing furiously over the floorboards, her arms wrapped tightly round her chest crushing the stiff ruffles of her bodice. Her voice mingling shame with bitterness, her plaintive excuses for him *... It is not easy being wounded in battle. For a military man to carry his scarring so publicly ...* Her gaze sweeping from the ceiling to the floor, as if she couldn't bear to look at her daughters, to see herself reflected in their eyes. *He has a bastard son whose mother's silence must be bought ... If only he'd had a legitimate son to inherit the baronetcy ... Such disappointment he has lived with ... All the endless oysters she had eaten – to the brink of sickness ... The gypsy who swore Frieda would be a boy ... Your fault, Frieda ... If only you had been the boy you should have been ...*

Frieda opened her eyes and pushed back the covers. The chill morning air shook her from her daze of semi-consciousness. She didn't want to think about the past. She didn't want to recall the move to a meagre, low-ceilinged apartment or how wrong it had felt – too narrow, too new, too parsimonious – or the endless ensuing discussions of who might marry them *without a dowry*. Her mother's voice filled her ears again. *Nusch will find a rich husband because she is beautiful . . . Elisabeth will be all right because she is brilliantly clever . . . but Frieda?*

She sat up quickly. I must think about the day ahead, she thought. I have things to do: instructions for Mrs Babbit, magazine subscriptions to be renewed for Ernest, a salve to be made for Barby's rash, an order for the butcher.

Later, as she yawned her way through her errands, she had a small moment of epiphany.

'Ernest,' she said, over dinner of mutton cutlets and fried potatoes. 'I want our children to grow up knowing courage is more important than appearance and intelligence.'

Ernest had a pile of exam papers beside him and was attempting to eat and mark at the same time. 'Whatever are you talking about, my snowflower?'

'I want them to know that courage is more precious than looking nice or being clever.'

His expression was one of such blank perplexity, she wondered if she should remind him of *his* courage, when he'd asked so boldly for her baronial hand in marriage. But then he looked up from his papers and answered her.

'I suppose courage is important if Monty wants a military career. I shall be happy if the girls are as pure and beautiful as you.' He patted her hand and turned back to his work.

She sighed and pushed her plate away. She was just about to ring the bell for Mrs Babbit, when Ernest said, 'Read Monty the stories of King Arthur. They're all about courage and bravery.'

'And the girls?' she persisted.

Ernest paused, his eyes lifting briefly from his papers. 'Duty, loyalty, morality. It's all in the Bible. It may even be in those Brothers Grimm stories you fill their heads with. Will you ask Mrs Babbit to bring my glass of stout to my study tonight?' He pushed back his chair, picked up the pile of essays and hurried from the room.

'Perhaps I will take Monty to Munich so he can remember his German courage!' Frieda called to his fleeing form. But there was no answer, just the sharp thud of his study door echoing through the house.

EIGHT

Monty

'Why do you keep answering me in English?' His mother's voice rose over the hubbub of the café. 'Don't you want to speak German to me now?'

Monty chewed diligently and said nothing. People stared when he spoke German and he didn't want to be called a hideous Hun any more. But he liked it when she spoke German at home. He liked the way German words came from deep in her throat, the way they rose and plunged and rattled from her mouth like gunfire.

'At home,' he mumbled, after a long silence.

'Very well.' She reached across the table for another slice of fruitcake. 'The cakes in Germany are really much better. I think you should come to Munich with me, Monty. Would you like that?'

Monty felt the tension slip from his shoulders and the tight knots fade from his stomach. 'Yes, please. Oh yes please!' Cake crumbs flew from his mouth but he didn't care. He was going to Munich!

'I don't feel quite myself and I think a short holiday in Munich will help.' She opened her book again, but she didn't seem to be reading. Her eyes didn't move.

Monty reached out and touched her forearm very gently. 'Have you a pain in your tummy, Mutti?'

She looked up and said, 'What would I do without you, Monty? You are such a big boy now.' Monty wished he wasn't such a big boy. He wanted to be small again, to climb into her lap and stroke her face and her hair and feel his skin melting under the soft heat of her palm. Like Elsa and Barby did.

'Oh look, Monty!' Her voice was suddenly silver bright and she was pushing her book back into her basket. 'Move up. Move up. We shall need more chairs.'

He looked up to see Barby's godfather, Mr Dowson, and his wife coming towards them. Mrs Dowson was pointing at him with the tip of her purple umbrella and Mr Dowson had a big smile on his face, so big it seemed to stretch from one ear to the other. Mr Dowson lived a few streets away and often came to visit. Monty liked his twinkly eyes which grew even brighter when Papa wasn't there. It struck him that perhaps Mr Dowson could be his mother's friend. Mrs Dowson wasn't much use – she was too busy embroidering banners for her committees.

'We're just leaving!' trilled Mrs Dowson. 'I have a women's meeting to attend. Emmeline Pankhurst is coming to Nottingham. You will come, won't you? We want to show her that Nottingham is taking women's suffrage seriously.'

'You don't need me, Helena. I'll join Mrs Weekley for a coffee.' Mr Dowson turned to Monty and his mother. 'You can tell me how my favourite goddaughter is.' He winked at Monty and squeezed in next to his mother on the banquette, even though the space seemed much too small and she had specifically said they needed more chairs.

'It is nice to see you, Mr Dowson.' Monty's mother put her head to one side, like a sparrow, and fixed her eyes on Mr Dowson. Monty was pleased. Perhaps she would tell him about the new baby. He stretched out his ears to make sure he didn't miss a single word.

'I've been busy, keeping out of mischief while Helena fills the house with her rabble-rousing suffragettes,' said Mr Dowson, rolling his eyes.

'They are doing important work and women should have the vote.' She hesitated for a second, stirring absently at her cold coffee. 'But when I went to a suffragette meeting they did not make me feel welcome. And now they are shouting and marching and behaving like men. I have a different vision.'

'Oh? Are you listening to your mother, Monty?' Mr Dowson prodded him in the arm.

Monty nodded and she continued, slowly, as if groping for the right words. 'They are not . . . inclusive enough. And it is not the vote that will bring us true freedom. It is much more complicated than that. We are powerful because we are different from men. We should be making our world more female, helping you men see things differently.'

'A more womanly world, eh? What do you think, Monty? Should women be given the vote?' But Mr Dowson was still looking at his mother so Monty wasn't sure if he was supposed to answer or not.

'Monty and I are going to Munich. It is more progressive there.'

'I hope you'll come back.' Mr Dowson gave a deep barking laugh. 'We all know what you think of Nottingham.'

'It is Nottingham that doesn't like me,' she protested. Monty turned away and fastened his eyes on the window where he could watch out for anyone from school coming in. It was then that he heard his mother's peculiar words.

'. . . Something inside of me . . . like a fire burning away . . .' She lowered her voice and ran her fingertips absently down the front of her dress. '. . . Feel as if I have . . . no meaning, no purpose. One day . . . dead!' She paused and clasped her hands against her stomach. 'And that is all.'

Monty recoiled. 'Why must my little brother die?' he blurted and he knew his eyes were very wide because his eye sockets ached.

'What?' His mother looked at him and the skin between her brows went into little pleats. 'Monty is obsessed with death at the moment. All morning he has been asking me about Heaven.' She shrugged, a big shrug, and kept her palms face upwards in the air for several seconds.

Monty suddenly felt very tired and his stomach was hurting. 'I have tummy ache, Mutti,' he said.

'I'm not surprised, young man. All the cake you've eaten.' But Mr Dowson wasn't looking at him. He was still gazing at Monty's mother, as if he'd never seen her before.

NINE

Frieda

Nusch's suggestion that Frieda and Ernest discuss literature together – to compensate for Nottingham's lack of salons – piqued Frieda. She had tried before, but that was years ago. Ernest had shown no interest in character or feeling, but wasn't it worth another attempt?

She found herself coming back to the idea again and again, albeit from different directions. Sometimes she imagined Elisabeth and Edgar crouched intently over *War and Peace*, perhaps beside a blazing fire or beneath a softly smoking lamp. She could see it clearly: Elisabeth with her chin resting in her palm, Edgar lifting his spectacles and rubbing pensively at the bridge of his nose. She could almost hear the opinions volleying from one to the other, the probing questions, the lively exchange of ideas.

At other times Frieda thought back to the early days of her marriage, when Ernest had come home each day with armfuls of books for her. After she struggled through them – her English wasn't so good in those days – he had smiled approvingly and kissed the side of her head before scooping them up and returning them to the library. When Monty was born Ernest became obsessed with working every minute of every day so that his growing family would never go hungry. He had stopped bringing so many books home for her, as if he thought reading and motherhood weren't compatible.

But he earned more money now, the children were older, and her English was vastly improved. Perhaps Nusch was right and some literary discussion would stave off this growing sense that her life was too slow, too empty, that she was missing out on the sort of *real life* her sisters claimed to have. And perhaps it would bring Ernest back to her, restore their intimacy even. So in the weeks after Nusch's departure she spent several hours looking for the perfect book, browsing the Nottingham Free Library and searching the shelves of the little bookshop behind the market. Finally she found it. A novel sufficiently similar to Elisabeth's marital reading material that Ernest could have no objection. But not the *same* novel, for she had no desire to ape her sister's choice. She kept the book hidden behind her sheet music, ready to surprise Ernest. Every afternoon she took it out and read for an hour, jotting down her thoughts in a little silk-covered notebook.

One evening as she was practising a Brahms sonata, her chosen book carefully propped behind the score, Ernest and Monty appeared in the drawing room.

'Monty, my love, you should be in bed.' She stopped playing but kept her hands hovering above the keys as she glanced at the wall clock. Half past eight. He should be asleep.

'He tells me he is too excited about Munich to sleep, my snowflower.' Ernest planted his hand on Monty's head. 'You will have to look after your mother, Monty. They say Munich is full of long-haired men and short-haired ladies these days.'

Frieda felt her hands tighten and her lips purse. Why did he persist in calling her *his snowflower*? Snow was cold and dead – and she was neither. I'm a thing of life, she thought. I'm not even much of a flower. A snowflower – whatever it was – sounded virginal, untouchable, arctic almost. Her gaze strayed to the vase of ruffled cream carnations he'd brought home the previous day. That is what he wants me to be, she thought, bitterly. He wants me to be a frilly white carnation. She took a deep breath.

'Ernest, I have been reading *Anna Karenina*. I thought we could talk about it once Monty is in bed.'

Ernest looked blankly at her. 'Isn't that what your ladies' afternoons are for? Your At Homes?'

'I – I've stopped them.' She could hear her words falling onto the piano, slipping between its ivory teeth. She wanted to explain how the local wives made her feel awkward and ostracised, that she found them dull and censorious, that their merciless struggles for superiority repelled her. But Monty and Ernest were staring at her with such undisguised surprise the words died in her mouth.

'I am reading instead. I hoped you and I could . . .' Her voice trailed off.

'I teach working men to read three nights a week, I teach in Cambridge every Saturday, I teach imbeciles at the college every day, I have a seminal book to write. What is wrong with the other wives?'

Frieda closed the piano lid. And what about all the time you spend arranging your book shelves, she thought, a hard tight lump rising in her throat.

'They are good Christian ladies. What will we say to them at church?' His face had an expression of baffled irritation. As if he was talking to one of his more difficult and foolish students.

She stared stupidly at the vase of frilled carnations, swallowing repeatedly at the ball in her throat. How could she tell him that she had nothing in common with the Christian ladies of Nottingham? That she felt like a different species? She riffled through them in her head . . . *Mrs Clark, the pawnbroker's wife, who inspects my clothes and finds them wanting. Mrs Black, the tea merchant's wife, whose relentless berating of her servants exhausts me. Mrs Burton, the factory owner's wife, who talks only of her latest hat.* No, she couldn't return to her Thursday afternoon At Homes. She would rather crawl on the floor with her children, or read, or pick wildflowers. She opened her mouth to ask Ernest, again, if he would discuss *Anna Karenina*, perhaps over supper, but he raised his palm to stop her. And in that single gesture, he seemed to push her not merely to the edge of his life but beyond. She felt the lump in her throat swell and grow. She clenched her teeth. She must not cry in front of Monty. Whatever the tears were – regret, anger, frustration, loneliness – she must not upset Monty.

'We'll continue this conversation later. When are you and Monty thinking of going to Munich?'

'A-as soon as his term finishes,' she said, trying to keep her voice high and bright. She had a sudden urge to hold Monty, to feel the reassuring softness of his hair against her cheek, the vanilla milkiness of his breath on her face, his skin comfortingly against hers. 'Come and give me a big hug before you go to bed, my love.' She opened her arms wide and smiled. But Monty didn't move.

'I think Monty's a little old for cuddles with his mother. I'll take him upstairs.' Ernest's hand pivoted on Monty's head, steering him towards the door. 'Say goodnight to Mutti.'

'Goodnight,' said Monty flatly. But Frieda couldn't speak. She turned back to the piano, tears pushing at her eyes, the lump in her throat chokingly large. Ernest had already told her, repeatedly, that Monty needed to become more independent, that she cosseted him, that he was too attached to her. She pressed her lips hard together, opened the piano lid and began playing a Beethoven piece. Her hands shook as the notes crashed around her, slamming into the walls and banging into the furniture. When Ernest returned and said she'd woken Barby and Elsa, she could not speak. She just shook her head and carried on. She felt as if the piano and the music she was thumping out were the only things holding her in place. And if she were to stop playing, she would shrink so far inside herself she might disappear. Who am I now? she thought. What am I? Nusch's words swam into her head . . . *Yes, Frieda. Come back to us, before it is too late . . .*

TEN

Ernest

Ernest wished Frieda would stop hammering at the piano. The storm of sound was making the panes in his study window rattle. Besides, she'd played the same piece continuously for three days now, and it was affecting his concentration. Perhaps if she had more musical talent it wouldn't have grated on his nerves so much.

He let out a long weary sigh and picked up his pipe, tamping it carefully with tobacco and placing it at the corner of his mouth. He moved aside some student essays, hoping to find a box of matches. Instead, his eye fell upon a copy of *Anna Karenina*. Frieda must have put it there. He'd begun to feel as if the wretched book was stalking him round the house. She clearly hadn't read it. She was obviously unaware of the plot and the characters, of their godless immorality.

He was about to push it to one side, when something made him open it and flick through the pages. Later he wondered if it was the binding: the quality of its maroon calfskin jacket and its flamboyant gilt lettering. He never could resist a beautifully-bound book. Frowning, he noticed that someone had written across the top of the opening page. Large, rounded letters that looped theatrically. He was certain it was the hand of one of the von Richthofen sisters, but was it Frieda's? Surely she wouldn't desecrate a book as handsomely bound as this.

'*Bevor es zu spät ist*,' he read aloud. *Before it is too late*. But too late for what, he wondered. He tried to recall how *Anna Karenina* ended but then remembered that he'd never finished it. Too late, he mused. *Zu spät . . . zu spät*. He leaned back in his chair and sucked on his unlit pipe, rather enjoying this cryptic moment.

And then it struck him, suddenly, blindingly. How could he have been such a dunce? Such a blockhead? He could feel everything falling into place – the message, Frieda's mood, her peculiarly inappropriate behaviour. Just the other day she'd fiddled, rather clumsily, with his shirt tails. And yesterday she'd tried to run her hands over his trousered buttocks while he wound up the grandfather clock in the hall. But now he understood. She wanted another baby. *Before it was too late*.

The moment of startled realisation passed almost immediately as he began listing the reasons for not having another child, under any circumstances. Too much noise. Too much fidgeting. Too many germs. Far too much expense. His plans to move to a more substantial house, with better quality garden soil, would be thwarted if he had to factor in funding a fourth child. And what about his book? His Cambridge Chair?

No – the whole thing was preposterous. He would resist her. He would remain immune to her feminine wiles. His gaze travelled across his desk and to the view beyond the window. Dusk. The last light hovering in the trees, on their greening leaves, their furled buds, the canopy of pale blossom. Spring, he thought with another jolt. Had the bounteousness and promise of spring caused his wife to dwell unduly on the subject of procreation? Yes, that must be it. The antics and agitations of spring: the budding boughs, the bursting blooms, the frenzied nest building. He glanced round his study, every wall lined with books, rows and rows of them rising from the floor to the ceiling. All in alphabetical order, starting with the Bible and ending with Zola. Each one catalogued meticulously in his own longhand. He had made his own nest, he thought with a sense of satisfaction. Perhaps his wife was merely wanting to extend her own nest. Perhaps the arrival of spring had some mysterious animal effect on a woman's body. A boyhood memory intruded sharply on his reveries: his nine siblings crouching over bowls of meatless soup, the cacophony, the chaos, the privation. No, another child was out of the question. He would never capitulate.

'Capitulate,' he said to the ceiling. The thin walls shook as Frieda thumped away next door, chord after chord. 'Capitulate . . . from the Latin, *capitulum*. Marvellous word . . . Copulate . . .' He stopped abruptly and then chuckled to himself. Words had an astonishing habit of doing that, of taking one effortlessly from one concept to another. He assumed it was the thoughts of procreation, of breeding, of spring, that had led him so subversively from 'capitulate' to 'copulate'.

An image of their wedding night dropped into his mind. The memory still haunted him – the shameful clumsiness of it, her unnatural enthusiasm. Somehow it wasn't what he'd expected the procreational act to be. She had displayed so little modesty, so little restraint, he had been forced to turn away, to feign sleep. He had a sudden urge to light his pipe, to smoke away this unwelcome memory. He scrabbled through his papers for a matchbox, guiding his mind adroitly into more pleasant territory. Their first meeting at that peculiar little fountain in the Black Forest where he'd taken the only holiday he'd ever had. What on earth had happened to him? He could remember, with absolute clarity, the greenness, the brightness of it all. The densely wooded hills, the slender pines leaning, line after line, into the afternoon light, the ravens whirling up from the treetops.

Looking back, it seemed as if this blast of freedom – from studying, from England, from his habitual metropolitan habitat – had given him a genteel swagger that quite belied his inner commotion

41

of nerves. As if he had become someone else for a fortnight. He remembered Frieda holding out her plump pink hand when they were introduced. Her glowing cheeks, her smile with its hint of truculence, the scent of lavender that rose from her white high-necked blouse. And her intriguing speech – such a strange mingling of Bavarian, Alsatian, Silesian, pocked with French patois. All those inflections had captivated him, seduced him. He'd known, almost immediately, that she was the only woman he would ever love. Although she was barely a woman at the time. Only eighteen. But so enchanting, so full of possibilities.

His thoughts swung back to the present. A fourth child was absolutely out of the question. He closed the copy of *Anna Karenina* and pushed it under some examination papers he was marking. Munich was the answer. A chance for Frieda to indulge herself in a little sensible introspection. A fortnight with Elisabeth would sort her out, put paid to any notions of a larger family. Elisabeth's exquisitely intelligent mind was permanently preoccupied with thoughts of economics and philosophy. Perhaps some of it would rub off on his wife.

'My wife,' he said aloud. 'My snowflower . . . My queen.' The word 'queen' made him pause. He'd always been intrigued by the word 'queen'. In most languages, the word for queen was the feminine derivative of the word for king. But not in English. He wondered if it was rooted in the Greek, *gynē*, meaning woman. Or perhaps from the Old Saxon, *qwan*, meaning wife. He looked out of the window at the particles of soot hovering like swarms of aphids. Frieda had stopped playing the piano and he could dimly hear the town's factories, clanging and clacking, hissing and spitting.

'My queen,' he repeated, smiling. How he loved the glorious lineage of language. How he loved the way words contained the entire story of a civilisation, the complete arc of man's progress from slavery to freedom. He lit his pipe, sucked away for a few seconds, then tilted back his head and puffed contentedly.

PART TWO

Munich 1907

'Her active life was suspended,

but underneath, in the darkness,

something was coming to pass.'

D.H. Lawrence, *Women in Love*

ELEVEN

Monty

It was dark when they finally arrived in Munich. Monty thought it must be the middle of the night. But then his mother said, 'We can go straight to Aunt Elisabeth's or we can stop for something to eat in the famous café your aunt insists we visit. Which would you prefer?'

Monty was immediately wide-eyed and awake. He liked the idea of going to a café very late at night, alone with Mutti, like a real gentleman. And he liked the way his mother was signalling to porters with such familiarity, holding herself very straight with her head held very high, like a queen. 'Please can we go to the café?'

'All right, just for a few minutes.' She turned, and while the porter loaded their trunks onto a luggage trolley, she took a deep noisy breath. Monty did the same. He could smell a funny yeasty smell and sweet meaty smoke. Munich smelled different from Nottingham, tantalising and exotic. And it struck him as odd that one city should smell so different from another.

He heard his mother giving directions for the 'Café Stefanie on Amalienstrasse' and felt a shiver at the roots of his hair, a shiver of pride and excitement. It wasn't like England, where the drivers didn't understand her and she'd have to repeat herself several times.

Or where, sometimes, they made rude comments about Germans under their breath.

'It is good to be home.' She ran her hands over her hair and then down the front of her dress, pressing at the creases of her skirt. 'Tomorrow you will drink Bavarian beer and eat proper food. So many good things we shall have. Now put your head on my lap.'

'Can we stay up past midnight? I'm not a bit tired.' He liked the feeling of Mutti's fingertips running through his hair. He liked the way she splayed her fingers so her hands looked like fat pink starfish. And he knew if they went to Aunt Elisabeth's, his mother would be too busy talking and unpacking to stroke his hair and he would have to go to bed by himself and the sheets would be cold and stiff.

She pressed her lips to his cheek and kissed him over and over, which made him think of his baby brother again. He adjusted his head so his ear was flat against her stomach. He would listen out for his brother, try and feel him inside her. But then the horse-cab stopped abruptly and she started speaking to the driver in her majestic voice again.

Monty sat up. He could hear singing and the strum of a guitar. In front of him people were spilling out of a foggy-windowed café, laughing and shouting. He remembered Papa's words about long-haired men and short-haired women and he tried to see what sort of hair they had. But it was too dark and all he could make out were blurred figures stumbling and waving.

TWELVE

Frieda

Frieda stifled a yawn as she asked the driver to wait. She could feel the dust and soot of the train sinking into her pores and when she moved too quickly the sharp reek of her underarms rose up. How ridiculous to have suggested going to a café at this hour.

'Monty, we should go to Elisabeth's. It is so late and we smell!'

But Monty had already jumped down and when she saw his face with its look of piteous indignation she didn't have the heart to make him get back in the horse-cab.

She took his hand, pushed open the glass doors of the café, and gave a silent gasp. For a second she wondered if they'd stumbled into a private drawing room by mistake. The café felt so intimate, so clandestine. It was panelled from floor to ceiling in rich dark wood, but for the windows which were draped in wine-coloured chenille curtains hung from brass poles. Lamps in fringed shades of fuchsia silk sat on each marble-topped table. Above, a brass chandelier swayed slightly as though caught in a draught. People were everywhere, standing in groups, bent over tables, clustered at the bar, their heads wreathed in a haze of blue tobacco smoke.

Frieda felt her fatigue fall away. This was nothing like the public houses of Nottingham where she and Ernest occasionally took a glass of his beloved stout. Nor was it like the Mikado Café with its silver cake stands and empty-eyed waitresses. She peered through the smoke into the heart of the room. A woman in a top hat, a cowbell round her neck, was going from table to table singing. A monocled man, with a guitar beneath one arm and strings of bright glass beads round his neck, trailed after her. Waiters, carrying trays high above their heads, wove their way between the tables where people were playing chess, writing, reciting, arguing. She caught snatches of what sounded like poetry, and heard the slap of hands on marble, spoons tapping on the rims of beer steins, boot soles drumming on the dark floorboards.

Monty's fingers dug into her hand, breaking her absorption. She felt her jaw hanging slackly and realised she was still standing in the doorway gaping while a waiter gestured to a table.

'*Bratwurst mit Kartoffeln bitt*e.' She shook her head briskly. She felt dazed and disorientated, as though she had stepped too quickly from one world into another.

'Why are these people so strange? Why aren't they in bed?' Monty asked in a loud whisper.

She squeezed his hand. 'They are artists, philosophers, writers. Even at this late hour great poems are being written and great thoughts are being discussed.' She paused, aware of something flickering inside her, like a tongue of fire. Beneath its fringe of smoke, and in spite of its soft lighting, the room was so splendidly colourful. Bare arms glinted and trilled with bangles of gold and silver. The women – sitting so alertly on the red plush chairs – were dressed resplendently in kimonos and embroidered dirndls. Even some of the men had red kerchiefs knotted at their necks.

'Why are they talking in funny voices?' Monty's fingers tightened over hers again.

She tilted her head and listened. She recognised French and German, of course, and something dark and lilting. Russian? Italian?

'What's in there?' Monty jerked his head towards the back of the café. The room opened out into another room, bright with the green expanse of billiard tables. She was about to explain the game of billiards when the singing woman leapt onto the table beside them and tossed her top hat to the monocled guitarist, revealing very short hair, cut high into the nape of her neck. The cowbell round her neck chimed as she moved and people began clapping and calling out 'Come on, Marietta!' The chess players paused and looked up idly. An aproned waiter threw her a yellow rose which she put behind her ear.

'I think we are about to have some lovely German music, Monty.' Frieda began clapping along with the crowd, thrilled at how invigorated she felt, at how swiftly the fatigue of their long journey had fallen away.

'Is she the short-haired lady Papa told us about?'

'Hush, listen.'

The guitarist strummed a few chords and grinned from beneath the ragged fronds of his moustache. The beads round his neck jangled as he beat time with his heeled boot. More people stood up and clapped, yelling at Marietta to 'Get on with it'. Marietta slowly unwound a chiffon scarf from her waist and tossed it into the audience. And then she undid her jacket and threw that too into the crowd, revealing a chemise edged with yellow lace. The cowbell tinkled encouragingly.

'What's she doing?' asked Monty and his voice was so loud and high that several people turned and looked at him.

'She is about to dance, but she is too hot.' Frieda began swaying to the music.

Marietta's fingers played with the ribbon on her chemise. Then she gave it a sharp tug, pulling it free and letting it float to the ground. The chemise ballooned round the swell of her breasts.

Frieda felt a pang of shock. She needed to get Monty out. Before he saw anything. Before this woman removed any more of her clothing. She began pushing at his chair, urging him up. The room seemed to be closing in on her, hot and crowded. All around them, men and women cheered and applauded. Next to her, two men began chinking their beer steins in time to the guitarist's chords.

Marietta's voice sung out, clear and reedy. 'We have no shame here, my fellow anarchists. And why should we feel shame? Our bodies are beautiful – as nature intended!' She seemed to look directly at Frieda as she tugged at the straps of her chemise, eeling her hips to manoeuvre herself out of the breeches she was wearing.

Frieda scrabbled for her shawl, thinking she could throw it over Monty's head. But her shawl had fallen to the floor and Monty was resisting her frantic pushes.

'I haven't had my sausage,' he wailed. 'I want my sausage.'

'We must go – immediately!' She pushed her fingers into Monty's shoulders and tried to turn him towards the door.

'My sausage,' he pleaded. 'What about my sausage?'

A tall man with rolled-up shirtsleeves and an open waistcoat pushed past them and reached up to Marietta. 'Will no one help this poor virgin?'

The crowd laughed as he eased his hand into the fly of her breeches and began flicking the buttons from their buttonholes.

'Repress nothing!' he shouted, as her lederhosen slipped down her thighs and puddled round her ankles.

'Thank you, my prince of darkness,' sung Marietta, kicking the breeches from the table and arching her neck, her eyes closed in an expression of bliss.

'We have to go!' Frieda began dragging Monty, pulling him towards the door. Ernest would never forgive her if Monty saw a naked woman dancing in a café. How would she ever explain it to him? The crowd was hollering now. She could hear feet stamping, the twanging of the guitar, the rattle of cutlery and crockery, Marietta's high rippling voice.

'Bring that boy back! What are you scared of? Let him see my beautiful bosoms. My beautiful arse!'

Frieda pushed at the glass doors and thrust Monty out towards the horse-cab. 'Oh – I have not paid! Driver! Help him up.' She turned back into the café to see Marietta's pale naked body spinning, the blur of her breasts with their rouged nipples, the crowd laughing and tossing coins into her top hat. For a few seconds Frieda stood and watched. She could feel her heart beating heavily behind her ribs and a slick of sweat building on her top lip. Marietta spun with such abandon that the horror of Monty seeing a naked dancer had been replaced by something quite different. A feeling Frieda couldn't readily decipher. There Marietta stood, high above everyone else, unashamedly enjoying their gaze. When she stopped spinning, she began plunging her hips into the air and running her hands up and down her thighs. And all the time she smiled, as though the sensation of her fingers against her skin pleased her, as if she revelled in her own nudity, in the freedom it brought.

Frieda flung some coins on the table and pulled herself away. She could feel her corset chafing at her ribs, rubbing the tops of her hip bones. The high ruffed neck of her blouse pinched at her throat. Her belt felt tight and constrictive. Her hairpins scraped against her scalp. Even her shoes gripped like tentacles at her feet. She had been travelling too long. She needed to get into her nightdress and go to sleep.

Later, after she'd put Monty to bed, she tried to sleep. But she couldn't get comfortable. Everything felt wrong. She pushed back the covers and tugged at her nightdress. The buttons were pressing into her chest. The cuffs and neckline seemed unusually tight, cutting into her wrists and throat. Perhaps Mrs Babbit had boiled it for too long, made it shrink. Or perhaps she'd eaten too much on the journey. Or perhaps . . . perhaps . . . She dropped her nightdress on the floor, walked to the window and opened it. Without thinking, she closed her eyes and spun and shimmied, her hips snaking and undulating. She ran her hands up and down her thighs and imagined an audience applauding and encoring. Tonight she would sleep naked. No more battling with her buttoned-up nightdress. She let her hands meander over her breasts and down her stomach. And as she did so, she heard the drifting strains of a guitar. She started swaying to its melody, her hair frisking freely over her shoulders. She felt a peculiar lightness in her feet, in her bones. As if gravity had released its claim on her. As if the earth could no longer hold her down. A slab of silver moonlight fell through the open window. She glided towards it, threw back her head and danced.

THIRTEEN

Frieda

Elisabeth moved efficiently round the dining room, smoothing the napkins, straightening the cutlery, brushing stray crumbs of black bread from the tablecloth. 'I'm glad Monty's sleeping. He must be exhausted.'

'Tell me everything, before he comes down. Your new lover – I want to know all about him.' Frieda looked round, checking the servants weren't in earshot.

'Don't worry about the servants. We have no secrets from them. They all know Otto, just as they know Edgar's lover.'

'Edgar has a lover?'

'Oh yes, of course. Fanny, the Countess zu Reventlow.' Elisabeth picked up the teapot and poured herself a cup of tea. Frieda noticed how steady and resolute her hand was, as if talking about her lovers over breakfast was perfectly normal.

'Fanny is a remarkable woman although she and I do not agree on how best to liberate women.' Elisabeth sipped pensively at her tea, then added 'Fanny thinks liberation will only be achieved when marriage is abolished and women become sexually free.'

'Sexually free?' Frieda blinked uncertainly. 'And how does that affect your marriage?' She spread a thick layer of yellow butter over her bread. She had woken ravenous, and oddly exultant after her naked sleep. But the exultation was fading now. Elisabeth talked about her life so openly, so matter-of-factly. How different it had been when they were children. The Baron's mistresses had been darkly hinted at by the Baroness, but they had never been named or discussed.

'I think free love makes for a stronger marriage. I adore Fanny, and Otto's wife is one of my closest friends. There's no cheating involved. Anyway,' Elisabeth paused and lowered her voice, 'Otto is different. He is a doctor. He understands a woman's body.'

Frieda raised an eyebrow.

'He has awakened me, Frieda.' Elisabeth slipped into the chair beside her, breathing damply into her ear. 'I never knew such exquisite pleasure. I have discovered my true nature with Otto. Such ecstasy, things I never knew with Edgar.' She gave a long swooning sigh and, as she did so, Frieda had a strange sensation of the room tightening around her, as if Elisabeth had claimed all the air and space for herself, as if Elisabeth had reached behind her and tugged the laces of her corset hard around her ribs.

She sat, silent. Somewhere deep inside, she felt an ache, a hunger for the things her sisters knew, that she had dreamed of but never known. And never would know.

'You've been spreading that butter for ages, Frieda. Would you like some cheese?'

Dazed, Frieda nodded. 'And the famously clever Weber brothers?'

'They're part of Munich's erotic movement too, of course. Max brings intellectual rigour to everything he does, even sex! But Otto – Doctor Gross – is so satisfying I have no need of anyone else at the moment. I feel as though I have been freed in some way.' Elisabeth leaned across the table, her eyes hard and bright like marbles. 'You may have seen him in the Café Stefanie. He runs all his talking cures from a table in the corner.'

Frieda forked a thick slab of cheese onto her plate, stabbing at it so hard the prongs went right through, leaving a neat row of holes in its hard white centre. 'What's a talking cure?'

'He cures sick people by encouraging them to talk. He's discovered that most illnesses are rooted in the mind. In the repression of emotions and memories.' Elisabeth paused then dropped her voice. 'But particularly in the repression of the sex instinct. Haven't these ideas reached Nottingham yet? You haven't heard of Vienna's Doctor Freud?'

'No.' Frieda's voice cracked very slightly.

'You would find Otto's analysis fascinating. That's the word he uses for his talking cures. He believes in the power of the female. His views are quite irregular. But he's cured hundreds of people.'

Elisabeth began scraping deftly at her cuticles with a neatly pared thumbnail. 'Why don't you try it? You might uncover the effects of all those oysters Mama ate trying to make you into a boy.'

'I'd like to go back to the café.' Frieda's heart thumped softly. What an unusual place the Café Stefanie was, she thought, hearing again the strumming guitar, the chinking cowbell. She'd felt so instantly at home there, but she wasn't sure why. Was it the absence of all that English affectation and restraint? Or was it because the air had seethed with novelty, with a sense of freedom? She could feel it tugging at her. Even now, over breakfast.

Elisabeth looked sideways at her, from under her lashes. 'Go and find Otto.'

Frieda sipped at her cold tea and stared at her uneaten cheese with its neat line of piercings. For a brief reckless second she imagined herself dancing, breathless, on a marble-topped table. Imagined the cool stone beneath her bare feet, the rampant eyes of men and women on her breasts and hips and thighs and . . .

'Frieda? Frieda?'

'All right. I'll go and meet your lover . . .'

'Good. Then I can send you home, content and cheerful.' Elisabeth ran her hand absently over her stomach. 'You're such a devoted mother, Frieda. You should have another baby.'

'I am more than a breeding cow,' Frieda replied, bridling at the casual indifference in Elisabeth's tone. As if Elisabeth could be something great because she was clever, but she, Frieda, was fit only for childbirth.

'I wish you would get involved with the English suffragette movement.' Elisabeth gave a weary sigh as if Frieda's political inactivity had disappointed her. 'Won't Ernest let you?'

'He has clear opinions on what women should do and be, as you know. He likes me to be a mother. But it's not that. It's . . .' Frieda paused and grimaced. She'd been to one of Mrs Dowson's suffragette meetings, of course she had. But when she spoke out, saying change wouldn't come from voting, they had turned on her. She had tried to explain – in her broken English – that a new society needed creating in the image of woman, that simply voting for laws made and controlled by men was insufficient, that behaving like angry men was the wrong way to get change. Afterwards they'd asked her to leave or stitch banners, and she'd overheard a woman describing her as 'the haughty stupid German'.

'Go and find Otto. You'll like him – he has your disobedient spirit.' Elisabeth coolly appraised her. 'The disobedient spirit you had as a child, before Ernest and the English stamped it out of you. But I haven't forgotten how you hurled rotten apples at those poor soldiers. Nor have I forgotten your naked diving and your unabashed peeing up the pear trees.' She paused and laughed. 'It never worked. Don't you remember how it ran straight down your leg?'

Frieda laughed. 'That was a long time ago.'

'Do you remember when you dived into that pool in the Black Forest and hundreds of frogs leapt out?' Elisabeth laughed again, her fingers skimming up and down the tiny pearl buttons on her blouse. 'I know a lovely place for swimming,' she continued. 'You won't need a costume. I often go there with Otto, Edgar and Fanny.'

'All of you . . . naked together?' In her mind's eye Frieda saw them: lying undressed on sun-warmed rocks, their smooth torsos flushed with sunburn and opening like blossom, clouds drifting lazily overhead, the shimmer of periwinkles and bluebells.

'You can dive there. It's quite deep.'

'Dive,' Frieda repeated slowly. And the word suddenly seemed the loveliest word she had ever heard.

FOURTEEN

Frieda

The Café Stefanie heaved and thrummed. Men in smocks and smoking jackets drank coffee and read newspapers. Women in velvet mantles and lederhosen, their hair loose, talked over slices of marble cake. She recognised several of them from the previous evening, some still scribbling and sketching. A bearded man worked at an easel, filling the café with the odour of paint and turpentine. In the room with the billiard tables she spied Marietta, in black breeches and a silk top hat, strutting round flicking a riding whip. Even the chess players seemed more alive than the people in the taverns of Nottingham, she thought.

'Where can I find Doctor Otto Gross?' she asked a waiter as he slid past, a tray of beer steins balanced high in the air. He tilted his head towards two women and a man bowed over a straggle of empty glasses and coffee cups. A thick shaft of silky sunlight draped itself across them, catching on the glasses and throwing spikes of brightness on the floor around them.

Frieda recognised Otto immediately: the man who'd called out 'repress nothing' as Marietta stripped. The man who'd put his hand so nonchalantly inside her breeches and unbuttoned her fly. He looked nothing like the doctors she'd met in Nottingham when Barby got a rash or Elsa had unexplained diarrhoea. She stared, enthralled, at his golden hair that stood in thick unruly spires, the heft of his shoulders, his long sinewy hands that rose above the table and hovered restlessly in front of his chest.

Marietta appeared, swayed past Frieda and stopped at Otto's table where she stood, pouting and flicking her whip. Otto laughed, caught the tail of her whip deftly in one hand and motioned her away.

'Excuse me, are you waiting for Otto?' A woman, her hair cut as short as a man's, tapped Frieda's arm. 'It must be your turn now, surely? And don't let Marietta jump the queue. She thinks her whip can get her anything she wants.' She laughed and thrust out her hand. 'I'm Fanny zu Reventlow.'

Frieda noticed, enviously, that Fanny was barefoot beneath her oriental gown and that her toenails had been untidily painted with purple oil paint. But before she could introduce herself Fanny's hand was in the small of her back, propelling her towards the table. 'Your turn,' she murmured.

Frieda swallowed, her mouth felt dry and gluey. 'I'm Elisabeth Jaffé's sister, Mrs Weekley.'

'Oh, Mrs Weekley from England.' Otto leaned back in his chair, sliding his hips forward and scrutinising her with a sharpness that excited and unnerved her. He patted the empty seat beside him. 'Come and sit next to me. You're more beautiful than your sister. She didn't tell me that.'

Frieda looked down at her long navy skirt, lying smooth over her corseted waistline. Suddenly she despised and hated her clothes.

'Nusch is the real beauty,' she said, recovering her composure.

'Crushed between beauty and brains then?' Otto opened a cigarette case and offered it to her.

'Not crushed,' she laughed, reaching boldly for a cigarette. Ernest didn't like women smoking. But she hoped the act of smoking would give her a more modern air and detract from the staidness of her outfit. As she took the cigarette she experienced a tiny thrill of rebellion.

'Tell me about your marriage.' He nodded in the direction of her wedding ring, his eyes fixed on her, expectant and curious. She could feel the warmth of his leg under the table, the softness of the velvet cushion behind her, the café clamour fading away. She was aware of the pulse in her wrist, of her heart staggering inside her, of her blouse clinging damply to her armpits.

'You like it here don't you, Mrs Weekley? Something's changing in your soul. I can see it from the light in your eyes.'

She drew back, startled.

'The world has descended on Munich. We have more poets, painters, philosophers, than anywhere in the world.' He blew out a thick plume of smoke. 'But at this moment I am interested only in you, Mrs Weekley.'

Frieda felt something shift and loosen inside her. And she was nine again. Standing beside the lake. Wind spiralling through her hair. The Baron urging her on, pounding the butt of his rifle on a toppled tree.

Show your sisters how to dive, Fritzl. Dive, my boy!

Fritzl? Boy? Yes Vater . . .

'Doctor Gross, can you tell me how a talking cure works?'

He leaned towards her, ran his finger over his lips. 'Only if you call me Otto. No formalities here. This is Munich, city of revolution.'

FIFTEEN

Frieda

The following week Frieda visited the Café Stefanie every day, talking with Otto then lunching with the artists and philosophers who spent their days there. Each time, Otto threw another idea at her, an idea so audacious it took her a few minutes to absorb. A world without war or armies . . . Countries without governments . . . Cities where women wore men's clothes and had their hair loose, where men wore women's clothes and grew their hair long . . . Communities where children were raised without knowing who their parents were . . . Societies without laws, religion or institutions, where people loved but never married.

At crowded tables beneath a warm fug of breath and cigarette smoke, she listened to Otto's friends extol his brilliance. Beer slopped impatiently from tankards. Runnels of coffee coursed across the marble tabletops. Crumbs of black bread flew exuberantly from plates and mouths. Linen napkins swabbed at sweating foreheads. Voices rose in a boisterous blur. Fists fell. Crockery rattled. Kimonos flapped.

'You have to come to Ascona,' said Fanny, as they all tucked into their *Wurstsalat* one day.

'Oh no,' replied Frieda. 'I have a husband and children in England.'

Fanny laughed so hard the bells round her ankles tinkled. 'How can you go back to all that? Don't be so ridiculous!'

And later, over coffee, Fanny leant into her and whispered, 'Haven't you slept with Otto yet?'

Frieda shook her head.

'He must be in love with you.' Fanny lowered her voice. 'You would be quite mad to go home without experiencing the full benefit of his cure. It's so very liberating. Surely your sister's told you?'

Frieda nodded. 'But my husband is a good man.'

Fanny snorted, her bangles clattering up and down her arms. 'You sound terribly old-fashioned! The only way women will achieve freedom is by becoming the sexual equal of men and not restricting themselves to one man who treats them like a chattel.'

Later, Otto had reached for her hand, pressed his lips to the back of her fingers. She'd felt the soft scratch of his moustache against her skin and a tingle had run over her body. As he lifted his head, the thought of sleeping with him hadn't seemed so wild or outrageous. Why else had Elisabeth sent her to him?

That night, as Frieda tossed and turned, the germ of an idea sprouted in the darkness. She tried to ignore it, then to smother it, and cast it away. But each time, it returned, more vivid, more enticing. Why shouldn't she experience the ecstasy that Elisabeth boasted of? Or the adulation and freedom that Nusch bragged about? Why shouldn't she? She slept fitfully, and when she finally woke, her whole body was aching with desire. She washed and dressed quickly, then hurried to the Café Stefanie. Monty and his cousins had gone to the zoo so the morning stretched, bright and seductive, before her.

The café was quiet. A few artists sat sketching near the window. Two chess players huddled over a chessboard in the corner. The waiters watered the potted palms and dusted the brass curtain poles. Frieda found a table facing the doors and ordered some coffee and a Wiener schnitzel. She felt as though something was slowly unspooling within her. As if she had opened an old book and found a long-pressed flower there. A little faded, a little flat, the petals slightly ragged at the edges. But still the same flower. Still in one piece.

The waiter brought her schnitzel and coffee and she began cutting up the meat, keeping her eyes on the door. She felt a sudden barb of guilt at what she was about to do. It wasn't too late to change her mind. She didn't have to betray Elisabeth and Ernest. She could leave now, go back and pack up their luggage. She tried to think of her mother, made bitter and vindictive by her father's philandering. Of the hatred that had seethed between them. But it was no good. She could think only of Otto, of his long slender body, of the way every word he spoke seemed to make her feel more alive.

The doors swung on their hinges. And there he was, pausing momentarily in the doorway so that sunlight streamed from behind him and skimmed round him, like a halo. For a second it seemed as if his body was outlined by a thread of darkness, as if he had an outer shell of blackness, but then he hurried towards her, and the effect was lost.

He slid onto a chair beside her, ground out his cigarette and fumbled in his pocket for another. Frieda took the opportunity to observe him and through the thin cotton of his shirt, she saw his chest which looked to her like the golden undulations of sand dunes, smooth and warm and yielding. He was so close she could smell the wood smoke that drifted from his pores, and something else – the smell of a man's skin, she decided. It was a scent she liked, that she hadn't inhaled for a very long time. Later, she wondered if it was the intoxicating smell of Otto's skin that had made her blurt out her next question so bluntly and gracelessly.

'Can I be your lover too?' She felt her face colouring immediately, the heat rising up the nape of her neck, flooding her face and scalp as she looked down at her plate. But even through her embarrassment she felt a thrill of triumph. For the first time she had reached out for something she wanted, without thought of decorum or propriety. Single-handedly she had made a choice, a decision, and followed it through.

'I like your boldness. I believe in repressing nothing, as you know.' He screwed a fresh cigarette into his ivory holder, lit it and blew out a thin jet of smoke. 'Sexual freedom is the only cure the world needs. Women like you – untainted by chastity, Christianity, democracy, patriarchy – are the future. Women who aren't afraid to ask for what they want, who have the courage to live in their bodies.'

She felt his words burn into her and as he spoke she had a sense of her past drawing, slowly, away from her. As if she were on the brink of something from which there could be no return. Otto's hand slipped onto her knee. And the touch of him also seemed to carry within it the promise of something new and different.

'I want to shed *all* my inhibitions. Will you help me?' She pushed away her plate, let her napkin fall to the floor.

'You'll have to share me with my wife, and your sister, and some of my patients. I don't believe anyone has the right to possess anyone else.' He studied her with his straight, steady gaze. A gaze that made her feel like a flower unfolding in the sun.

She nodded. There were gaps where his shirt buttons were missing and she could see through to his skin. She yearned to touch him, to slip her fingers into his shirt and feel the warmth of him. An image of Ernest came to her, pinched into his favourite brown chair gripping his glass of brown beer, his hands roped with veins and mottled with age spots. How was it that Otto understood her wholly and yet she was married to a man who barely knew her, who looked at her but did not see her?

'You are capable of so much, Frieda. But you must overthrow the patriarchs in your life, before they destroy you.' He traced the outline of her lips with his thumb then drew back. 'I'm writing a paper on personality types. Will you read it for me?'

She wondered if she'd misheard him. Ernest had never asked her to read any of his work. She'd volunteered repeatedly in the early days of their marriage, asking him to share his research or discuss his students. He'd batted at the air and laughed, as if such an idea was unimaginable, preposterous even. On one occasion he'd said her mind was 'not sufficiently trained', a turn of phrase that still sent a chill down her spine.

'Come home with me.' Otto took her hand, held it between his, letting her feel the current that ran from him to her and back again. 'I've never wanted anyone as much as I want you.' He pressed her hand against his heart so that she felt its strong unbroken beat beneath her palm.

Suddenly she was aware of the nakedness beneath her dress, her petticoat, her chemise, her corset, her drawers. 'Yes,' she said. 'Yes.'

SIXTEEN

Frieda

'I must tell Elisabeth.' Frieda drew her finger down Otto's chest, over his palpitating heart, through the woven line of hair that bisected his stomach. Her two nights with Otto had transformed her in a way she could barely articulate. She felt as if small sparks of electricity had replaced the sluggish blood in her veins, unleashing a new person, a new Frieda. After they first made love, she had opened her eyes and seen her surroundings as if for the first time. As a newborn baby takes in its first view, she thought. While she lay, dazed and panting in Otto's embrace, her thoughts had turned back to Monty's first minutes of life. The way his minute-old eyes had looked in wonder, at her, at Ernest, at the candles guttering on the window sill. How bright and radiant everything must have seemed to him. As it did to her at that moment.

For the minutes – no, the hour – that followed, she'd had the strange experience of being outside time and space, as if everything existed in suspension. Otto had continued to talk of revolution and anarchy and how psychoanalysis would change the world, while she had lain in a haze of bliss, hearing only the wind rolling up against the window panes, the throbbing of a church bell, the chime of milk churns being unloaded from a cart. But now she had to think about her sister.

'You haven't told her yet?' Otto looked up from his notebook, surprised. He was sitting up beside her scribbling frantically, noting down everything about her for the paper he was writing on personality types.

'No, but I must.' She lay back against the bolsters and closed her eyes. Being with him made her feel gloriously invincible but the feeling fled when she thought about confessing to Elisabeth. She had a dim sense that her sister wouldn't be happy, that she'd attempt to assert her authority somehow. As she'd always done as a child.

'She won't mind. She believes in free love.' Otto ran a careless hand through his hair, pushing it into sunlit spikes. 'She'll be happy to share me with her own sister, just as she's happy to share me with her best friend, who is of course my wife.' He laughed and pulled Frieda towards him. 'Here in Schwabing we all believe absolutely in the sexual revolution and the death of patriarchy.'

'Tell me about that place in Switzerland, Ascona.' She leaned into his chest, nuzzling its hollows with her nose. She loved it when he talked about the revolution. She loved the way words tumbled and flew from him, like acrobats in a circus.

'The revolution has started, Frieda. We're breaking down the old patriarchy of family in Ascona. All food and possessions and children are shared.' Otto pushed away his notebook and lifted his face to the light. 'It's the only place in the world where women are liberated – because families aren't dominated by the father there. There's no loneliness either, because everyone is equal and everyone truly cares for each other.'

'No loneliness?' She shivered, recalling her time in Nottingham. The long years when only books had made her feel less alone. The startling realisation, one wintry day, that marriage had made her *more* rather than *less* lonely.

'None,' he said emphatically. 'We shall be so happy there, Frieda, my love.'

67

She picked up Otto's pen from its pool of ink spreading across the stained sheet. 'Are children happy there?'

'Everyone is happy. No one is tainted by property or ownership or authority. People are truly free!' He took the ink pen from Frieda's fidgeting fingers and refilled it from the inkwell beside the bed. 'Roll over.'

She turned onto her front, felt the nib of his pen scraping over her buttock, breathed in the smell of the bolster. I could wear lederhosen in Ascona, she thought. And pea-green stockings. She had a fleeting glistening picture of Monty, Elsa and Barby wading naked through shallow streams, shoals of silver fish swimming between their limbs and nibbling at their toes.

'Ernest never let our children run around without clothes on,' she said, twisting her head from the bolster. 'Once I took them on a beach holiday and they spent the whole week naked. I was terrified they would tell him.'

'Bring your children. And we'll be free to do exactly as we want, to follow the call of our bodies, our hearts, our instincts. We shall be free spirits. We shall be truly ourselves!'

That's all I want, she thought. To be myself. Only myself. Why is it so hard? So complicated? She felt Otto's warm breath blowing against her bottom. 'What have you written?'

'Woman of the future.' He blew another soft jet of breath onto her behind. 'I've been dreaming of you all my life. I didn't know it was you – but now I see it was a prophetic dream of how perfect a woman could be. Your suffragettes don't understand that women can't be liberated until they free their sexuality. The act of love is an act of revolution.' His voice rose and plunged and spun. 'I've never met a woman as sexually free as you. To be so at ease in your skin, to delight in giving while the rest of your sex have been squeezed dry and flattened by repression. It's a form of genius, Frieda.'

She laughed. 'Genius? Me?'

'Yes, a genius for living. You've kept it locked up in . . . in . . .'

'Nottingham,' she said flatly.

'The very word stinks of hell. Come and fly with me!' He pulled her to him with such force, she couldn't breathe. And he pressed his mouth on hers and kissed her as though this was to be his last kiss, as though he wanted to imprint it forever on his memory.

SEVENTEEN

Ernest

It was after ten o'clock when Ernest arrived home from teaching his regular Wednesday class to the local pit workers and labourers. It hadn't been his best class. He had done his utmost to inspire the men, but fatigue had rather taken the shine from his performance. Nor had he managed to curb his yawns when the poetry readings began, despite their being marvellous examples of England's finest poet, Lord Tennyson.

Mrs Babbit had left him a glass of stout and a cheese sandwich, but he felt so overcome with tiredness he couldn't eat. He wondered if it was the extra class he'd taken on and the extra exam papers he'd agreed to mark. Perhaps he'd overstretched himself. But the responsibility of his family weighed more heavily than ever on his stooped shoulders. And he was quite determined that Frieda should have a lavish London hat with feathers stitched around the brim. If it was ordered in time, she could wear it to the Church's harvest festival service in September.

Recently he'd been dreaming of the workhouse that he lived next door to, as a child. He had no idea why it had returned to haunt him. But since Frieda and Monty's departure not a night had gone by in which he didn't wake, cold and sweating, from a dream in which he and his family were dragged, barefoot, to the workhouse.

Perhaps if he slept in the marital bed tonight, he thought. Perhaps his sleep would be improved with a little more space and a softer mattress and the smell of his wife on the pillow. He missed Frieda. He missed the way she moved round the house, with the negligent, large-boned grace that only the upper classes can muster. He missed the thumping piano notes, the slightly toneless singing. The house felt too quiet and empty – and dull.

He went upstairs and looked at Barby and Elsa, marvelling at how peaceful and contented they looked. He'd always enjoyed watching his children sleep. He rarely saw them awake these days, he thought, with a stab of nostalgia. He slipped into Frieda's bed and breathed in the smell of her. He wondered if *she* was thinking of *him*, as she lay in Elisabeth's guest room. She was probably snoring in that soft way of hers, he thought with a smile.

Or perhaps she and Elisabeth were drinking tea and discussing *Anna Karenina*. Or babies. He hoped Elisabeth's superb logic – and her superior grasp of economics – were at work on Frieda's addled brain. Bridge, he thought with a start. He should find her a bridge club. He didn't usually tolerate card games but Professor Kipping's wife had mentioned that bridge was very fashionable amongst Nottingham's most elegant ladies. Yes, he would look out for a bridge club.

Later, when he hadn't managed to fall asleep, he crept to his room and found his Bible. His father had read the Bible to him every day. And now, when he was plagued with insomnia, he would open the Bible at random and read until sleep washed over him. He had to be vigilant, otherwise a single seductive word could send him scurrying down the philological and etymological paths that so excited him, making sleep still more elusive. It wasn't only words: inflexions, numerals, pronouns, prepositions, conjunctions – any could send his mind spiralling through space and time, riffling through all the tongues known to him.

He turned up the lamp and opened the Bible . . . *But I say, walk by the Spirit, and you will not carry out the desire of the flesh. For the flesh sets its desire against the Spirit, and the Spirit against the flesh; for these are in opposition to one another, so that you may not do the things that you please . . .*

EIGHTEEN

Monty

Monty woke to the raised voices of his mother and Aunt Elisabeth. He knew it was late because there was no light coming through the shutters and he still felt very sleepy.

He yawned and stretched, and rubbed his eyes. His book was still on his bed. He must have fallen asleep while he was reading. He pushed back the eiderdown. He wanted to go and see his mother – she hadn't been home all day and he knew Aunt Elisabeth was cross because she'd made a lot of noise clearing up the tea things. She didn't normally touch the crockery because the servants did that. But yesterday she had cleared the table herself, bashing the plates and clanging the cutlery and pulling the tablecloth sharply from the table with tight, angry hands.

He walked quietly to the hall. Aunt Elisabeth's voice was very loud. And very cross.

'I can't believe it, Frieda! How could you do that?'

'But you believe in free love. I thought you would be happy for me.'

Monty strained his ears. He liked the sound of free love.

'He has me! And he has a wife who is my best friend. And sometimes he has to help his patients. But he has no need of you.'

73

He could hear the furious *swoosh-swoosh* of his aunt's skirts and the stab of her heels on the floorboards.

'But – but I thought that's what you meant when you encouraged me to have the talking cure with him?'

'That's not what I meant at all! You have Ernest to think of.'

Monty crept along the corridor until he was standing by the door to the drawing room. He knew eavesdropping was wrong but he wanted to tell his mother about Friedel's train set and ask if he could have one for Christmas.

'Can't we share him? I'm not asking you to give him up . . .'

'It's out of the question, Frieda. Two sisters with the same man – it's almost incest.'

'No, it's not.'

'You don't know the half of it. You should leave him alone.' Aunt Elisabeth's voice sounded different now – wobbly, as though she was going to cry. Monty stood very still. He didn't want to see his aunt crying.

'What don't I know? He wants to take me and the children to a place called Ascona. Frankly, I'm very tempted. It sounds a revolutionary place to live. I love the idea of living communally . . . not owning things . . . not having a scalp full of hairpins and my ribs imprisoned by a corset every day. Anyway, he thinks I'm wasted in Nottingham.'

Monty froze. What was she talking about? Taking him and Elsa and Barby to – to where? And why was she talking about her underclothes?

'Don't be such a fool, Frieda! The truth is . . .' There was a long silence. Monty could hear the blood drumming in his ears. And then his mother spoke in a loud, angry voice.

'You're jealous! You don't want to share anything with me. Your love isn't free at all! You're a hypocrite, Elisabeth. An envious hypocrite!'

Monty shrunk against the wall. He had never heard her shout like this. He wanted to slip back to his room, but if they heard him they'd think he was snooping and he'd be in trouble. So he stayed there, rooted to the spot. And then he heard Aunt Elisabeth speaking very quietly, so quietly he had to stretch his ears to hear.

'I am having a baby. Otto's baby.'

There was a long silence, so long and deep Monty wondered if they could hear the beating of his heart through the wall.

'Does Otto know?'

'Of course he knows! Half of Munich is having his child.'

'Will you leave Edgar?' Monty could only just decipher his mother's whisper.

'Of course not. Edgar will bring the child up as his own. Did you know Otto's wife is also having his child?' He heard Aunt Elisabeth sigh and the scraping of a chair against the floorboards, as though she was sitting down. He started inching back up the corridor. He didn't want to hear any more. And he didn't want to be caught eavesdropping. He wanted to read his book. Suddenly he imagined himself as Robin Hood, mounting his steed, pulling up the reins, galloping and galloping through the green glades of Sherwood Forest. Over the bluebells he went, through the dells with their banks of old man's beard, ragged robin, cow-parsley, on and on into the woods. Swallows swooped alongside him, magpies scattered from his path, buzzards wheeled overhead. On and on he went through the forest.

'Monty! Whatever are you doing here?' Aunt Elisabeth's voice was like glass.

'I wanted some water.' He looked down at his feet, his face burning.

His mother came out and put her arms round him. 'Oh *mein Liebling*. Come on, back to bed. It's very late.'

He clutched at her and breathed in her smell. But she didn't smell right. There was no scent of lily-of-the-valley or the violet soap she liked to use. And all the arguing with Aunt Elisabeth wasn't right either. Mutti never raised her voice or argued. Not with anyone. Later, Monty wondered if he'd dreamt it all.

NINETEEN

Frieda

The news that Elisabeth was carrying Otto's child made Frieda feel a sensation that, at first, she couldn't identify. Of course she'd felt fury at her sister's possessiveness. It went against the grain of everything Otto espoused. It went against the grain of all the ideals Elisabeth professed to believe in, the ideals she, Frieda, was embracing so eagerly. But beneath the anger at her sister's jealousy, something reared sour and green. It was envy, she realised eventually, reluctantly. Envy that Elisabeth was having Otto's child. Envy that, yet again, Elisabeth had managed to grab something Frieda desperately wanted for herself. And now it gnawed away at her new sense of freedom. At her new sense of self. Demeaning her with its grubbiness.

She knew the baby changed everything. How could she continue with Otto if her sister was carrying his child? If her sister forbade it? Her hand fluttered to her stomach. But what if she had already conceived too? She had an intense desire to be carrying Otto's child, to have part of him inside her, something that would bind him to her. It was a strange feeling, she thought, and not something she'd had with Ernest. Monty, Elsa and Barby had appeared like small miracles, but entirely unconnected with the distantly functional act that had produced them. But a child with Otto was different. The child would be a symbol, a sign of hope and love.

Otto felt the same way. The day before he'd thrown himself at her feet, begged her to produce *our baby*. It would be a genius, he'd said. A free spirit that could grow up with all his other children at Ascona.

His unwavering respect for motherhood, for matriarchy, was something she'd never seen before. She couldn't help thinking how much better the world would be if more people adopted Otto's philosophy of a matriarchal society, as they had in Ascona.

Ascona . . . the word was like nectar on her tongue. She couldn't shake off the image of her children running barefoot through streams, the wind in their hair, the sun on their pale skin, and above them a vast sky yellow with light. Instead of the grinding dirt of Nottingham, they would have alpine peaks of jewelled ice, lakes leaping with diamonds, sun-swept shores. She could almost see them, growing freely like mountain flowers.

The next morning, as she sat on Monty's bed stroking his hair, she was aware of her envy slipping away and a deep serenity taking its place. She realised that for the first time she felt able to hold her son without the sense of desperation she'd experienced in Nottingham. She could touch him now, without needing to cling to him. It was a strange blend of detachment and love that she couldn't explain. A sort of deep contentment, she decided.

'Would you like to meet my new friend at the Café Stefanie?' she asked. She harboured a hazy hope that they might all go and live in Ascona. How and when, she had no idea. And at some moments the idea seemed ludicrous and impossible. But every now and then she let the fantasy take hold of her and instil a new gust of hope into her.

Monty's head bobbed up. 'Yes! And can I have some cake there?'

The café was busy, its air thickly intoxicating with the lingering smoke of cigars and Russian cigarettes, its tables still sticky from the previous night's spilt schnapps. The anarchists in the corner were debating as vigorously as ever and at the bar poets exchanged scribbled verses. Otto leapt out from the billiard room with a great cry.

'Frieda!' He clicked his fingers at a waiter. 'Coffee. And something for the boy . . . Apple strudel!'

'This is Monty, my eldest child,' she said.

'Hello, Monty! How fine and tall you are, as handsome as your mother, eh?' Otto ruffled Monty's hair. 'How would you like to be part of a revolution? How would you like to live in Paradise?' Otto beamed at him, then added 'You look like a genius, Monty. But genius is destroyed by domesticity, by patriarchy, by fathers. Sons must rise up and revolt. We must eradicate fathers in all their guises. Will you join me?' He clapped his hand on Monty's shoulder.

'Don't take any notice, my love. My new friend is very excitable. Let us sit by the window.'

Otto joined them at the table, his feet tapping restlessly on the floor as he called out to friends and acolytes. Frieda had an overwhelming desire to throw her arms round his neck, to tell him she loved him, that she could feel the pattern of her life changing, but that she didn't know what to do now, what sort of woman or sister she should be. She looked at Monty pouring a large puddle of cream over his apple strudel, and her emotions swung back to him. I'm like the wavering needle of a compass, she thought, being pulled from one person I love to another.

When Monty went to watch the chess players, Otto leaned in to her and whispered, 'I've been invited to speak at a conference in Amsterdam. Can you meet me there? In September?'

Frieda nodded. She would find a way.

'And we can plan our future together. I don't have a future without you. My genius is entirely dependent on you, my beloved. I like your son very much – bring him, bring all your children.'

79

'And the child that you are to have with my sister?' she asked, keeping her tone calm and even.

'It will grow up with our child, Frieda. All of them can grow up in Ascona. There is only love in Ascona.' He lit a cigarette for her, pausing to stare into the match's flame. 'The psychology of the unconscious is the philosophy of revolution, a revolution that must be led by women . . . the first true revolution will be the one that unites woman and freedom and spirit in a single whole. You, my beloved Frieda, will help forge our new world in Ascona.'

Frieda closed her eyes. The café with its swallowing-and-chewing sounds and its coffee-and-bread odours slipped away to nothing. For a few seconds she could think only of this promised paradise. Of herself – her new, true self – in this Eden where she would work alongside Otto on his brilliant ideas, where only the cry of peewits and her children's laughter would disturb them.

'I have some patients for my psychoanalysis,' Otto announced, standing up abruptly. 'I'll be back later.'

Frieda nodded and closed her eyes again so that her dream of Ascona swam back, clear and splendid.

'What does er-eradicate mean?'

She opened her eyes. Monty had returned and was wiping anxiously at his trousers.

'It means to get rid of.'

'Why does your friend want to er-eradicate fathers?'

She laughed. 'He wants to change the world so that men are not always in charge. He wants to eradicate patriarchy.' She patted the space beside her. 'Sit down and I will tell you about a brave new world where there are no armies, no wars, no hate, only love and good things.'

TWENTY

Frieda

A day later Elisabeth announced she was returning to Heidelberg to help Max Weber with his book on Eastern religion. Frieda took her sister's words as covert permission to spend time with Otto. But, more significantly, she noticed this was the first time Elisabeth had flaunted her intellectually superior life without it evoking in her the slightest feeling of envy. She attributed her serenity to Otto who had involved her in every aspect of his work but particularly his new theory of personality types. Their evenings followed a regular pattern now. At his corner table in the Café Stefanie, she would read over his ideas on personality traits, adding and underlining with red ink. After much animated discussion, desire would come over her, like an unendurable hunger. And they would retire to his rooms for a few hours of frenzied lovemaking.

Two nights before she and Monty returned to England, Frieda came home to find Elisabeth waiting in the drawing room, her hands cradling her stomach.

'I thought you were back tomorrow.' Frieda hastily smoothed her hair and tried to make it lie flat against her head. The smell of Otto rose up from her, potent and musky.

'Edgar and I want you to end this ludicrous affair.'

Frieda's cheeks flushed. And something snapped inside her. 'I am helping him with his work, giving him greater insights into the human mind. He says I am the only truly uninhibited woman he has met.' There – she had said it. The words hung like wire between them.

Elisabeth's lips tightened into a thin white line. She crossed her arms on her chest. '*I* am having his child, not you.'

'I think I am too.' Frieda stared grimly out of the window, her hand moving instinctively to her abdomen – something had been moving and shifting inside for the last three hours.

'Don't be ridiculous! How could you possibly know so soon?'

'Why won't you share him with me?'

'Because you are my sister!' Elisabeth moved towards a vase of lilies and snapped the wilting head of a bloom between her finger and thumb. A haze of yellow pollen tumbled to the floor. 'And Ernest will never agree to an open marriage.'

'But Otto and I love being together. I know he loves you too, but –'

'Otto has no idea what love is. He's an intellectual genius and an incomparable lover, but that is all he's good for.' Elisabeth tapped her stomach in an exaggerated manner. 'Why else would I ask Edgar to bring up this child?'

'You have Otto *and* Edgar. And those Weber brothers. Why shouldn't I have someone who values me, who inspires me? Why shouldn't I have pleasure and happiness?'

Elisabeth gave a scornful laugh. 'If you're thinking of suggesting an open marriage to Ernest you must be quite deranged. It would be madness, a crime.'

Frieda rubbed angrily at her temples. 'I'm thinking of taking the children to live in Ascona.' Where people support each other, and live freely, equally, without resentment and jealousy, she thought, bitterly.

Elisabeth glared at her. 'Don't be ridiculous! He has no money and he has no concept of responsibility.'

'He includes me in his work, Elisabeth. We work *together* on his ideas, his papers. Just as you and Edgar do. Just as you and Max Weber do. It makes me feel as if I matter, to him and to myself.' She could hear the supplication in her voice, but Elisabeth was still glowering at her. So she carried on. 'All the thoughts and ideas I had in Nottingham – germs of them really – but I couldn't articulate them. He has helped me to understand myself, to see who I am.'

Elisabeth gave a disdainful shake of her head. 'Very well. If you insist on pursuing this affair I cannot stop you. But Ernest must never know. I do not particularly like Ernest but he is a good provider. And we women are nothing if we are not provided for. Unless you intend to provide for yourself?'

'And how exactly could I do that? With three children and no qualifications!'

A silence fell over the room. Outside a dog yelped and Frieda heard the rattle of its chain being loosened. She thought of the long-lost Frieda who'd run, panting, alongside the Baron's bloodied hounds. Otto had rescued that girl, unchained her, brought her back from the dead. How could she leave him now? How could she let the trap snap shut on this bright seam of hope?

PART THREE

Nottingham 1907

'How to act, that was the question?

Whither to go, how to become oneself?'

D.H. Lawrence, *The Rainbow*

TWENTY-ONE

Frieda

'You're not our old mother. You've got our old mother's skin on, but you're not our mother that went away.' Elsa's blue eyes briefly met Frieda's over the dining table.

'Of course I am the same! Maybe my hair has grown thicker from the German food.' Flustered, Frieda put a hand to the hair piled up on her head then shook her napkin onto her lap. 'Has my hair changed, Ernest?'

'What?' Ernest peered at her.

'My hair, is it thicker?' Her hands lingered under the table, fidgeting with the napkin, plucking at its hem. Elsa's words had stung her but she knew Elsa was right. She was not the same.

'I think you both look splendid. Was it very warm?' Ernest turned to Monty. 'And what did you think of the food in Munich, young man?'

Frieda watched Monty arranging his boiled potatoes, so that they circled his pork chop with its thick grey rind. She pondered Elsa's words: *not our old mother*. In spite of the exhausting return journey, she felt as light as pollen. The giddy joy of her time with Otto, as *herself*, clung to her. She wondered if that was how an escaped canary felt when returned to its cage. Did the exuberance of its rebellion, the joy of its soaring flight, nourish it even as it returned to captivity? Or was it the prospect – the dizzying, tumescent hope – of absconding for a second time that kept the bird singing? She thought of Otto's promised trip to Amsterdam. She thought of their child that might, at this very moment, be growing in her womb. Her body tingled and, for a second, she felt so light, so buoyant, she had to hold the seat of her chair.

'And what is the talk in Munich? Other than the military might of the Kaiser.' Ernest sipped cautiously from his glass of water.

Frieda saw her chance. Perhaps if she could introduce her husband to the new ideas fermenting in Germany, he might change. Like Edgar. At the very least, she would have someone to talk to. She heard a voice in her head call out: *Courage!* She took a long, deep breath. 'Have you heard of a man called Doctor Freud? All Munich is talking of him and his ideas.'

'Oh – a medical man? Has he found a cure for typhoid fever?'

'Oh no, much better than that. He understands everything about our repressed feelings, our frustrated longings and urges.'

'Our what?' Ernest stiffened and put his water glass down.

'All the urges we have buried in us. Our need to love. Doctor Freud believes we have repressed it all in our unconscious.' She spoke slowly, determinedly. Perhaps she could help him slough off the layers of inhibition and restraint that governed his life. Perhaps she could help him see who she was now, who she had become. She saw now that it wasn't fair to continue this charade in which she played at being someone she wasn't. It wasn't fair on him or her. Particularly if there was another child, Otto's child. She wondered, briefly, if Ernest would be as generous, as honourable, as Edgar had been to Elisabeth.

'Many people in Munich are vegetarian. They eat no meat,' she persisted, hoping this idea might get a better response.

'The weather has brightened. You should take the children for a walk after luncheon.' Ernest was gripping his cutlery so hard his knuckles had paled.

'I want to go to the minnow stream with my jam jar,' Barby trilled. 'Please!'

'Of course, *mein Liebling*. What fun!' Frieda pulled Barby into her arms and buried her nose in Barby's soft flossy hair. The scent of her daughter's hair – lilac and wet grass – eased the pounding of her heart.

As soon as the children had left the table to find their hats and boots, Ernest turned to her. 'Do you think that was appropriate, Frieda?'

She pushed her plate to one side and put her hands back under the table. Her fingers ground at the napkin lying across her lap. 'I wanted to tell you, Ernest – and you asked what Munich was talking about. They are talking about our deepest longings and repressed urges.'

She tried to catch his eye, but he was staring at the cruets. And when he spoke, his voice was nipped and strained. 'We will have no more talk of this Doctor's idiotic sex ideas. Not at the dinner table, not in the drawing room and not in the bedroom.'

Frieda felt a twist of anger. How could he be so small-minded? So intolerant? She opened her mouth to remonstrate but then decided to swallow her irritation. She was resolved not to let Ernest destroy her new mood, not to let the cage door swing closed behind her. She would hang on to this wondrous feeling of weightlessness and happiness for as long as she could, at least until she got to Amsterdam and saw Otto again.

She ploughed on, her fingers milling ceaselessly at her napkin. 'They are also talking about bringing back the principles of pagan society, where men worshipped women and all their feminine mysteries.'

'Shall I sell the house and get rid of the servants and relocate us to a cave?' His voice was dry and bare. 'You could spend your days making sparks from flints while I pursue wild boar for you to skin. Or would I spend my days worshipping at your shrine?'

He gave a mocking laugh. 'If this is the talk of Germany I see no need for us to fear the Kaiser.'

'Why do you never take me seriously?'

'I thought there might be talk of the Kaiser's plans. The *Daily Mail* has a sabre-rattling headline about him every day. And so does *The Times*. Apparently a German invasion is imminent. Although it would appear the people of Munich are oblivious to this.' He sighed, as though her replies to his questions had disappointed him. As though *she* had disappointed him.

'I smoked in Munich, Ernest. Everyone there smokes. The Munich doctors say tobacco is very good for a lady. I would like to continue smoking here.' She felt an angry tear at the back of her eye. She squeezed the napkin in her fist, determined to persevere, determined not to cry. If he refused to let her smoke, she would ignore him. Defy him.

'As I smoke a pipe it would be ungenerous of me not to allow you to smoke the occasional cigarette.' Ernest paused and his jawline softened. 'I don't find it becoming in a lady but if it will aid your health, I can have no objection, can I? But not in public please. And perhaps not in the stone-age cave we are shortly to inhabit.'

He stood up and kissed her perfunctorily on the cheek. As the door closed behind him, Frieda bit down on her lower lip and threw her napkin to the floor. Why did he always laugh at her? Why wouldn't he discuss anything with her? She wondered if it was the way she presented her ideas: not eloquently enough for him, too much feeling and not enough form. And why did he only want to discuss war and newspapers when the world was humming with new theories of how to live, of how to *be*? His reaction – so curt and sneering – suggested her new ideas were an affront to him. But perhaps they frightened him in some way? Was that it?

A sudden twinge in her stomach halted her meandering thoughts. She put her hands on her abdomen. Could it be . . . ? Or was it just Mrs Babbit's cooking making its circuitous journey through her intestines? She moved her hands from her stomach to the neckline of her dress, slipped one hand into her chemise and pulled out the letter. It had been waiting for her when she got home, in an envelope bearing Elisabeth's handwriting. Otto must have written it before she left Munich. She unfolded it, saw his wild scrawl, felt her pulse quicken.

There had been a second letter too. From Elisabeth's husband, Edgar. She'd read it and dropped it quickly into the fire. Edgar's letter had been brief and to the point, asking her to burn all Otto's letters. She would reply, agreeing to his request. She knew if she didn't, he and Elisabeth would refuse to forward Otto's letters. And she didn't think she could go on without hearing from him. But she had no intention of burning his letters. It had taken a day of cajoling to persuade Elisabeth to act as messenger. Edgar had been more forthcoming. Eventually both of them had agreed to forward Otto's letters in envelopes handwritten by themselves to ensure Ernest didn't become suspicious. Frieda ran her fingers lovingly over the envelope, then slipped it back against her breast.

'Mutti, it's raining. Can we still go out? I want to show you my minnows and Elsa has a baby frog.' Barby tottered into the dining room clutching a jam jar.

'Of course we can. I love the rain!' Frieda bent down, pulled Barby to her and smothered her with kisses. 'Put that jar down and dance with me, my love!' Together they twirled round the table, Frieda lifting Barby so high her booted feet skimmed the floor. Her anger and frustration diffused into the air, and she felt, again, as light and bright as a splinter of sunshine.

'You are still our mother. Elsa was being silly . . . you are still our old mother that went away.'

'Of course I am,' Frieda said soothingly. But she knew she wasn't.

TWENTY-TWO

Monty

Three weeks later, Monty came home to find his mother crying. She was sitting at the piano playing a new piece he hadn't heard before. Her eyes were pink and wet and her face was blotchy. A tear was rolling down her cheek. He didn't like seeing his mother sad. Especially now that he was happier. The boys at school had stopped calling him a Hun. He wasn't sure why, but he thought it might be because of the new boy with no toes who was being taunted instead. Monty was still being very careful. He was keeping his head down and pretending he couldn't speak German.

'Mutti?' He touched her gently on the arm.

'Oh Monty . . . Shall I tell you why I am sad?' She wrapped her arms round him and buried her face in his hair. 'You remember asking about a baby brother?' Her shoulders went limp and she gave another heaving gulp. 'There is no baby brother.'

'Would you like to see my new stamps? There's a nice one with a parrot on. Would you like to see it?'

She nodded and pulled a handkerchief from her pocket. 'You must not tell Papa I was crying. He would only worry about me. I will have a cigarette and look at your new stamps.' She mustered a small smile and patted his arm.

As Monty climbed the stairs to his room, he wondered how she knew there was no baby. Had she read it in a letter, he wondered. She got lots of letters now. She always smiled when she read them and said, 'More news from Aunt Elisabeth!' Sometimes she got *two* letters from Aunt Elisabeth on the same day.

He pulled his stamp album from under his bed. He knew the parrot stamp would cheer her up because it was full of bright colours – red, yellow, green – and came from a long way away. He flipped through the album until he found it, mounted in the very centre of a blank page, with extra hinges to keep it in place. But when he looked more closely, his limbs set slowly rigid. It seemed to him that in the eyes of the parrot, piercing and spare, he saw the eyes of a man. A particular man. Doctor Gross, with his golden-yellow hair and his brilliant blue eyes. He carefully removed the parrot stamp from its hinges and slid it beneath the rug. He would only let her see his English stamps today. And if she asked where the parrot stamp was, he would show her his set of English bird stamps – a robin, chaffinch, linnet, bunting and wagtail. He knew they lacked the panache of the parrot. But they were beautiful, all the same.

TWENTY-THREE

Ernest

When he heard the knock on his study door, Ernest assumed it was Mrs Babbit bringing tea. Frieda never bothered knocking, and the children were too intimidated to come to his room when he was working. Which was a good thing. A father needed to be a figure of authority and respect.

His eyes travelled to the photograph of his wife which he kept, in a polished mahogany frame, on the mantelpiece. She'd come back from Munich so radiant, so palpably glowing, he'd felt a pang of sadness. It was clear the German climate and food agreed with her so much better than their English equivalents. But at least she'd stopped groping at his shirt tails. Elisabeth – her mind trained so assiduously at Heidelberg University – must have convinced her that another child would be a grave mistake.

The knock came again, a little louder this time. Too timorous for Mrs Babbit, thought Ernest.

'Papa? May I come in?'

'Monty?' He turned to the door, surprised and pleased. 'I'm glad you've come. I have some more stamps for you that I quite forgot about. Professor Kipping gave them to me yesterday. From America.'

'Thank you, Papa. Mutti is going back to Germany tomorrow.' Monty stood by the door, shifting from one foot to the other.

'Yes, she's going to see Aunt Elisabeth. Your aunt's been unwell. Come and look at these stamps.' Ernest beckoned Monty into his study. The boy looked pale and apprehensive and Ernest wondered, again, if he was becoming too attached to his mother. He'd warned Frieda before, told her that boys who couldn't stick up for themselves got bullied, and boys who spent too much time with their mothers became inverts. He'd seen it before. And it never ended well.

'I – I – don't think we should let her go to Aunt Elisabeth's.' Monty's eyes flickered to his shoes, then to Ernest and then back to his shoes.

'Why not?' Ernest's arms longed to reach out for his son. Instead he folded them squarely on his chest and gave a small, dry cough.

'She – she might catch Aunt Elisabeth's illness.'

'Your wonderful Mutti is as strong as an ox. She's only going for a week.' Ernest gave what he hoped was a reassuring nod of his head. 'We have to remember that Germany is her home and we need to let her go whenever she wants.'

'But travel is dangerous. She might meet someone who – who . . .' Monty's voice petered out. He put his thumbnail to his mouth and gnawed at it.

'Someone who . . . what?' Ernest watched Monty carefully. His son was behaving most peculiarly. This attachment to his mother was distinctly unhealthy.

'Who wants to er-eradicate fathers!' Monty stared at Ernest, wide-eyed and flushed.

Ernest frowned. 'Don't worry, Monty, she is travelling first class. Now take these stamps and put them in your album.'

Monty shuffled off and Ernest tried to resume his work. He had twenty student essays to mark before tomorrow, but he couldn't concentrate. He kept seeing Monty's small, white face, so wan and fearful. And when Monty's face faded, Frieda's bounced into view, so ruddy, so lustily glowing. Suddenly, in the very back of his mind, a thought began to form, embryonic and dark. But no, that couldn't be right. It was too unpleasant, too unsettling, to think about. He pushed it away. Monty had been reading too much . . . his imagination was too vivid . . . he was excessively fond of his mother. Perhaps he should spend more time with his son, playing sport or fishing. But he didn't have time. If he was to keep Frieda happy, in the clothes and hats she liked, with plenty of domestic staff, he had to keep working.

Ernest's gaze sidled back to the photograph of her with a baby Monty in her arms. She was as beautiful now as she was seven years ago. A little larger, but he liked that. She would be happier in Cambridge. If he kept working, perhaps he'd be offered a Chair at Cambridge University. He knew Frieda would prefer it there: quieter, a more erudite population, none of the black industrial miasma that hung over Nottingham. And when his etymological tome was complete there might be enough money for a holiday.

He turned back to his marking, but the writing on the page seemed to twist and turn like a snake so that the meaning of the words evaded him. He picked up his pipe and packed it with tobacco. He tried to concentrate on the feel of it in his hand, smooth and reassuring, the mouthpiece between his lips, the warm nimbus of smoke in his mouth. But still that kernel of a thought kept creeping back, as though it was colonising inside him, like mould spreading over a damp wall.

He pushed away the papers and stood up, his knees creaking. He would go and find Frieda, offer to help with her packing, broach the subject of Monty perhaps. He went upstairs to Frieda's room.

She was standing over her bed, head on one side, looking at the dresses and hats spread out across the lace counterpane. 'I cannot decide what to take, Ernest. The yellow satin or the lavender muslin?'

'I prefer the yellow. It suits your sunny disposition, my snowflower.' He remembered abruptly that she no longer liked being called his snowflower. But she didn't snap at him, as she had before. He felt a swift sharp pain beneath his ribs as he recalled the brief exchange before she'd left for Germany. She'd suggested – in a distinctly snappish tone – that he think of a new term of endearment, one more in keeping with her character. He'd been so dumbfounded, so hurt and confused, a fog had fallen on his brain. In the ensuing seconds nothing had come to mind but a carnation. When he suggested *my carnation*, she'd drawn in such a long painful breath, he'd known it wasn't right. And since then he'd reverted to snowflower. After all, he'd called her *his snowflower* for nearly nine years. It sat elegantly on his tongue and he liked it.

'If you prefer it, I shall take it.' She skipped round the bed, picked up the yellow dress and dropped it into her travelling trunk.

'You're in high spirits, my love.'

'You know I adore going to Germany, Ernest. Even if I am to be nursing a sick sister.'

'Monty's worried. He must be reading a very lurid book at the moment.' Ernest sucked on his pipe and watched his wife. She was inspecting her hat with particular scrutiny.

'Oh you know Monty.' She placed the hat in a hatbox and fiddled with the strap. 'He is always imagining things. Perhaps he will be a great poet.'

'Yes, perhaps.'

'You're filling my bedroom with pipe smoke. Have you finished your work?' Frieda moved towards him and kissed him on the cheek as though she was kissing him goodbye, or dismissing him.

Ernest cleared his throat, looked at his feet. He wanted to tell her he loved her but the words clotted on his tongue. 'We'll miss you, Frieda,' he mumbled. Even those few words sounded odd and stilted, as though he was reading them from a book, as though they were someone else's words. Why was he unable to tell his wife how much he loved her?

'I know, I know, you silly old thing.' Frieda patted him on the chest. 'But I am only going for a week. What a lot of fuss you are all making.'

He gave a small, parched cough. 'I'm sorry I haven't been able to give you more. But I have my hopes pinned on Cambridge. If I can just finish my book.' He wanted to take her in his arms, to hold her tightly to him. But it was the afternoon and Mrs Babbit and the maid were downstairs and the children and Ida were around somewhere. And Frieda was back at her chest of drawers tossing underclothes into her trunk.

'Yes, yes. Now go back to your work. Go and finish writing your book.'

Ernest turned and walked towards the door. And as he did so he caught sight of something that made his step falter, very slightly. On her dressing table was a stack of letters folded in a messy pile and bound with a purple silk ribbon. He wanted to look again. Perhaps they were from him, his love letters of nine years ago. Or letters from her sisters. Or letters from her mother. If he looked again he could verify this, put his trembling heart at rest. But a small voice in his head told him to keep moving, to return to his study, to keep working. Cambridge! He must get her to Cambridge. And he wiped the letters from his mind in the same way he wiped chalk from a blackboard. One quick, deft movement – and gone.

TWENTY-FOUR

Monty

'I s Mutti coming home today, Papa?' Monty carefully spread butter onto his toast, making sure it went right to the crusts.

His father lowered his book and sighed. 'I can only give you the same answer that I gave you yesterday, and the day before, and the day before that. She is coming home tomorrow.'

'Will there be a postcard today, Papa?' Monty cut his buttered toast into five fingers and lined them up beside his boiled egg. He hoped Mrs Babbit hadn't undercooked the egg. He didn't like it when translucent strings, like bits of phlegm, appeared on his toasty soldiers.

'I am not a prophet, Monty. You'll have to wait for the postman.' He lifted his book again.

Monty dipped a finger of toast into his egg. His mother always sent postcards when she went away. But this time there had been no postcard, no letter, no telegram. Nothing.

'Is Aunt Elisabeth better?' He lifted the toast from his soft-boiled egg and examined it for uncooked globules. There was only yolk, deep yellow and runny, just how he liked it. He put it in his mouth and concentrated very hard on chewing.

'I do not know that either.' His father closed his book and looked at him down the line of his nose. 'There'll come a time when you won't see your mother for long periods of time, Monty. I have decided to send you to boarding school.'

Monty squirmed on his chair. 'Can't I go to school in Nottingham?'

'I think you'll benefit from boarding school. It'll help you become a man.'

'How does a boy become a man?' He peered into his eggshell to see if there were any yolky bits at the bottom.

'Well, you grow big and tall. And you might meet a girl you like . . .'

His father shifted impatiently on his chair and Monty knew he was getting cross with Mrs Babbit for not bringing his coffee.

'How old will I be when I like girls?'

His father's eyes opened very wide as though he was surprised by Monty's question. 'It's different for everyone. Ah, my coffee. Thank you, Mrs Babbit.'

Mrs Babbit put the coffee pot on the doily. Then she picked up a napkin from the table and wiped the cup and saucer and polished the coffee pot, so everything gleamed and shone. His father picked up his book again. A smell of mildew rose from its pages and a small silverfish flopped from its spine and wriggled across the tablecloth.

'Will I like *all* girls?'

For a moment there was silence, then his father said, 'No, just one.'

'And she stays with you forever?' Monty chewed thoughtfully on his last square of toast. It was cold now and he wished he'd put some marmalade on it.

'That's right, Monty. That's what marriage is.' His father turned back to his book and began reading, his eyes going from left to right, zig-zagging across the page.

Monty felt a bit better now, but he wasn't sure why. Perhaps it was because his tummy was full of egg and toast. And then, with an involuntary shudder, the image of Doctor Gross flashed before his eyes. The keen blue eyes like skewers, the wild hair in bright spikes, the peculiar talk of destroying fathers and living in Paradise.

He heard the sudden clatter of his buttery knife hitting the wooden floor, then the crashing of his eggcup and the clanging of his teaspoon as they too tumbled to the ground, spinning and skimming towards the Persian rug.

'Good God, Monty! What on earth are you doing? Mrs Babbit!' His father leapt up, shaking his head in an anguished way. 'It appears to be impossible to have a quiet breakfast in this house.'

Monty pushed his chair back and surveyed the floor around him. Eggshell lay in shards across the parquet. Strands of egg white stuck to the rug. The spoon, with its smears of yolk, had spun right across the room and lay, disgraced, by the door. Monty felt hot tears pushing at the back of his eyes.

'It's all right. Nothing is broken.' His father picked up the eggcup and raised it to the light. 'Not even a crack.'

As Monty looked with relief at the yolk-stained china, he saw, from the corner of his eye, his father watching him, staring at him with an odd expression. He thought he saw his father's arm nudge jerkily towards him, but then it abruptly changed direction and picked up the butter knife instead. Monty felt the lump in his throat choking him.

'Why don't you go and play outside?' His father's voice was soft and kind, but Monty's face was flaming with shame and the lump in his throat was so big he couldn't breathe. He turned and ran up to his bedroom, crying out 'S-s-stamps.' But his voice came out all strangled and he didn't want to look back for fear his father would think him still a baby.

TWENTY-FIVE

Frieda

The train back to Nottingham passed through woods and fields of bronze and copper and gold. The trees were on fire, flashing scarlet, amber, mustard-yellow. And the October sky was so high and blue that when Frieda looked out she felt dizzy. But mostly she looked down, at her hands twisted in her lap, at her feet, at the rattling floor of the train compartment. She felt stricken with a feeling of loss. As if something precious had slipped through her fingers and shattered into a thousand pieces.

She had fallen in love with Amsterdam, with the way it basked defiantly in the early autumn sun. She'd loved the surfeit of leaves, rolling along the bridges and streets, floating like old gold on the surface of the canals, piled – crisp and russet – in the gutters. She'd loved the shimmer of light on water, the endless curving bridges, the narrow houses with their stepped gables, the smell of pickled herrings that rose up, sharp and briny, from the fish carts. But not everything had been as alluring.

In Amsterdam she'd learned that Elisabeth had ended her relationship with Otto and found another lover. And now she couldn't help seeing Otto as something Elisabeth had passed on, discarded, unwanted. A broken piece of jewellery. She's taken his child – the child I wanted – and tossed him to me, she thought. As our father tossed rinds of fat to his dogs.

Ascona seemed the thin ghost of a dream now. Not only because Elisabeth had dispensed with Otto, but because Frieda had come to see the truth of her sister's words: Otto had no understanding of responsibility. During their week in Amsterdam he'd behaved more and more erratically. Losing his hotel keys, forgetting where to meet her, leaving his shoes beside a canal, falling asleep mid-sentence over breakfast, talking constantly – of Elisabeth's betrayal – as they made love, writing lengthy letters to Doctor Freud which he then set alight in an ashtray.

Nor did he have any money now his father had disowned him. In Amsterdam she finally realised that Ascona, with its heady promise of freedom and adventure, required money. Without money it would never be the idyll she'd imagined, her children splashing naked among drakes and swans and rainbow trout. It was all very well in summer. But in winter they'd need clothes. And hot food. And a fire. The combination of Otto's penury and volatility made it plain that all her dreams of a bohemian life were exactly that – dreams. And nothing more.

As the train approached Nottingham, the landscape changed. Furrowed fields became black smoking pits, gaping quarries, factory chimneys that jabbed like scolding fingers into the sky. She thought of what she was returning to. Ernest, shuffling round between his books, his pipe hooked between his teeth, his lungs creaking. Telling her how to behave, how things are done in England. Laughing when she wanted to talk of philosophy or poetry. Fastidiously smoothing strands of hair over his polished head.

She thought back to Munich, the spring of her affair with Otto. Through him – his body, his love for her, his ideas – she had been able to cast off the lost and lonely Nottingham Frieda. She'd rediscovered an old Frieda on which she'd stamped a new image of herself. How could she grip on to this in Nottingham? She knew now that she was Mrs Weekley in name alone. She stared at the carriage floor, with its stains and crumbs. She hated the name, she hated everything it stood for. In Germany she was a Baroness with a name that carried weight, meaning, history. In England, she was nothing.

'Mrs Weekley, Mrs Weekley,' she murmured, her fingers knotting and unknotting. The name had never felt so wrong, so alien. 'Ernest Weekley's snowflower,' she added with a soft snort. It had never felt right but today it felt more incongruous than ever. All at once she yearned for her own name, to be herself again, the Baroness von Richthofen. An image of Fanny, Countess zu Reventlow, hovered into view. Fanny, with her dislike of suffragettes, her loathing of marriage, her steadfast belief in sexual freedom for women. Fanny had kept her own name, lived on her own terms, stayed true to herself. For a minute Frieda longed to be Fanny, but then she wiped her hand over her face, wiping Fanny away along with the soot flecking on her cheeks. It was no good wishing to be someone else. Whoever she was, she was mother to Monty, Elsa and Barby now. She must find a way of being herself while being an English mother.

It crossed her mind that perhaps she should never have gone to the Café Stefanie. Perhaps its taste of freedom had thrown into sharp relief the bolts and bars of her Nottingham life. But she knew that wasn't true. Her Munich encounters had merely magnified the loneliness, the meaninglessness, of her English life. She thought back to her first visit to the café, that sudden sense of stepping into the bright glare of life. She turned to the window and stared across the scored black fields and the reeking canals, up to the sky. How bright and high and spotless it was.

When she arrived home, Ernest was carving roast pork, handing out platters to the children. Barby and Elsa hugged her, returning quickly to the table. But Monty held on to her for a long minute and when he finally pulled away she saw his eyes were wet with tears. *My beautiful children*, she said to herself. *I must try, somehow, to find my purpose in them.*

'Is Aunt Elisabeth better?' Elsa asked.

'Oh yes. It was only a touch of flu. Nothing serious.' How easily, how smoothly, the lie sprang to her lips. She felt a prick of shame at her ability to lie with such ease, followed swiftly by indignation. It wasn't fair that her sisters could be as honest and brazen as they liked while she had to demean herself with untruths.

'So why did you go?' Elsa fixed her sharp eyes on Frieda.

Guilt flashed through her. Elsa knew. Elsa had guessed. No, that was ridiculous. Elsa was five! Her duplicity loomed up in front of her. Perspiration pooled in her armpits. Heat rose from her ribs. Otto. Suddenly she could smell him on her, like the muted odour of old scent. She twisted away from the table. Stooped. Pretended she'd dropped her handkerchief. She had to compose herself. This was England. This was her family.

'My godfather came!' Barby's voice rang out across the table. 'He brought me a present.'

'Mr Dowson came, did he?' Frieda caught Monty's eye on her, staring at her with a most mawkish expression. For a brief second she wondered if Ernest was right. Perhaps he was too attached to her . . . Or did he know she was lying? Was that it? She turned quickly to Barby. 'What did Mr Dowson bring for you, my dear?'

'A lamb made of real lamb's wool,' crowed Barby.

'I wasn't here when he visited. Ida and Mrs Babbit looked after him.' Ernest inspected the blade of the carving knife then laid it beside the oozing remains of the pork knuckle.

'So, which of you entertained Mr Dowson? Surely you didn't leave him to Ida and Mrs Babbit?'

'I did! I did!' shouted Barby. 'I picked some flowers for Mrs Dowson because she's hurted herself. I picked them all by myself.'

'Good girl.' Frieda put a forkful of meat into her mouth. The familiarity of it soothed and distracted her at the same time. But then she thought of Otto and the meat lost its flavour and turned to cardboard on her tongue. She looked round the table, her mouth sculpted into a smile. Her children and Ernest sat with backs as straight as bars. Everything about the room seemed rigid, colourless, wrong. 'I would like to redecorate this room,' she said, pushing her plate away. 'Make it brighter. It is too dark and stuffy.'

'Not too bright. We don't want our eyes strained,' Ernest said.

She looked across the table at her husband, noticed the deliberation with which he ate, with which he dressed. His tie, with its perfect knot. His cufflinks, polished to a shine. His cuffs and collar, stiff with starch. There was something so bland and clipped about him. From his naked head all the way to his patent leather toecaps. Had he always been like this, she wondered? She thought back briefly and it seemed to her that Ernest had chosen a role and an image – that of an English gentleman – and set himself in it, with quiet determination. She almost envied him for his certainty. Why had she not been able to do the same?

She glanced at her children, hoping for a surge of affection. But Elsa was glaring at her, Barby was pushing sprouts round her plate with the prongs of her fork and Monty was carefully separating his potatoes from his carrots.

Otto's words began ringing in her ears, like a fugue urging her back to life. *Don't let them destroy you . . . Don't let yourself die . . . You're the woman of the future.* She glanced over at Monty, hoping he might smile. He seemed quiet and vaguely puzzled, as if he was mirroring her own feelings. But then he shot her one of his elfish smiles and she returned it with a conspiratorial wink.

'Sit up straight and eat with your mouth closed, Monty,' said Ernest before turning slowly to Frieda. 'I'm not sure Mrs Babbit will let you into her kitchen, my snowflower. In your absence she's become terribly territorial about her kitchen and her pantry and her scullery.'

'*Her* kitchen? It's *my* kitchen!' But she wasn't thinking about the kitchen. Or Mrs Babbit. She was thinking of the letters Otto had promised, wondering when they would arrive. She knew now that his letters were her lifeline. His letters and her children. There was nothing else now.

•

Café Stefanie
Amalienstrasse
Munich

My darling Frieda

You must take a lover immediately. Do not wait or it will be too late. Cast aside any misjudged loyalty. Do it for me. It will restore your spirits and remind you of the revolution to come. Death to monogamy!

Find someone you can trust. Find someone who can keep you alive. I must have you alive, Frieda.

Never forget that you are the woman of the future and that monogamy is the tool of patriarchy.

Your loving and devoted
Otto

PART FOUR

Nottingham 1908

'The mighty question arises upon us. What
is one's own real self? It certainly is not
what we think we are and ought to be.'

D.H. Lawrence, *The Lost Girl*

TWENTY-SIX

Ernest

Ernest sat at his desk looking out onto the garden. The daffodils had pushed their way out of the black soil and now their yellow heads were shifting and swaying in the breeze. Crocuses sat like splendid mitres of yellow and purple amongst the clods of earth and he could just make out tiny, downy buds on some of the trees. He was pleased spring had come. It had been a long, cold winter and the children had been plagued by a succession of coughs and colds. Frieda had worn a brave face but he knew she was troubled. Anxiety about the children, he assumed. And about Elisabeth who had given birth to her third child in December and written constantly to Frieda all winter. He saw the envelopes in the waste paper basket although he had no idea where the letters went.

He reached across the desk for his pipe and, as he did so, his fingers brushed against the manuscript of his seminal work on etymology, reminding him that it needed a title. Something that would express his passion for words, for their linguistic roots, their provenance. It saddened him that people cared so little about the source of words. Such a wealth of meaning, such historical riches, such an abundance of humour lay in the roots of even the most commonplace words and names. He hoped his book would bring language back to life, excite people about the simplest and dullest of words. He smiled, rocked his head, tamped a little more tobacco into his pipe. Cambridge University would beat a path to his door and Frieda would blossom like the daffodils outside. He glanced at his manuscript's blank cover page. He would ask her to help with the title. He would run his ideas past her, include her a little more in his great oeuvre. Perhaps when she got back from her drive with Dowson.

He stared at the vacant page. A title . . . He needed a title . . . He concentrated all his powers of thought on the empty page, putting everything else out of his mind . . . A name was starting to form in the back of his brain . . . coming to him . . . slowly . . . like a spectre emerging from the gloom . . . Romance . . . Words . . . He would call his book *The Romance of Words*.

●

Café Stefanie
Amalienstrasse
Munich

My darling Frieda
I am so happy your lover is giving you a little pleasure. Stay with him, for me. Now you must do the same for your repressed husband, before the weight of his moral conscience becomes too much and makes him fatally ill. You must wean him from the tyranny of monogamy. He too is a victim of patriarchy and you must free him, as you have freed yourself. If he cannot respond to you, you must find someone else to show him the transformative power of the erotic. And then he will understand the new world we are creating. And you will be released from his possessive grip forever.
    And then you must come to me.

Otto

TWENTY-SEVEN

Frieda

Frieda folded Otto's latest letter and slipped it inside her chemise. Elisabeth had written to her earlier, explaining that Otto was suffering from a cocaine addiction, and she had begun to see the effects in his letters. Sometimes they were almost illegible – long rantings about Elisabeth's desertion of him written in an untamed scrawl so difficult to decipher they made her eyes ache. Or lengthy tracts on the psychopathic constitution or the pathogenic consequences of power structures, scored and ripped where his pencil lead had broken through the paper. But at other times, his letters were all of her: her passion and exuberance, her courage and beauty. And these letters reminded her not only of the joy he'd brought to her life, but of who she was now.

She felt, more than ever, as if she was someone different, someone quite altered. She knew that a fresh Frieda had burst forth, but it seemed to her that the old Frieda – Mrs Weekley, the respectable wife of Professor Weekley – lingered, urging her on, encouraging her into a covert defiance of her husband beneath his very nose. She had recently propositioned Mr Dowson, Barby's godfather and Ernest's friend. Of course, it was the newly liberated Frieda that had put her hand casually on his knee, explained that she no longer believed in monogamy, that her passionless marriage was slowly killing her.

He'd responded with an unexpected alacrity. As they kissed for the first time, in his motor car, she'd had a peculiar sense of her old self looking on with a deep admiration. And she'd kissed Mr Dowson with a greater fervour, as if she was showing off to her old self. As she and Mr Dowson tugged and hurried at their clothes, the words *I am the new Eve* had rushed, exulting and thrilling, into her head. Otto's phrase – *the woman of the future* – was all very well, but it was *his* description, *his* expression, *his* dream. 'I am the new Eve,' she'd whispered, over and over, as Mr Dowson shuddered inside her.

But it was Otto's suggestion for healing Ernest that intrigued her. She thought about it as she read, as she shopped, as she played dominoes with Monty, as she helped Elsa with her embroidery. But she thought about it most of all as she watched Ernest. She saw how he gripped his spoon as he ate Mrs Babbit's habitual raspberry custard pudding – gripped it so tightly the tendons in his hand rose up in white ridges. She saw the stiff line of his jaw as he said prayers before Sunday luncheon. She watched as he inadvertently picked up one of her menstrual rags from the floor and then dropped it as though it were a burning ember, fleeing to his study with his face inflamed.

Clearly she hadn't been able to help him. God knows she'd tried. A few years ago she'd hesitantly suggested they make love naked, instead of in their nightshirts. She remembered the expression of shock on his face, how he'd drawn back from her as though she was diseased. Yes, Otto was right. The weight of such repression was too much for any mortal.

But could someone else help him? Perhaps someone more anonymous, someone who wasn't his wife or *his snowflower*. She'd heard stories of English noblemen preferring parlour maids and prostitutes to their own wives. Was it possible Ernest might feel the same way? Was there someone out there who could release him from his huge burden of inhibition? She remembered how expertly

Otto had stripped her of any vestiges of decorum. Could someone do the same for Ernest?

A week later, as she lay with Mr Dowson in the bluebells in Sherwood Forest, she thought again of Otto's idea. Questions crowded in on her. Could Ernest be freed of his repression? Could he be made happy?

'Do you think Ernest could be seduced by another woman?' She looked up through the spreading branches of the oak, at its newly green leaves, at the pearly sky beyond. The air was heavy with the scent of bluebells. Her ears were full of the chafing and scraping of insect wings. She tried to imagine Ernest lying beside her, but the image kept fraying and tearing. He would never enjoy the feeling of damp grass against his spine or sunshine on his skin. Unless she could free him.

Mr Dowson snorted with laughter. 'I hope you don't have Mrs Dowson in mind?'

'Would you mind?' Frieda sighed. Why was it always one rule for women and quite another for men?

'There is someone I know. Mrs Gladys Bradley. But are you sure Ernest is the sort of man who could be seduced? It always seems to me that he's completely besotted with you.'

'He does not see me. He sees someone else.' Frieda closed her eyes. The light felt like velvet on her eyelids. The breeze lapped at her body, crept through the roots of her hair. How good it felt to have her skirts hitched up to her waist, to feel the air on her legs, on her skin. Next time she'd take all her clothes off. Next time she'd come on her own and sunbathe completely naked with the bluebells swaying around her.

She stared up at the sky. The sun was straining to break through, giving the pale clouds an iridescent quality as if they were a silver bloom on a glinting jewel. She liked gazing at the huge expanse of sky. It gave her a sense of freedom, of escape. Sometimes her desire to run away overwhelmed her. All this brightness she had to display, for Ernest, for the children, for the neighbours. Yes, she must help liberate Ernest and then perhaps he would understand her.

'How will you engineer this seduction of Ernest?' Mr Dowson sat up and offered her a cigarette.

'It is more of a healing than a seduction. This woman – Gladys Bradley – will visit when I am out.'

'I'm not sure Ernest would comply, not with the children and the servants there.' Mr Dowson inhaled deeply, then blew a long plume of smoke up into the half-white sky.

'I will take the children out and give the servants a holiday and Mrs Bradley will call on Ernest.' Frieda watched the smoke waver and shift and disappear into the air. How calculating she sounded, how dully functional. She wished she could bring more poetry and passion into her plan but perhaps Mrs Bradley would bring those qualities. 'Is she a woman of passion? Of romance? And she needs to be clean. Ernest can be quite fussy.'

'Mrs Bradley is clean enough. I think you'll like her.' Mr Dowson blew a puff of smoke into Frieda's ear. 'She's like you . . . liberated . . . fun-loving.'

Frieda rolled away and pulled down her skirt. Fun-loving, she thought. *He calls me fun-loving.* He didn't understand that this *fun* was a first small step in an almighty revolution, a revolution that would cure the world of so many of its ailments and neuroses, that would make every man and woman equal and honest and happy.

'This is not just fun.' She could feel the bluebells, damp and cool and crushed beneath her. She saw them stretching out into the wooded distance, a vast reach of violet-blue. 'Doctor Gross believes monogamy exists only to control women. He believes we should all be able to do whatever we want with whomever we want, even men with men. And I agree.'

'Whoa! What exactly are you suggesting?' Mr Dowson sat up in alarm. 'He sounds deranged.'

'Oh no,' Frieda gazed wistfully back at the sky. A pair of green woodpeckers plunged and soared above her, carving bright-green arcs through the air. 'He is a genius. One day we will live in a world where men and women can love each other without being married, where men can love men if they want. Where people can make love with lots of people, not just one. And where such things will be talked about, in the open. He calls it a sex revolution.'

'I can't see that happening in England,' Mr Dowson snorted.

'You should hear him. He has seen what happens when people repress their sexual instinct.' She put her hand over her eyes. The sun was pushing through the cloud, forcing its thin, raw rays upon them. She could feel Otto's letter beneath her chemise, pushing at her breastbone. She wanted to read it again, to remember the world he'd painted so vividly for her.

'When shall I introduce you to Mrs Bradley?'

'Tomorrow. Bring her to the Mikado Café.' Frieda sat up. It was time. Ernest needed help. Before it was too late.

TWENTY-EIGHT

Ernest

'Do you know where the word "money" comes from?' Ernest fastened a keen eye on his son who was sprawled on the floor playing with a model fort. 'It comes from one of those fascinating linguistic accidents that so excites me and I wish would excite you.' Ernest stopped. He could feel a large sigh swelling inside him, like an ocean wave. Try as he might, his family showed no interest in his great passion. At least Monty had the right temperament, and an instinctive enthusiasm for precision and order. It was a good start, he thought.

'It probably comes from the word "mint", which can be traced back to Roman times when the Temple of Juno was very close to where they made coins. Do you know who Juno was?' Monty wasn't even looking at him now, just staring at the rigid rows of soldiers he'd arranged in front of his fort.

'Goddess of war,' Monty muttered. He closed one eye and looked sideways down the line of soldiers.

'They were so grateful to Juno for warning them about forthcoming disasters, they called her Moneta – from the Latin word to warn, *moneo* – and they made a temple in her honour. From the name Moneta, we get *Münze* in Germany, *monnaie* in France and mint in England, as well as words like monetary.'

Monty yawned.

Ernest felt a stab of disappointment. Perhaps he should try a different approach. 'What about the word "dollar"? Any ideas?'

He could feel his throat tickling and prickling as though he had a pin cushion lodged in his larynx. He coughed but it made no difference. He'd had a sore throat and an irritating cough all winter and all spring. For some reason he hadn't been able to shake it off.

Ernest looked over Monty's bowed head and out of the window. The sky looked watery and tired. He closed his eyes and listened to his son making rifle-shooting sounds. Then he gave a small, parched cough and his eyes snapped open. Wasn't he supposed to have a visitor this afternoon? Some woman who was interested in the etymology of names and wanted to discuss the source of her own name. At least there was one person in Nottingham who shared his interests.

He could hear Frieda's heavy footfall in the corridor, and then the soft swishing of her skirts. She began calling for Monty, telling him to get his hat and shoes on. Monty sprang to his feet and darted from the room, like a small animal bolting for freedom. He finds me dull, thought Ernest. My own son finds me dull. He tried to clear his throat. Something was trapped there, sitting on his chest, weighing him down.

'I am taking the children out,' Frieda announced. She was standing in the doorway, a broad scarlet belt pulled tightly round her waist and a bright blue shawl around her shoulders. She looks beautiful, Ernest thought. So healthy and glowing, her tawny-green eyes sparkling, her blonde hair springing thickly from her well-made head. His eyes flicked round the room, over the damp stains on the ceiling with their scummy brown rings, the parsimonious fireplace, the narrow skirting boards. How unworthy of her this house was. How out of place she seemed, like a diamond dropped on a cinder path. He looked up at the stains from the children's spilled chamber pots. He must work harder, save more money. He had to restore his beautiful wife to her natural habitat.

'Mrs Bradley will be here soon, Ernest.' Frieda moved swiftly towards him, ran her hand over his thinning hair and then smoothed down his moustache with her index finger.

Ernest exhaled laboriously. 'I don't feel quite myself, my dear. But I will do my best for Mrs Bradley. She wishes to discuss the etymological roots of her name, is that right? Bradley? Or her maiden name?'

Frieda batted at the air, as though any name would do. 'Just show her how brilliant you are with word history.' And she elongated and emphasised 'word history', as though she was talking to a small child or a deaf person.

'Etymology, my dear, etymology.'

'Yes, yes, of course.' Frieda turned to leave and then stopped at the door. 'Mrs Babbit has left early and Ida is coming with me. Can you make Mrs Bradley some tea?'

Ernest frowned. 'Why has Mrs Babbit left?'

'Some family business. Goodbye, Ernest. We will be gone all afternoon, but we will be back before you leave for your evening class.'

'But . . . But . . . I cannot entertain Mrs Bradley alone. With no servants in the house . . . oh no! That's not done!'

'Don't look so alarmed. She is coming to talk to *you*, Ernest. Not Mrs Babbit or Ida. I am sure you will manage.'

He tried to get up, but fatigue swept over him. He gripped the arms of his chair and let himself fall back so his head lay prostrate. He closed his eyes and prayed Mrs Bradley would not come. What on earth would she think when he scuttled off to the kitchen to make tea? He, a Professor of Modern Languages, entertaining while alone at home. Why did his wife have so little understanding of English etiquette? If anything, she had regressed. Ever since she got back from Munich, her head full of nonsense, she had shown a distinct disdain for decent behaviour. She had stopped wearing a corset . . . She had refused to go to church . . . She had been seen alone with Mr Dowson in his motor car . . . She had upset Mrs Babbit by coming down to breakfast with her hair loose . . . She had confused Ida by asking the poor girl to call her Frieda instead of Mrs Weekley. He suspected she was sleeping without a nightgown. He couldn't be sure but one morning he'd gone into her room to say goodbye and seen a dimpled buttock protruding from beneath the quilt. He would have a word with his sister, see what Maude suggested. She was a little more modern than his mother . . . Yes, this needed a woman's touch.

The house was silent now. He could hear nothing but the ferocious buzzing of a bluebottle at the window and the strident tick of the clock in the hallway. His throat felt scratchy and swollen and his chest seemed to be sinking as though a great weight was upon him. He hadn't felt this tired, this exhausted, since the old days – the days of working all day and studying all night. Perhaps all that effort, that grinding graft, had finally caught up with him. But if he hadn't worked so studiously, so diligently, what would he be now? A clerk perhaps, on a paltry income, living in a hovel with an outside privy, and a cemetery of dead children. He thought back to his own childhood, his nine brothers and sisters crammed together in a stinking cottage adjoining the workhouse. It was the image of the workhouse that had driven him on, night after night, year after year, as he taught himself German and French by the skimpy light of a spitting gas lamp.

It seemed to him that every minute in the last forty years had been pushing him towards this moment. His wife, his children, his house, his professorship were like markers, arrows, pointing him onwards. He was nearly there. His book and a Cambridge Chair were his final destination. And then he could pause and draw breath. Spend time with his family. Perhaps travel with Frieda. At times he felt so close to his destination, it was as though he could smell it in the air. He could smell the pages of his newly printed book, the glue and leather of its binding, the clean, bracing air of the Fens, the musty parchment of the Old Library at Trinity Hall.

A sharp tug of the bell-pull dragged him from his reveries. He shuffled to the door, suddenly aware of how he must appear, servantless and stooped. He pulled himself up, squared his shoulders.

'Good afternoon. I'm Mrs Bradley to see Professor Weekley.' The woman wore a hat trimmed with silk roses the colour of skin, and a blue dress with a lot of Nottingham lace at the neck. She had sunken blue eyes and a large mole that sat on one cheek like a third eye.

'I'm Professor Weekley. Please come in.' He stood aside and gestured down the hall. 'I thought the drawing room would be more comfortable, but we can retire to my study should we need access to my books.'

Mrs Bradley gave a delicate cough that slipped into a simper. Ernest wondered if she was nervous. There was something slightly jittery about her. He was obviously coming across as *too* professorial, *too* intimidating.

'What a lovely house, Professor.' Mrs Bradley's eyes skimmed across the walls, down to the floor, up to the ceiling and then along the hall to the stairs.

'Is it the name Bradley you're interested in, or your maiden name?' Ernest could feel his throat protesting. It didn't want him to talk, it wanted him to drink something hot and lie down somewhere quiet. He held open the door of the drawing room and Mrs Bradley sidled past him. She smelled of wood violets. Pleasantly agreeable, he thought.

'Bradley will do very well, thank you, Professor.' She sat down on the chaise longue and began easing off her gloves. Her pouchy eyes gazed at him in a way that unnerved him, but he wasn't sure why.

'Can I get you some tea, Mrs Bradley?'

'Your throat sounds hoarse, Professor. All those lectures, no doubt. You should take a little whiskey, warm with a teaspoon of honey.'

'I'm afraid our cook is not here.'

'Oh I don't need anything. Please don't go to any bother on my account.' Mrs Bradley lowered her eyelashes then inclined her head and looked up at him. 'I just thought you might like a little whiskey.'

'Yes, perhaps I might. Excuse me a minute.' Ernest went to his study and found the bottle of whiskey he kept under his desk for emergencies. He poured himself a small glassful and returned to the drawing room. How thoughtful this Mrs Bradley was. She'd noticed his dry throat, which was more than Frieda had.

'Is your husband interested in the etymological root of his name?' The whiskey ran down Ernest's throat and made him feel better, reinvigorated and soothed at the same time. He wondered why he hadn't had some earlier.

'You should have it warm, with honey. If you point me in the right direction I'll make you a proper hot toddy.' Mrs Bradley was already on her feet, speeding towards the door, her face alight. She didn't seem at all perturbed by the emptiness of the house or the lack of servants.

And suddenly Ernest felt like letting her go to the kitchen on her own, letting her make him a proper hot drink, letting her look after him. If only Frieda were more like Mrs Bradley. That, he supposed, was the drawback of marrying nobility. He waved his hand vaguely in the direction of the kitchen. 'Honey should be in the larder. Matches on the shelf. Can you light a gas stove?'

'Of course I can, Professor. Leave it to me.' She took his whiskey glass and disappeared.

Ernest lay down on the sofa. He felt very tired all of a sudden. Extinguished. Snuffed out. He arranged a cushion under his head and closed his eyes. *Just for a few seconds*, he told himself. The minute he heard Mrs Bradley's step he'd sit up. Straight. Upright. Like a professor. Like a distinguished etymologist. But when he opened his eyes, Mrs Bradley was already back, kneeling on the floor beside the sofa, her fingers in his hair.

He pulled himself upright, jerking his head free of her hands. How long had he been asleep? How long had Mrs Bradley been kneeling beside him, weaving her fingers through his hair? He looked down and saw his shirt had come free from his trousers and was hanging loose. And where was his tie? Had he forgotten to put it on? Mortified, he stood up and began apologising with as much dignity as he could muster. But Mrs Bradley just nodded and held up a glass of once-warm whiskey. He took the glass and sipped at it. It was laced with something sweet that he couldn't identify. It wasn't honey. Sugar perhaps. Or jam.

'That's very kind of you, Mrs Bradley. I'm awfully sorry. I think I'm unwell.' He blinked several times, hoping he could blink the woman away. But instead, she got up from the floor, came towards him and pulled him down onto the chaise longue. He didn't have the energy to resist. Every molecule in his body was telling him to recline, to find a horizontal position for his weary bones, to close his eyes.

'I know exactly what's wrong with you, Professor.' Mrs Bradley's voice was soft and murmuring and gentle. She was kneeling on the floor again, at his side. She took the glass of whiskey from his hand, tilted his head back and eased the rim between his desiccated lips. He felt the liquid warming his throat, travelling through his veins, round his body. How good it felt! Was she a nurse? Or perhaps she'd nursed a sick husband or invalid parents. There was something so sure about her hands. She'd put the glass down now and was sliding her fingers inside the collar of his shirt.

'It's your chest, Professor. I can feel it on your chest.' Her hands began making circling motions on his ribs.

'Bradley,' Ernest stuttered. 'I must explain the source of Bradley.' He felt stricken with shame. He could feel the colour rising in his pallid cheeks. He didn't want to offend Mrs Bradley. Besides which, the warmth of her hands was making him feel better, more relaxed. She seemed to be easing the weight from his chest. She must be a properly trained nurse. Her movements were so deft, so competent. He could feel the breath starting to flow more freely through his lungs. But a voice in his head was telling him this was all wrong. He shouldn't be allowing it. It was neither becoming nor professorial. And what if Frieda and the children returned? Or Mrs Babbit?

He tried to pull himself up, struggling against the pressure of Mrs Bradley's endlessly orbiting hands. But he was too weak. Mrs Bradley, with the pressure of her palms, induced him back into a horizontal position. She had undone all the buttons on his shirt. How had she done that without him noticing? 'Are you a – a nurse?'

'I trained at the Liverpool Royal Infirmary.' Her hands worked away at his flesh, her fingertips moving in whorls and spirals round his nipples. Stroking away the tightness in his chest. He felt his eyelids closing. A warm haze hovered over him, like a blanket. Her fingers were gently kneading his stomach now, moving down and down. He felt a whimper rising from his throat, slipping from his lips. He needed to focus . . . be more commanding . . . more eminent . . .

He tried to think about etymology, about her name. 'Bradley may have originated from broad wood . . . it's an ancient name . . .' He tried to make his voice imposing, but it came out thin and breathy. 'Your husband probably came from a forest clearing . . .' How ridiculous he sounded! Even to his own, sympathetic ears, he sounded ludicrous. And why was his voice warping and straining?

'Hush,' soothed Mrs Bradley and her fingers crept into the waistband of his trousers. He could smell the wood violets on her and the tang of whiskey on her breath. She must have helped herself to his whiskey. How had he missed that? What on earth was she doing? Her fingers were tugging at the buttons of his fly. Tremors of excitement rippled through him. He could feel the blood rushing to his face, to his groin, pulsing hotly beneath his skin.

'No!' he shouted. And in a surge of energy he pushed aside her hands and pulled himself up. He stood stiffly, doing up his shirt buttons. 'I apologise, Mrs Bradley. I'm not well. Perhaps you could see yourself out.' He indicated the door then returned to fumbling with his buttons. His hands were shaking and his breath coming in scratches.

'There's gratitude! I only wanted to help you, Professor.' Mrs Bradley's voice was grating and shrill now. Ernest couldn't look at her. Instead he listened to her departing steps, to the slam of the front door, to the squeal and thud of the garden gate. And then he slumped down on the chaise longue. Every movement, even the lifting of an eyelid, exhausted him. He had never felt so weak, so depleted, so empty.

He closed his eyes. Birdsong. Rising and falling. The crow of a cockerel. The barking of a distant dog. All these sounds drifted through his head in snatches. Fading in and out. And all the while his limbs ached, his muscles ached, he ached in every inch of his body. He had to write some more of his book. He had to finish it. He tried to move his arm, but it wouldn't lift. It lay as if glued to his side.

He closed his eyes again. Listened to the sounds of the birds, the rumbling clop of a horse and cart from the street. They seemed to be coming from such a long way away. His mind looped back to Mrs Bradley, the nurse. What a strange dream that had been. So lifelike, so real. And yet he knew his mind wasn't working as it should be, that his body had been sapped of everything, and that something wasn't right. Yes, even his dreams were peculiar now.

'Ernest?' Frieda had returned and was standing, towering, on the threshold.

He opened his eyes a fraction. How bright it was. How glaringly bright.

'Don't you have to teach a class tonight?' She stared. Looming. Frowning.

What day was it? What time was it? He tried to turn his head towards his wife, to acknowledge her presence. But he couldn't. He closed his eyes again. His throat burned. His mouth felt dry. He wanted her to leave him alone. He was too tired to talk. Too tired . . .

'Monty! Run to Mr Dowson's house. Ask him to call a doctor. Ida, come and help me carry Ernest!'

He heard the low buzz of Frieda and Ida discussing how to move him, where to put him. He didn't want to be moved, but his arms didn't have the strength to push them away and his jaws wouldn't open to speak. So he let the two women manoeuvre him to the couch, his feet pulling behind him, dragging across the floor like two dead fish.

Later, when he opened his eyes, he was in his bed and there was a strange man standing beside him, talking in a hushed voice. He was too tired to listen. So he closed his eyes and heard the breath wheezing in and out of his throat, rattling and laboured. And when his eyelids shut, strange images filled his head. He was holding a swaddled creature and it was Frieda. No sooner had he recognised his wife, all bundled up in a woollen shawl and tucked under his arm, than a dog leapt up from the shadows and bit her head cleanly from her body. He tried to wrench Frieda's still-throbbing head from the dog's jaws, but he was too slow and the dog swallowed the head and bounded off.

He heard Frieda crying and tried to force his eyes open. But his lids were great boulders on his eyes. He felt himself pulled back – and this time he was lying on a table and flies were swarming over him, buzzing and swarming in black knots, and then Mrs Bradley appeared bearing yards and yards of pale bandage. Behind the bandages that fluttered from her hands, Mrs Bradley was naked. She began wrapping him in bandages. And now the bandages were all over him and she was binding his neck, unravelling the bandage towards his mouth, his nose, his eyes . . . He couldn't breathe! Ernest gasped and flailed and Mrs Bradley's breasts swung above him, suffocating and smothering him. Bandages and breasts and Mrs Bradley . . . He couldn't breathe!

His eyes snapped open. He tried to gulp air into his lungs. Everything in the room was blurred as though someone had put a gauze veil over his head. He felt drumming inside his chest. Was it his heart? Was he alive? Through the gloam he could see the outline of a person. He tried to lift his head from the pillow, but it was too heavy. Why was his head so heavy? He tried to reach his arm out, to touch his head, to check it was still there. But his arm had no feeling, just heaviness, so much heaviness. He closed his eyes. He tried to remember who he was, where he was. But he couldn't think and the torpor was pulling him away, beckoning to him, telling him to . . . to . . . to what? Yes, to stop moving, to stop living. It was his time.

TWENTY-NINE

Monty

Monty kept chewing. And when he finished his mouthful, he crammed in another forkful of meat, of mashed potatoes, of boiled carrots. He had to keep chewing. If he stopped chewing, he would cry. He didn't want to cry, not in front of his sisters. Not now Mr Dowson had told him that he would soon be the man of the house. His bottom lip quivered. He could feel Aunt Maude's gimlet eyes on him. He quickly gored a piece of stewed lamb with his fork, hurried it into his mouth, concentrated on chewing.

'Is Papa dead yet?' Barby's eyes were silvery with tears. 'Has he gone to Heaven?'

'Why does he make that horrible noise?' whispered Elsa as she pushed lumps of mashed potato round her plate.

'Don't play with your food, Elsa,' said Aunt Maude. 'It's his lungs making the noise.'

'Who will be our Papa when he dies?' asked Barby.

'Stop this nonsense! Ernest will be fine,' Aunt Maude said, but her face was dark and her tone so full of forced joviality that Monty knew she was lying.

'Can Mr Dowson be our daddy? He's nicer than the other godfathers and he always brings me presents.' Barby pushed her plate away. 'What's for pudding?'

Monty's shoulders shook. He pushed his lips tightly closed. He had an overwhelming urge to pray. He knew if he didn't pray, he would cry and all manliness would disappear forever. He leapt from his chair and ran up the stairs.

'Don't you want pudding, Monty?' Aunt Maude's words pursued him, chasing him towards the curtained comfort of his room.

Inside his bedroom, he kicked the door closed and pressed his hands together in prayer. His lips began moving, silently, as he begged God to let Papa live. He promised to do anything God wanted. Anything at all. He would give his toys to poor children. He would share his stamp collection among the church choir. He would never forget to say his prayers. He stopped and waited. The sobs that threatened to burst from him subsided. He opened his eyes and looked out at the sky. It looked like blackberry jam. Streaks the colour of butter ran through it. And above, the sun flared and boiled. Monty felt God's presence. God was there, in the sky, watching him through his orange eye.

He flung open his window and dropped to his knees. He had never felt so close to God. Ribbons of light plunged from the sky, crimson, gold, violet, like rung-less ladders to the Almighty.

'Please, God, can you let Papa live?'

He had a sudden need to be somewhere holy, somewhere he might hear God's reply. He ran down the hall, past his father's bedroom with its odour of disinfectant and sickness, down the stairs and out of the front door. He heard Ida asking where he was going. But he didn't stop. He ran all the way to the church, knowing the blazing eye of God was behind him, watching him, urging him on.

The churchyard was quiet and still. He looked at the orderly rows of graves and felt calmer. The colour was draining from the sky as the sun rolled away. And without God's eye on him, Monty felt less frantic. He walked round the tombstones looking for a good spot to pray. In the quietness, he thought he could hear the dead groaning and turning beneath the earth. And as he walked, he was sure he could feel tiny vibrations beneath his feet, as the dead shifted and twisted in their coffins. Around him the air felt heavy with their hovering souls. He shivered. The light had gone from the sky now and he had goosebumps all over his bare arms.

'Monty! Monty!'

He turned and there was his mother in her nursing apron, running towards him, weaving in and out of the tombstones. He fell into her arms and the two of them clung to each other.

'You must be brave, Monty. Courage is the most important thing in life.'

'More important than God?'

'Courage is the most important thing. Come. We don't want to spend the night with the phantoms, do we?'

As they left, Monty turned back to look at the sky. And God's eye had gone. Completely gone.

•

8 Vickers St
Nottingham
10 July 1908

Dear Elisabeth
What a terrible time we have had! Ernest has been very ill and I have been too busy nursing him to write to you.

He had very bad pneumonia in both lungs. The Doctor said he had probably been ill for weeks and weeks. I knew he was not quite himself. But when the Doctor said he was on the verge – yes, the very precipice – of death, I was quite taken aback. But you know Ernest. He just carried on and said there was nothing wrong with him.

The Doctor has prescribed rest, fresh air, gentle exercise (a short daily walk and a little gardening) and a pint of fresh milk every day.

*I have decided to devote myself, once again, to my family.
I want to be the best possible wife and mother, so I have ended
my liaison with Mr Dowson and my correspondence with Otto.
While Ernest is at home I cannot risk any more of Otto's wild
letters arriving. I feel so grateful to him for awakening my radical
spirit and showing me my true self – but now I must focus all my
energies on returning Ernest to good health.*

*I have been offered the chance to translate Yeats, an Irish
poet, into German, working with a most distinguished scholar.
This will keep my restlessness at bay. But it will be easier if you
could refrain from telling me too much news of Munich. I must
put all that behind me now.*

*Your loving sister
Frieda*

*8 Vickers St
Nottingham
20 July 1908*

*My dear Maude
Finally I am sufficiently strong to put pen to paper. I want to
thank you for all you have done in our hour of need.*

*Frieda's ministrations continue to be exemplary. She pays
such close attention to every word the good Doctor Mellors utters,
even writing it all down in a little notebook she keeps expressly
for the purpose! It has been marvellous to see her doting on me
like this – such a tonic for my health.*

*I am now intent on finding us a new house, with more generous
proportions, a larger garden for the children, electric lighting for
Frieda and French windows! I know Frieda will enjoy creating
a new home, particularly if it has French windows. Of course, it
is only until we get to Cambridge. But as the Doctor says I may*

not return to work for some time, it would appear that Cambridge will have to wait.

I am itching to get back to my book. I have a title: *The Romance of Words*. Do you like it? Romance – from the Old French, *romanz* (meaning a story in verse) and before that from the Vulgar Latin, *romanice scribere* (meaning to write in the Roman style).

I do hope Frieda didn't enlighten you on the ideas of a certain Doctor Freud while you stayed? If she made any mention of unconscious forces or repressed desires, I beg you to eradicate them from your mind immediately. They are ridiculous ideas that her mind is not sufficiently trained to understand. Thank goodness such ideas are confined to Munich. I can't imagine them getting any attention here – we English are far too sensible.

Maude, could I ask you to do something? I don't know how much you noticed while you were here. No doubt, you were very busy with the children and managing Ida and Mrs Babbit. But Frieda, in addition to taking up smoking, has stopped wearing a corset (corset – originally from the Latin, *corpus*, meaning body). Could you possibly write to her and explain the appropriateness of a corset for a woman like herself? I do not feel it is my place to raise such a delicate and feminine matter.

Your loving brother
Ernest

PART FIVE

Nottingham 1912

'And how could she start – and how
could she let go? She must leap from
the known into the unknown.'

D.H. Lawrence, *The Rainbow*

THIRTY

Monty

M onty sat next to his mother on the couch. He could feel the beginnings of a knot in his stomach. Like the knots he'd had when he was little and they'd lived in their old house. He was nearly twelve now and his past seemed blurred and distant. Except for his stomach. His stomach was still the same, with its propensity for lumps and aches and funny little spaces that gurgled at night.

'We have a guest coming for lunch, Monty.' His mother paused and looked at the gold carriage clock sitting stoutly on the mantelpiece. 'I think Ernest has forgotten. So irritating!' She put her book down and lit a cigarette. She smoked all the time now, sometimes lighting a new cigarette while the previous one sat smouldering in the ashtray.

'Who's coming for lunch?' Monty turned the page of his encyclopaedia of wildfowl. He was trying to memorise every breed: the maned goose, the marbled teal, the wandering whistling duck, the black-necked swan, the spur-winged goose, the red-crested pochard. Such beautiful names they had.

'An old student of your father's. A Mr Lawrence. He wants to get a job in Germany and your father invited him for lunch so we could help him. I expect he will be very dull and I would prefer to read my book.'

'I can help,' offered Monty. 'I can talk to him. Or I can see if Papa's on his way.'

She ran her hand over his hair and down his cheek. 'I do love you, Monty. What would I do without you? Your father says Mr Lawrence is a young genius.' A cylinder of ash fell from her cigarette onto her skirt. She brushed it away with an air of distraction and added, 'He's an author and a poet apparently. We don't get many of those in Nottingham, do we?'

Monty turned pensively back to his book. He loved sitting and reading with his mother, just the two of them, sitting so closely he could hear the air wheezing softly in and out of her nose. 'Have you heard of the white-faced whistling duck, Mutti? Isn't that a wonderful name for a duck?'

'You and your names. You are turning into your father.' She sighed and inhaled deeply on her cigarette. 'And now I am about to meet Nottingham's only poet, so I can help him escape to Germany. Ironic, *nein*?'

Monty sprang up. Footsteps. Crunching on the gravel path. Papa? He waited for his father to call out. Papa always opened the door and called 'I'm home', exactly as the heel of his right foot landed on the hall mat. Instead he heard the long, steady chime of the bell.

'Oh no! The poet has arrived and your father has indeed forgotten.' She heaved herself from the couch and ran a hand across her hair. 'Go and let him in, Monty. I want to finish my cigarette.'

Monty cleared his throat expectantly. In Papa's absence, he was the man of the house and it was important he behave as such. He pulled himself up to his full height and opened the door, keen to see what a real-life poet looked like.

'Is this Mr Weekley's house?' The poet had reddish-brown hair, combed so it lay flat and thick along the top of his forehead. His moustache was the colour of marmalade and he had very bright eyes that twinkled like the sapphires in Aunt Nusch's rings. Monty thought he looked like a fox, a thin hungry fox.

'Please come in, Sir. Papa's not back yet but my mother's here.' Monty examined the poet. He had very shiny shoes with thin soles. But he had no hat or cane which meant he wasn't a proper gentleman.

'No need to call me Sir. We're not in school now, are we? Are those your sisters out there?' Mr Lawrence nodded in the direction of the garden but his blue eyes flickered round the hall.

'Yes, Sir. Barby is seven and Elsa is ten.'

'And you? How old are you?'

'I'm Monty and I'm eleven and three quarters.'

'What do you like doing with yourself, Monty?' The poet's eyes were fixed intently on him now, as though he hadn't seen a boy before.

'I have a very valuable stamp collection, Sir. And I'm learning all the names of wildfowl off by heart.' Monty wondered if he should mention poetry somehow. He knew a genius wouldn't be interested in stamps or wildfowl. 'And sometimes I read poems, Sir,' he added quickly.

'Bah! Poems are dull for a boy. But wildfowl – that's interesting. Have you a favourite?'

Monty stared at the poet. 'The wandering whistling duck, Sir.'

The poet stooped so his twinkly eyes were right in front of Monty's. 'That's a good name for a duck. What does it do?'

'It roams and makes a curious noise. There are quite a few whistling ducks, Sir. Would you like me to recite their names?'

'I would. That I would. But I think Mrs Weekley might be waiting.' He looked over Monty's shoulder and Monty was suddenly aware of his mother, standing silently at the door of the drawing room.

'Ah, Mrs Weekley, I'm Mr Lawrence. Your husband was my favourite professor when I did my teaching certificate. It's very kind of you to have me for lunch. Monty and I were just discussing wildfowl.'

'Do come in, Mr Lawrence. Monty is obsessed with fowl at the moment, aren't you, Monty?'

'I was a teacher until a few months ago. I know all about boys and their obsessions.' Mr Lawrence laughed, a soft whooshing laugh that sounded like wind in the chimney. 'I wanted to study botany at one time. So I can see why you like wildfowl, Monty. Another time you can recite wildfowl to me and I can recite the names of flowers to you. The names have such magic in them, don't they?'

'Do not stare so, *mein Liebling*.' His mother gestured in the direction of the garden. 'Why don't you go and play with your sisters. Mr Lawrence and I have to talk about Germany. It will be boring for you.' She turned to Mr Lawrence and Monty noticed how bright and shiny her eyes had become, how one of her hands fluttered blindly at her throat like a moth.

'But . . . but . . .' He wanted to ask if Mr Lawrence would recite a poem. He'd never heard a poet speak with a Derbyshire accent. At school they only learned about grand poets like Lord Byron and Lord Tennyson. Perhaps Mr Lawrence would recite an exciting poem about battles, like 'The Charge of the Light Brigade'.

But when he turned and looked, beseechingly, at Mr Lawrence, he saw that Mr Lawrence was no longer interested in him. Mr Lawrence was looking very attentively at his mother. As if she was a new and exotic stamp that had arrived, unexpectedly, through the post. Monty was reminded of an envelope his father had given him with a beautiful red-and-yellow stamp that needed steaming off. So he shrugged and let his mother kiss him noisily on the cheek. Perhaps Mr Lawrence would recite a poem over lunch.

THIRTY-ONE

Frieda

'Please, do sit, Mr Lawrence,' Frieda gestured to the brown velvet chair with the clawed feet. It was Ernest's chair but it was the most comfortable, the plumpest, and the young man who stood awkwardly before her looked in need of comfort. He was so thin, his legs like pencils. And so pale, as if he had risen from his coffin. And yet his eyes, behind their curious blue gaze, had a fierce glint that belied the wan gauntness of his body. He reminded her of something, but she could not think what it was.

'Thank you, Mrs Weekley. It's very good of you to have me.'

His voice – its warmth and eagerness, the roll and lilt of it – made something pinch deep inside her belly. She reached for her cigarettes and noticed a tiny inexplicable tremor in her hand. As if remote parts of her were stirring, unfolding.

'My husband tells me you are the son of a miner, but you do not look at all like a miner's son.' She lit her cigarette and tossed the spent match into the ashtray.

'I've been ill,' he said, pushing his knees together and leaning forward as if Ernest's chair was a trap about to close its jaws around his limbs. 'But that's very dull. Tell me, how did you imagine a miner's son to look?'

'Big and strong and muscular,' Frieda replied without hesitation. 'You don't look as if you could lift a wandering whistling duck, as my son would say.'

A look of surprise crossed Mr Lawrence's face but then he laughed as if her words had pleased him. 'Professor Weekley tells his students you're of noble birth. Is that right?'

Frieda frowned, briefly confounded by this piece of information, but Mr Lawrence was still laughing, even as he spoke and his mood seemed to sweep her up. She smiled and tossed her head. 'Of course. I am the daughter of a baron. And here we are – a baron's daughter and a miner's son – conversing like normal people. What do you think of that, Mr Lawrence?'

'It's against the rules,' he replied, no longer laughing. 'I lost my best friend when his parents discovered my father was a miner. He wasn't allowed to talk to me again.'

'That makes me so angry! How could they do that to a child?' Frieda had a sudden pitiful image of Mr Lawrence as a child, small, slight, friendless. A sadness caught in her throat. She took a long drag on her cigarette and blew out a thin jet of smoke. 'My husband tells me you are a writer. What are you writing?'

Mr Lawrence leaned further forward, his hands twisting in his lap. 'A novel about a man growing up. A man from round here. His mother dies and he's very close to her. He struggles after that.' He paused and coughed, then stared, searchingly, at her. 'Do you think my book will find any readers, Mrs Weekley?'

Frieda felt a quiver run along her insides. Suddenly she had to stand up, to move. The room with its black-and-gold carpet, Ernest's gilt-framed certificates, the endlessly ticking clock, felt choking and oppressive. She began pacing, aware of Mr Lawrence's gaze following her, never leaving her.

'A son who is obsessed with his mother?' Ideas and words from her time in Munich swam into her head, like goldfish biting for air. She punched out her cigarette and drew back her shoulders.

'Have you heard the new ideas from Doctor Freud in Vienna? Do you know the story of Oedipus? Or Hamlet? Doctor Freud believes all boys are caught between hating their fathers and desiring their mothers.' She paused, expecting him to flinch, to look away in disgust. When he didn't, she continued, a faint mocking note in her voice. 'Would that apply to your character?'

'I've no knowledge of any Doctor Freud.' Mr Lawrence stood up and moved to the French windows where the red velvet curtains were gusting in the wind. She noticed how lightly he moved, how quickly and certainly. Not like an invalid, she thought. Not like a labourer or a miner. More like an animal. A wild graceful animal. Or a bird. A slender darting bird.

'I'm just rewriting a scene where the son kisses his mother and begs her not to sleep with his father. The mother character's called Gertrude, same as in *Hamlet*. But I want nothing more to do with women – nothing, nothing, nothing. I'm through with women! What would Doctor Freud say about that?' He turned back to her, his eyes glistening and his skin tinged pink.

Frieda threw back her head and laughed. His words were ridiculous, spoken to provoke her. She could see it in the eagerness of his gaze. She recognised then the light spiking behind his pupils. It was desire. And she knew it was for her. The knowledge pleased and emboldened her. 'Doctor Freud would agree with me, that there is not a man worth having nowadays. They cannot get away from their mothers. Their mothers are all in love with them, and they are all in love with their mothers. What are we women to do?'

'Do you do so badly?' Mr Lawrence's voice mingled inquisitiveness with amusement, so that she could not tell if he was laughing at her or prying. And the not-knowing piqued her.

'Yes! It's all true. They are all mothers' little darlings, all Hamlets, obsessed by their mothers. And we are supposed to be Ophelias and go drown ourselves.' She stooped for a cigarette, jabbing it between her lips.

143

'Are you about to drown yourself?'

'No, but a mother's love is so very powerful. Although I must say Professor Weekley is no Hamlet. His mother did not swamp him with love.' She reached for the matchbox but as she did so, Mr Lawrence's hand shot out, so that for a second their fingers touched, like hot coals.

He rattled the matchbox and grinned, as if he had secured a small victory. 'So what is Professor Weekley in this German scheme of things?'

'He loves the idea of me. He calls me his snowflower. But I'm not a snowflower. I am more of a dandelion. Give me a light, please.'

'And do you blaze as brightly and forcefully as a dandelion?' Mr Lawrence struck a match and Frieda plunged her face into its flame so that she felt its heat against her mouth, her nose, her chin.

'Why shouldn't I be a weed? I don't want to be worshipped, I want to be loved. But you cautious Englanders want a little white snowflower in your buttonhole. You do not know how to love! Isn't that so?'

'That is because most Englanders want a life without intimacy, without intensity of feeling. I prefer a dandelion, myself. I love the way their petals are pressed back with such urgency.'

She repeated his words swiftly and silently in her head, ash tumbling from her cigarette ... *intimacy ... intensity ... petals pressed back with such urgency*. For a second the room seemed to tip around her, as if she were a bee crawling out of a windblown rose, intoxicated and drunk on pollen.

'Yes,' he continued, rocking on his heels. 'I'm very partial to dandelions, they're like great golden jewels, clusters of 'em, that yearn restlessly for the heat of the sun. They take such pleasure in being themselves.'

She felt the hairs rise on her arms. There was a force behind his words, something more than his dialect, his poetry. Hurriedly, she put her cigarette to her lips, waited for him to continue.

'A dandelion's not *for* anything, is it? It's not for putting in a swanky vase. Or frying with onions. It's just itself, proudly and pleasurably itself. We humans should be more like 'em.'

'Oh yes! You are right!' She was conscious, in that moment, that their minds had met and crossed and understood. That this miner's son – so strange and unknown, so young – was more like her than anyone she'd ever met.

'And dandelions are full of vigour and poetry and courage,' she added, not wanting the conversation to end.

'They answer only to their own God. And with a sensuality all of their own, that golden throat, the long green neck . . . I once compared myself to an empty dandelion stalk in a poem. Do you see why?'

She paused. A thick lock of Mr Lawrence's hair had tumbled over his eyes so that she could no longer see him. Before she could stop herself, her hand had shot out and smoothed the lock from his face.

Mr Lawrence coughed and stepped away. Ernest was standing in the doorway, breathless and wiping the perspiration from his forehead, folders and papers clenched beneath his arm. How had she not heard the crunch of his feet on the gravel or his key in the lock?

'I am so very sorry, Mr Lawrence,' he said, straightening his papers and putting them on a side table. 'Please forgive me for my inexcusable tardiness. Quite inexcusable.'

Frieda felt the room sink awkwardly, clumsily, around them. The air, that had been thick and charged, was all at once strained and sober. The sounds of domestic life – Mrs Babbit sharpening a knife on a whetstone, the children laughing in the garden – came to her, sharp and tyrannical.

'We were talking of dandelions,' she blurted, her fingers fretting at her neckline.

'Dreadful things, impossible to dig out,' Ernest said, shortly. 'Mrs Babbit has just told me luncheon is served. Come to the dining room, Mr Lawrence.'

Only then did Frieda realise what Mr Lawrence reminded her of. He reminded her of a wildcat her father had brought home from a hunting trip. An escaped lynx, said the Baron, as he'd dropped the slatted wooden box carelessly on the floor. The cat had beautiful dappled fur but its back leg was broken where it had been wrenched, half-starved, from a snare. And yet its eyes had flared, furiously and desperately, with life. The Baron had offered ten marks to anyone brave enough to put their hand inside the cage and touch the snarling beast. 'Go on, my little Fritzl,' he'd urged. Frieda had closed her eyes and thrust her hand into the box, stroking its twisting foaming head with a single finger. She didn't do it for the ten marks. Or for the approval of her father. She did it for the cat. To comfort him. To help him. Later the Baron opened the box to shoot the cat but, somehow, the cat evaded his bullet. She could still remember her father's vicious curses. But most of all she remembered the cat, its supple sinuous haunches leaping through the moonlit orchard, as if its broken leg was no impediment to escape.

'Mutti? Is it roast beef for luncheon?' Monty appeared beside her, a trail of stamp glue across his chin.

'Yes, *mein Liebling*,' she said. 'It's your favourite roast beef today.'

She reached for his hand, gripping it tightly in hers. His cool sticky fingers seemed to moor her, to reattach her to their mutual world: roast beef and stamp glue and Mrs Babbit's blancmange. She was still Mrs Weekley. Mother of Monty, Elsa and Barby. Wife of Professor Ernest Weekley. But with a stranger in her dining room. A stranger she had never felt so close to, so in thrall to. A stranger with the vim and spirit of a wildcat. She felt her knees weaken, and the running swell of her blood. Quickly she braced herself. 'Mrs Babbit's excellent roast beef. Aren't we lucky, *mein Liebling*?'

THIRTY-TWO

Frieda

'I think that went very well, my snowflower.' Ernest stood up slowly from the sofa, wincing and kneading at the small of his back with a spidery hand. 'He should find the lecturing position he wants in the Rhineland. A most promising young man.'

Frieda nodded, her eyes fixed on the French windows. As if she expected Mr Lawrence to reappear. Their conversation, which had so thrilled and intoxicated her, had changed course when Ernest arrived home, switching to more mundane subjects. But Mr Lawrence's words, his questions, the rich inflection in his voice, played over and over in her head.

She'd been aware of his gaze throughout lunch. Following her over the silver cruets, the toughened joint of beef, the bowl of wet cabbage. Lingering on her face and throat. Tracking the movement of her hand as she reached for the boiled potatoes. On several occasions she'd caught his clean blue eyes seeking out hers. She'd held his gaze for as long as she dared, felt the space between them recede, tauten, quiver; sensed a curious gravitational pull that seemed to come from his presence.

'No notion of etiquette. Did you see him trying to work out the cutlery? Perhaps I should offer him a little guidance before he moves to Germany.' Ernest brushed a speck of dust from his lapel and looked at the clock.

'Germany . . . yes,' Frieda echoed, her voice low and soft. She stared out at the garden. The salmon sun of earlier had shrunk behind the factory chimneys and a sooty mizzle of March rain was falling on the lawn, the shrubs, Ernest's newly planted rhubarb crowns. And yet she felt exhilarated, as if her blood was sprinting through her body, as if her ribs had burst from the corset Ernest insisted she wear on Sundays.

'I'm sorry I was so late. I hope the conversation wasn't too awkward?'

'He spoke to me like no Englishman has ever spoken to me.' Frieda's eyes rose above the black chimneys to the grey billowing sky. Mr Lawrence's words – so direct, so without tact or charm – had seemed to jump, naked and unadorned, from his very soul.

'You mustn't be too hard on someone bred in a miner's hovel.' Ernest shook his head, sympathetically. 'And his mother passed away recently, poor man. Now, I really must get back to work.'

Just as he was about to close the drawing room door, Ernest turned back into the room. 'Oh, that reminds me, Mr Lawrence asked if he could come back on Sunday, wants you to look over his application letter, check the grammar for him. I'll be in Cambridge, of course. Would you mind terribly, my dear? I know he's not the class of gentleman you're accustomed to, but his poetry is quite exceptional.'

THIRTY-THREE

Frieda

Three days later, Frieda received a letter. It had one line and was unsigned. But she saw the address, a small mining village called Eastwood, and knew instantly who it was from.

You are the most wonderful woman in all England

She laughed and folded the thin sheet of paper into a small square before tucking it into her cuff. She had thought of Mr Lawrence constantly since that lunch. Of his voice that had been soft and harsh by turns, of his words that had seemed to well from some place deep inside him, of his eyes that had fixed on her with such naked eagerness. She had this strange sense that she would never fully know him, that somehow he was un-knowable. Had Ernest been like that when they first met? She thought back through the haze of years and remembered how exotic he had seemed, how the promise of adventure and travel and independence had called to her, how he had rescued her from the fierce hatred of her home. But even then she had felt the predictability of him, the finality of him. As if, in that first week of meeting, she had seen and understood every little inch of him.

She waited, impatiently, for Sunday when Mr Lawrence was coming for tea. And by the time Sunday arrived and Ernest had left for Cambridge, she was fizzing, every nerve vibrating with expectation. She spent an hour choosing her outfit, unsure what to wear, who to be. As she riffled through her dresses and skirts and blouses, it seemed that none were right for Mr Lawrence, that none were *her*. They were right for her with Ernest but not for her with Mr Lawrence. Eventually she settled for a navy skirt with a yellow high-necked blouse that felt all wrong but was, she thought, something a miner's wife might wear.

When Mr Lawrence arrived, she motioned him to the kitchen where he pulled out a chair at the scrubbed pine table and laid out his German application letter. She saw how much more at ease he was here and decided against tea in the drawing room.

There was an awkward silence as she hunted for the teapot and then fiddled with the gas stove, unable to light it. Suddenly he pushed back his chair and stood up, shaking his head so hard his hair fell louchely from its neatly brushed parting.

'You can't turn the gas on, can you, Mrs Weekley? And nor can you find the tea things. I should scold you!' He moved her aside, turned the dial on the new gas cooker and put a match to it. The blue flame roared noisily into life. Frieda watched him as he found the teapot and cups, the sugar bowl and the silver sugar tongs, as he measured leaves from the tea caddy and poured water from the kettle. He seemed so deft and efficient, even in an unfamiliar kitchen. The way he opened the cupboards and drawers with such surety. The way he wrapped the tea-towel so neatly round the handle of the kettle. She should have felt embarrassed at her inability to light the stove or find the cups. Instead his competence sent a shiver of desire through her. She watched his hands scooping tea leaves and pouring milk – and they reminded her of lilies, delicate and white. The hands of a poet, she thought, her eyes sliding up to where his jacket pinched at his narrow shoulders and strained against his long neck.

'Are you always this lazy?' he asked, bluntly. 'Or is it because you're from the ancient and famous house of Richthofen, and not accustomed to housework?'

'I like the way you talk to me,' she said, looking him straight in the eye. 'And I liked your letter. You do not trifle with small talk, do you?'

A shaft of light caught on the teaspoons as he arranged them on each saucer, making slender beams of silver that jiggled on the ceiling. 'No,' he said. 'And nor should you. I prefer the swift lash of your tongue to any niceties.'

'But Nottingham is all small talk,' said Frieda, bemused.

'And I want none of it. I want a rapturous life, not one of polite affectation and lies. But what sort of life do you want, Mrs Weekley?'

'No one has ever asked me that.' Frieda thought for a minute, her lips chewing. 'I want a courageous life. A free life. I want to be myself.'

'And what is yourself?' He gestured round the kitchen, with its lines of shining pans, the gleaming new gas cooker, the window that looked onto the scrupulously clipped garden in all its shrubberied seclusion. 'I don't think this is yourself.'

'And how would you know, Mr Lawrence?'

'Because I can see through your hard, bright shell.'

Frieda felt something inside her fall away. As if a curtain had been dragged too soon from a stage set, leaving a tangled clutter that couldn't be concealed. She busied herself stirring at her tea. She felt ashamed of her lack of contentment, ashamed of her loneliness.

'Yes, I want to be myself. I would like a life of rapture too. I had it once, for a fortnight.' She faltered, briefly assailed by memories of Munich. 'But I have the children to think of and I want to be a wonderful mother. That is myself too. Just not all of myself.' She gave an irritated shake of her head, frustrated that she could not properly explain how she felt.

Mr Lawrence leaned across the table, a blue light flaming at the back of his eyes. His hands inched across the scrubbed pine, edging spontaneously towards her.

'I want to live like a flower, to just be myself. My dandelion self. You put it so well last week.' Her fingers pulsed, as if each one had its own beating heart. She sensed their impulse – to reach for his hands, to grip them tightly in her own. She felt the air between them, stiff and bristling with tension. Before she had time to consider the propriety of such an action, her hands had shot across the table and snatched at his.

He took her fingers into his cloistered palms. 'Tell me,' he said, simply.

For the next hour she spoke of Otto and Ernest, of her longing for passion, of her need for intimacy, of her belief in freedom, of Munich and the Café Stefanie, of the strange workings of the unconscious mind, of her boundless love for Monty, Elsa and Barby. At each pause, he threw her a new question, his eyes always alert, never glazing over, never softening with mock sympathy. Only once did he look away. When she told him of her affair with Otto, he looked down at the table and was silent for a second, as if unsure what to say.

'Do you hate me now? For telling you the truth about me?'

'No,' he said, quickly. 'I'm shocked, but I like you even more. Your husband has no idea?'

She shook her head so frenziedly a hairpin clattered to the floor. 'I want so much to be loved. To be a *full* part of someone's life. To have passion. Children cannot give that. And I must use my brain! Men keep all the brainy work for themselves.'

Mr Lawrence took the cups and saucers to the sink and began washing them up.

'Leave them,' she cried. 'Mrs Babbit will do that tomorrow.'

'I can't sit idle,' he said, carefully wiping the tea things dry and replacing them in the cupboard. 'Is there no passion in your marriage?'

'No! He has made an image of me. He knows nothing about who I am. And if he did, he would only jeer and sneer and hate me.'

'You're not like any woman I've ever met,' he said later, reaching for his coat and cap. 'You're so fine, so perfectly unconventional.'

She gestured at his application letter, lying unread upon the table. 'I haven't checked the grammar yet.'

He brushed the letter away. 'Forget the grammar. Who cares about grammar when we can converse like we have? With real passion, with honest feeling . . .'

Hope swept through her. Perhaps he would stay in Nottingham. Perhaps they could continue their friendship and it would sustain her, feed her.

He plunged his hands into his pockets, as if to still them. 'You've helped me with my novel, Mrs Weekley. You've helped me understand how a mother feels, the force and mystery of it all. You and your mad German ideas.' He grinned and his mouth seemed to pull and stretch until it covered the full width of his face.

After he left, Frieda could not settle. She walked the house, trying to understand what had just passed between her and her husband's student. She felt as if she had been split open, as if Mr Lawrence had peered deep inside her, seen things she had hidden from the rest of the world. It was a marvellous feeling, she decided, to be explored and understood. And yet she felt plagued by restlessness.

What if he turned out to be like any other English man? The disappointment would be crushing, she thought. And yet she detected something puritanical in him, a stringent morality that rose up and briefly revealed itself. Sometimes in a turn of phrase. Sometimes in a faint expression of disapproval so fleeting she wasn't sure if she'd seen it or not. He seemed so awed – impressed even – by her lack of inhibition. But what if he was simply prying for story material? What if he was as priggish and patriarchal as the next man?

His mettle must be tested, she decided. She would wait a week, spend a little more time with him – he'd mentioned seeing a play at Nottingham's Theatre Royal and a return visit to work on his German grammar. And then, if she was still as dazzled by him, she would take him to the woods and show him who she truly was. She would let her body speak, in the boldest possible way. It was so rare to find an English man untouched by prudery or repression or lasciviousness. But she must know that he was free of those traits, that he was as open-minded as he claimed. Yes, she would take him to the woods and put him to the test.

THIRTY-FOUR

Frieda

She could feel the cool, spongy moss beneath her back, soft and faintly damp against her bare skin. She closed her eyes. Mr Lawrence had stopped talking and she could hear the whisper of insects in the tangled grass and the screech of a jay in the trees above. The smell of spring was everywhere – a sappy, green smell tinged with something loamy and fetid that reminded her of Ernest's compost heap. The one at the very back of the garden that he turned every Saturday after he got back from teaching. She wondered if he was digging over his compost at this very moment, in that neat, precise way he had. A shiver ran over her.

When she looked back at the thirteen years of her married life, she saw it as something that had happened *to* her. Life had happened and she'd been swept along, a piece of driftwood picked up by the tide and tossed out to sea. It wasn't a life she'd made or created for herself. It was the life Ernest had built. A set, compressed life rigid with respectability. And she was bobbing around at its periphery, consoling herself with Monty, Elsa and Barby. But without purpose or meaning of her own. The children were growing up. Soon they wouldn't need her. What would she do then? She knew women weren't supposed to have purpose outside the home. But times were changing. Even Mrs Dowson had purpose with her suffragettes. And then there was Elisabeth. In her last letter, Elisabeth said she was helping Max and Alfred Weber write books so radical and exciting she could barely sleep, books that would change society forever.

She'd had her chance with Otto, of course. But one had to be practical and think of the future and he'd turned out to be wholly unreliable. But now, with Mr Lawrence, she was coming back to life, bursting into bud like the ash, oak and elm trees that circled them. And she thought again of Otto's words: her genius for living, for inspiring men to greatness. If she could just persuade Mr Lawrence to stay in Nottingham as her new lover . . .

She twitched. Something was moving in her pubic hair.

'Don't move, Mrs Weekley. Keep your eyes closed.'

'What are you doing?'

'I'm threading violets through your pubic hair, making a floral tapestry.'

Frieda laughed. She had invited him to come and lie with her in the woods, told him she had a special secret place. After scrambling through the bracken and gorse she'd flung off her clothes and let the frugal April sun fall upon her skin, smiling as Mr Lawrence's expression tipped from shock to awe to pleasure. Mr Lawrence had then gazed at her with such adoration she'd felt herself swell and expand, as if to accommodate the surfeit of emotion inside them both.

Eventually she'd coaxed him out of his jacket. Then his worn-down shoes and heavily darned socks. And when he was quite sure they wouldn't be discovered, he'd begun kissing her all over, small panting kisses so full of wonder and tenderness she'd been quite startled. But when she pulled his head to hers, tried to press her mouth on his, he pulled away and said, 'Not my mouth. My bronchials are playing up and I shan't want you to catch anything.' Otto had never displayed such delicate or tender feelings. Yes, he'd been completely uninhibited, shown her things she'd never imagined. But Mr Lawrence was quite different. His ardour was restrained and gentle and yet it quivered all around him.

'Can you smell the air, Mrs Weekley? The smell of tree bark and lambs' wool and life erupting all around us. Isn't it splendid? The smell of intercourse between heaven and earth, the smell of creation.' He sniffed vigorously at the air as he teased the limp stems of violets through her pubic hairs. 'Isn't the sunlight mad today? Have you noticed how it leaps and jumps like a Morris dancer? Open your eyes. The sun has gone quite crazy.'

Frieda opened her eyes. Sunlight glittered and shook from the boughs above them. And beyond was the sky, pale blue and shiny like the inside of a wet seashell. She lifted her head. Mr Lawrence was still crouched between her legs and when she looked down she saw a mound of purple violets below her belly button.

'I cannot believe you can sit there and not want to make love to me, Mr Lawrence.'

'Oh but I do, I do. I'm always thinking of you, of how it will be. I can't get free of it, of the desire for you.'

She pushed herself up on her elbows, struck by a sudden thought. 'Are you still a virgin, Mr Lawrence?'

He rubbed the ball of his foot absently in the grass, his eyes down. 'Not quite, but almost. Nothing satisfactory at any rate. But it's not that.'

She lay back and closed her eyes again, trying to stifle the smile creeping across her face. The thought of teaching someone like Mr Lawrence, just as Otto had taught her, was gratifying.

'The problem is you're still Weekley's wife, his territory. And I won't take you out of inflamed necessity.'

She felt her breath empty out of her. *Weekley's wife . . . his territory.* She wanted to leap up and shout 'I am no one's territory! I am not a horse to be bought and sold!' But she held her tongue. Mr Lawrence would come round. She would enlighten him, introduce him slowly to her own ideas of liberty. And anyway, something about his self-restraint impressed her. She thought briefly of Mr Dowson's meaty hands, how they'd prowled over her body at every opportunity, as if he had no control of himself. And then she remembered her father, whimpering incontinently after losing everything at the gambling tables. Of course, Ernest had discipline. Bags of it. But no passion. Mr Lawrence had passion *and* discipline, emotion *and* restraint.

After a protracted pause, she asked 'But you like this?'

'Oh yes, very much.' Mr Lawrence flushed. 'I love the nakedness of you, the wild recklessness of you.'

'Next time you will take all your clothes off too. You will love the feeling of sun and air on your skin. Such a magnificent feeling of freedom.' She threw back her head and stretched out her arms, turning her palms up to the sky. She remembered the first time she came here. Just after her return from Munich when she could think of nothing but Otto. She hadn't intended to lie naked in the open air but as she walked through the woods, a sudden breeze had rushed up her skirt, rattling and pulling at her underclothes as if trying to prise them off. The breeze had become an August wind, chasing her further and further into the undergrowth. Finally she'd stumbled into this secluded pool of sunlight and, with her mind in turmoil, impulsively thrown off her clothes and sunbathed. Afterwards she'd felt better, clearer and calmer, as if soothed by the sun.

'How splendid you are!' Mr Lawrence paused and then added, almost shyly, 'Would you like to read my novel? I'd appreciate your opinion.'

Frieda kept her eyes closed. She didn't want him to see the welter of feelings his simple request had provoked. In her most composed voice, she replied, 'I'd be delighted to help you. I think I should go home now, the children will be wondering where I am.'

'You can't go home with bloomers full of violets, Mrs Weekley.' He began removing the violets and placing them, one by one, on her upturned palms. 'I've never met anyone like you. I feel as if you've planted yourself inside my soul.'

'Yes,' she murmured. How right he was. She felt exactly the same but could never have articulated it as he did.

When her palms were full of violets he reached for her underclothes which he'd folded and placed on a branch. Even that small gesture had surprised and delighted her. He'd picked up every bit of clothing from where she'd flung it on the mossy earth. Then he'd shaken out the creases, folded each garment and laid it carefully on the branch of an oak tree.

'Let me dress you. Let me do it.' As he buttoned and laced her chemise and then her petticoat and dress, he kept his eyes down and asked 'Is there too much of the woman in me? I'm none too manly, am I? Be honest, Mrs Weekley.'

'You're fine and strong,' she replied running her hands up and down his trousered legs as she spoke. 'You have a fine strong body and you should never be ashamed of it.'

That evening, as she tickled Barby, as she admired Monty's new stamps, as she plaited Elsa's hair, she couldn't stop thinking about Mr Lawrence. She tried to push him from her mind. But he wouldn't shift. She couldn't erase the sweet sensation of his kisses up and down her spine, the roughened tips of his fingers as he'd traced the arteries that ran along the insides of her arms. She recalled his words – *you've planted yourself inside my soul* – and smiled to herself. Yes, and he has planted himself in *my* soul, she thought. And now he's like a seed sprouting in the darkness of me.

'Mutti! Did you hear what I just said?' Barby tugged at her sleeve.

'I'm sorry, *Liebling*. What did you say?'

'Oh never mind.' Barby climbed off her knee and walked away.

Frieda nodded absently. She had to work out how to keep Mr Lawrence in Nottingham. How to keep him as her lover. Because she couldn't go back to the drifting lethargy of the last few years. Not now.

Ernest

'Analogies . . .' Ernest paused and gazed out of his study window at the billowing, white sky. It had a strangely undisturbed quality today, a virginal quality, as though no one had taken any breath from it, as if undefiled by factory smoke or railway steam or ash from the pits. He frowned. He mustn't let himself be distracted by air or clouds or poetic notions of virginity. What was he thinking!

'The form of a word is often affected by association with some other word.' He spoke out loud, even though he was alone. The emptiness of the house made him feel oddly abandoned and the sound of his voice was reassuring. Ida had taken the children out, it was Mrs Babbit's day off and Frieda was out with Mr Lawrence. Ernest coughed as if to puncture the silence. He'd grown up subjected to the interminable din of a large family and, although he'd longed for peace and quiet then, he now found the silence of an empty house slightly unsettling.

He began speaking aloud again. 'Hence the word "bridal" comes from the coupling of bride and ale – a liquid refreshment frequently consumed at marriage festivities.' He and Frieda had drunk German ale at their wedding. What a long time ago it seemed . . . Thirteen years . . . And what happy years! She was as lively and cheerful now as she'd been at eighteen. She still laughed in the same way, with a slightly mocking undertone, and arched brows, and eyes that flashed green and gold. He remembered, with a sudden stab of nostalgia, how she'd once listened to him with the eagerness of a disciple. And he remembered how her talk of strength and courage had piqued him. Later he attributed it to the military environment she'd grown up in. But then she'd just seemed exotic, quite unlike the demur English girls he saw at church.

His mind drifted back to his proposal letter. How impudent, how audacious he'd been. In England no man of his class would dare propose to an aristocrat. In England he would have been pilloried. But for some reason Germany had emboldened him. And to his surprise, Frieda had agreed. Even now, he couldn't quite believe his luck.

'Marriage . . . must be from the Old French, *marier*. To marry . . .' Ernest looked up at the photograph of Frieda he kept on the mantelpiece. He'd had a few words with her, the previous evening. Not a chiding, just a gentle warning. 'I had to say something,' he murmured to himself. 'I had no choice. For her own good, of course.' His great friend, Professor Kipping, had mentioned – just in passing – that Mrs Kipping had told him of a little gossip circulating. Regarding Mrs Weekley. That Mrs Weekley had been seen a little too often with a poorly dressed young man in a flat cap. At the theatre. Walking in the country. Inappropriate for a married woman. Inappropriate for the wife of a professor. Inappropriate for a baroness.

Ernest had protested, of course. He'd explained to Professor Kipping that the man was a poet, that Frieda wasn't English, that she was a German aristocrat who had grown up in quite a different milieu. He'd even informed his good friend of Frieda's youthful presentation to Kaiser Wilhelm, of the stir she'd created at Court with her beauty and spirit. Professor Kipping had nodded in his mild-mannered way and said he intended no disrespect, he was merely passing it on at his wife's request.

'I have no wish to curtail her,' Ernest continued, aloud. 'She is not a butterfly to be pinned to a board.' Besides which, Mr Lawrence was departing imminently for a teaching position in Germany, so there was no cause for concern.

He'd placed a kindly hand on Professor Kipping's shoulder and told him he appreciated the confidence but Mrs Weekley was a loyal and devoted wife and mother, and anyone who cast aspersions on her good character was greatly mistaken. He'd still felt impelled to let Frieda know people were talking about her. He'd relayed Kipping's words as gently as possible. Frieda had flounced round the drawing room, expressing outrage at 'old-fashioned English people obsessed with rank.' With tobacco smoke streaming from her nostrils, she'd declared herself 'finished' with English women. A few minutes later, she ground out her cigarette and perched on his knee. 'You should not listen to this stupid gossip, my dear.' And she had stroked his hair and his moustache and told him with maternal pride that Monty had beaten her at chess, again.

Later that evening, he'd gone into his wife's bedroom to say goodnight. He'd found her propped up against a pile of pillows, a cigarette tucked into the corner of her mouth, reading from a stack of handwritten papers. With even more pride, she'd told him that Mr Lawrence wanted her to read his new novel. 'It is inspired by his own life and he wants me to go through it, line by line.' Her voice had shimmered with pleasure and satisfaction. 'He needs my help because he does not understand women, and it is all about women.'

'He has chosen the right reader then.' And Ernest had kissed her on the top of her head, noticing the neat determination of Mr Lawrence's handwriting as he did so.

He gazed at her photograph again. He must get her to Cambridge. He picked up his pen and looked at the last sentence. 'Marriage. From the Old French, *marier.*' He paused and sighed. 'In considering the Old French element in English, one has to bear in mind a few elementary philological facts.' Yes, he nodded, if only everyone realised that most French nouns and adjectives were derived from the accusative. And nor were they from the French of Paris but from old dialects like those of Normandy and Picardy.

THIRTY-SIX

Frieda

Not since her discovery of the Café Stefanie five years ago, had Frieda felt so alert, so alive. Every morning she woke with a shock of excitement. An image of Mr Lawrence leapt into her head, making her feel light-headed with joy. Somehow, he imbued everything with colour. Things that once seemed flat and turgid were now draped in brilliant hues. Even the puffball of smoke that hovered over Nottingham was tinged with a luminous mauve, like the wing of a wood pigeon.

Each day she flew from her bed, whipped round the house like a dervish, gathering up children and school books and sheet music, tossing instructions to Mrs Babbit and Ida, breaking into song or some impromptu dance steps – and waiting anxiously for the postboy so she might find out when Mr Lawrence was next free.

She knew his youth and genius excited her, that his words of poetry made her melt inside, that he seemed to understand her like no one else. But there was something else about him that thrilled her. Something she could not put into words. One afternoon, a week after they had lain together in the woods, he took her to Sherwood Forest. There she saw clearly that he was quite unlike any man she had ever met.

He bounded from streams to rocks to fallen tree trunks, pulling her by the hand, exclaiming at everything. He seemed to see the smallest things: a drop of dew in the crease of a leaf, a ruff of mottled fungus round a branch, roots that twisted forth from the ground, light refracting on a puddle of rainwater, a single red ant marching up a blade of bright green grass. It was as though he had not two eyes but a hundred. He made her look at the stamens of a celandine and describe the colour to him.

'Why, yellow of course,' she laughed.

'No, Mrs Weekley!' he exclaimed as he pulled her to the ground. 'Look again. This was Wordsworth's favourite flower, and you must do it justice. There are a hundred different yellows. You must find the right one.'

'Yellow, like butter? Or the flesh of a yellow plum?'

He nodded and then his eye caught something else and he tugged at her hand and gestured fervently at the sky. 'That was a green woodpecker. Did you see it? Watch how it flies . . . how it rises and drops. No other bird flies like that. And did you hear its cry? I love the way it flashes through the sky, a streak of green with that brazen dash of scarlet at its throat.' And he swooped his hand through the air mimicking the bird's flight so gracefully Frieda almost felt herself flying.

A second later he was crouched over a rotten tree trunk, prodding and sniffing. 'Come and look at this,' he called. 'Jelly ear fungus. Isn't it a beauty?' He took the tip of her finger, guiding it gently over the ears of crimson fleshy fungus as if it were a bolt of the finest silk.

'You are so – so alive,' she said later, as they sat against the trunk of a vast oak tree.

He pulled his knees up, so that his trouser hems rose revealing narrow, bony ankles. 'I want to start a new community where everyone shall be truly, richly, deeply alive. A new way of living, away from industry and cities.'

She smiled as her thoughts turned instinctively back to Metz. Its flat fields of rippling rye. The purple plums with their milky bloom. The cherry blossom, tender and pink. How had she ended up in a city that palpitated with industry and grime?

'Have you seen how the trees of London burst through the pavements? We can all do that. We've enough life to break out of this system, to create a new world, a better world. I know it in my heart.' He knocked his fist against his chest as though he was willing it to open. 'In my writing I want to explore the very depths of the human soul, the male *and* female soul. I want to know how the heart works, Mrs Weekley. I want to see inside the human unconscious.'

She nodded, thinking she could listen to him, on and on, and never have her fill. She had an odd feeling that she was waiting in the wings, waiting to take her place on a blossomy sunlit stage, listening for her cue.

'I want my life to be an adventure. A real adventure into the unknown. Come with me! I don't need any of the usual trappings. Just clean water and simple food. Objects don't matter – it's the magnificence of our dreams that matter. And who needs luxuries or possessions when we have all this?' He threw out his arm to indicate the blossom crowding on the boughs, the crows rawking overhead, the wisps of cloud in the pale blue sky.

'They say the Italian sky is the colour of lapis lazuli, every day for months on end. Hot and pure and blue. Wouldn't you love to see it?'

'I would,' Frieda replied, wistfully. She thought of her comfortable house with its jealously guarded grounds, its neatly edged lawn, its carefully pruned rose beds, its steady, even habits. She thought of Ernest. Crouched over his work. Sipping at his nightly glass of stout. Winding the clocks each week, on the same day, at the same hour.

'I can achieve so much with you by my side, Mrs Weekley. You're the woman of a lifetime!' Mr Lawrence gripped her hand. 'Come and see the world with me. Help me create a bonfire of life!'

'I have three children whom I love deeply.' She summoned images of Monty, Elsa and Barby, as if to anchor her, to remind herself of her role, her place. She tried to swallow the lump that had risen in her throat and wedged itself there like a fishbone.

'Bring 'em. I'll make a home for us all, I promise.'

'Ernest is a good man.'

'He's stifling you, smothering you to death. Bring your children and come away with me. I'm all yours, Mrs Weekley!'

'It is not so easy.' She paused. The ground seemed to be shifting beneath her, as if the plates of the earth were moving and colliding in great jolts.

'Come away and be separate in your own soul. And live!' He leapt up and scooped at the air with his cupped hands. 'Look at this damselfly.' He squatted beside her and opened his hands. 'The males are always brighter. Isn't he a beauty? Look at the colour of his body. Like the ocean, like the Mediterranean sky.'

Frieda examined the damselfly as it sat in Mr Lawrence's hands. And in that second she had a fleeting glimpse of a life with Mr Lawrence. How rich it would be. How full and wide and deep. How dazzling! She suddenly felt giddy with exhilaration. The wings of the damselfly seemed more beautiful, more intricate than any insect wing she'd ever seen, as if her nerves had expanded and come to the very surface of her skin, her eyes, her brain, her heart. She was aware of her breath scratching round the lump in her throat, the beating of her heart, the fluttering motion in the damselfly's lacy wings, the vibrant turquoise of its markings.

He spread his hands and the damselfly whirred into the sky. 'I can't let you go, Mrs Weekley. I want you. I need you. It would be wrong to send you back to *him*. Come away with me and be free.'

Frieda let the idea play in her mind. Mr Lawrence wanted her as she was, for who she was. Otto had wanted her, of course. But she'd never felt completely needed by him. She'd never felt his life, his genius, depended on *her*. He'd had ample inspiration

167

elsewhere . . . cocaine and morphine . . . other women. Sometimes she wondered if Otto had wanted her for who she was or for what she represented, the 'personality type' that he'd wrapped her in, like a cloak of his own weaving . . . the eager pupil who'd been so responsive to his tutelage. Ernest was no different. He wanted her as his snowflower and had appropriated the bits of her that suited him, ignoring the rest. He too seemed to have no need of her. His small successes had disappointed her, as much for the self-sufficiency with which he'd achieved them as for their insignificance.

But Mr Lawrence was different. He'd already published one novel, *The White Peacock*. His second, *The Trespasser*, was about to be printed. She'd read the draft manuscript of his third novel and seen, with her own eyes, the depth of his imagination, the mutinous disobedience of his mind. To be with someone so *alive*, who loved her with such passion after a mere fortnight, who was destined for greatness. It's as if he's offering me not only my freedom and his love but his vast talent, she thought. And a life that is fulfilled, impetuous, intense. The life she had dreamed of since Munich, since Otto. The life she had dreamed of as a girl.

'Did you hear me? I can do so much with you by my side! People are calling me a genius. But I need you with me. I can't do it without you.'

Frieda's mind flipped back to her childhood. The Baroness and her friends pecking at marble cake. Sipping their schnapps from engraved glasses. Clucking like trussed hens. The scrape of cake forks on porcelain. The creaking of whalebone corsets. She, Nusch, Elisabeth, waiting behind the big wooden door with the brass handle. Mother calling. Nusch first. Isn't she pretty? Oh how lovely she is! What a fine figure. What a good match she'll make. Cluck cluck cluck. Elisabeth next. My Elisabeth is writing a book. My Elisabeth is raising money for orphaned children. Oh how worthy! How clever! How industrious! The perfect wife for a high-ranking official. Peck peck peck. Frieda last. Silence. Raised pince-nez. The

Baroness's eyes like currants. This one plays in foxholes and climbs trees. Eyes rolling. Chests heaving. Tut tut tut.

'What are you thinking about?' Mr Lawrence looked tenderly at her.

'Oh nothing,' replied Frieda. 'I think I shall call you Lorenzo. I want to have my own name for you.'

'Lorenzo.' Mr Lawrence rolled the name round in his mouth and smiled. 'I like that.'

'I know others call you Bert, but I like Lorenzo.'

'I must have a name for you too. What did your folks call you when you were little?'

'I never had a special name. My little sister, Johanna, was called Nusch and Elisabeth was called Else. My father called me Fritzl for a bit, but my mother didn't like that, so I was always just Frieda.'

'Isn't Fritzl a boy's name?'

She nodded.

'Well, I shall call you Queen Bee. Because you're so very *queenly*, so imperious. But I insist you tell Weekley about us. Tell him the truth and then come away with me. Bring your children and I'll make a home for you all, a new heaven on earth. I promise!'

Frieda closed her eyes. It was a blissful idea. *A heaven on earth*. But it was impossible, of course. She had only known him for three weeks. Or was it impossible?

'Can we take Elsa and Barby out next week? Monty is still at school.' She would watch Lorenzo with Barby and Elsa, see if they liked him. See if he realised the enormity of his offer; the wild rashness of his promise. Once he'd spent some time with them, no doubt he'd retract everything. And then perhaps they could be simple lovers. She just needed to persuade him to stay in Nottingham. That was all.

THIRTY-SEVEN

Frieda

'Who are we waiting for?' asked Barby.

'We are meeting a friend of Papa's – of mine – and together we will take a walk to a farm where you can feed a lamb. He is coming on the next train, *mein Liebling*.'

Frieda watched her daughters skipping in and out of the sunshine that streamed, golden, across the station platform. It was a glorious blue day, the sky scrubbed clean after the morning's mist. The fields stretched, green-and-blond, into knotted bands of trees. Even the shadowy copses were splashed with sunlight and vibrant with bright moss and yellow lichen. Frieda turned her gaze to the railway track, and began pacing the platform.

She hadn't seen Lorenzo for a few days. During that time she'd become restive and unsettled. It was beginning to dawn on her that something more powerful than she could have imagined was evolving between them. The feeling frightened her, the compelling and inevitable force of it. She likened it to the eerie lull before a storm, everything in flux, the air teeming with electricity, but all of it mute and invisible. Only *felt*. She knew she should stop seeing him, that she should beg him to go. And yet she felt powerless to do this. *It would be like asking the clouds not to rain and the wind not to blow*, she said to herself as she tried to make sense of it. Besides, a small voice, obdurate and hungry, kept hissing in her head. *If he was my lover, here in Nottingham, perhaps he would give me the physical love I crave . . . perhaps his attention would sustain me. Until . . . until . . .* But until what? Until Ernest changed? She wasn't even sure she could convince Lorenzo to stay in Nottingham. He seemed so determined to leave.

And all the time he was imploring, pleading with her to leave Ernest and join him in a new life. Tempting her with his beautiful words of adventure and the *wonder of living*. How could she resist the wild lure of his poetry, his ideals, his genius? Or his promise of a heaven on earth? She would watch him with the girls. And then she'd see.

The train's whistle split the peace, scattering her messy thoughts. Lorenzo bounded onto the platform, his head turning this way and that. As soon as she saw him, she felt the ache of desire. She'd found herself thinking constantly of his body in the last few days, imagining the carved blades of his shoulders, the stipple of freckles across his chest, the long reach of his spine. He was lean and lanky, without muscle or heft, but she liked that. Something about his thin frame, his long fingers, the stark whiteness of him, appealed to her. She longed to fold herself into his slender body, to feel the grip of his arms around her, to have the smooth heat of his skin fusing with hers. She felt a frisson of anticipation. One of the reasons Lorenzo had suggested this particular outing was because he wanted to show her a farm that he had keys to, and whose owners were often out. 'I know you're still Weekley's,' he'd said. 'But I've a violent desire for you and I can't hold back any more.'

They walked through the fields, Lorenzo darting to and fro, pointing out flowers in the tousled green verges – speedwell, milkwort, meadow saxifrage – and plucking the sunny heads of dandelions.

'Girls! We can float these like rafts, dandelion rafts,' he called, throwing the petalled heads to Elsa and Barby. 'And I've brought paper and matches so we can make a Spanish Armada and sail it down the stream. Follow me.' He began running up a pebble track, calling out 'I bet you don't know what the Armada is, do you?'

'Yes, we do,' said Else huffily. 'It's ships, of course!'

Frieda sauntered behind them, swinging her parasol and smiling. He had all the makings of a natural father, she decided, pleased and relieved. His enthusiasm and energy and curiosity – what child wouldn't fall in love with him? As I have, she thought happily. How marvellous it was to feel herself coming back to life, able to breathe again.

She leant on a narrow stone bridge and watched Lorenzo and the girls, crouching beside a shallow stream. Lorenzo had pulled a folded sheet of paper from the inside of his jacket pocket and was doubling it over, carefully pressing the creases between his fingers. He looked utterly absorbed, as if he'd left the whole world behind. Elsa and Barby were pushing and shoving and making faces at each other behind his head. When he finally dropped his paper boat into the water, the current whisked it away and spun it into the bank where it became entangled in a mass of slippery weed.

'Let's get it, let's rescue it!' Barby ran towards the bank, scrambling through brambles and reeds, her neatly booted feet slipping in and out of the marshy ground.

'Watch your dress,' called Lorenzo as he climbed back to the bridge.

'It is only a dress. It is not important,' Frieda laughed. 'Isn't Mr Lawrence clever, girls?'

The children didn't reply. They were too busy prodding at the soggy boat and beating at the weed with the long, knuckled twigs Lorenzo had cut from an oak tree.

'I am dying to see this cottage, where we can have a little tryst,' she whispered into Lorenzo's ear. 'Can we have a peek while they are rescuing the boat?' She breathed in the scent of him – coal-tar soap, ink, a faint spicy trace of hair oil – and felt a shudder of desire.

Lorenzo nodded and pointed ahead with a stick. 'It's through those trees, Moorgreen Cottage. You go and look and I'll stay with Elsa and Barby.'

She walked into the copse and squinted into the drowsy gloam. Beyond the trees she could just make out a house, low, with a red tiled roof and latticed windows. As she got closer she saw the house was surrounded by an orchard, and among the fruit trees were flowering currant bushes. Swallows dipped and dived in and out of its eaves. Thick ribbed logs had been stacked against its brick walls. Chickens pecked in the long grass and a ginger cat sat upon a water butt, sunning itself. Behind the house stretched slumberous fields where goats grazed on pink-flowering clover, and lambs tottered beside their bleating mothers.

'How beautiful, how simple and divine,' she said, beneath her breath. She had a sudden longing to live somewhere like this. Her own large detached house seemed anonymous and bland, a house made in Ernest's image. Of course, she'd chosen the red velvet curtains herself and it was *her* Bohemian glass and Persian rugs that gave it a little character. But the garden was all Ernest: the vegetables in orderly rows; the tightly pruned shrubs carefully chosen to shed as few leaves as possible; the square clipped lawn. She pictured herself here, with Lorenzo and the children . . . him writing beneath a pear tree, the children chasing chickens. And herself, big and bloated with love and happiness.

She scanned the windows, wondering which one hid the room where she and Lorenzo would finally make love. There was one window that seemed to lean out of the building, its drunken frame tilting into a vast pear tree so dense and lavish with blossom it was entirely white from the trunk up. Like a gauzy lace wedding veil. She imagined being there with Lorenzo, the windows flung wide, pear blossom drifting in, great tufted clouds of it. She laughed and twirled her parasol in delight.

When she got back to the stream, Lorenzo was squatting beside her daughters in the mud and lighting matches, one after another, and tossing them into a paper boat. A wave of tenderness washed over her. How could she ever have doubted his competency as a father?

She knelt and picked some little bunches of violets and stuck them jauntily behind her ears. She gathered dandelion heads and arranged them on the spokes of her parasol. Then she picked a shiny hart's tongue fern and jammed it into the top of her bun. Later, when Elsa asked her, with a grimace, why she had flowers and leaves stuck in her hair, she said 'It just came over me. Don't you like them?'

'You look silly,' said Elsa.

But Frieda didn't care. As they walked to the farm her feet seemed to spring from the ground, as if air had been pumped into her boots, so that the violets bounced and shook around her ears, and her nose swam in their violet scent.

174

THIRTY-EIGHT

Frieda

Two days later, she and Lorenzo returned to Moorgreen Cottage. Lorenzo unlocked the front door and led her up the creaking wooden stairs which were narrow and in darkness. His fingers shook in hers.

'Everyone's out,' he explained. 'We have at least an hour.'

In the little room that opened on to the pear tree, they made love for the first time. His body was as delicate, rangy and oyster-pale as she'd imagined. His skin burned, white-hot, beneath her fingers. But in their fever of nerves, it was without finesse and over too soon. He crawled away, apologising and ashamed. She pulled him back and locked her arms around him. As they lay there, she felt a sudden, unexpected compassion for him. 'There will be more times, good times,' she murmured, stroking his hair and kissing his neck.

Afterwards Lorenzo leaned out of the window and cut great swathes of pear blossom with his pocket knife. He laid the boughs over her naked body and shook the blossom on her hair, her face, her breasts.

'God, I love you,' he said. 'I'll always love you.'

She looked into his eyes and it seemed to her that they shone like liquid silver. She felt tears massing behind her lids. 'We must be happy today,' she declared as she brushed petals and tiny insects from her cheeks and brow.

'Aye, but where will it end? The world is so full of mean, brutal people.'

'Enough! I will teach you nude dancing.' She leapt up, throwing the boughs off the little wooden bed and shaking her head so that white pear blossom flew like a halo of confetti round her hair. 'And then we can make love again. And again. And again.'

He looked at her, askance. 'What the deuce is nude dancing?'

'Like this.' She began to spin around the little room with its leaning walls, its uneven floors, its sloping ceiling. Blossom tumbled from her, as she spun faster and faster. Her breasts bounced. Her unpinned hair streamed from her head in thick blonde ribbons. 'Dance with me!'

Lorenzo started to jig, his stiff white body moving in awkward angular jerks, his hands clumsily cupping his genitals. She watched him, all elbows and knees, then burst into peals of laughter.

'Perhaps I will teach you to make love instead.' She took his hand and pulled him back to the feather mattress. 'But this time I will be on top. I will show you how.'

From the corner of her eye she saw the pear tree and its clouds of pale blossom, beckoning through the little lopsided window. 'Actually, I have a better idea. If I bend and hang from the open window, and you are behind. I will show you.'

'B-but . . . if someone is outside and sees?'

'No one will come. Trust me. I want to feel you inside me as I breathe in the living pear blossom.' She ran her hands over his chest and felt him quiver beneath her touch. She had this vague feeling that, somehow, she was putting him together again. As if he were the dispersed pieces of a jigsaw puzzle and she must make him whole, complete.

'Oh Queen Bee, you are so perfectly splendid. So perfectly utterly splendid!' He buried his head in her breasts and did not move or speak for a long time.

Cowley
Victoria Crescent
Nottingham
17 April 1912

Dearest Elisabeth
I have so much to tell you about Mr Lawrence. We have fallen deeply in love. So deeply I do not know how to extricate myself.

He keeps insisting I tell Ernest the truth about us. He is very moral and honest, and will not tolerate deception or secrecy or hypocrisy. And he is quite desperate to marry me. He is going to Germany to stay with his cousins in two weeks' time. Which is exactly when you and I are going to Metz for Father's military anniversary. Is that not a coincidence? Mr Lawrence has suggested that he and I travel together and have a few days holiday. Perhaps you can meet him? I do not know what will happen between us, but I think the best result would be a blissful affair and then – who knows? Perhaps our passion will burn itself out. That would be most convenient. I have a little fantasy of him and me and the children living together. Is that very wrong? Very foolish? He has returned me to life, as Otto did. So I must enjoy it while I can. After all, I could be run over by a tram tomorrow!

But tell me, do you think I might be able to start a new life with him? He has promised me – yes, promised! – a new heaven on earth with my children. Doesn't it sound beautiful?

Nusch says Alfred Weber is living with you and Edgar, like a second husband. Is that true? I wish Ernest would be as accommodating as Edgar. Nusch also tells me you are sleeping with Alfred's brother, Max, at the same time. Do they both know? What a very full life you have!

Your loving sister
Frieda

Unter der Schanz 1
Heidelberg
25 April 1912

Meine Liebe Frieda
Please stop this nonsense. Please grow up!

If Mr Lawrence refuses to skulk and lie, then you must either end things with him or tell Ernest and hope he will let you continue the affair. I do not, for a minute, believe Ernest will comply with such a request. You do not mention whether Mr Lawrence is happy to share you, only that he wishes to marry you. You cannot be married to two men at once.

England is a backward country and remarkably intolerant, it seems to me. Here, in Munich, Fanny (the Countess zu Reventlow) has her son and a most colourful love life. But any thoughts of leaving Ernest for a coal miner's son are ludicrous, unthinkable. Do not bring him to Metz. Father would kill him. Let him find his teaching position in Germany and then find yourself something in Nottingham that will make use of your energy and talents. Why must you always behave like such a child?

Yes, Albert, Edgar and I are living in what the French call a ménage à trois, although my marriage with Edgar is over and we both know it. As for my relations with the eminent Weber brothers, I beg you to be discreet. I am helping them develop their philosophies of society and history, and I am assisting Max with his revolutionary books.

Otto has been locked up in the Mendrisio mental institution. Such a waste of talent. I do not know what will become of him now.

With sisterly affection
Elisabeth

THIRTY-NINE

Frieda

Frieda tapped softly on the study door. She'd spent all morning feverishly folding and unfolding, packing and unpacking. The velvet evening cape? Her silk dress with the lilac trim? The fringed paisley shawl? It was hopeless. She couldn't think clearly. She would speak to Ernest, unburden herself. And then perhaps she would be able to pack.

'Can I come in, Ernest? I need to talk to you.' The words that had been trapped in her throat for so long crept out, slipped reluctantly through the keyhole, settled in her husband's ear.

She heard the scraping of his chair and his voice: 'Yes, yes, if you must.'

He sat, stooped over his desk, surrounded by books. Their smell, papery and slightly mildewed, hung in the air. He looked up briefly as she entered, then turned back to his work. 'Nearly ready for publication. You should be proud of your old husband.' He spoke to his desk, picking up his pen and nodding at the same time.

Frieda stood in front of him, her hands pressed tightly together. She could taste bile in her mouth, bitter and sour like the pith of a lemon.

'I doubt we'll make our fortune with my book. It's a little too obscure for that.' He paused and scrutinised the nib of his pen.

'But it'll help secure a professorship at Cambridge. Could you buy me some more nibs when you return from Metz?'

Frieda gripped her hands a little harder. She could feel her nails cutting into the skin, her body shaking violently. Why didn't he notice? Why didn't he say something? She started shuffling backwards in the direction of the door, her lips moving anxiously over her teeth.

'And some ink too, please.' Ernest looked up, directing his gaze out of the window. The children were playing with a kite they'd made from an old sheet and a ball of wool. Frieda followed his gaze, out of the study with its oppressive collection of books, its wall of framed scholarships, commendations, distinctions – out to the garden where Monty was flinging the kite into the air and watching it land with a thud. Barby and Elsa looked on and then all three collected in a huddle, examining it, arguing about how to make it fly. Their voices drifted in through the open window, Monty saying the kite was too heavy and Elsa saying the wind was blowing in the wrong direction.

'They look like gypsies, my dear. Is there any reason none of them have brushed their hair this morning?' Ernest turned to Frieda with a look of mild disapproval.

'It is the wind.' Frieda briefly caught his eye then looked away, her heart fluttering wildly. Surely he could see how her body shook? How bloodless her face was?

He peered again at the nib of his pen as if examining it for a crack. 'Cotton is too heavy for a kite. Monty should know that. I really must get back to my work. I'm so close to finishing now. When it's done, we should throw a small party. What do you say, my snowflower?'

Frieda could feel herself edging nearer the door, her palms grinding together. She mustn't leave his study – not without telling him, not without saying something. She had promised Lorenzo. She had promised herself. She must speak before she went to Metz.

What had happened to all those words? All the words she'd practised through the night, over and over. *Ernest dear, I'm not who you think I am. We are living a lie – and I cannot lie any more. I love someone else now. I will take the children away but I promise you will see them whenever you want.*

She stood there, trembling, a feeling of nausea swilling inside her. She could hear Lorenzo's voice burrowing its way into her head, urging her to speak before it was too late.

'Ernest?' She stopped and took a long breath.

'Oh yes, you wanted to speak to me. Is it about Mrs Babbit again?' He held his pen up to the light, narrowed his eyes and inspected it again. 'I know she's a tyrant but she *can* cook, and that means more time for you to do whatever you want.'

Frieda felt the sweat in the pits of her arms and on the back of her neck. This was her moment, her cue. But her tongue had frozen and her mouth refused to move. The children's voices came to her in fragments, as though she were trapped in a dream. She heard Barby saying they should pray for God's help, then Monty saying there was too much wool and the kite would never fly. And their voices were so relentlessly cheerful, so decisive, she could not speak.

The clock on the mantelpiece struck the hour and Ernest looked conspicuously at it. 'I really must get on,' he repeated.

'I had a lover in Germany, Ernest.' The words shot from Frieda's mouth so quickly she wasn't sure if she'd said them or not. She waited for Ernest to respond, but he said nothing, just sat staring at the clock. Monty's voice came through the open window again, telling Elsa and Barby the kite should be launched from an upstairs window. And she heard all three of them running towards the house, shouting and laughing.

'I had a German lover,' she repeated, her voice a little louder, a little more emphatic. She had to finish before the children came into the house. Why didn't Ernest look at her? Why didn't he say something?

'I'm not who you think I am, Ernest.' Her voice trailed off. Ernest turned back to his nib and nodded in a distracted way. She could see him looking past his nib at his papers, and the expression on his face was so calm she assumed he hadn't heard her.

'I've had lovers,' she blurted. Ernest's face seemed to freeze for a second but he said nothing. She could hear the children racing up the stairs and then Mrs Babbit shouting at them to be quiet and make less noise.

'She certainly is a tyrant.' His voice sounded stiff at the edges but then he cleared his throat and looked pointedly at the clock again. 'Don't worry, dearest. I know Nottingham hasn't been easy for you. I know you're better suited to Cambridge, but if I can just finish my book, we'll be there very soon. I promise. Now I really must get on.' He turned over a sheet of paper on his desk, dipped his pen into the inkpot and wiped the nib carefully on his blotter.

Tears welled up in Frieda's eyes. She had failed. She had tried to tell him about Lorenzo, but she had failed. She turned and reeled towards the door, desperate to escape, to get air into her lungs, to get away.

But Mrs Babbit was standing outside looking harassed and red-in-the-face. And before Frieda could push past her, Mrs Babbit started complaining about the children, saying they'd been in her kitchen pestering her for food and their noise was giving her a headache.

Frieda blinked hard. She bit her bottom lip to keep the tears back. She didn't want to cry in front of Mrs Babbit. And then Mrs Babbit humphed and clucked and went back to the kitchen. And Frieda ran up the stairs to her bedroom, locked the door and threw herself onto the bed. She couldn't do it. She couldn't leave him. Why ever had she thought she could? She tried to make sense of Ernest's strange response to her confession. Was it that he didn't love her? Or was it that he loved her so much, he didn't care? Or was he so immersed in his work he hadn't heard her?

She sat up and leant against the bedhead. Nothing made any sense. She rubbed at her head, as if to rub away the questions churning in her mind. Outside she heard a wood pigeon cooing softly and then a blackbird joined in, its song clear and melodic. As she listened to the blackbird's plume of notes, elliptical and dazzling, the wood pigeon's gentle cooing seemed to fade away. And she knew the wood pigeon was dull and monotonous and would never sing like the blackbird.

She reached into her bedside cabinet, her fingers crawling blindly to the back of the drawer. She felt the trailing ribbon first. Then the paper, worn as thin and soft as silk. She pulled out Otto's letters and re-tied the purple ribbon with a little flourish. Then she placed the bundle of letters at the bottom of her travel bag.

She stood up and angled her ear to the window. The blackbird's song soared and scissored through the air, bright and glittering. Calling to her: Courage. Courage!

FORTY

Monty

He was playing with his new spinning top when she appeared at the back door. He spun the top again and again, watching the brightly painted metal as it threw splinters of light across the stone terrace, whirling and spinning until it made his eyes ache.

'Monty?'

He looked up, squinting into the sun. She was wearing her best hat, her gloved hands clasped in front of her.

'I'm off now, to Germany. And your sisters are going to Hampstead to stay with Granny Weekley and Grandfather Charles until I return.'

He nodded and turned back to his top which was lurching towards the flowerbed. He didn't want mud on his gleaming new top so he sprang after it, catching it just in time.

'Won't you come and give me a hug?'

Monty looked up at the sun, already blazing like a giant torch in the sky. It would be too hot for Papa today. If Papa spent all day in his study, he would be able to play with his spinning top all morning, perhaps all afternoon too.

'Will you bring me a present?' He pushed down hard on the spinning top sending it spiralling so fast all he could see was a blur of yellow and green and orange. His mother moved towards him, her arms outstretched. But as she crossed the terrace, his top began zig-zagging towards the grass. He chased after it but he was too late – his top was careening across the lawn, throwing up small divots of earth in its wake. Monty grabbed at it, but the top was reeling too fast and when he looked back he saw a thin furrow across the lawn and knew his father would be cross.

His mother was still pursuing him, so he hurriedly offered her his cheek then he set to work repairing the furrow, carefully pushing the clods back into the rift and wondering what she would bring him from Germany. Perhaps she'd bring him some tin soldiers. Or a drum. Yes, he'd like a new drum.

Overhead, the sun rose and flamed and motes of soot and dust danced in the light. And far away at the edges of the sky, small white clouds appeared like rabbit tails. Monty finished patching up the trough in the lawn and decided it was too hot outside. He'd go inside and draw pictures of the presents he wanted. Perhaps he could post them to her so she'd know exactly what to buy.

FORTY-ONE

Frieda

As the train pulled out of the station, Frieda stared into the black smoke drifting past the window. The carriage was airless and smelled of sweat and face powder but she felt paralysed, unable to stand up and open the window, unable to look at Barby and Elsa who were dividing up the bag of liquorice shoestrings she'd bought them at the station. Something seemed to be unpicking inside her, as though a needle was slowly gouging out a seam of tight stitches – stitches that had held her together for twelve long years.

Outside, the narrow Nottingham houses with their garden privies and ragged fences and sagging lines of laundry, row after row of them, bled into the black cloud that hovered eternally over the city. And as the train quickened, and the scraping of its wheels and pistons settled into a steady rhythm, the rows of houses became green banks of tangled nettles and brambles and buddleia, and beyond lay fields of grazing cows, oak forests, silver streams. She smiled, thinking of her rambles with Monty in the bluebell woods, the thick scent of their crushed heads as they trampled over them playing at Robin Hood and Maid Marian. Monty had always made her stand by a tree trunk pretending to be tied up so he could rescue her.

'I don't want to stay with Granny.' Barby's voice cut into Frieda's thoughts. 'Grandfather Charles always tells the same story about the fires of hell and he has black teeth.'

'How long will you be gone, Mutti?' Elsa coiled a liquorice shoestring neatly round her finger and sucked at it.

'Two weeks.' Frieda looked at her daughters' wide blue eyes and their raspberry cheeks, and felt a heave of love for them. They were so delicious in their pink-and-white striped dresses and their matching hats.

She turned back to the window. Ploughed fields rushed past. Birds banked and swooped in blurred flocks. The speed of it all seemed to mirror the thoughts racing through her head. She would go to her father's party, have a week with Lorenzo and then return to Ernest and discuss the future again. And this time she wouldn't flee in tears. And if – if – Lorenzo came back from Germany, he would be as a father to her children. Exactly as he promised. The train took her words, echoed them, spun them back at her. *Promised. Promised. Promised . . .*

She gave a small toss of her head, as if to rid herself of all the voices in her brain. She'd had enough of thinking about everyone else, wondering what was going on in Ernest's head, worrying about whether she should do this or that, or what *he* or *she* or *they* would think of her. She loved her children and they loved her. Everything would sort itself out.

'When I come back we will go to London Zoo and watch the parrots and the monkeys. Would you like some lemon sherbets?' Frieda opened her travel bag and started rummaging through it and as she did so her fingers stumbled over Otto's bundled letters. Her heart gave a small lurch. She wanted to take them out, to smell them and stroke them and read them – all over again. His letters reminded her of who she was, of what she could be. She closed her hand over them and it seemed to her they pulsed beneath her palm. Briefly she shut her eyes and let the pounding of the train wash over her. She would read Otto's letters again, draw strength from them. He had known she was destined for something bigger, for a life with purpose and passion. And in the drubbing of the train tracks, she heard his words again . . . *Woman of the future* . . . *Woman of the future* . . . *Woman of the future* . . .

She pulled out the letters and deftly slipped them into the fold of her skirt. Then she brought out a bag of lemon sherbets and told Elsa to share them equally with Barby. While the girls counted their sweets, Frieda unfolded the top letter and placed it inside her book, sliding the others underneath her bottom.

She held the book in front of her face, smiling as Otto's wild declarations of love unrolled from his ramshackle handwriting. She seemed to smell, dimly, the Café Stefanie on the notepaper. And in that second she was returned to Munich. She caught, again, its mood of excitement and hope. Words from the Countess zu Reventlow rushed into her head, pushing Otto aside. Love is not property or ownership or possession. Love should be free. The body should be free. Women should be free. *She* must be free.

FORTY-TWO

Barby

Barby saw them first, their black-hatted heads bobbing up and down as they scoured the crowds spilling from the train. Granny was short and stout with folds of flesh that toppled from her chin. Aunt Maude was tall and bony with thin pendulous earlobes.

'Your train is very late, Frieda,' barked Granny as she wiped at her face with a handkerchief. 'This heat is terrible! It's much too hot for May. Where is your porter? We have a cart waiting outside for the girls' trunks. Maude, take their hands!'

Aunt Maude's hands scuttled from her dress and grabbed at Barby and Elsa. 'Hello, girls,' she breathed. 'How was your journey?'

Barby felt Maude's stringy fingers lock around hers. 'We had liquorice shoestrings and lemon sherbets and peppermint drops and –'

'You spoil those children, Frieda.' Granny made a series of angry clicking sounds with her tongue. 'I've told you before and I'll tell you again – it's not good for them. Children shouldn't have sweets before dinner. You're lucky Ernest earns such a good wage. Now, Frieda, can we tempt you back to Well Walk for some tea?'

She said she didn't have time, that she had to take a taxicab to Charing Cross Station and really didn't want to miss her train. And as she said this, her hand fluttered at her collarbone and her eyes zig-zagged here and there. Barby thought she was looking for the porter but the porter was standing right behind them waiting for his instructions.

Barby squeezed Aunt Maude's hand again and when Maude dipped her head, she whispered, 'Mutti is taking us to the zoo when she gets back.' And she felt Aunt Maude's long earlobes quiver very slightly against her mouth.

'I don't want to be late either. Charles is waiting for us at home.' Granny's forehead shone and small pearls of sweat had gathered in the corners of her nose. 'The house is even hotter. Charles insists on keeping a fire going. And, as you know, I like the curtains closed. Now, when can we expect you back? Not that there's any rush, of course. Maude needs something to do, something to keep her busy and stop her moping around all day.'

'A couple of weeks.' Frieda smiled brightly and kissed Granny on her sheeny cheek. Then she kissed Aunt Maude and turned to Elsa. 'You will be very good, won't you, Elsa? And look after Barby and make sure she behaves herself and isn't any bother to your grandparents. I love you both, very much.' She hugged and kissed them while Granny tutted and rolled her small eyes.

'Goodness me! Is it really necessary to make such a fuss, Frieda? You show these children too much affection – they'll grow up to be soft. Now, off you go.'

'We'll be very busy. You can help me with the spring cleaning,' murmured Aunt Maude. 'And tonight we shall go to church.'

Barby twisted her head, hoping to wave at her mother. For a minute she was gone, lost in a rolling bank of heads and hats and smoke, all of it shifting and heaving under the heat. But then Barby saw her, standing on tiptoes, waving furiously and shouting 'I love you! I love you!'

PART SIX

London, Metz and Nottingham 1912

'He wanted her, he wanted to be
married to her, he wanted to have her
altogether, as his own forever.'

D.H. Lawrence, *The Rainbow*

FORTY-THREE

Frieda

The taxicab swung down Oxford Street and into Charing Cross Road. Frieda sat with her travel bag on her knee and her suitcase at her feet. Her stomach turned over and over in a frenzy of anticipation and nerves. What if he'd changed his mind? What if he'd decided that having an old mother-of-three as a lover was too constraining, too much responsibility? And if he turned up, he'd ask about Ernest. How would she explain herself?

She opened her bag. Otto's letters were on the top where she'd put them after the train journey. She decided to keep one inside her blouse, like a piece of secret jewellery. Just as she had five years ago, when she returned from Munich. She slipped the topmost letter between the mother-of-pearl buttons that ran down the front of her blouse and eased it inside her corset. Her skin felt damp and she hoped her perspiration wouldn't make the ink bleed. If only she didn't have to wear all these ridiculous clothes. If it wasn't for the disapproval of her mother, she'd have left her corset behind. On the bonfire for the gardener to burn. She could feel it chafing, squeezing at her ribs, scraping at her hipbones.

She stepped out of the taxicab into a snarl of traffic: omnibuses, horses, motor cars, bicycles, an ice-cream cart, a distillery wagon. Through the haze of heat hovering over the traffic, she spied Lorenzo scanning the crowds – his back held very straight, his hair neatly parted and combed. Her heart pitched and rolled. Why had she doubted him?

'Lorenzo!' She should have smoothed her hair and powdered her nose, wiped away the sweat and grime collecting in the seams of her skin, but it was too late now. He would have to take her as she was.

'I am here, Lorenzo!' She wanted to throw her arms around his neck, right there in front of the defecating horses swarming with flies, the stiff-lipped, bowler-hatted men queueing at the Bureau de Change, the uniformed nannies with their starched faces and their gleaming perambulators, the thin-ribbed cats watching from the shadows.

'Thank the Lord, you've come!' Lorenzo pressed her to him. 'I've been in such an insane whirl, like a stupid scattered fool.' He pulled back, with a long rattling cough. 'How was Weekley? What did he say?'

Frieda dabbed her forehead with a handkerchief. She had a sudden urge to be on the boat: cool salty air on her skin, gulls wheeling and diving overhead, the white cliffs of Dover shrinking and receding into the distance. 'Don't you have any luggage?'

'I have a notebook and a change of clothes.' He had a small case in his other hand, barely large enough for a few underclothes. 'Will Weekley give you a divorce? I want to be married as soon as possible. You know how important marriage is to me, don't you?'

Frieda swallowed. She felt very hot, as though she was burning up. Her throat felt dry and prickly.

'We must be married, my Queen Bee. He must give you a divorce. I don't care a damn what it all costs.'

'The children?' Her mouth seemed to be full of pins and needles, so that her words came out like a single, broken note.

'Did he say we can have them?' He gestured towards the platform. 'You can tell me everything on the train. And when we get to Germany we can be together, openly and honestly.'

Frieda nodded. She needed more time to compose her answers, to muster the right words, to prepare him for disappointment. The faces of her children kept swimming before her: Monty in the garden with his spinning top, Elsa and Barby in their striped dresses doggedly devouring lemon sherbets. A dull ache rose up from the pit of her stomach. How could they possibly live off Lorenzo's paltry income? No – it was ridiculous, impossible.

'We must call a porter,' she said, gesturing at her suitcase and travel bag.

'Nonsense.' Lorenzo picked up the luggage and strode towards the platform, his voice floating back to her, high and strident. 'I hate England and I loathe London. It's like some hoary massive underworld, an inferno where the traffic flows like the rivers of hell. Come on, Queen Bee!'

She followed him, feeling the heat in the air and the heat in the tiles beneath her feet and the heat pulsing through her veins and pushing up through her skin. 'Germany will be cooler, I hope,' she said, quickening her step as Lorenzo's long black legs disappeared through the crowd. Perhaps she would be able to think more clearly without this infernal heat to contend with.

And then he was beside her again, his blue eyes snapping and his pale face tinged a soft pink. 'In Germany we can be together properly – an absolute union, spiritual and mystical. We shall be as two stars, balancing each other. D'you understand?'

Frieda nodded, but inside she felt the shift of something dark and dubious. And all at once she knew why she hadn't been able to speak fully to Ernest, why she hadn't told him about Lorenzo. She didn't want to be married any more. She didn't want to swap one married life for another. She needed more time. She opened her lips, searching for the right words. But she was too late. Lorenzo had his mouth to her ear and was talking with such urgency she felt unable to interrupt.

'I've been so afraid, so worried. I thought Weekley might kill you. He's a man in whom the brute can leap up. It's in his eyes. Like an eel which bites out of the mud and hangs on with its teeth. But he's let you go – and now we're free!'

She winced and caught her lower lip between her teeth. Ernest had displayed none of the brute or the biting eel. The possibility came to her that Ernest had never loved her, that he would let her and the children go without a struggle, relieved at their departure. Then he could concentrate entirely on his book and his collection of first editions. She felt a prickle of pain. Had the last thirteen years been for nothing but show and convenience?

'In Germany I will love you to madness, all for the pure wild passion of it!' Lorenzo plunged back into the throng.

She felt a shiver ripple over her scalp and down her spine, so that every inch of her body seemed to tingle. His lanky body was thrusting forward through the crowd, but his words seemed to jump and hop in front of her face . . . *all for the pure wild passion of it* . . . Yes, that was how she wanted to live, not for show or convenience but for *pure wild passion*.

FORTY-FOUR

Barby

Barby wrinkled her nose, bracing herself for the familiar smell. She noticed it as soon as Granny pushed open the front door, more pungent than ever in the heat. She glanced at Elsa behind Maude's back and pinched her nose theatrically, hoping Elsa would laugh, hoping for a small moment of intimacy, something that might fill the tiny hollow she felt inside. But Elsa glared and shook her head, as if she had suddenly grown up and was someone else now.

'In you go, girls.' Aunt Maude stood to one side and Barby noticed her shoulders had risen and hunched forward, as though her aunt was carrying an enormous invisible box. And when she and Elsa stepped into the narrow dark hallway, Aunt Maude lingered outside, fumbling with her gloves and the shabby embroidered reticule she always wore on her wrist.

'Charles? Charles? They are here. Safely arrived from Nottingham even in this awful heat. The driver has left their trunk outside. Will you help Maude bring it in? I don't know what Frieda has packed in there. It feels like a library. Is that trunk full of books?' Granny wrenched the hatpin from her hat and stabbed accusatorily at the trunk with it.

'Papa wanted us to keep up our studies and our reading,' said Elsa quietly.

'Ernest is no suffragette so I've no idea why. Or has Frieda become a suffragette now? Maude is going to break her back getting that trunk up the stairs. Charles? Are you coming?'

Grandfather Charles lumbered into the hall. His beard, once threaded with grey, was now entirely white. His owlish eyes had sunk into his head. He was tall and thin and as he loomed over her, Barby felt the solemn piety of him. Being in his presence was like being in church, she thought.

'Kiss your grandfather, girls,' commanded Granny. 'Hurry up! Maude is waiting to bring in your trunk.'

Grandfather Charles slowly bent his head towards her and she heard his bones crack and felt the soft brush of his beard on her cheek. 'Thank you for letting us stay with you, Grandfather,' she said, remembering what Papa had told her to say.

'You're welcome, Barbara.' Grandfather Charles dipped his snowy beard towards Elsa.

'Thank you for having us in your lovely home, Grandfather, and we promise to be as helpful as we can.' Elsa's words came out tonelessly and in a single breath as though she'd been memorising them. Barby shot her a look of disgust. It wasn't a 'lovely home'. It was a horrible home that smelled of dead mouse and boiled-to-death cabbage and camphor all mixed together.

'You're a good girl, Elsa.' Grandfather Charles patted her stiffly on the head, his forehead glistening with sweat.

'Maude and your grandfather will take your trunk upstairs and then you can accompany your grandfather on his administrations.' Granny paused as if to let the significance of this sink in. 'It'll be good for you to see how the poor and homeless live.'

Barby knew what this meant: an afternoon with their grandfather as he gave coins to paupers or helped homeless families move their scant belongings into the workhouse. And when they returned home, Granny would quiz them on what they'd seen. 'That will stop you getting airs and graces,' she'd say, her nose tilted towards heaven. 'Your mother may have been born with a silver spoon in her mouth but you're just like the rest of God's flock and don't you forget it.'

FORTY-FIVE

Frieda

As the boat-train left London, a breeze coaxed out the hot stale air, replacing it with cool air smelling faintly of grass clippings and freshly turned earth. The passengers stopped fanning themselves with newspapers and pushed their handkerchiefs back into their pockets. Frieda waited for Lorenzo to begin his questions about Ernest again.

Instead he stared at her, scrutinising her as though he wanted to commit every line of her face, every freckle, every dimple, the contours of her lips and cheeks, all of it, to memory. Normally she loved it when he gazed at her, but now it unsettled her. There was something about it that made her think of a lion with a carcass, licking and tearing every shred of flesh and membrane and marrow before gnawing obdurately at the bones. She pulled back her lips, bared her teeth and feigned a lion's snarl. 'You remind me of a lion, Lorenzo,' she laughed. 'The way your eyes are so full of intensity.' She could feel the stares of other passengers, sneaking furtive looks at her ring finger, speculating about her German accent, wondering why a well-dressed older woman was behaving so intimately with a younger man who talked in dialect, wore cheap ill-fitting clothes, carried a cardboard suitcase with warped struts.

'And when did you see a lion's eyes?'

'At the zoo. When they are eating you know they are thinking about nothing else. Only eating. But I am always thinking about so many things.'

'So what are all these thoughts milling around in your beautiful baronial head?'

'Oh, they are mostly very dull. Curtains that need cleaning. Invitations and letters I must reply to. Socks that need darning. Things I have to buy: ink for Ernest, birthday presents, a new hairbrush for the girls.' She sighed and flapped her hands as if she wanted to scatter these dismal thoughts across the train compartment, pass them to the eavesdropping passengers crushed around them.

'Tell me how you feel.' His gaze – straight, guileless, blue – seemed to bore into her and she had, again, that strangely thrilling sensation of being split open, like a fig. She wondered if he could actually see inside her, if he already knew what had happened between her and Ernest the previous day. No, that was impossible. She pondered his question. If she ignored the turmoil of her marriage, how *did* she feel?

Like a diving bird, she thought. *I feel like a diving bird*. A memory floated towards her . . . the Baron dropping her head-first into a lake of brothy water. How old had she been? Seven? She remembered the rush of air against her skin, her scalp splitting the surface, her bones slicing through the silty water, the mingle of fear and exhilaration. And the leaping pulse of light that had swept across the lake as she surfaced, gasping for breath.

'I want to know everything about you. I want to know every thought that crosses your mind, every feeling that runs through your heart, every sensation that passes over your skin. I want to know it all.'

'Why?'

'Because I want to understand what you *are*. Not just what you feel or think. But what you truly *are*. Deep in your soul.'

Frieda moved her mouth to Lorenzo's ear and whispered, 'Then I will tell you. I will start with my thoughts because right now I am thinking about the woman opposite who is watching us and pretending to read her Bible. I am thinking that I have had enough of England where everything is so small and mean. I am wanting to run my hands all over your body which is too thin. So I am also thinking that I will make you eat good German food in Metz. *Blutwurst* and *Pfefferkuchen* and *Buttermilchsuppe*.'

'What else?'

She leaned into him, felt the buttery warmth of his breath, smelled the clean odour of shaving soap on his cheeks. 'I am hoping Monty had a good lunch today. And I am thinking how much I love you. And I am panicking about what to say to my parents. And I am hoping my hat will not be too crushed for my father's big party, and that Elisabeth can lend me a dress.'

'At least you don't need to think about Weekley any more. You can put him behind you – all the socks and curtains and ink.' Lorenzo took her hands and held them tightly in his. She stared at the burst of freckles on his knuckles and the blue veins that ran beneath his pale skin. But then Monty's solemn face appeared and seemed to hover before her. She saw the freckles that ran over *his* nose, *his* cheeks, and hoped Mrs Babbit would make him wear his hat every day.

'You did tell him, didn't you, Queen Bee?' He was gripping her hands now. She could feel the blunt edges of his nails scoring her palms.

'We have to separate at Metz station, you know that, yes?' Her eyes followed the web of veins up his hand and over his wrists and into the frayed sleeves of his shirt. Monty's face had floated away only to be replaced by Ernest's. She saw his open mouth, his pale gums and scrupulously brushed teeth, heard him say *Everything will be all right when I get you to Cambridge, but now I must get on*.

'What d'you mean? We agreed to stay as man and wife.'

'No, we didn't. Nothing is agreed!' She tore her hands away from his and folded them in her lap. She could feel the ground rushing beneath her, hear the railway sleepers rattling into the distance. Outside, fields and farms and forests zipped past, and the blue sky pushed down on the horizon, flattening it into a thin, bruised line.

'My parents know nothing. I cannot just arrive with a man they know nothing about! I am going for my father's anniversary. He has been fifty years with the German army, it will be a big party and I do not want to spoil it for him. You must understand that?'

'We agreed. We agreed to be true to ourselves.'

'Yes, yes, Lorenzo. We will have a few days alone together but let him have his party first. Please?' She unclasped her hands and reached out for his in a gesture of conciliation. 'You can easily find a room in a hotel.'

'Oh very well.' Lorenzo shook his head. 'And how did Weekley take the news?'

She paused and chewed her bottom lip. How could she tell Lorenzo that she'd tried to inform Ernest but failed? That she'd told him of her lovers and he'd said nothing, not a word?

'He will give you a divorce, won't he? I must have you as my wife!'

'Hush, we can talk later. Why don't you sleep now?' Frieda adjusted her skirts and settled herself into her seat as if she too were going to attempt some sleep. Lorenzo's merciless demands were beginning to vex her, revealing a pugnacious streak that sat uneasily alongside the traits she so loved and admired in him. No doubt he was anxious, she thought, letting her lids drop over her eyes.

'If you're not going to tell me about Weekley, tell me about your father, the Baron, and the Baroness, and all your aristocratic family.' His voice had acquired a deferential tone that surprised her.

She nodded, and as she did so she slipped two discreet fingers between the buttons on her bodice and stroked the softened edge of Otto's letter. 'I will tell you everything. I shall start with my sisters, but you must remember that I was the only one who could dive.'

FORTY-SIX

Monty

As soon as Monty pushed open the front door, he knew something wasn't right. There was no smell of gingerbread in the hall – or of scones or sponge cake or bread – no baking smells of any sort. And when he listened he couldn't hear the usual sounds of Mrs Babbit huffing and puffing, or the thump of her rolling pin or the vicious hiss of the steam iron. Perhaps she had nipped out. But hadn't Mutti said she was always to be here when he got home from school? He unslung his satchel from his shoulder and went into the kitchen. Mrs Babbit wasn't there. He tried the pantry and the scullery but she wasn't there either. And the kitchen was all neat and tidy, everything in its place. Perhaps Mrs Babbit had gone home early.

Monty took an apple from the bowl and bit into it. He wandered back into the hall and towards the staircase. Everything was still and quiet. For a second he wondered if he'd gone into the wrong house by mistake, pushed open the wrong front door, taken someone else's apple from someone else's kitchen, climbed someone else's staircase. There were no shoes or dolls or tea sets spread out in make-believe picnics, no creases in the rugs for him to trip on, none of the wildflowers his mother loved to have around. It was all too neat and tidy, too quiet. He took another bite of his apple and chewed it very thoroughly with his mouth open. And when he walked up the stairs he stamped his feet loudly, and the sounds of his own footsteps and the crunching noises in his mouth made the house feel less silent.

That was when he heard it. An odd stifled sound, like a gasp. He stopped on the stairs and took the apple from his mouth. The sound came again. Only this time it was followed by a long, heaving noise, as though someone was struggling for breath. Monty turned back down the stairs. Someone was in the house! Had someone broken in and attacked Mrs Babbit? Was she lying somewhere, bound and gagged? In a pool of blood perhaps? His heart raced. He'd never come across a dangerous person before. What if the thief was still in the house?

The sound came again, loud and choking and followed by a peculiar whistling noise. This time it was so loud Monty knew exactly where it had come from. Was Mrs Babbit lying in her own guts in Papa's study? Or was it Papa? Had the robber attacked Papa – and left him to die?

He flew down the stairs and flung open the door to his father's study. He was supposed to knock, but there was no time for that. He stopped abruptly. There were no pools of blood, no evil thieves wielding sabres, no Mrs Babbit bound and gagged. Just his father. With his head on his desk. And all his papers strewn around him like a ragged halo. Sobbing.

Monty stared. His father's shoulders heaved and shook. Rasping, choking, strangled sounds ripped from his mouth. His father's hands were on the desk, around his head, balled so tightly his knuckles looked like white marbles. Even though his fists were clenched, they were shaking as if his father had lost control of them, like a palsied old man.

'Papa?' His voice came out thin and high. He wanted to go to his father and put his hand on his father's clenched, shaking fists but something stopped him. So he just stood there, bewildered. 'Papa?'

'Leave me alone! Leave me alone! For God's sake, go away!'

Monty turned and left the room. His heart was beating fast against his ribs. Like the time a cricket ball had hit him in the eye and everything had spun black around him and he hadn't known what had happened or how it had happened or why it had happened.

He lay on his bed and stared at the ceiling. He tried to think of other things but the image of his crying father stalked him. Even as he recited the names of wildfowl, he heard his father's hideous, shuddering sobs. He wondered if there was a way of undoing what he'd seen and heard, some scientific means of tipping time back and putting these things from his mind. He felt a sudden twinge in his belly and slipped his hand into the waistband of his trousers. Beside his jutting hipbone, something protruded, ridged and hard. He laid his hand on it and felt it shift beneath his touch, as though it were alive. As though he had a burrowing creature inside him. He would pray. He would ask God to stop his father crying. He would ask God to stop this thing writhing inside him.

FORTY-SEVEN

Frieda

Frieda's first few days in Metz passed in a blur of activity. Her parents' apartment hummed with the comings and goings of friends and relatives staying for the Baron's party. She had to admire her mother's floral arrangements; she was needed to look over the dinner menus; the Baron's new hat had to be collected from the milliner; his military guests needed entertaining; she had to stitch buttons on cuffs and sew up drooping hems. Through all this, she yearned for Lorenzo, remembering over and over how they had lain together, drenched in pear blossom in that low-slung rickety cottage.

After two days in his hotel, he started sending her notes, asking when he could see her and when he could meet her family. She saw the bewildered impatience in his handwriting and was terrified he'd appear on the doorstep, or jump out in front of her as she escorted the Baron's guests round town.

And then a cable from Ernest arrived. She was in the drawing room, drinking tea with Nusch, when the Baroness marched in and dropped a telegram in her lap.

'What is the meaning of this?' The Baroness spoke in a voice tight with disapproval.

Frieda looked at the telegram. Two lines: *Are you with someone? Wire me yes or no.* It was as if there had been some peculiar delayed reaction to her aborted confession. As if he had heard her words then but only now understood their meaning. Somehow Ernest knew she was in Metz with another man.

She buried her face in her teacup. Her insides were shrivelling and cringing.

'Explain yourself,' barked the Baroness.

'I think perhaps my life with Ernest is over.' She could barely drag the words from her throat.

'Over?' Nusch crowed. 'Let me see that.' She plucked the telegram from Frieda's lap, her smile spreading as she read it. 'Oh you wicked girl. Is your lover here in Metz?'

Frieda sucked nervously at her bottom lip and nodded. She couldn't think what to say, or how to say it. Sentences formed in her mind and then broke off and disappeared. She cast around the room as if the right words might come to her from the swagged chintz curtains or the paintings of bloody battlefields in their twisted gilt frames.

'Don't be silly, Frieda.' The Baroness crossed her arms and pulled her eyes, nose, mouth into a disapproving knot. 'You cannot leave your husband. It is simply not done. You keep your lover, say nothing and carry on being a good wife. How stupid of you to have been found out.'

'But Mr Lawrence refuses!' Frieda wailed.

'Who's Mr Lawrence? Is he your lover? I was rather assuming you'd chosen an English duke.' Nusch's voice wavered with disappointment.

'He's very moral and very honest. He wants us to be completely open about our affair and not hide things from Ernest. And he's not a duke.'

'This Mr Lawrence is a fool then. You cannot possibly leave your husband for a fool.' The Baroness walked stiffly across the drawing room, her black silk skirts rustling, her corset creaking, her breath coming in small irritated bursts.

'Is he very rich?' Nusch leaned forward, eyeing her sister with a sly curiosity.

Frieda took a deep breath. 'He's poor. He's a writer . . . I love him.'

The room fell silent. Nusch gaped, cup and saucer poised mid-air. The Baroness stopped pacing and turned to the tea table. All the colour had drained from her face. Frieda ploughed on. 'His father's a miner. He has no money but he's a genius. He's going to be a celebrated writer but he needs me, he needs my help.'

'Ridiculous! You are the daughter of an officer and a gentleman. Even as a lover, he sounds quite inappropriate.'

'He sounds even worse than Ernest.' Nusch put her teacup back on the tray and made a show of examining each of her rings in turn. 'Sometimes I think you are quite mad, Frieda. It's really very remiss to get caught by your husband.'

'I didn't get caught. I told him. I wanted him to know who I really am.'

'That's even more stupid.' Nusch began polishing the diamonds and sapphires on her fingers with a small silk handkerchief. 'No husband should know who his wife *really* is.'

'We need to be practical. Ah, here comes Elisabeth, thank goodness.' The Baroness hurried to the door and whispered to Elisabeth as she stood unpinning her hat.

'I wrote and told you not to bring him to Metz. You write to me for advice. I give it to you. And you take no notice whatsoever. Whatever were you thinking?' Elisabeth swept across the room, tugging impatiently at the fingers of her gloves.

'You knew about the miner and didn't tell me?' Nusch said, aggrieved.

Elisabeth ignored her. 'There is only one thing we can do.'

'I knew Elisabeth would come up with a plan. It is so useful to have a good thinker in the family.' The Baroness began bustling round, rearranging the slices of marble cake on its wreathed plate and smoothing the backs of chairs. 'We must have everything sorted as quickly as possible. I cannot have your father being distressed at his own party. Fifty years in military service! That's what we should be thinking about, not your escapades, Frieda.'

'We mustn't mention anything to Father. Not yet. If Mr Lawrence was rich, I wouldn't hesitate to support you. But he has no money. He cannot maintain you or your children.' Elisabeth perched on the edge of the sofa, looking punctilious and efficient. 'You must stay as Ernest's wife. If he thinks you're an adulterer he may be able to claim custody of the children. Then you have nothing – no children, no reputation, no money. As good as dead.'

'But I don't love Ernest. He doesn't understand me and I'm so miserable in Nottingham. My whole life there is a lie.' A lump rose in Frieda's throat but she swallowed it down defiantly. 'Anyway they're *my* children. Of course I can keep them. I'm their mother.'

'Yes, yes.' Elisabeth flapped her hands as if everything Frieda had said was irrelevant. 'You need to deny everything to Ernest before your reputation is destroyed. And you need to tell this miner to stop any thoughts of informing Ernest. He's just trying to force your hand.'

Frieda felt her throat constricting, her palms prickling. She imagined returning home. To Ernest and to Nottingham. Mrs Kipping and Gladys Bradley turning away from her in the street. The simmering suppressed fury of Ernest and his family. Their silent pious superiority. The snide sneers, the slights, the snubs. Ernest would never forgive her. He would break her. They would live the empty deadly lives of her parents. Her children would grow up as she had, in a house made savage with hatred. 'He's promised me a heaven on earth with my children,' she whispered, too softly to be heard.

'If only you'd found a nice military man. They're terribly obliging when it comes to this sort of thing,' Nusch simpered.

'If your father hadn't squandered all our money, you could have had a dowry and married an officer and we wouldn't be having this conversation,' said the Baroness, with sudden bitterness.

'You have two choices.' Elisabeth turned briskly to Frieda. 'To keep this Lawrence man as your secret lover, as you did with Mr Dowson and Doctor Gross. Or to end it with the Lawrence man. But leaving Ernest is simply not an option.'

'Elisabeth is right. Now, I have things to organise so I want no more talk of this silly affair. And you must ask the man to leave Metz immediately.' The Baroness pushed her palms together and raised her eyes to the ceiling. 'Does he look like a miner?'

'I assume he's extraordinarily handsome? He must have some redeeming feature.' Nusch gave a kittenish arch of her neck and then glanced sideways at Frieda. 'Excellent in bed, is he?'

'He's handsome to me. And no, he's not covered in soot. He's a writer, not a chimney sweep.' An image of Lorenzo came to her, lodged itself in her mind's eye. The day he'd made paper boats for Elsa and Barby. Something about the bend of his neck, the curve of his spine, the soft enthusiasm of his voice. That was when she'd felt the first strike of pure absolute love. How strange that she could pin it down to such an exact moment. How wonderful that she had captured the moment so concisely in her mind. Imprisoned it almost, like a photograph.

'Are you listening, Frieda?' The Baroness moved purposefully towards the door and then stopped. 'It's decided then. You will wire Ernest to say you're going home very soon and you will ask this miner to leave. Is that understood?'

'If he was an aristocrat he would never make such demands. Only working men have that sort of . . . of . . .' Nusch gave a short toneless hum as she searched for the right word. 'Cheek! Yes, cheek.'

Frieda didn't reply. She put her hand into her pocket and let her fingers curl around Lorenzo's latest note, another scrap of paper pleading to see her. She felt an unexpected spill of irritation.

Even Lorenzo was being demanding and truculent. Why was he so impatient? Why was he so adamant that Ernest know the truth immediately? She felt as though everyone was pushing and pulling at her. All of them telling her what to do.

She chewed her lip. The love that should have freed her seemed to be turning upon her. As if the bones of her children, her family, Lorenzo – their spines and ribs and thighbones – were now the bars of a cage from which she couldn't escape. She had a sudden violent longing for freedom. She wanted to pull the pins from her hair and feel it swinging down her back. She wanted to rip off her clothes and kick off her shoes and race along the canal. For miles and miles. Away from Metz, away from Germany, away from everything and everyone.

FORTY-EIGHT

Frieda

'How do I reply? My sisters say I must deny everything and go home.' Frieda hugged her knees to her chest and tried to blot out the intrusions of Metz: the drums and trumpets of a marching band, endless volleys of rifle shot, the dagger beak of a woodpecker.

'Tell him the truth. Wire him straight back and say you're with me.'

'Must I? Already?' She lapsed into silence. During the days of her father's party, she'd felt as if she were trapped between two lives, amorphous and flaccid, like a fat mollusc between two rocks, its tentacles drifting this way and that with the current.

'We must be detached. And impersonal.' Lorenzo lay back on the grass, his hands clasped behind his head. 'It's not the time for emotions. I'll write a letter you can send to Weekley. We must be cold and logical.'

'Cold and logical? Must we?'

'I need certainty, Frieda. I can't live in this state of flux. I need certainty to write. We mustn't make this about emotions. It's about our future together.'

She lay back beside him, easing her shoulder blades into the warm ground. 'Have you told your family?'

213

'No. I shan't tell them 'til it's sure and certain. 'Til the divorce papers have come from Weekley.'

'But *my* family knows so why won't you tell *your* family?'

'They're not ready for a shock like this. But I'll fight for you. Tooth and claw if I have to.' He paused and turned his head towards her. 'I love you, Frieda. When I'm with you I feel as though I have sunlight turning inside me. I shan't give you up. Not for anyone or anything. My genius depends on you, Queen Bee.'

Frieda plucked at a dandelion and blew softly on its seed heads. They rose uncertainly into the pollen-thick air. *Sunlight turning inside me . . . sunlight turning inside me . . .* no one can live without sunlight. She closed her eyes and shook her head. There were too many thoughts – clamouring, clashing, colliding. 'I can't think about all this mess, Lorenzo. Give me some poetry, describe the hedgerow to me. You know how I love to hear your words.' She opened one eye and pointed a finger in the direction of a hawthorn hedge, dredged white with blossom. She could just see the shape of a man, dressed in navy blue. She frowned, wondered who he was, why he wasn't moving. Closed her eyes again. Felt the sun, like warmed silk, on her lids. *Sunlight turning inside me . . .*

'Rich, motionless blooms, very fragile and white, in tight little bunches . . . twinkling like manna . . . evanescent . . . gentle . . . a smoke of blossom.'

His words washed over her, meandering and melodious, each one holding the promise of something more. 'Don't stop, Lorenzo. Describe the sky for me.' She sighed contentedly and reached for him, running her fingers over the rasping wool of his jacket, tracing the poverty of his childhood in the coarseness of its thread.

'Pale and high and drifting . . . swallows swooping in rainbow arcs of ecstasy . . . heaven and earth teeming around us. The barren ugliness of Nottingham gone forever.'

She felt, again, the thrill of escape, and knew this was her chance to consign her old life – with its dreary routines, its unendurable loneliness – to the past. But then a pang of guilt struck at her. She would celebrate her escape once she had agreed the details with Ernest, once she had Monty, Elsa and Barby with her. In the *heaven on earth* Lorenzo had promised.

She opened one eye again. The man in blue was striding officiously towards them. She closed her eyes, ignored him. He was probably on his way to some military celebration. Metz was full of them this week. Prussian officers everywhere, the smell of saddle soap and gunpowder in every gust of wind.

Lorenzo unhooked his hands from behind his head and reached for her fingers. She felt his energy, his verve, streaking through her, racing from the tips of his fingers through her palms, up her arms, tumbling down to her heart, along the poles of her ribs, skimming her hips, thighs, calves. And then the flash of fire she always experienced when he touched her now.

'I don't want to think of life without you,' she murmured. 'But everything has been so sudden and I am worried about my children.'

'Don't think about them now, my Queen Bee. I'll make a home for us all.'

'What sort of home?' She smiled as an image came to her: pristine blue skies and meandering pewter streams, the sun stretching its buttery haze over them, insects riding on the warm air, whistling wandering ducks for Monty, swallowtail butterflies for Elsa, mistle thrushes for Barby.

'A home without possessions. One for living in, not stewing in. We mustn't be dominated by material things. There must be no tyranny in our lives, no possessions to constrain us.'

Frieda thought back to her Nottingham home. The house Ernest bought after his illness. She thought of all the nights he'd worked to buy her a gold carriage clock, all the student essays he'd marked so she could have red velvet curtains to draw across French windows. How proud he'd been of his French windows. How lovingly he'd gazed at his musty collection of first editions. Yes, they had lived in thrall to possessions, bullied and controlled by them. A feeling of lightness came over her, as if a vast weight had rolled from her.

'You see everything so clearly, Lorenzo. But I'd like a piano, and the children will need their toys, of course.'

His fingertips crept to the emerald ring she always wore on her middle finger. He began turning it, slowly, carefully. 'Don't think about them now, my Queen Bee. Is this the gem from your great-grandmother? I'll describe its mysterious depths for you, make you forget everything. I'll make you swoon with my poetry.'

'*Nein, nein, nein*! The man in blue was suddenly looming over them, shouting at them, the hard German vowels of his speech cutting through the air. '*Er ist Engländer! Er ist ein Spion.*' He jabbed repeatedly at the grey wall behind them. '*Festung! Festung!*'

Frieda leapt to her feet, pulling at Lorenzo's hand. 'Get up! Stand up! Apparently this is an important garrison and he thinks you're a spy.'

Startled, Lorenzo stumbled to his feet. 'I wouldn't know a fortress from a factory. What's he talking about?'

'*Kommt! Kommt!*' The man pulled a whistle from his pocket, his eyes bulging fanatically. He blew into the whistle and a second later, soldiers appeared from every direction, running towards them, pikes raised, rifles aloft.

'For God's sake what is this?' Lorenzo gripped Frieda's arm. 'What are they saying?'

'They think you're a spy,' she hissed. 'Just do what they say.'

'Tell them I'm not a bloody spy!'

'Just go with them.' She gave him a gentle push in the direction of the soldiers. 'I will get my father and he will have you released.' She turned to the soldiers and in her haughtiest voice said, '*Mein Vater ist der* Baron von Richthofen.'

'*Ja, ja,*' laughed the man, pointing at Lorenzo's ill-fitting jacket. '*Und ich bin ein Hund!*'

'We will come and get you very soon, my darling Lorenzo.' She turned to the man and gave a disdainful toss of her head, her nostrils flaring with contempt.

The soldiers formed a tight knot around Lorenzo and led him away. As he turned his blanched face back to her she felt a great gush of love. His sudden helplessness, his eloquence, the paucity of his past, the promise of his future, the unpredictability of him – so much that excited her, thrilled her, unnerved her. She waved and he returned it with a flutter of his fist, a gesture that seemed at once vulnerable *and* valiant.

She watched him walk up the hill, slightly stooped and circled by scarlet-and-gold soldiers. From nowhere words filled her head, swarming in her ears . . . *I am with you such a short time . . . I am going where you cannot follow now, though you will follow me later . . . would you lay down your life for me? Believe me, you will disown me three times before the cock crows . . . I am the man . . .*

She turned and ran. She would find her father. Then she would compose a letter to Ernest. In her own words and her own time she would tell him – kindly and calmly – that she was with Lorenzo. And when she felt sure, quite sure, she would post it.

•

Deutscher Hof Hotel
Metz
7 May 1912

Dear Professor Weekley
You will know by now the extent of the trouble. Don't curse my impudence in writing to you. In this hour we are only simple men, and Mrs Weekley will have told you everything but you do not suffer alone. It is really torture to me in this position. There are three of us, although I do not compare my sufferings with what

yours must be, and I am here as a distant friend, and you can imagine the thousand baffling lies it all entails.

Mrs Weekley hates it, but it has to be said. I love your wife and she loves me. I am not frivolous or impertinent. Mrs Weekley is afraid of being stunted and not allowed to grow, and so must live her own life. All women in their nature are like giantesses. They will break through everything and go on with their own lives.

The position is one of torture for us all. Do not think I am a student of your class – a young cripple. In this matter are we not simple men?

Mrs Weekley must live largely and abundantly. It is her nature. To me it means the future. I feel as if my effort of life was all for her. Cannot we all forgive something? It is not too much to ask. Certainly if there is any real wrong being done, I am doing it, but I think there is not.

D.H. Lawrence

FORTY-NINE

Frieda

'Frieda!' The Baron's voice ripped through the house. 'Come to my study. Now!'

For a second she was ten years old again, standing in his study beneath the great pairs of curving antlers, the mounted hunting rifles, the stuffed head of a bear with yellow glass eyes. Beneath her feet the grey, greasy pelt of a wolf. The odours of saddle wax, cigars, smouldering logs. Her childish hands brushing fitfully at her skirt. And he, with his gleaming brass buttons and scarlet epaulettes trimmed with gold thread.

'What the hell is going on? I have a letter from Ernest begging me to send you home. Says you've run off with a penniless lout.' The Baron's Adam's apple vibrated visibly in his throat. His red face shone. Spittle caught in the corner of his mouth. 'Not that shabby chap I just rescued from a police cell?'

Frieda hung her head. So Lorenzo had done what he had threatened. He had posted a letter to Ernest. Without her knowledge. Without her permission. Stupefied, she stared at the wolf hide beneath her feet.

'He says he will lose his job and the children will starve. Says they can no longer live in Nottingham. Says he will kill himself.' The Baron's fingers worked furiously at the ends of his moustache, twisting and curling them. 'Have you forgotten you're the daughter of a nobleman?'

'Ernest is being histrionic. But it is true. I don't think I can go back to him.' She didn't say that Lorenzo had promised to make her a new home – not the numb, blank home she'd shared with Ernest but a home of joy and rapture, a home for her body and soul. She didn't say that Lorenzo would never let her return.

'You will go back to Ernest. And that's the end of it. No daughter of mine behaves like a loose woman!' The Baron glared at her, his chest heaving inside his gold-braided jacket.

But you were a loose man and that was all right, thought Frieda sourly, recalling his mistresses, his illegitimate son, his gambling addiction that had lost them everything. She opened her mouth to remonstrate but the Baron raised his bloodless, withered hand. The sight of it, shaking, dangling like a small dead squid made her choke back her words. He seemed utterly pathetic now. No longer the idol she'd worshipped as a girl. Barely worthy of her respect, let alone her admiration. She'd once been so grateful when he praised her courage and bravery. But as he stood there, his shrivelled hand hanging limply in the air, she saw him for what he was: a failed soldier, a hypocrite, a fraud.

'Why can't you be more like your sisters? They've both made successes of their marriages.' He waved his withered hand at her. Small beads of spit seeped from his mouth and loitered on his chapped lips. 'Or have you become one of those insufferable English women who want the vote?'

A feeling of defiance flamed in her. She refused to hear another soliloquy on the superior qualities of her sisters and their houses. She refused to be coerced and circumscribed by her hypocrite-of-a-father. Nor would she be threatened by Ernest. 'Mr Lawrence wants to marry me. If I agree, the children will come with me. No one will starve or kill themselves.'

'I brought you up to be brave, like me! Now show a man's mettle and go home to your husband.' He turned irritably back to the rifle on his desk, pushed a cartridge into the barrel and cracked it shut.

Dazed, she turned to leave. She felt paralysed by the welter of emotion swirling around her. Some words of Otto's stumbled into her head: *You were born for freedom.* But there was no freedom in this tangled scrum of feelings. She had a sudden impulse to read Otto's letters again. She would take his letters and a few clothes and visit Elisabeth in Munich. She would revisit the Café Stefanie, perhaps some of the other Munich haunts that had once inspired her. She'd be able to think more clearly there.

'Look at me before you leave,' growled the Baron.

Frieda turned and immediately shrank back against the wall. Her father stood there, the barrel of his rifle pointing at her, his finger hovering over the trigger.

'Put it down,' she shouted.

He dropped the gun and turned away, his shoulders suddenly sagging, his chest deflating, as if all the air in him had been sucked away. She felt a stab of compassion for him. How old and hollow he seemed, like a defeated dog that slinks abjectly into the shadows. Behind the embellished pomp of his uniform he was nothing.

'Go back to Ernest. Do your duty, Fritzl.' His voice was subdued now, as if his earlier anger had exhausted him. 'Do it for me, Fritzl.'

'I am not Fritzl. I am Frieda.' She turned on her heel, letting his study door thud closed behind her.

FIFTY

Monty

Monty knew it was too early to be awake. The light edging through his curtains was thin and raw. He felt weary in his limbs, and his eyes seemed to dangle in pockets of darkness, as though they had shrunk in their sockets. He went to the window and pulled back the curtains. To his surprise, someone was in the garden. Someone was digging in his father's vegetable plot. Monty could just make out the grey outline of a man bent over a spade. He wondered if someone was stealing the potatoes, but then he realised the man was digging the bed being saved for tomatoes.

Monty rubbed his eyes and looked up at the sky. The moon still hung there, like a silver cutlass. Swallows were diving and swooping through the grey air. He had to go to school but he had no idea what time it was. If his father was gardening it must be later than he thought. He went to the hall to look at the grandfather clock. No one had wound it up and its hands were stuck at half past two. He couldn't hear the rattling of crockery and pans that signified Mrs Babbit's breakfast preparations. He couldn't hear anything except birdsong and the dull thwacking of spade on soil.

His father hadn't spoken to him for three days. He'd been working very hard and Mrs Babbit had been leaving trays of food outside the study door. But then Mrs Babbit had brought the trays back to the kitchen, with their plates of cold soup and congealed cutlets and bread that curled at the edges. Eventually he'd asked Mrs Babbit why his father wasn't hungry and Mrs Babbit had said perhaps he wasn't feeling quite himself.

On the first day Mrs Babbit had been very nice to him, making all his favourite things: apple pie and custard, lemonade, scones with gooseberry jam and cream. But on the second day, Mrs Babbit had been quite different and Monty wondered if she too wasn't feeling quite herself. So he'd spent the evening making a list for Mutti of all the things he'd like for his twelfth birthday, which was only four weeks away.

He went downstairs and out into the garden. There was his father, in his striped nightshirt and rubber boots.

'Papa?' He wondered if his father was digging for treasure or perhaps for something he'd lost. He wasn't working the soil properly, not like he normally did, from right to left. He was just turning over the same forkful of earth, again and again.

'Papa? I need to go to school.' Monty could feel a heaviness in his stomach. His father's mouth was moving, as though he was talking, remonstrating with himself. But Monty couldn't hear anything above the sound of the digging. He made his voice louder. 'Papa? Papa?'

His father stopped digging and looked up, a dazed look on his grey face. His eyes were red and beneath them were dark crescents. He stared at Monty as though he didn't recognise him. And then he said, 'What? What did you say?'

'I have to go to school and I don't know what time it is. No one has wound the clock.'

'School? Today?' His father leaned heavily on the spade as a small trickle of sweat slid down the side of his face.

'Yes. It's Friday. Shall I wait for Mrs Babbit?'

'Mrs Babbit isn't coming today.' His father lifted the spade and swung it hard into the earth. And as he did so, a choking noise burst from his throat.

'Oh.' Monty didn't want to look at his father any more. So he looked up at the sky. A thin vein of yellow pallor had appeared, pinched by ruts of the palest pink. A hideous thought was beginning to take shape in his recently woken brain. A great flock of starlings flew overhead, rising and plunging like a dark wave, and as they disappeared over the rooftop, Monty knew he had to ask.

'She's d-dead, isn't she?' Monty felt icy fingers curling round his insides, gripping and squeezing.

'No, she's not dead but she says she can't work for us any more.' Papa wrenched the spade from the earth, spraying soil all over his bare legs and into his rubber boots. His throat made another strangling, choking sound and Monty saw his eyes were shining with tears.

'Not Mrs Babbit . . . Mutti . . . She's d-dead, isn't she?' Monty's legs crumpled and he sank down onto the dewy grass. He felt as though he couldn't breathe, as though there was no air left.

'As good as dead, yes. She must be dead to us now.' With tears streaming down his face, his father plunged the spade back into the soil.

'I don't understand, Papa. What do you mean?'

'We must live as if she's dead, Monty.' He paused and gulped, then added, 'You are not to say anything. Not to your sisters. Not to anyone.'

'So she's still alive? She's not dead?' Monty felt a surge of joy and relief. He jumped up from the grass, as light as a bubble now. He wanted to punch the air and shout and dance. His mother was alive!

'She has gone to be with Mr Lawrence. She has left us.' Papa gave a great sob and threw the spade to the ground.

'What?' Monty gaped at his father. 'No, Papa. Mutti is at Grossvater's party in Metz. Have you forgotten?'

'She wants to marry Mr Lawrence.' His words came out in a mangled sound, and sank like stones to the bottom of Monty's stomach. He lunged for the spade but then fell onto the black earth, sobbing and keening like a gull.

'We must get her back! She's married to you. She can't marry Hungry Fox . . . She can't!' Monty reached for his father's hand and began pulling him. He was angry now. Filled with rage and fury at his father's weakness. Why was his father digging the garden in his nightshirt when he should be rescuing Mutti from the clutches of Hungry Fox?

He pulled at his father's hand, tugging him up from the ground and towards the house. There was no time to lose! He would take his bow and arrow and shoot Horrid Hungry Fox. Why had his father not thought of that? They could take Mrs Babbit's sharpest bread knife. Or perhaps they could buy a shotgun.

'Come on, Papa! We can take the train.' Monty's fury at his father's feebleness was swelling inside him. Why couldn't his father be more manly? Like Robin Hood or King Arthur. Why was he snivelling like a baby?

'No!' he sobbed, shaking off Monty's hand. 'You do not understand!'

'She's not his! She's ours!' Monty's voice erupted, louder and clearer than he'd expected.

His father stopped sobbing. Threads of snot and spittle ran down his chin. Sweat and tears glistened in the creases of his face. He leant against the wall of the house with his eyes closed, as if he was trying to compose himself before going inside.

'I will not allow her back, Monty. She has disgraced us. She has dishonoured her marriage vows. She has destroyed my family, my career, our reputation. Everything!' He began pulling off his rubber boots with his thin, trembling fingers.

'What will happen to us?'

'We'll sell the house and you'll move to London and live with your grandparents and go to a new school, where no one knows us.'

'I don't want to live in London. I have friends now.' Monty's eyes welled with tears.

'You will do as I say!' His father raised his clenched fist and hit it hard against the brick wall. Monty recoiled. He didn't want to be with his crazy father any more. He wanted to go to school and sit in his Latin lesson and listen to the master droning on and on.

His father slumped against the wall and examined his hand. It was grazed all along the side and blood was beginning to leak from the broken skin. And then he started crying again and his chest heaved so that horrible, garrotting sounds came from his throat, slicing open the morning air and scaring all the birds from the sky.

'Shall I go to school now, Papa?' Monty whispered. His father was frightening him. And he needed to get to school so he could think clearly and calmly about how to rescue his mother, how to bring her back. And only then would he think about Horrible Hungry Fox. And the punishment he deserved.

•

Cowley
Victoria Crescent
Nottingham
12 May 1912

Dearest Maude, my dearest sister
Brace yourself for terrible news. Frieda has left me and gone to Germany with another man. I am too cowardly to tell the old folks. I beg you to tell them. I know this will be ten thousand times worse than death for them.

I am in a terrible state. I cannot see Frieda's handwriting without trembling like an old cripple. To see her again would be my death. I would kill myself and the children too. It is terrible when one so longs for death and still must live for others. I will not kill myself but I wish she would leave me in peace.

Today I hoped that the clatter in my head had half disappeared, but then I received a letter from her suggesting a compromise and it robbed me of my little reason – again.

For her and the children's sake I must keep my local position although the place is more hateful to me than hell. Today I had to lecture for four hours and then take part in a long meeting. I had desperately to stretch every nerve in order not to cry out hysterically.

And then I am as weak as a child and can only lie there and think and think – if only I could stop thinking for a quarter of an hour!

I will fight with my despair and find the best way out.

Please break it to the old folks as gently as you can. And please say nothing to the girls. They are not to know. I will write again with my instructions for Elsa and Barby.

In great anguish
Ernest

PS I beg you to make the children God-fearing Christians. All traces of HER must be stamped out. There is to be absolutely no bohemianism.

PPS The children are never to speak another word of German. Ever.

FIFTY-ONE

Barby

Barby and Elsa stood on the landing, listening to their grandmother's voice rising up the stairs. 'What do you mean, Maude? . . . No! . . . I will not believe it!'

Aunt Maude's voice followed, timorous and hesitant. 'Gone . . . I am to take them to church . . . he has instructed me . . . remove all bohemianism . . . all traces of her . . .'

'How do we tell Charles? I cannot do it . . . We are not to tell them? What are we to say?' Granny's voice trembled, then swelled, angry and outraged. 'Vile woman! Disgraceful . . . little more than a . . .'

'Why is Granny being so mean to Aunt Maude? She's being even more mean than normal!' Barby whispered indignantly.

Granny bellowed up the stairs. 'Elsa! Barby! Get your hats and gloves. We are taking you to church this instant.'

'Church? It's not Sunday. It's the morning. Why must we go to church?' Barby asked.

Granny carried on shouting. 'Brush your hair! Blessed are those who practise righteousness at all times.'

While Elsa went to their room for their hats, Barby began edging down the stairs, keeping her back against the wall and her ears strained. She peered over the banisters. She could see Granny straightening her lace cap and Aunt Maude untying the strings of her apron. Granny started making angry clicking sounds with her tongue and they began talking again, in hushed tones. 'Depraved German stock . . . they are half-depraved stock . . . The work of Satan himself . . . She will see the righteous anger of God!'

Granny squinted up into the gloom of the stairwell. 'Hurry up, girls! You must put on the whole armour of God that you may be able to stand against the wiles of the devil.'

'Why must we go to church now?' Barby protested.

'Hush,' soothed Aunt Maude. 'We'll attend morning service at eleven o'clock and then you'll enrol for the choir and for Sunday school.'

As soon as the church came in sight, Granny marched towards its open doors with her back very straight and her black skirts billowing. 'We must pray these children can resist temptation, that all bad blood is exorcised.'

After the service Aunt Maude and Granny made Barby and Elsa sit in the back pew while they huddled with the vicar. Barby leaned in to Elsa and asked 'Have we done something wrong?'

Elsa carried on staring at her prayer book, running her index finger carefully over the embossed letters on its title, tracing them as if she had lost her eyesight and was trying to read them with her hands. 'I think so.'

'Come along, girls.' Aunt Maude scuttled up the aisle, her straw boater askew on her head. 'The vicar says you can attend both sessions of Sunday school and he's letting you join the junior choir without an audition. You will find the singing of psalms most comforting, most reassuring.'

'And properly pious,' snapped Granny. 'Let us not forget the Lord's great mercy.'

'But we're going home soon. Why must we join the choir?' Barby asked, perplexed.

'Because the Lord loves everyone, even when *she* does not. You and Elsa shall attend Evensong this evening.'

'Is it because we're full of sin?' asked Barby in a small voice.

'Yes, you are. And your dear, good father has asked Aunt Maude to eradicate it. And eradicate it we will!' Granny tramped out of the church, her footsteps hard and sharp on the stone floor and her head held very high. Aunt Maude loped along behind.

Barby reached out for Elsa's hand. 'I don't understand. Does Papa think we are full of sin?'

But Elsa didn't answer. And all Barby could hear was the sound of the weather vane swinging violently in the wind and Granny's grating chant. 'Let no man pull asunder what God has joined together.'

•

Cowley
Victoria Crescent
Nottingham
25 May 1912

Frieda
I am prepared, under extreme duress and as a gentleman of indisputable probity, to restore you to the position of Mrs Weekley. For the sake of our family and our children. I would, of course, require your fidelity and loyalty. I would expect you to honour the marriage vows we swore at our wedding and in sight of God.

If this is not acceptable, I would consider offering you a London flat where you could live with the children. I would expect your behaviour to be of the highest moral standards. I do not wish our children to be tainted by scandal or exposed to immorality. Thus it goes without saying that all association with other men must end, immediately.

I cannot compromise any more than this.

Ernest

230

FIFTY-TWO

Frieda

'You're being ridiculous, Frieda. Of course you must go back to Ernest and the children.' Elisabeth perched neatly on the edge of her smoke-coloured sofa, watching her sister over the rim of her teacup.

'But Lorenzo needs me. He cannot bear to be away from me, even for a few hours.' Frieda sucked hard on her cigarette and stood up. She wished she could find the words to explain the *rightness* of Lorenzo, of their future together, of how she felt this rightness with a brilliant intensity, as if she held a finely cut diamond in her hand.

'You barely know him. You ran off with him after a mere eight weeks. How can he have become so dependent on you in eight weeks? It's quite absurd.'

'I didn't run off with him.' Frieda blew out a tail of smoke and walked to the window. She ran her hand down the butter-yellow curtains. How sumptuously silky they were. How heavily they fell. How right the yellow looked against the grey velvet upholstery. In front of the window was a vase of yellow Gloire de Dijon roses. How fragrant they were – and how artfully positioned in a ripe shaft of afternoon light. Everything in Elisabeth's apartment was so precisely placed and well appointed, so perfectly paired, so ordered.

231

It should have soothed her, but it didn't. Instead it threw into sharp relief her own turmoil.

'He sent that letter to Ernest behind your back, without your agreement. He forced your hand. He tricked you.' Elisabeth moved to the vase of roses, adjusted a bloom, then stepped back to inspect it. 'But more importantly, he has no money. You know Papa calls him an ill-bred, common, penniless lout, don't you?'

Frieda's blood simmered. Her father didn't have an ounce of Lorenzo's heart or honesty. Not an ounce of his talent or brilliance. She inhaled savagely, letting her lungs fill with calming tobacco smoke. 'Lorenzo is a genius. Even Ernest spotted that.'

'But how will he keep you?' Elisabeth deftly plucked a monogrammed handkerchief from Frieda's pocket. 'Why did you get handkerchiefs embroidered with our coat of arms if you want to live like a pauper?'

'It was a whim.' Frieda lapsed into silence. She couldn't explain – even to herself – the precipitous feeling she had, alone and back in Schwabing, that this tiny interval in her life was a chance to be herself again. Here she was neither Mrs Weekley nor a future Mrs Lawrence. Of course the handkerchiefs made no difference to her mangled state of mind. But she gleaned a certain inarticulate comfort whenever her fingers fell upon the embroidered crest.

She stared out at the street. Two boys were chasing a dog down the road and as she watched them, she felt a tear bubble up in her eye. What was Monty doing? Was he sorting his stamps or playing with his spinning top in the garden? She pictured him squatting on the grass, mud on his knees, the spinning top pirouetting round the lawn. Or perhaps Ernest had taken him to Sherwood Forest to practise his archery. And the elderflower would be out and the chestnut trees would be in bloom and the briar buds would be unfurling. And Ernest would be showing Monty how to split an arrow.

'You know I dislike Ernest, but you must go back to him.' Elisabeth placed Frieda's newly monogrammed hanky conspicuously next to the vase of roses and went back to the couch. 'Have your affairs. Come to Munich for your fun. But with no reputation and no money you are nothing and no one.'

Frieda turned back from the window, blinking away the image of Monty. 'But I can be someone with Lorenzo. He wants me to help him with his writing. He has so many plans – to see the world, to change the world – and I'll be part of that. I don't want fun!' She felt the old swill of envy inside her: Elisabeth was allowed a full life but she, Frieda, must return to a dry dutiful marriage with a husband who would never forgive her transgressions.

'Well, just take the London flat Ernest's offered you. At least then you'll see the children.' Elisabeth gave an impatient sigh, as if Frieda's prevarications were beginning to irritate her.

'I cannot. Ernest changes his mind every few hours so I hardly know if the offer is genuine. Anyway it comes with a condition that is unacceptable to me.'

Elisabeth raised her eyebrows. 'And what is that?'

'He demands that I give up Lorenzo. And I cannot.' Frieda looked down, rubbed a weary hand over her face. 'I have been lonely for so long. Only reading made me feel less alone. And now, with Lorenzo, I am offered a future without loneliness.'

'Mr Lawrence must step aside now. This is nothing to do with your loneliness.'

'He refuses. He says why should *he* be sacrificed? He says the children will suffer and feel forced to live for me not for themselves, to pay me back for my sacrifice . . . they will be my emotional slaves. He says their lives will be ruined if I give him up for them.'

'What utter nonsense!'

'He is making me calico bloomers. Sewing them himself. And he trimmed my hat the other day. We will survive without money.'

233

'Calico bloomers!' snorted Elisabeth. 'What is wrong with the French lace Mama brought us up with?'

'Lorenzo prefers plain cotton. He's rather good at sewing.' Her voice softened with tenderness. How could she explain to her rational and sensible sister the thousand different loves she felt for Lorenzo? Elisabeth would never understand. Elisabeth who had chosen a marriage of lucrative convenience and now kept herself fortified with her salons and her lovers. Elisabeth who had never felt alone.

'Be sensible, Frieda. Go back to Ernest.'

Frieda turned back to the street. The boys had gone and the street was deserted except for a few pigeons pecking half-heartedly at a crust. Perhaps she should go back to Ernest. The ache of being separated from her children was becoming unbearable. An image of Nottingham's stagnant canals, bile-green, with their floating tongues of liquid sewage, rose before her eyes. And she thought of Ernest pedantically picking over the meaning of obscure, obsolete words. And that endless, awful emptiness.

'Be Ernest's wife in public.' Elisabeth put her teacup on its saucer with a conclusive clink. 'And keep Mr Lawrence as a secret lover. Ernest need never know.'

'Lorenzo wouldn't agree to it. He refuses to do anything involving subterfuge.' Frieda stabbed out her cigarette and took a fresh one from the box on the table. A thin streak of resentment wound through her half-formed thoughts. She was tired of being lectured by Elisabeth, tired of the way everyone assumed that Elisabeth knew best. 'I don't know what to do. I need somewhere to stay while we sort this out. Somewhere with peace and quiet.'

'Men are so selfish.' Elisabeth bent down and straightened the edge of a Persian rug. 'You can have Alfred's place in Icking. It's empty at the moment. It's so beautiful there, by the river, with the Alps in the background. I'll give you some money.'

Frieda's nostrils flared. She didn't want to take Elisabeth's money or Elisabeth's lover's flat. But what choice did she have? She thought

234

of the mountains streaked with blue snow and the opal light flashing over the River Isar. And Lorenzo. She would have time to rest and think. Then she would make her decision: Make a home for her children with Lorenzo or return to Ernest?

•

The Beuerberg Inn
Beuerberg
26 May 1912

Dearest Elisabeth
Lorenzo and I are staying for a few days in an old inn in the charming village of Beuerberg, on our way to Alfred Weber's flat that you so generously offered. All the houses here have white gables and black balconies and there are bluebells everywhere. I was beginning to feel my sanity returning.

But something has happened. Or rather something has not happened. My menses has not come. I think I am to have a child with Lorenzo. It makes me nervous. How I can return to Ernest and the children with a little Lawrence baby? And if I stay with Lorenzo and we have no money, how will we raise a child? I have told Lorenzo, of course, and he is very excited. He tells me now that he has a 'definite desire' to have children with me. I did not think he would respond like that.

I must admit that a part of me likes the idea of another child. One that could grow up with Monty, Elsa and Barby. I would have four children, like you!

Lorenzo is still pressing me to marry him. I do not wish to be married. I do not wish to be a possession. I do not believe in fidelity or monogamy. But then he plays his trump card: reminding me that Ernest will never let the children come to us if I am not married. Of course, if there is a little Lawrence baby I will be compelled to marry him. I suppose.

I cannot think clearly any more. Why must the lives of we women be so hard, so complicated?

From your loving sister
Frieda

FIFTY-THREE

Monty

Nんone of the clocks in the house ticked any more. When Monty returned from school each day, the booming silence echoed through the empty rooms. He made himself toast in the kitchen, scraping out the dregs of the jam jars. And then he went to his room and rearranged his stamps or drew pictures of wildfowl.

Some evenings his father was at home, either digging frenziedly in the garden or locked in his study, talking and arguing with himself and hurling books at the wall. His eyes were permanently glazed with tears these days, and he and Monty sidled past each other, like strangers.

Sometimes Monty stole into his mother's room and lay on her bed, breathing in the tobacco smell of her pillows and spreading himself out on the lace counterpane. Or he'd sit at her dressing table and run her hairbrush through his hair and arrange her hatpins and hairpins in orderly lines and straighten up her perfume bottles and check the lids of her powder and rouge pots were tightly screwed on. And then he'd plump up her pillows and smooth down the coverlet and check her spittoon and chamber pot were neatly placed beside her bed. All ready for her return.

Once he found Papa in her room, lying on her bed, face down. He was wearing nothing but his underclothes. Monty gawped, shocked at how thin his father was. He looked gnawed to the bone, as if he'd been extinguished, his insides drained right out of him so that he was hollow and empty. That was when Monty realised his father was no longer his father. He looked the same, but he was a different man. Quite a different man.

There were constant reminders of *her* everywhere. Her hats and gloves sat on the shelf in the hall. Her buttonhook hung from its nail by the front door. Her books and sheet music were piled up in the drawing room. Her embroidery box sat open in the dining room, with its spools of coloured thread and her china thimble with the von Richthofen crest on it. She seemed to haunt the house, her presence in every room, in every cranny. The smell of her still lingering, strands of her blonde hair snaking over the sofa, the piano stool, the rim of the bathtub.

One afternoon, as Monty was eating toast in the kitchen, he heard his father calling. He finished his mouthful and went through to the hall. His father stood leaning limply against the study doorframe.

'Monty, have you been telling the boys at school that your mother is coming to collect you, to take you to London?' His father's eyes sharpened to needle-points.

Monty flushed and looked down at his scuffed, unpolished shoes.

'Has there been talk at school? Amongst the boys?'

Monty nodded and kept his eyes on his shoes. The laces were fraying and his fallen trouser hems flapped untidily round his ankles.

'What have they been saying?'

'That Mutti has run away to Europe.' Monty felt the whatever-it-was that lived inside him begin its meanderings through his gut.

'What else?'

'That she's gone with a coal miner,' he mumbled.

'What else?'

'That he's young enough to be her son.'

'Anything else?'

238

'That there's a baby coming,' Monty muttered. He heard his father swallow loudly.

'And what do you say to them?'

'I tell them they're liars.' Monty lapsed into silence. His face felt hot and he couldn't meet his father's eye.

'And then what do you say?'

'I tell them she's coming to collect me . . . to take me to London to live with her . . . and you . . . and Barby and Elsa.'

'You know that's a lie, Monty.' His father's voice was like eggshell. 'I think it might be better if you stop going to school. Finish the term early.'

'Not go to school?' Monty repeated. A shiver ran through him. Although some of the boys had been saying mean things about his mother, school was all he had now. He thought of his history lessons, his Latin lessons, the masters with their familiar faces, his wooden desk with its smoothly whittled ducts where he laid out his pencils each morning.

'The gossip isn't good for us. There's every chance I could lose my job.' His father leaned more heavily into the doorjamb, as if his emaciated legs could no longer bear the weight of him.

'But you can go to Cambridge now.' Monty brightened. 'They don't know about Mutti in Cambridge.'

'That dream is dead. No one will have me – not with the whiff of scandal that hangs over us. I only wanted it for your mother. Not for me.' His face twitched and his mouth wobbled, as if he was about to cry. But then he closed his eyes and gave his head a sharp shake.

'What is to happen to us, Papa?'

'I've found a new school for you, Monty. St Paul's in West London. I'll buy a house near the school and you and your sisters will live there with your grandparents and Aunt Maude. I will join you at weekends.'

239

'So you'll stay here during the week?' Monty's eyes flashed hopefully round the hall. He would come and stay at weekends, see his friends, wait for her.

'No. I'm selling the house. I'll rent a room near the University.'

'You can't! What about Mutti's things? She'll be back for them!'

'She is not coming back,' his father shouted. And he raised his palm and slapped it hard against the doorpost. 'Why am I cursed with an idiot for a son!'

The lump in Monty's throat seemed to swell and grow and rise up towards the roof of his mouth. He tried to swallow it, but instead an odd popping noise like an exploding chestnut escaped from his larynx.

'I'm sorry.' His father reached out and clutched at Monty's arm. 'Sometimes I think I'm going quite insane.'

'Papa?'

'I need to get back to my work. The proofs are here from my publisher.' He gave a long stuttering sigh that made his chest heave.

'It's my birthday soon, Papa.' Monty felt bad mentioning his birthday but he needed to say it. Because if he didn't, it might disappear. Like everything else in his life. And he might stay eleven forever.

'Is it?' His father frowned and dug his fingers tighter into Monty's arms. 'How old will you be?'

'Twelve.'

'Twelve?'

'Yes. On June fifteenth.' He wished his father would stop squeezing his arm. It was starting to hurt.

'And what would you like for your birthday?'

'A new bow and some more arrows please.' There was silence. Monty heard the breath hissing in and out of his father's nose. He shuffled awkwardly from one foot to the other. There was a question he wanted to ask, had to ask. It crouched there – on the tip of his tongue. And then out it spilled. 'Will Mutti come back for my birthday?' She had never missed his birthday. Never.

His father dropped Monty's arm and his white face filled with blood. 'She is not coming back. Never! Not for your birthday. Not for Christmas. Not for anything!'

Monty flinched. 'Not even for Christmas?'

'Not for anything. And you are not to write to her. I forbid it!'

Monty tried to swallow the lump in his throat but this time he couldn't. It rose up and burst from him in a startled sob. He gulped it back down but tears were ramming at the backs of his eyes and there was no air in his lungs. If he didn't cry, he would choke. He turned and fled up the stairs. When he got to the landing, he stopped and shouted down to his father, 'But how am I to remember her? How am I to remember her?'

•

The Beuerberg Inn
Beuerberg
30 May 1912

Dear Elisabeth
Menses arrived! No little Lawrence baby.

I feel relieved and sad at the same time. Lorenzo was disappointed but is now resigned and is striding, lithe and lanky, round our horrid bare room (we sleep beneath a gruesome oil painting of Christ bleeding on a crucifix) telling me that he will change the world for the next thousand years. He really believes it!

We leave for Alfred's flat tomorrow.

Your loving sister
Frieda

FIFTY-FOUR

Frieda

Alfred Weber's flat was on the fourth floor and looked over distant blue-black mountains with snow-covered peaks that turned a rich golden in the afternoon light. Frieda and Lorenzo breakfasted each morning at the local *gasthaus*, beneath a horse chestnut tree that shed its pink petals in their coffee, on their slices of black bread, into the butter dish. After breakfast they walked high into the mountains or through the surrounding valleys and beech forests. One day, Lorenzo became particularly excited at the profusion of wildflowers, bending to examine every bloom that crossed their path.

'What are those gold bubbles?' He pointed, enthralled, at a cluster of globular flowers the colour of ripe quinces. 'If you don't know the name, we must make our own.' He slithered down the bank to where the flowers grew beside the jade green river. Returning with a flower in hand, he presented it to Frieda with a small bow. 'I name this flower the Brilliant Bachelor's Blooming Button and I give it to you, my empress.'

Frieda laughed. 'I love that name! They are exactly like gold buttons. But why the buttons of a lonely bachelor?'

'Because bachelors need their spirits kept up while they search for the woman of their dreams.'

They stumbled, hand-in-hand, through ferns and alpen roses to the riverbank where the Bachelor's Buttons grew in huge yellow boluses, beside the primulas and harebells, the willows and white poplars.

'Look at this one, Frieda. Look at its stamens. See how they reach out, how hungry they are for life and sun. You name this one.'

Frieda paused and looked at Lorenzo, his pale face flushed with excitement and spattered with new freckles. The bright beam of his eyes seemed to bring everything to life and saturate everything with colour. She loved the way he found beauty in the greyest of clouds and the rankest of weeds. The previous day he'd brought home a brown medlar, hard and unripe. But as he took her finger and laid it gently on the medlar's leathery pitted skin, she'd felt a sudden breathless soaring. That something so worthless could be made so exquisite.

'How about Lover's Lament?'

'Far too sad. There's nothing lamenting about this little beauty. Take off your shoes, come and paddle with me.' Lorenzo began untying his shoelaces, pulling off his worn shoes and coarse socks. His feet were thin and white and red flakes of skin clung to his toes. As she looked at them, Frieda longed to kneel in the damp earth and cover them with kisses. There was such pathos in his feet. But Lorenzo was already slipping over the rocks, splashing and gasping.

'Come to this pool. The water's not so cold here . . . Oh and breathe in! Can you smell the wild peppermint? I feel as if we're on the slopes of Heaven.'

'These waters come direct from the Alps. It is melted snow.' Frieda kicked off her shoes, unrolled her stockings and threw them carelessly over a branch.

They spent the next hour dangling their feet in a small pool of sun-warmed water, smelling whatever the breeze blew their way. When their feet started to go numb, she pulled the rings off her fingers and told Lorenzo to give her his feet. Obligingly he placed them in her lap. She gently stroked his crooked toes, then she kissed each cold, pale foot and began slipping her rings onto his toes. 'Your feet are like two cod fillets,' she laughed. 'But there is something about them that fills me with love for you. Now, put them back into the water and see how they come to life.'

Lorenzo obediently submerged his feet in the milk-green pool. The ripples distended and distorted them, and the light caught on the gold bands and the precious stones, making everything glimmer and glint beneath the surface.

'Your feet are so superior, so well-nourished and healthy. Your grand, baronial feet next to my poor Nottingham feet.'

She poked his flat, bony feet with her rounded, pink feet and laughed. 'I would rather have one of your callouses than all the rings in the world. Come on – take your clothes off and swim with me!'

'Here?' He glanced round then wiped his palms nervously on the knees of his rolled-up trousers. 'Naked?'

'Why not? So what if a peasant sees us? I don't care if the woodcutter sees my breasts. All women have them, they are all the same.' Frieda peeled off her dress and petticoat, then tugged down her bloomers. She stood on the rock, her chin tilted to the sky, her back arched, her skin gleaming mother-of-pearl.

'Come on,' she commanded. 'I did not leave Ernest to have prudery from you, Mr Lawrence.' And with that she stepped down into the pool, gasping as the ice-cold water rose up her legs, turning her flesh a blotchy blister-pink. She looked back at Lorenzo. He was folding his trousers with quick anxious movements, his eyes swivelling left and right, his frail white body bowed over himself.

'You silly shy thing . . . You must be naked! The shock of it will make you feel most magnificently alive.' She plunged her head beneath the freezing water. A second later, he was beside her, a splashing gasping tangle of limbs. She found his hand, pulled him into the arctic heart of the pool. Then she put her arms around his neck and asked 'Do you not feel good and alive now?'

'Oh Lord, yes!' He tugged himself free of her and began scooping at the water, flinging it over himself. 'I'm washed clean! This pale-green glacier water has washed me quite clean!'

They warmed themselves in the glare of the sun and returned to the flat. Lorenzo set up a makeshift desk on the balcony overlooking the wheat fields that stretched, green and bristling, into the valley. He wrote fast and furiously as though a forest fire was crackling behind him. Every now and then he paused and massaged his hands, looking out at the passing bullock wagons, the mules laden with huge wheels of cheese, the stooped women threshing wheat. And then he dipped his pen into the inkwell and started writing again, the words streaming across the paper as if his pen could barely keep pace with his thoughts.

Eventually he stopped and called to Frieda, 'I never knew life could be so great – so godlike. I have proved it! I have proved that life can be wonderful and beautiful and good beyond one's wildest imaginings.'

'Oh my dear, and how have you proved it?' Frieda came out to the balcony and put her hands on his shoulders, felt the knots and lumps beneath her fingers.

'I am so fearfully happy, my empress, my Queen Bee. Being in love is the greatest thing that can happen to a man and I want to tell everyone, all my bachelor friends, everyone!'

She opened her mouth to speak, to tell him that she hadn't decided what to do yet, that she would do nothing without her children. But the words crumbled in her throat.

'You know I love you more every morning and every night.' Lorenzo leaned back, let his shoulders melt into her warm hands, rested his head against the softness of her stomach. 'Oh Frieda, where will it end? I know I'll love you all my life but what if Weekley won't release you?'

'Let's not think about him, Lorenzo. Not today.' Another letter from Ernest had come that afternoon, saying he would never give her a divorce. Frieda had opened the letter at the door, said nothing. She knew how Ernest's letters angered Lorenzo, how bitter he became when he saw her crying for her children.

'But I must marry you, my empress.' He pushed his head further into the folds of her body.

'We can carry on like this, no?' She looked across to the mountain peaks. They had lost their morning glimmer and were bathed apricot-gold in the syrupy afternoon sun.

'I believe in marriage, my Queen Bee. I want you to be my wife. I don't want you being turned away from people's houses because you're not respectable, because you live in sin. Anyway, Ernest will never let your children stay with a fallen woman.'

Frieda stroked Lorenzo's hair. She didn't want to be a wife again. She wanted to be like Fanny zu Reventlow – with her own name and her independence. But she wanted her children and she knew Lorenzo was right. She turned her gaze from the grizzled ridges in the south, back to England. She looked across the little white village, beyond the white church, beyond the woods and wheat fields, and thought again of her children. What were they doing now? Was Monty playing chess with Ernest? Was Barby drawing pictures of fairies under Aunt Maude's admiring eye? And Elsa – what was Elsa doing? Helping Granny with the meal? Yes, Elsa, always so helpful . . . She would be laying the table. And they would be thinking about their trip to London Zoo. The trip she'd promised . . . Her eyes filled with silent tears.

She felt Lorenzo's hand tugging at hers. 'We can't let Weekley destroy us. We mustn't let him. Our life together is going to be so good!'

She stepped back from the window, not wanting him to see the watery film on her eyes. 'But we can still make a home for my children?'

Lorenzo picked up his pen, positioned his index finger above the nib, circled his thin wrist in the air. 'I want to travel into the

wilderness of human experience, with you at my side, as my wife.'
He paused, then pushed the nib onto the page and held it there,
the ink bleeding out into the paper.

Frieda blinked rapidly and turned her tearful gaze back to the
window, back to the north, back to England.

FIFTY-FIVE

Frieda

'Just one week without pain and indecision,' he pleaded. 'A week we can call our honeymoon? And then we'll sort out the mess, we'll get your children back.'

She went out to the balcony. Dusk was deepening into night, and on the track below woodcutters and charcoal burners sang as they trudged home. She called over her shoulder, 'Very well, for one week I promise not to think about Ernest or England or my . . .' She could not say the word. But she would put them all to a distant corner of her mind. Just for a week. 'The truth, my darling Lorenzo, is that I am very happy with you. So very happy.'

He came and stood beside her and pointed into the darkening Milky Way. 'Look at Sirius, the dog star. See how he drapes a green tinge over everything, how he looks back at you. Look! He's staring at us!'

Frieda smiled and wrapped her arms around him. 'I think he's looking at me!'

'Bah! He's looking at me. I call him the Hound of Heaven.'

'Oh, I love that . . . the Hound of Heaven.' She turned the words over on her tongue. It was the first time anyone had ever pointed out a star to her and she had a sudden desire to stay up all night, to track every star, learn its name, follow its path through the galaxy.

She tugged on Lorenzo's hand. 'Come to the beech woods now. Come on!'

He screwed up his eyes. 'It's late. And I'm in my slippers.'

'No, it's not late. Come barefoot. Like me. We can lie on our backs and watch the stars.' She pulled him through the sitting room, through the kitchen, out of the front door. The village was silent. The darkness hung like an inky cloak across the roofs, the trees, the bristling fields of rye and corn.

'Let's run – all the way through the woods!' She grabbed the skirts of her scarlet pinafore, lifting them high above her knees, and ran, the pink soles of her feet flashing in the moonlight.

'You're such a child,' he called. 'It's impossible to see and my feet will be cut to ribbons!'

'I am much older than you,' she yelled back, as she ran, faster and faster, up the pale curving path that wound into the beech woods. An owl streaked past, white and silent, and from far away she heard a long shrill cry as if a small mammal had fallen into a trap.

She turned and called to him, 'Come on! I know a place where we can look through the branches at your Hound of Heaven.'

She ran through the trees, her bare feet sinking in and out of the leaves that spread, damp and pulpy, across the forest floor. For the first time since leaving England she felt the freedom she'd been yearning for. It swept her up in a blast of exhilaration, so that for a few minutes she forgot Lorenzo and felt herself to be absolutely alone. She felt the air gusting in and out of her, with its pungent black odour of fungi and earth. She felt the breeze whipping through her hair, drawing her up and up, as if she was being tossed high into the elements.

'I can breathe,' she sang out. 'I can breathe!'

Lorenzo was cussing behind her, twigs snapping and leaves rustling as he laboured through the darkness.

'I can't see a damn thing,' he said, appearing with one hand clamped against his chest, his eyelids blinking rapidly.

'I want to lie in the dark of the moon,' she said, flinging herself onto the ground, burrowing her spine and bottom deep into the mulchy leaves. 'This is how I need to live! Tell me about all these stars.'

Slowly, cautiously, he lay down beside her. 'We are between the mud and the heavens,' he murmured. Then his arm darted up. 'There! Follow my finger . . . That's the great plough.'

She stared up into the firmament, at the wheeling stars, at the moon looming large and white like an enormous milky pearl. She turned to Lorenzo and pushed her head into his chest. She could feel the pumping of his heart, like a piston against her cheek. He brought his lips down to hers and kissed her in a way she'd never been kissed before. By turn hectic, then gentle, then with a fierce determination, his tongue thrusting at the roof of her mouth and his hands in her hair, scrabbling at her neck, at the hooks and buttons of her clothes.

Afterwards, she whispered in his ear, 'Bury me in leaves! I want to feel like a plant, like the root of a dandelion.'

He dug out huge handfuls of leaves and mud, spreading them carefully over her body and patting them down, as if she was a child having a sand burial at the seaside. When the damp started to seep into her bones, she burst from the leaves throwing sodden clods high into the air and laughing with delight.

'Well, now I know how it is to be a flower root. I prefer to be myself.'

Lorenzo wrapped her in his arms, then lifted her hair and began kissing her neck. 'I never loved anyone except my mother. I wasn't sure I could. But I love you more and more.'

'I want you to tell me that every day.' She lay quiet and sombre for a minute. No one had spoken to her like Lorenzo did, not since Otto. She couldn't recall if Ernest had ever spoken to her like that. 'Will you say that to me every day?'

'No,' said Lorenzo. 'I can't. It's the English in me. But I do know that life with you will be all richness, nothing but richness.'

He stroked her hair, picking out dead leaves and small bony twigs and flipping them into the undergrowth. 'If my mother had lived, I could never have loved you. She wouldn't have let me go.'

Above them the trees reared up, soughing softly in the wind. Frieda didn't want to think about his mother or the past or England. She'd promised him a week of honeymoon, and so she put her fingers to his lips and said, 'There's a hunter's ladder if we go deeper into the woods. We can climb into a tree and sleep there. I always slept in trees when I was little.'

'Did you?' Lorenzo reached for their clothes that he'd folded into a tidy pile.

'No clothes,' she said, imperiously. 'Follow me. I'll take you there.'

'But . . .' He stared at her, aghast. 'What if . . .'

'Chase me!' She leapt to her feet and ran, deeper and deeper into the woods, batting away the spiked limbs of trees and the long tendrils of ivy that fell from above. She could hear Lorenzo bounding lightly after her and laughing in disbelief.

They climbed the huntsman's ladder and sat swinging their legs from a broad branch while moths brushed blindly against them.

'Have you noticed how beech trees *rush* into leaf? As if they can't wait for spring, as if they must be first,' said Lorenzo.

'No,' she replied, amused. 'But I will now.'

'That's how I feel with you. You have such a genius for living.'

She smiled. 'Otto Gross used to say the very same thing to me.' A thought struck her and she glanced sideways at him. 'You should read Otto's letters to me. They are like scriptures, mad crazy manifestos of love.'

'I've read 'em,' he said lightly. 'Every heart is entitled to its secrets, but you left them out for me to read. Remember?'

'Did I? I suppose I did.' She heard the note of wistfulness in her voice and wondered if it was for the Mrs Ernest Weekley who once wallowed in secrets and mystery but now had none. Oh, but there was one remaining secret, she reflected.

She blinked it away and laid her head on his shoulder. 'I wish we could be like this forever and ever.'

'We can,' he said, with urgency. 'We can.'

She felt his lips brush the side of her head and his fingers trail over her bare shoulder, soft and sweet. And in that second she felt closer to him than she'd ever felt, an intimacy deeper and more profound than she'd felt with anyone.

He pointed into the distance where a crack of pale light was rising from the edge of the earth. 'Look! An apple-green dawn seething on the horizon.'

She smiled. 'I love your words, Lorenzo. You are so full of poetry. I don't think I want to share you with anyone, ever. I want your poetry all for me.'

'Do you?'

'For me and the children,' she said, her voice ringing with a renewed sense of hope. 'How they will love to run through moonlit woods and hang from trees and hear your fine words.'

Lorenzo stared distractedly into the boughs, black and green, embracing above their heads. 'The moon . . . a golden petal . . . Her eyes, green . . . like flowers undone.'

The leaves rustled in the silence.

FIFTY-SIX

Frieda

A few days later, she awoke to find the bed empty, the sheets on Lorenzo's side neatly turned back, his bolster smoothed of rumples. She stretched and smiled. It had been Lorenzo's idea not to open any post in this week of *his honeymoon*, as he called it, and she felt lighter and happier as a result. For five days now, he had scooped up Ernest's spiteful, indecisive letters and locked them away, unopened. And, somehow, she had managed to suppress the constant inner struggle that had so blighted the previous weeks. But tomorrow she would find and open Ernest's letters. She harboured a secret hope that one of them might deliver the children to her, a hope that had nourished and sustained her all week.

She kicked back the sheet and laughed. They had been to the beech woods again the previous evening and the bed was full of dried leaves and crumbs of soil and a long white feather that Lorenzo had found in the woods and laced into her pubic hair. She threw the feather up to the ceiling and was just lunging for it, when Lorenzo burst into the room, a gale of papers and notebooks and rose petals.

'I couldn't sleep, my Queen Bee, not a wink.' He tossed a sheaf of papers onto the bed. Rose petals – pink, white, yellow – fell from his hair and his shoulders. 'Get back into bed and read these, will you?'

Frieda pulled a blue silk dressing gown from the hook on the door and slipped it on. 'What are they?'

'Poems, short stories, ideas for travel pieces and essays and more stories. I feel . . .' He paused and seemed to search for the right word.

'Inspired?' she suggested. She had noticed how manic, how hectic, he had become recently. He worked with a febrile energy, as if his body couldn't keep pace with his mind, as if his pen raced to keep up with the ideas that spilled, insatiably, from him.

'The woods, last night and the other night . . . that's how I want to live, Queen Bee.'

She laughed. 'Trying to sleep in a cold, scratchy tree?'

'I want to rough it and scramble through, free, free. I don't want to be tied down.' He began pulling handfuls of rose petals from his tattered pockets and flinging them on the mattress.

'So we do not have to get married?' She clambered back into bed, the scent of crushed roses everywhere, heavy and luxuriant.

'Of course we must be respectable and married,' he said, coldly. 'Now read my work while I bring you a tray of food.'

She began reading though his poems – so many of them, so frank and candid – and then his sketches and story ideas. She didn't pick up her pen until she came to a short title-less story. Everything was about *her* – the poems, the story ideas – but this piece included her exact words, the very words she'd used a week ago. How had he remembered them all so precisely? She grasped the pen, plunged it into the inkpot and began crossing out the words that weren't right, that weren't *her*.

She was so engrossed she didn't hear the ring of the postboy's bicycle, or his sharp rapping on the door. When Lorenzo appeared, clutching a parcel, she looked up, startled. 'We agreed not to open the post this week.'

'It's my manuscript. Back from my publisher.' His voice was strained and uncertain.

'They probably want a few revisions,' she said cheerfully. 'You said yourself it is the best book you've written.'

'It is,' he said. 'It's a damn fine book.'

'So open it,' she replied. 'And tell them you want to change the title to my idea. *Paul Morel* is a rotten title. I like my idea – *Sons and Lovers* – much better.'

He undid the string, carefully looping it into a neat coil before sliding off the brown paper.

'Just tear it! Why must you save every bit of string and paper?' She sighed, exasperated. They needed the money from *Paul Morel* and here he was, painstakingly tying up string!

He put aside the huge hulking manuscript and began reading a letter that had come with it. She watched as the blood slowly drained from his face, then surged back in a crimson rush of rage.

'What is it, Lorenzo? I can help you revise it.'

But Lorenzo didn't answer. Then he hurled the letter on the bed and beat at the air with his fists. 'The blasted jelly-boned swines! The slimy, belly-wriggling, miserable, sodding rotters!' His voice rose, shrill and strident. His fists pounded faster and faster. 'The snivelling, dribbling, dithering, palsied, pulse-less bloody English!' He stormed from the room, slamming the door so hard the shutters banged against the walls.

She could still hear his voice, forcing its way through the floorboards . . . 'I can write bigger stuff than any man in England . . . It's a great novel . . . A bloody great novel . . . curse those rotten-boned, pappy-hearted swine . . . Let them stink in sourness . . .'

She picked up the letter from Mr William Heinemann and scanned it: *Your novel lacks unity without which the reader's interest cannot be held . . . no sympathy for any character in the book . . . poorly structured . . . a lack of reticence . . . must decline to publish . . .*

She put her head in her hands. If Lorenzo didn't sell this novel, how would they eat? How would they feed and clothe the children?

His last book of poems had only sold a hundred copies. Not enough to feed a carp.

Lorenzo burst back into the room, his face a livid puce. 'Get up! Honeymoon over!'

'It's all right,' she soothed. 'I will help you. We can do this together.'

He tossed a bundle of envelopes at her. 'And these bowel-twisting letters are yours, from that monstrous, vile husband of yours.'

'Where are you going? Don't leave me to read these alone,' she begged as Lorenzo marched out of the room. She found Ernest's letters agonising and contrary and often shocking in their brutality. Already her hands were shaking and her mouth felt hard and dry.

Lorenzo's reply came, clear and sure, from the stairs. 'I'm going to rewrite my bloody good novel and make it even bloody better.'

•

Bei Herrn Professor Alfred Weber
Icking
Bei München
28 June 1912

Dear Ernest
Thank you for offering to take me back as your wife and for your offer of a London flat. Your offers seem to change daily so I am unsure how to respond. However, with the many conditions you attach to all your offers, you make it impossible for me.

You demand that I give up Mr Lawrence. I cannot. He relies on me entirely. He says he would die if I were to leave him. And his genius would be destroyed forever.

I would like to spend the school holidays with Monty, Elsa and Barby – every year for as long as they wish to do so. I miss them desperately and I hope you will agree to this. It does not seem much to ask and children should know their own mother.

Frieda

•

Bei Herrn Professor Alfred Weber
Icking
Bei München
1 July 1912

Dear Elisabeth
I cannot take much more of this! Last night I sat and banged my
head against the floor, over and over – so wild and bitter was
my grief. Being apart from one's children is like having one's
flesh torn away, ripped cleanly from one's bones. I have tried not
to think of them, and for a few days (which Lorenzo called his
'honeymoon') I managed not to, but now the pain has returned,
sharper and more acute than before.

    What I cannot understand, dear Elisabeth, is why so many
must suffer so that I can live. You have a life and no one has
suffered. Why must others suffer so that I can live? So that Lorenzo
can live?

    Ernest refuses to understand why I left. I am sure if he better
understood me, the true me and not the Mrs Snowflower-Weekley
he invented, he would be more forgiving, more sympathetic.

    So I am changing my approach. I have sent him Otto Gross's
letters, so that he can see who I truly am, the honest and genuine
Frieda. As you can imagine, it was like pulling out my own heart
and sealing it in an envelope. For five years those letters have
affirmed who and what I am! But what choice did I have? If Ernest
knows it was Dr Gross that inspired the change in me and not
any deficiency on his own part, he may be more compassionate.

    And now I shall post my copy of Anna Karenina to him. If
Ernest reads this, perhaps he will be more merciful, more tolerant.
Perhaps he will see there is no shame in being a cuckold. And
perhaps he will understand the consequences of refusing to give
me a divorce.

Alfred wants his apartment back, so Lorenzo and I have decided to walk over the Alps to Italy. I will try and forget all this misery I have caused. Perhaps the hike will clear my head so I can make the right decision. Every time I think of my children I am reduced to tears – which I must hide from Lorenzo as it makes him very angry. Yesterday he slammed a door in my face, shouting 'I shan't put up with another moment of misery!'

He promised me a home with them ('a heaven on earth' as he so beautifully put it) but as time goes by I see how rash that promise was. I am beginning to see a different side to Lorenzo. He wants me all to himself. I do not think he wants a home with my children, in spite of his promise.

Your unhappy sister
Frieda

PS I hear you are now referring to yourself as Frau Jaffé-Richthofen. How very emancipated. I long for my own name, more and more. Sometimes, when Lorenzo makes me very cross, I take a sheet of Mama's letterhead with our coat of arms (she gave me a stack of it – which Lorenzo loves to use!) and write I am Baroness Frieda von Richthofen all over it. You will think me foolish. But you are not being coerced into becoming Mrs Lawrence!

FIFTY-SEVEN

Ernest

Gardening was the only thing that stilled his mind now. No, not gardening – digging. His weeks of sleepless insanity had passed. The days when Monty had looked at him with fear and disgust. The days when he had run his forefinger along the blades of kitchen knives, garden shears, his razor. The days when he had searched the garden shed for arsenic or carbolic acid. He knew now that he mustn't die. He had to live. For his children. *His* children.

The Romance of Words had been published and become an overnight sensation (the publisher's words, not his) but he cared nothing for it. One sleepless night when madness rampaged through him, he lit a fire and burnt every copy the publishers had given him – ripped the covers from their spines, tore the pages into shreds, threw them to the flames. And as he did so, blasphemous curses spilled from his mouth in a way that both horrified and pacified him. As the flames died to embers, he asked himself what had happened to the man he once thought he'd be, to the life he'd predicted for himself – to the Cambridge Professor of his dreams? Where was that man?

The insanity had passed but the bitterness and humiliation were still with him, jostling uncontrollably with the love that refused to die. He couldn't understand why he still loved her. Why he loved her more now. She had betrayed and deceived him. She had humiliated and shamed him. But at times his desperate love for her overwhelmed him. And he sent her grovelling letters begging her to return. Afterwards, he hated himself, despising his weakness. Despising her for reducing him to this feeble, hollow man. And a great gush of ungovernable anger would wash over him. He'd post another letter – it was all over, he never wanted to see her again, she'd never see the children again, he'd never give her a divorce. And so his days had passed, veering from one violent emotion to another.

He preferred it outside. Where there was no trace of her. Where he could dig and dig. The house was littered with her things, her odours, memories of her presence. He could smell her cigarette smoke, her perfume, her soap. Sometimes he pressed one of her shoes to his nose, so he could smell her feet. Sometimes he picked up one of her hats and inhaled the smell of her hair. And then, ashamed of himself, he'd run out to the garden and begin digging again.

Every now and then he'd catch his own smell – the odour of turned earth and suffering and desertion. And on the odd occasions when Monty stood beside him, he'd smell something similar on his son. That was when he decided to clean the house. He was supposed to be preparing for the removal men. They were coming to take all the furniture to London. But he'd been too busy digging and nothing was packed. He pushed his spade into the soil and went inside to the scullery. He found a bucket, a box of soda crystals and a rag and was about to return to the kitchen when he noticed Monty's sheets and nightshirt hanging from the rack on the ceiling. He blinked uncertainly. Monty must have been doing his own washing. The parlour maid was the only servant who still came and she hadn't been in for a few days. Said she was sick. Ernest hadn't believed her. But what could he say? No one wanted to work for him now. He stared at the sheet with its stains and marks and suddenly images of his red-haired student and his green-eyed wife, fornicating, raced through his mind. One after another.

He went back to the kitchen and tried to read the instructions on the box of soda crystals. The words jumbled and jumped and he couldn't concentrate. All he saw, everywhere, were Frieda and that loathsome man kissing and copulating. Their tongues rammed down each other's throats, up each other's orifices, all over each other. When these pictures stuck in his head, there was only one thing Ernest could do. And he did it now. He lifted his forearm to his jaws and bit down. Hard. Harder. Harder still. He bit until the pain was unbearable. Afterwards he looked at the deep ring of purple teeth-marks, and nodded, satisfied. On one occasion he'd drawn blood and Monty had asked why he had a bandage on. He told his son he'd accidentally dropped hot coffee on his arm and Monty had shaken his head sympathetically.

He poured the crystals into a bowl, added hot water and stirred the crystals with a wooden spoon until they dissolved. He was going to eradicate the smell of his wife. Exterminate all traces of her. He rinsed the rag in the water and wrung it out. He'd start by wiping down everything she'd touched: the piano, the door handles, the light switches, the taps, the insides of her shoes.

He was giving the rag a final twist when the doorbell rang. He looked at the front door with its garish panels of stained glass. He didn't want to see anyone. Nor did he want anyone to see him. He'd already burst into tears in front of Professor Kipping's wife. The bell rang again. Ernest could just make out the shape and uniform of what appeared to be the postboy. His heart leapt. She had written, begging for forgiveness!

He opened the door very slightly and pushed his head round the side. The postboy thrust a parcel and a letter at him, gave a cheery wave and went back to his bicycle. It was her handwriting . . . On the parcel *and* the letter . . . She wanted to come back to him . . . She'd had enough of being poor and she wanted to come home. Thank goodness he hadn't got started on his cleaning.

Ernest took the post to his study, found his letter opener and with trembling fingers opened the envelope. He would read the letter begging forgiveness first and then he'd open the package. Perhaps she was congratulating him on the success of his book. News of the extraordinary success of *The Romance of Words* must have reached Germany.

To his surprise, there were several letters in the envelope. Folded very small. Tied with a thin purple ribbon. His forehead buckled. There was something familiar about the ribbon, something that made a slick of nausea rise up inside him. He looked again. Most of them were in a hand he neither knew nor recognised. A messy, sprawling hand with jagged lines and shaky loops. And long slashes in the paper where the nib had pushed right through. He felt his pulse slow. He'd seen these letters before. In her bedroom. Five years ago. So this wasn't the contrite letter he'd hoped for. Only one note was in Frieda's handwriting and it was two lines long:

> *To help you understand me, I send you these letters from my old lover, Doctor Otto Gross. Please try to understand who I am.*

Ernest read it again. His brain was exploding into scarlet shards. His heart was hammering at his ribs. The blood zipped through his swollen veins. He reached for his pipe. He must calm himself. He found his tobacco pouch but his fingers were shaking too much to fill his pipe. He wouldn't read them. He would put them straight on the fire. No, he would send them to that filthy lout, Lawrence.

Then he remembered the parcel. It was still sitting on his desk. He took a long deep breath, cut the string and pulled off the brown paper. It was a copy of *Anna Karenina*. And with it a short note:

> *I beg you to read this. See what terrible things happened to Anna after Count Karenin refused to divorce her. I beg you to let me see my children.*

All the emotion drained out of Ernest. He felt a cold, empty space inside him, saw the dead gaps in his thoughts, the great void of all the days ahead. It was odd how that happened. One minute he was wild with fury. And two minutes later he could be hollow and emotionless. And two minutes after that he could be crying and begging her to return, wishing he could rest his head against her and forget all this had ever happened.

He picked up the book and took aim at the empty grate. It could sit in the ashes until he next lit a fire. Or perhaps he'd light one now and burn the book and her ridiculous letters. But just as he was about to fling the book into the fireplace, something fell out of it and fluttered to the floor.

Ernest bent and picked it up. It was another letter. But it wasn't Frieda's handwriting. And nor was it the manic scribble of the German doctor. He paused. Frowned. He knew that handwriting. He knew it well. He saw it every year in a birthday card to Barby, accompanying a lavish present labelled in the same hand. Why was a letter in William Dowson's handwriting inside Frieda's copy of *Anna Karenina*? His old friend, Dowson . . . He hadn't seen him for a few months, always too busy buying and selling lace factories. And Mrs Dowson always so busy marching and campaigning . . . Must be some old note that got stuck in the pages. He felt an unexpected lurch of affection for Dowson. Perhaps he should drop by and see him, tell him everything. Trade some of his dignity for a friendly hand on his shoulder, a sympathetic ear.

Ernest unfolded the note. Froze.

If you had to run away with someone, why not me?

Underneath was Dowson's signature. *William*. And the intimacy of that single word told Ernest everything.

He sat in stunned, disbelieving silence, his eyes going from the note to the bundled letters in their purple ribbon and then back to the note. Who was this woman? What sort of woman had

263

he lived with for thirteen years? What sort of woman cuckolds her husband with a family friend, with the godfather of her own daughter? He leant his head in his hands. How many more were there? Professor Kipping? Edgar Jaffé? How many of their friends had his wife had? He was surely the laughing-stock of Nottingham, the cuckold of the county. His lips and mouth felt dry. His chest felt tight and crushed as though poison ivy was binding and twisting round his heart. She was a stranger to him. He had never known her. He felt something rising in his throat, a sob of such magnitude he couldn't breathe. He groped across his desk for an envelope. He would post Dowson's note to that swine, Lawrence. Let him see what sort of woman she really was. He tried to lick the seal on the envelope but his tongue was too dry, too cracked. Instead, he put his head on his desk and wept. He wept until there was nothing left inside him. No anger, no pain, no humiliation, no hate, no love. He wept until he heard a knock at his door. He didn't want to see Monty. He couldn't face Monty. And he didn't want Monty to see him like this – with his red-rimmed eyes and his vocal chords pulled so tight he couldn't speak.

'Papa? Papa?'

Ernest didn't move. He tried to call out, to ask Monty to leave him alone. But his tongue withered in his throat. He raised his head and looked out at the trees. Their green leaves drooped as if under the weight of his grief and shame. He put his head back on the desk and closed his eyes. The dogged tapping at his door started again, quietly at first but then louder.

'Papa? Are you in there?'

Ernest slowly opened his mouth. 'Not now,' he croaked.

'Papa? It's my birthday. I bought us a cake from the Mikado. Papa? Are you in there?'

FIFTY-EIGHT

Barby

M onty arrived first. Then tea chests – hundreds of them – containing all the crockery, cutlery, curtains, cushions, clothes and books from the Nottingham house.

'Wherever are we to put it all?' asked Aunt Maude, wringing her red hands, as the chests were unloaded from carts and hauled into the house.

A week later, the furniture arrived – chairs, tables, wardrobes, beds. Every room at 40 Well Walk was stacked with furniture. Tea chests lined every wall so that the eight inhabitants had to flatten themselves and slide rather than walk. Reversing, waiting, manoeuvring, simply to pass each other or to get in and out of the front door. Granny pushed mouse traps into the crevices between the chests but then forgot where she'd put them and so the smell of festering mouse carcass grew and the buzzing of a thousand flies added to the household cacophony.

Tempers frayed in the summer heat and Monty, Elsa and Barby took every opportunity to slip off to church. The cool air with its perfume of lilies and freshly starched cassocks, the silence, the triangles of coloured light that fell through the stained glass, the huge, unfilled space – all this calmed them. Besides which, when their father returned on Friday evenings he smiled when they told him how often they'd been to church. Peculiar smiles that stretched tightly over his teeth. But smiles, all the same.

Elsa and Barby stopped asking when their mother was coming home. Aunt Maude told them she was ill and would return when she was better. Monty had stomach-ache most of the time and said nothing. And when his sisters asked, he just shook his head and said Mutti was still in Germany.

'But why doesn't she write?' asked Barby when Monty had first come to London.

'She's too ill, I suppose,' Monty said. And then he'd doubled over with tummy pains and had to lie down in the bedroom he shared with their father.

One Friday evening, Ernest arrived back from Nottingham and asked the three children and Aunt Maude to join him among the tea chests in the front parlour. He lowered himself carefully into an armchair and Aunt Maude and the three children squeezed onto the couch. Granny lurked at the door like a fat black spider.

'I have bought a new home for us all. Much bigger . . . With a garden. In Chiswick, near the River Thames.' He paused and cleared his throat. 'We'll start moving next week.'

'Will Mutti like the house?' Barby asked.

'Elsa and Barby will share a room and Monty will have his own room. I'm hiring a cook so there'll be less work for your grandmother and Aunt Maude.'

'Aunt Maude and Granny are coming to live in our house?' Barby asked, surprised. She could feel Elsa stiffen beside her. And on the other side of her, Monty belched softly and put his hands to his stomach. She shifted slightly. She didn't want Monty to be sick on her. He'd been sick on her shoes the day before and she could still see the splash marks.

'Yes. And your grandfather of course. Which brings me to my next point.' Ernest's gaze rose until he was staring at a point above their heads, like the vicar did when he was sermonising. 'From now on you are to call Maude "Mama".' And he gestured vaguely at Aunt Maude with his bandaged arm.

'Mama?' Barby echoed, startled. 'Why are we to call Aunt Maude "Mama"?'

There was a short silence while Aunt Maude squirmed on the couch. Monty retched and gulped. Elsa stared at her father with wide, suspicious eyes.

'She is to be called Mama from now on,' he repeated, his gaze still fixated in space. There was something about the rigid line of his jaw that stopped Barby asking any more questions.

'When is Mutti back?' Elsa asked.

Papa gave a terse shake of his head. His eyes looked sore and watery, as though he had something in them. A small fly or a grain of sand perhaps. 'I have work to do now. Maude, could you take them to church?'

'Your mother is ill,' hissed Aunt Maude. 'How many times do we have to tell you!'

Granny stood in the doorframe, hands on her hips, nodding with feigned solicitude. 'Stop bothering your father, children. If we go now we'll be in time for Evensong.'

The five of them walked to church in silence, Aunt Maude and Granny in front and Monty trailing and belching. But just as they got to the gates of the churchyard, they heard the sound of retching and turned to see Monty bent over the gutter, vomiting.

'He's not well!' Elsa exclaimed. 'He shouldn't be here!'

'That's enough from you, young lady,' snapped Granny. 'Do you know why your mother isn't here? Do you?'

'It's because she's ill in Germany. She's probably got what Monty's got and I bet Grossvater isn't forcing her to go to church,' Barby said plaintively.

'How dare you talk back to me! No wonder she doesn't like you. That's why she's not here. She-that-was-Frieda doesn't love you. And now we must love you. And if your father wants you to call

Maude "Mama", then you will!' Granny strode towards the church, her black skirt skating out behind her. 'It's up to God now and he smiles only upon the righteous.'

Elsa reached instinctively for Barby's hand, pulling her into the churchyard. Monty limped behind them, groaning faintly and wiping his mouth. Barby felt Elsa's fingers gripping and pressing the bones in her hand. What had Granny meant when she said their mother didn't love them? Why had she called her *She-that-was-Frieda*?

That night, Barby climbed into Elsa's bed, and snuggled tight against her.

'Mutti wouldn't leave us, would she?'

'No,' agreed Elsa. 'I think she's gone mad and they've put her in a lunatic asylum. They're too ashamed to tell us. And that's why they're saying beastly things.'

Barby moved in closer so that they lay like conjoined twins. 'I think she's lost her memory and doesn't know where she is. *They* think she's run away but really she's walking round lost in a big German forest. Like a princess under a magic spell.'

She smiled in the darkness. 'D'you remember when she used to tell us the story of Sleeping Beauty? D'you remember how she would leap up when we kissed her and all the pictures would rattle and shake on the walls?'

Elsa giggled. 'D'you remember when she did such a huge leap, she broke my bed?'

The sisters squeezed each other, and when they awoke the next morning, they were still pressed tightly together like the two shells of an oyster.

PART SEVEN

Lake Garda, Italy 1912–1913

'He hated her, truly. She hated him.

Yet they held hands fast as they walked.'

D.H. Lawrence, *The Witch a la Mode*

FIFTY-NINE

Frieda

The Villa Igea, in the village of Gargnano, looked out across the vast, blue expanse of Lake Garda, and beyond to lemon groves and the silver-veined mountains of the Monte Baldo. Peach, orange and persimmon trees jostled in its small garden. Vines and jasmine scrambled, wild and dishevelled, over its surrounding walls. Beyond, sprawled a profusion of trees – olive, chestnut, fig – and row-upon-row of bony vines, rising high into the hills.

When they first arrived, Lorenzo raced through the villa opening every window, every door, exclaiming at everything – the charcoal braziers and copper pans in the kitchen, the blond rush matting on the dining room floor, the roses that fell through the bedroom window and left their strewn petals on the quilt. Frieda draped her shawls over the tables and arranged her hats and necklaces in colourful compositions on the empty walls.

It was September then and the village air had been sharp with the smell of crushed grapes and fermenting wine. The days had started early with the sound of peasant song as the grapes were trodden. But now the village was full of soldiers with extravagantly plumed helmets and long, gleaming boots. They reminded Frieda of her childhood and she often sat at the window watching them strut and swagger. When they returned to their barracks, she would stare out over the lake, at the steamers festooned in bunting and the boats with their yellow and pink sails, and wonder where to put the children's beds when Monty, Elsa and Barby finally arrived.

She oscillated between the thrill of escape and the wretchedness of suppressed grief. Letters continued to arrive from Ernest, sometimes daily. His moods fluctuated wildly: some letters begged her to return home, others offered a divorce if she agreed to leave Lorenzo, but many more refused her a divorce – ever. Seven months after her departure he still seemed distraught, and this shocked her. He had always been so stiff and wooden. Why had he never loved her like this before? Why had he never shown her any emotion in Nottingham?

She blotted out her misery by throwing herself into Lorenzo's work. He was still revising *Paul Morel*, and would sit in the garden, his spine against a peach tree, and an expression of anguished concentration on his face. She'd watch him until the bones of his face began to move beneath his skin. Then she'd hurry out, offering to help in any way she could. She saw herself as a candle, shining light into the gaping holes littering his manuscript.

'You have missed the point,' she said, throwing down the latest version of a chapter he'd rewritten three times.

Lorenzo hovered, pale and drained. 'How have I missed the point?'

'Paul really loved his mother, more than anybody. You must make that clearer. It's like Oedipus.'

'Oh not all that Otto Gross stuff again!' Lorenzo flung himself onto the couch. His eyes had lost their usual curiosity and seemed flat and glassy. 'Help me, Frieda. Help me understand it.'

'As the sons grow up, the mother selects them, one by one, to be her favourite. That is the point. She urges them into life with her love and they love her back.'

Lorenzo sat up, leaned forward. 'Go on.'

'It is not a problem when the sons are small.' She paused. A memory of Monty flew before her. Fat, pink fingers clinging to her skirt. *Mutti, when can I marry with you?* She shook the memory away. Obediently, his baby face receded, like a balloon drifting over the horizon. She faltered for a second, then continued. 'But when the sons grow up, they cannot love. Not properly.'

Lorenzo's gaze sharpened. 'When can they love properly? I mean love with passion, with their bodies and souls?'

'When the mother is dead, of course.' Frieda clapped her hands. 'Only when she dies are they truly free to love.'

Lorenzo leapt from the couch, his fingers running wildly through his hair and his eyes flashing kingfisher blue. 'Yes! Because the mother is the strongest power in their lives. She holds their souls. So when they meet other women, there's a split in them. But the mother is always stronger. Isn't that so, Frieda? She's always stronger.' Lorenzo's hair stood upright now in messy spires of copper. A sheen of sweat bloomed on his forehead.

'Yes, she is always stronger, because of the blood tie. It comes back to the blood. But the lovers, the women, will fight the mother. We women do not give up so easily.' Frieda gave a short toneless laugh, relieved she'd not had to fight the indomitable Mrs Lawrence for Lorenzo.

'But the fight . . . the battle . . . there must be a victor.' Lorenzo started pacing the room, his voice rising and dipping, his fists clenching and unclenching at his sides. 'If you and my mother had battled for me, it would have killed her. Perhaps the battling for her sons kills the mother?'

'Of course. It's in the mother's unconscious. She sees her son leaving her for another woman. She fights for him. If she thinks she cannot win, she dies. And then he is free.' Frieda watched Lorenzo as he paced, his shoulders hunched forward like a wildcat. She worried when he became this excited, but she also knew it was what he loved best, what kept him alive and inspired. A week before, Lorenzo had coughed into the bathroom sink as she stood quietly behind him. Unaware of her presence, Lorenzo had calmly turned the tap on to wash away the phlegm. But not before she'd seen the globule of blood that lay in the sink, curled round the plughole like a crimson serpent. She'd turned away, not wanting him to know that she'd seen.

'Won't you sit down, Lorenzo?' She patted the cushion beside her, but he continued his feverish circling of the room.

'And the father . . . How would the father be?'

'The sons hate the father, of course. They are jealous of him.'

'Because he once had the mother's full passion . . . Yes, of course!' Lorenzo dropped to his knees in front of Frieda. He cupped her face in his hands, pushing the blunt ends of his fingers into her cheeks. 'And when the mother dies, the son is left naked of everything, drifting towards death . . . it's the tragedy of thousands of young men of England . . . I can see it in so many of my friends. Their mothers have choked the very souls from them.'

'He must not drift towards death, Lorenzo. He is finally free, when she dies. It is the victory of the son over the mother.'

'No!' Lorenzo leapt to his feet again. 'That's rubbish, Frieda! First he must want to die. He must seek death. He must be lost without his mother.'

'That's not right, Lorenzo. It must be a great liberation. He must fall in love and experience true passion. It should be immediate, as if he is on the rebound, like real love.'

'No, I won't have that. He must drift towards death. But he must experience other women along the way.' Lorenzo strode towards the small desk where he kept his pen and ink and a stack of paper. He picked up his pen and thrust it savagely into the inkwell. 'This is my story. Stop meddling!'

'The mother is really the thread, Lorenzo. She is the domineering note. She has to be. Let me write this section, where the mother is talking to Paul about Jessie.' Frieda picked up the revised chapter and shook it at Lorenzo. 'I understand a mother's love.'

Lorenzo snorted, then gave a thin rattling cough. 'Very well, have a go. But if I don't like it, I'm not using it.'

Frieda smiled and reached for her cigarette box. She loved it when they worked together. She loved the feeling of collaboration, as if they were wrestling together with an unwieldy lump of clay. She'd already rewritten great tracts of his novel, secretly scribbling them down on scraps of paper and hiding them behind a loose skirting board in the bedroom.

'This is what I love you for, Lorenzo. You are so honest in your work. You come out and say things that other people dare not even think. You are the only revolutionary worthy of the name, my dear.'

'So I have finally overtaken Otto Gross in your league of revolutionary heroes, have I?' Lorenzo threw a box of matches at her and began writing, his pen moving so fast across the sheet of paper it was as if it had a life of its own and Lorenzo was merely keeping the nib steady on the page.

'You have.' Frieda drew on her cigarette. Although Otto seemed a distant memory, she knew a part of him was still inside her and would never leave her, like bacteria colonising deep within her. And she knew this bacterial snippet of him was now making its way into Lorenzo, into his books, into the ideas he grappled with each night.

His pen stopped its rasping and scratching. 'You know what we did this morning . . . he taught you that, didn't he? You didn't do that with Weekley, did you?'

Frieda laughed. 'Why are you blushing, Lorenzo? Why should you be ashamed? Ernest would never have done something as ungodly as that.' A distant memory of Ernest flitted before her – his functional lovemaking, the way he'd shunted at her like a plunger unblocking a sink. The one time he'd referred to their lovemaking he'd lowered his voice, coughed and asked if it was a good day to 'indulge in the procreational act'.

'So it was Gross?'

'Look at me, Lorenzo. I won't have any shame or fear or embarrassment between us. Why are you so shy now?'

'This talk of my mother I suppose.' He looked at her. 'I love the way you make me spiritual and bestial at the same time.' He turned back to his page, chewing abstractedly at the end of his pen.

'Good. Pleasure is important, Otto showed me that.'

'I want to write about it, Frieda. I want to shock the English public out of their sanctimonious propriety.' He put his pen down and carefully blotted a dribble of ink that had leaked onto the margin of his page.

'It would be banned and burned – and you know it.' She paused and took a deep inhalation of her cigarette. And as the smoke drifted from her nostrils, she added, 'But there is a way you could do it. You are so clever and brilliant with words. You could weave a veil of poetry over it, a veil so light the pleasure of the act can be glimpsed by those whose minds are open, but not by the prosecutors and the priests. I can help you. But not in this book.' She jabbed her cigarette in the direction of his manuscript. 'In your next book.'

'I want my next book to be about two sisters, like you and Elisabeth, how they experience love and sex.' He stopped blotting the ink stain on his manuscript and looked at Frieda. 'You're so good for me, Queen Bee. I have to have a woman supporting me. I daren't be in the world without a woman behind me.'

'I have replaced your mother then?' Frieda blew a long plume of smoke up to the ceiling and picked up her book from the floor.

'I can only write what I feel strongly about. And that, right now, is the relationship between men and women. But it's not just that. It's that you keep me in contact with the unknown.'

A smile twitched at the corners of her lips. She liked thinking of herself as a conduit of mystery, a channel to *the unknown*. She opened her book. Dust rose from its yellowing pages and a flattened fly flipped from the spine.

'What are you reading?' Lorenzo shot her a look of mild enquiry.

'The Bible. I've nothing else left. Anyway, I rather like Christ and I think he would have liked me too.'

SIXTY

Frieda

Three days later, Lorenzo brought up the subject of Otto Gross again. He had arranged his oil paints, jar of turpentine, rags and brushes in a neat line and was adjusting the angle of his easel, his head bent down and away from the pearly November light filtering through the window. His canvas of three naked men was propped against a wall from where it glared into the room.

'What did your mad Austrian doctor think about – about love between men?'

'He's an anarchist. He thinks nothing of it.' Frieda lifted her head from her book and looked curiously at him. There was something about his question, the uncertain tone of his voice, that made her sit very still, her breath held. She waited for him to respond but he didn't. Instead he picked up his canvas, placed it on the easel and began wiping at one of his brushes with a rag.

Frieda put down her book and lit a cigarette, shaking out the match with a single, sharp turn of her wrist. 'Otto believes you have to act out all your sexual desires and fantasies to rid yourself of repression, to be truly free.'

Lorenzo started swiping vigorously at the canvas, filling in an area of shadow in the corner. She had a sudden urge to see his face rather than his back. She took a long drag of her cigarette and said, 'It is against the law of course. Look what happened to Oscar Wilde.'

Lorenzo swallowed loudly but said nothing. The room seemed evasively quiet. She could hear the dragging of his brush on the canvas and the spitting of a log in the fireplace. But the usual sounds from the street – babies crying, dogs barking, the marching of soldiers, the clanking of buckets and churns – had stopped. In the silence an image returned to her, as sharp and clear as glass: Lorenzo watching a vine grafter mixing lime and dung and earth with his hands. As the grafter bent over his bucket, his breeches slipped down his narrow hips, revealing a strip of glistening, bronzed flesh. A peculiar light had come immediately into Lorenzo's eyes. A light she knew and loved. A light she thought was reserved for her. For other women even. She had looked away, not wanting to see or know. As she stared dumbly at the rows of vines, a passage from Lorenzo's first novel had crawled, uninvited, through her mind. A scene in which two men swam together in a millpond, then towelled each other dry. The exact words pressed into her head – as if her unconscious had stamped them on her memory . . . *he put his arm round me and pressed me against him, and the sweetness of the touch of our naked bodies one against the other was superb . . . our love was perfect for a moment, more perfect than any love I have known since . . .*

She rubbed hard at her forehead. She could feel a dull throbbing in her temples. As if a headache was coming on. She didn't want to think about such things any more. As if she didn't have enough to occupy her thoughts. She suddenly wished she'd kept Otto's letters. Why had she sent them to Ernest? Why hadn't she copied them out first? She ground out her cigarette and stood up. She would go and lie down. Shake off this headache.

As she passed Lorenzo on her way to the bedroom, she touched him lightly on the shoulder. 'I am going to rest for a bit, my dear.'

279

He turned to her and nodded in a distracted way. She felt the bone of his shoulder against her fingers. Then she saw his face, twisted and contorted as though his facial muscles were moving, almost gyrating, beneath his skin. As if he were a small animal with its paws caught in the teeth of a trap.

'Oh my dear, I love you. I want everyone to love you. You deserve it.'

'I love you too, my Queen Bee.' But he would not look at her, just continued trailing his brush down the canvas, long black lines like gashes round the buttocks of his subjects.

When she got to their bedroom she lay down in bed, pulled the covers over her head and cried. An hour later, she got up, blew her nose and pulled her carpetbag from under the bed. She listened for any sound of Lorenzo and when she heard nothing she opened the wardrobe and began pulling clothes from hangers, hurling them into her bag. A dress, shawl, blouse, skirt. As she opened and closed drawers, she said the names of her children over and over. *Monty, Elsa, Barby. Monty, Elsa, Barby.* Into the bag went her red stockings, her purple stockings, her string of glass beads, a stained flannel, a threadbare towel. She went through the pockets of Lorenzo's jackets, taking all the notes and coins she could find.

She kneeled down and fumbled with the clasp. And as she did so a memory of her wedding night returned in a frozen flash. The small hotel on the shore of Lake Lucerne. The room with its faded wallpaper of twisting ferns. Her crouching, naked, on top of the armoire. Ernest's nervous pacing in the corridor. The jangling of coins in his pocket as he opened the door. The smell of sweat and whiskey as she leapt upon him, pressing herself against the rough tweed of his jacket. She'd pushed her mouth, clumsily and eagerly, against his. Only to feel him pull away. Only to see his expression of mingled shame and disgust, to hear his stuttered protestations . . . *the flesh must be subdued, my snowflower . . . the flesh must be subdued . . .*

Afterwards, he'd thrust briefly, dutifully, joylessly in and out of her. She'd spent the rest of the night on the balcony, staring at the grey moths stumbling beneath the bright scoured moon, watching the dawn creep up from the lake. She could still recall that dawn – the wan bar of light and then the sun itself like a pale gold bullet hole, streaks of pink and yellow and orange spilling out and bleeding into the air. When the dawn chorus began, it was as though all the birds were singing from the bottom of the lake. Muted. Smothered. Nine months later Monty had arrived.

Frieda felt a tear roll down her face. Slowly, she began removing her things from the carpetbag, returning them to their hangers and drawers, putting Lorenzo's money back into his jacket pockets. She wiped at her tears with the sleeve of her dress and walked to the window. The lake was a vast sheet of wrinkled gleaming green. Beyond it rose the hills, pink and silver beneath the tapering light of the sinking sun. How beautiful it was. How humbling. She wondered where Lorenzo was. Perhaps he too was looking at the same view. Perhaps he was writing about it, in those supple, sinuous words of his. As if, somehow, he was at the very heart and kernel of the lake itself. Inside its bowels, its lungs, its blood. No one else could do that, she thought. No one at all.

SIXTY-ONE

Frieda

One morning, as Frieda sat wringing wet sheets over a tin pail in the garden, Lorenzo came rushing up from the village shouting, 'One hundred pounds, Queen Bee! One hundred pounds!'

She dropped the sodden sheets and ran to meet him, wiping her soapy hands up and down her apron.

'Duckworth is to publish *Sons and Lovers*!' He swept her into his arms and began to jig, his face pressed into her soap-sudded hair. 'I bet you think it's all because of you, don't you?'

'Yes,' she said, laughing and pushing him away. 'I wrote most of that book with my own blood.'

'Poppycock! But I shan't fight you today.' He picked up a wet sheet from the ground and threw it over her head, so that she was draped in dripping white. 'They're cutting ten per cent of it, but I don't care because they've paid me a hundred bloody quid!'

She threw off the sheet, tossed it over the wall and wiped the wet from her face with her apron. 'So what is being cut?'

'All that stuff you made me write about your breasts.'

'You wrote that! You are obsessed with my breasts . . . What else?'

'Bits with the mother. They thought it was too *oedipal*,' he said, making his voice shrill and sneering on the word 'oedipal'. 'They can do what the hell they like with it. I have my hundred pounds.'

He began jigging round the garden, his bony knees and elbows jabbing wildly at the air.

'We must celebrate, Lorenzo! Shall we buy wine for everyone in the village?'

'Later.' He stopped jigging. 'First I shall write an introduction to *Sons and Lovers*, a sort of manifesto . . . How we find God in the Flesh, in Woman . . . Through Woman we go back to the Father, but blinded and unconscious.'

Frieda tore the sheet from the wall and resumed wringing it over the pail. 'You are terrified of women,' she declared, twisting brutally at the sheet. 'You know we are superior, and more powerful, and it terrifies you. You hate it that you have to love me, that you can do nothing without me. I have seen right through you, like glass.'

'I won't fight you, not today.' Lorenzo gave a long cackling laugh. 'I'll write my manifesto and then we'll get drunk with the peasants.' He jigged into the house, his fingers clicking loudly above his head, like castanets.

Frieda struck at her forehead. He could be so infuriating! So exhausting! But his vitality, the sharp light in which he saw everything, his wild poetic fury, they made her feel as if she could breathe again. All at once she thought of Ernest's bed in the spare room. The sheets tucked tightly round the narrow mattress. The grey blankets. The single puny pillow, its feathers flat with age. If only she and Ernest had spent time together, unwed and free. Perhaps she would have had the foresight to see, to guess at the trajectory of their marriage. And all this pain could have been avoided. She shook out the wet sheet and tossed it over a bush. Yes, she thought. Otto, Fanny and the free love crowd of Munich were right: chastity was wrong; monogamy was wrong; marriage was wrong.

SIXTY-TWO

Frieda

It was ten months since she'd seen her children. Christmas day had been the worst, a day of such whistling emptiness she spent most of it grinding her face into the pillow. The doorbell had rung once, and Frieda had dashed to answer it, only to find the usual village boys plying their threaded strings of dead songbirds. Something about the tiny feathered bodies, so limp and lifeless, so casually killed and strung, had sent her back to bed in paroxysms of grief. But she could say nothing, tell no one. She and Lorenzo were almost entirely alone, friendless, outcast. Or so it felt to her.

She hoped to see her children at Easter. Ernest's last letter, after accusing her of betraying her noble birth, had implied this might be possible, and now her head was full of plans to return to England. There was nothing she longed for more than to hold her children. Sometimes she woke in the morning hearing their laughter floating up the stairs. For a brief second she wondered if she was back in Nottingham, if Monty, Elsa and Barby were about to knock on her door and burst into her room, as they once used to. Then she realised it was the local children on their way to the village school, jostling and laughing outside her window. The first time this happened she grabbed a sheet of paper and began writing a letter to Ernest, asking if she could come back. After two sentences, she'd torn the letter into pieces and thrown it into the grate. How could she ever go back? No one would speak to her . . . Ernest hated her . . . She would make it worse for the children, having a pariah as a mother. Besides which, Lorenzo couldn't survive without her. She would see them at Easter. They were *her* children and no one could prevent a mother seeing her own children.

But then a letter came from Ernest, thicker and stiffer than usual. Inside was a photograph of Barby and Elsa holding hands. How beautiful they looked – with their long curls. And they both had new hats on, with velvet ribbons round the crown and big brims to keep the sun off their faces. Frieda felt a sweep of grief. How could she wait until Easter? Easter was too late! She should go *now*. She should go to Hampstead and just knock on the door. Granny Weekley would have to let her in. She turned the envelope over. Read the single line in Ernest's careful, spiky handwriting. Felt the earth sway beneath her feet. The photograph fell from her hands and fluttered to the floor. Frieda gasped for air and stumbled to the ground, scrabbling for the picture. As she lay, facedown on the stone tiles, she felt a howl rise from some raw, bloodied place deep inside her. It burst from her, ripping through her body with such torment Lorenzo ran in from the garden where he'd been splitting firewood.

'What's the matter? What is it? Are you hurt?'

Frieda continued screaming but he couldn't make out the words. He knelt down beside her and was just about to touch her when he saw the photograph in her hand. He snatched it, glanced at the picture then turned it over. 'You will never see them again,' he read, his voice mincing and sneering. He stood up and flung the photograph at her.

Frieda's screams turned to hoarse sobs punctuated by gulps and gasps. 'They . . . are . . . my . . . children!' She twisted her head towards Lorenzo. Her face was red and raw, riven with snot and tears. 'Hold me – please hold me! I need you to love me!'

'No!' He reached down and began pulling her arm, dragging her across the floor. 'I never want to hear about those brats again!' He tugged her towards the couch, then dropped her arm so it fell heavily at her side. 'Stop footling with the idea of Ernest and those children – and your loathsome, detestable duty. I love you! I need you! More than they do!'

Frieda's sobs stopped abruptly. Startled, she turned to look at him and saw his fist raised above her, as though he was about to strike her. The muscles in her face froze. Her body braced itself. Something had changed in Lorenzo. She'd never seen him so altered before. This wasn't weary irritation. He was shaking with anger and bitterness, his face a spasm of hate.

'Why don't you just go back to Weekley! Go on! Take your fat arse and just go! Why should I put up with all your snivelling and moaning?' His fist swiped through the air, towards her. But then he drew it back towards himself, thumped it hard against his breastbone. 'I am the man in your life now! You chose me! Me!'

She stared at him, unable to speak. She felt as though he was swallowing her up with his rage. He had taken her away from everyone and everything. To this villa in the mountains, miles from anyone and anywhere. As if he wanted her expunged from the world. And now he was turning on her.

'Why haven't you forgotten them yet? Ten months! What's wrong with you?' His voice rose to a shriek.

Frieda buried her face in the velvet of the couch, trying to make sense of the strange, shifting emotions within her, and Lorenzo's crescendoing anger. He had been kind and sympathetic at first. Then peeved, and then annoyed. But now he was about to explode – as if he was jealous of her children, enraged by her love for them. When she realised this, Frieda felt a tenuous, inarticulate thrill. There was something about his aggression, the implied power and strength of it, that exhilarated her in an odd and confusing way.

After that, Frieda and Lorenzo argued often and violently. About her children, when she couldn't hide her grief. But also about his work, about books, about why the bellows didn't work properly or why the weather had turned. Other than the fights over her children, she relished their battles. The sound of Lorenzo's voice tearing through the air, fraying with emotion, made her feel curiously alive. And she knew their fights impelled him on to greater creativity, greater courage in his writing. She wasn't sure why this happened, but it did. He needed a little time to cool down (sometimes only a few seconds) and then he'd be back at his work, his pen hurtling across the paper. As if their arguments were a form of exorcism, a catharsis that freed him in some way. Believing this enabled her to bear the abuse he threw at her, the cruel taunts and humiliating insults that spewed unprovoked from his throat.

'I don't want us to be always cooing like two lovebirds,' he said after one particularly bitter argument about whether fireflies and glow-worms were the same thing. 'I need to be waging an inner war, with someone I love and trust. How else am I to experience the hinterland of the soul?'

'I know, I know,' Frieda crooned. Even as they fought, she felt the tugging of a secret thread between them, an infinitely elastic thread that bound her to him and him to her. Sometimes it seemed that he was wrestling with his own soul, and that she was helping him, much as a midwife bears the fury and pain of a birthing woman. But she refused to use her children, her grief, as fodder for his work. No, that was all hers.

'It takes strength and courage to love like this, my empress,' he added. 'Men aren't brave enough to love properly now. But we are. We are!'

'Yes, we have courage,' she murmured, her hand moving instinctively to her cheek. She could still feel the burn and fizz of his palm. She would try and keep her sorrow to herself. She would wear it like an iron chain around her heart. She would fight him over anything. Even fireflies. But not her children.

SIXTY-THREE

Frieda

The rain had been falling for three weeks when the first divorce papers arrived, with Ernest's allegations of adultery. They were delivered in hand by the English Consul, bowing, simpering, rubbing at his little oily beard, as the long scrolls of paper sheered from his briefcase. Lorenzo was on his hands and knees scrubbing the floor, but he leapt up, crying 'Don't be scared, Queen Bee. This means we can be married, at last!'

When the Consul pointed out the critical words, the accusation, Lorenzo chuckled and then repeated the words over and over, wiping his wet, foamy hands up and down his apron. 'It says we've "habitually committed adultery together" . . . I like that . . . "habitually committed adultery". So that's what we've been doing, eh? Habitually committing adultery!'

A day later, a final letter came from Ernest. Frieda opened it with trembling fingers, unable to forget the photograph with his punitive words on the back. But this letter was worse. Far worse.

I have done with you. I want to forget you and you must be dead to the children. You know the law is on my side.

So this is it, she thought. I have lost my children. A great cry of anguish rose up inside her. She'd never thought it would come to this. How could *her* children be taken from her? How was that possible? She bit down hard on her white lips and dropped the letter onto the fire. She didn't want to become hysterical again. She didn't want to infuriate Lorenzo. But she couldn't keep her pain to herself. She felt her body sink to the ground and then a rush of despair ran, unrestrained, through her and she pummelled her fists against the floorboards.

'You must make your choice!' Lorenzo shouted. 'It's either me or them!'

'The law!' she shrieked. 'Can they undo the fact that those children are mine?' She twisted round to see his booted foot hovering above her head. Shock ran over her, but was quickly engulfed by a wave of pain so immense, so sharp she could not quell it. How had it come to this? She threw her head hard against the floor.

'Those brats don't love you! And you don't love them. Get up!'

She could feel his boot, the heat and force of it, just above her head. But she didn't care. He could kick her and beat her and shout at her. She didn't care.

'They are my children! I brought them into the world, I loved them. How can he take them from me? It's not right! You promised a home for them. You promised!'

'It's not up to me. It's that fucking Weekley! Now get up and shut up!' And she heard Lorenzo's boots slapping against the floor and the thunderous slam of the front door.

Later he returned, chastened, with a bouquet of sodden winter roses and some persimmons. 'My empress, if you choose your children over me, how would they grow up with that burden of expectation, the weight of your sacrifice on their puny shoulders? I've seen the stifling love of a mother. Let 'em go free.'

That night Frieda sat smoking cigarette after cigarette, using the last one to light the next one, as she stared out over the black emptiness of the lake. The moon was very pale and fragile, a dimpled sliver of ice. In the darkness the lake looked gouged-out, like a vast crater. And yet she could hear the slop and slur of its waves as they chewed relentlessly at the shoreline. And she could feel the porcelain chill of the lake mist, clinging to her, settling inside her.

She shivered and looked up at the sky, sprinkled with tiny white stars. Her mind jolted back to their night of stargazing when they'd sprinted naked through the beech forest behind Alfred Weber's flat. Their *honeymoon*. Lorenzo still talked of it . . . those few idyllic days when they'd hidden the post, when she'd assumed Ernest would be kind and honourable, when they'd revelled in long days of lovemaking and blotted everything else from their minds. She raised her arm to point at the stars, to remind Lorenzo of that deliriously happy night, but then he slammed the vase of winter roses on the table and began talking again, one hand rapping on his chest.

'You must see sense. *I* need you now. They have their grandparents and their father. But I have no one. And I can't live without you.' His voice lapsed into morose silence and then he abruptly changed tack. 'I've had enough of this! You need to choose. Me and poverty or your children and comfort.'

She turned away from the lake. 'They are my children. *My* children! How can he refuse me?'

But Lorenzo's eyes flared with fury again and he picked up an ashtray and hurled it to the ground. 'Why aren't you going then? I wouldn't try to stop you!' He lunged for the fruit bowl, spittle flying from his mouth. 'If you really want to leave me, you can go back to England today. Go and do your filthy duty!'

Frieda heard the air whistle as the fruit bowl flew past her head. And then the sound of china smashing against the wall. Dazed, she surveyed the room. Thorns of broken crockery lay scattered across the tiles. Lemons, their skins split and gaping, reeled dizzily across the floor. She reached for another cigarette, waiting for the combative frisson that inevitably flared when Lorenzo turned on her. But she felt nothing. Just a dull weight pressing on the back of her neck. So this, she thought, is my life now. I have sacrificed my children for this.

'No more misery!' Lorenzo kicked viciously at a spike of china, sending it spinning into the corner of the room. 'I may hate you, I may rage against you, I may sneer at you – very well! It doesn't alter the fact that I love you.'

Frieda put the cigarette into her mouth and tried to strike a match but her hands were trembling and it took several scrapes before a flame was mustered.

'Say something!' Lorenzo balled his fists and boxed at the air. 'I love you with every fibre in my measly body. I love all of you. But only half of you loves me! I want all your love, not a paltry fraction of it!'

Frieda inhaled deeply and watched him in his impotent rage. He was shaking his fists as though he meant to thump her or beat her. 'I have left everything for you, Lorenzo, everything! How can you not see that?' Ragged wisps of smoke escaped from her mouth and hovered wearily in the air.

'But you haven't! You think about them all the time. Your wolfish mother love is like some demon, drawing you away from me!' His voice rose and pricks of light flared in his eyes.

She shook her head, refused to respond.

'Half your love is spent on those Weekley brats. How can you fully love me when you're always thinking about them? How? How?' As Lorenzo danced before her on the balls of his feet, his fists raised, his face red with fury, she was reminded of the goblins she'd read about as a child. Evil creatures who became so enraged they made terrible rash promises or committed hideous acts of malice. Her childhood had been full of stories about such creatures. And now she was living with one, had deserted her children for one. What had she done?

For two days, Frieda didn't speak. Lorenzo spent his time copying out Ernest's letters and chortling to himself. He tried to engage her by talking about the play he was writing, a play that would make full use of Ernest's diatribes. But Frieda didn't respond. And as she slunk around the apartment an idea started to take shape in her mind, slowly and reluctantly. An idea she couldn't throw off. It attached itself to her and spread. Until she could think of nothing else.

SIXTY-FOUR

Frieda

'Come and look, tell me what you think.' Lorenzo was standing at his easel drawing a landscape of cypresses, olive trees and a vaulting bridge. He gestured at the easel with his pencil. 'Have I got the bridge right?'

Frieda put down her book and stared out across the lake – purple, green, cobalt blue, foaming whitecaps racing over its surface. She didn't want to live without her children. How could she do it? How could she bear it?

'Won't you look?' Lorenzo pleaded.

She slowly raised herself from the couch. She'd positioned it in front of the window so she could watch the quaking fractals of silver light on the water but today there was no light, just rushing wind and squalling gulls. And everywhere her children's faces. 'Not quite soft and misty enough for me. But the bridge is good.' She knew her words sounded toneless and flat. She knew Lorenzo would be disappointed.

The smallest of things threw her back into the past now. Yesterday she'd seen a baby swaddled in a blanket being paraded by its proud mother. And as she looked at the baby, she'd seen Monty. Such a beautiful baby he'd been . . . his face as round and shiny as an apple, his fine golden hair like thistledown, his pale eyelids criss-crossed with violet veins. She had traced them with her finger as he slept, and thought him the most beautiful baby she'd ever seen. Until Elsa came. Elsa with her strawberry cheeks and little fat arms like sausages. Such a pretty baby. Prettier than all the other babies in Nottingham. And then Barby, with her big brown eyes and her button nose and her small gnarled head, like a walnut. Such a dear child, so affectionate. How her eyes had flashed! Not like a baby's eyes at all. Ernest had called them imperial von Richthofen eyes.

She stood up, took her coat and hat from the nail by the door. 'I'm going for a walk.' She saw Lorenzo look up, uncertainly, from his easel. She saw his mouth stiffen and the rigid set of his jaw. He hated it when she withdrew into herself, made herself unreachable like this. But what else could she do?

She walked until she got to the shore of the lake, until she felt its damp breath on her skin. A stiff wind blew across its surface, whipping the water into white waves and bucking seahorses. Stones. She knew you needed stones to weigh the body down. They must be big enough to hold the body underwater but not so heavy it sunk to the bottom without trace. She wanted her body recovered. She didn't want to sink to the bottom of the lake and rot with the fish, among the lost oars and rusty tins. She didn't want to be buried among slimed stones and tangled fishing lines.

She found some stones and put them in the pockets of her coat. Then she walked to the shore and stood staring across the water. Everywhere she looked she was reminded of her children. Beneath her feet were tiny pebbles, white and polished smooth, like babies' teeth. And she thought of her children's wobbly teeth. Remembered how Monty had sucked and probed with his tongue, until they were loose enough to pull. How Elsa had scrubbed at hers with the nailbrush to make them shine like pearls. And Barby's teeth? Had she lost the big ones at the back yet? Perhaps she had a wobbly tooth at this very moment.

Under the water, thick fronds of vegetation wavered like tentacles. Frieda crouched down and put her hand into the water, stroked the weed. How she longed to feel her children's hair again, to feel it sliding beneath her palm, to brush it and stroke it. Who was brushing their hair now? Was Aunt Maude doing it the way they liked, carefully without pulling at the knots? Was Granny Weekley bandaging their feet when they got blisters? Was Ernest reading to them at night and doing all the voices in the way they liked? She could feel the tears pooling in her eyes, like the rain that was falling from the sky in cold darts, pocking the surface of the water.

She unbuttoned her boots and peeled off her stockings. Then she took a tentative step into the water, gasping at the coldness of it. She felt its frozen fingers on the hem of her dress, its icy tongue lapping at her toes, the arches of her feet, her ankles. She put her hands into her pockets and gripped the rocks. Were they weighty enough? Should she find more? No, the huge heft of her grief would pull her under, hold her there.

She waded out a little further and the water rose to her calves, then her knees, then her thighs. Her skirts ballooned around her. She felt the water sucking against her skin, the coldness of it anaesthetising her limbs, making her flesh erupt into goosebumps. She looked out at the dark clouds curling on the horizon, and thought of Anna Karenina. She had read Anna's final soliloquy so often it was imprinted on her mind. Anna had given up everything for love, to feel fully alive again. And yet love had been both blessing and curse. And Anna had paid the ultimate price, made the ultimate sacrifice. Now she would do the same. She took another step and felt the sharp edge of a rock cut into the heel of her foot. Mud shifted, oozed, rose up between her toes. She was shivering now. Her feet and legs were becoming numb with cold. The wind and rain had disappeared quite suddenly and the lake was strangely quiet, still and unbroken. As though God had plucked the wind and the fishermen and all the wildfowl from its waters so she could die in solitary peace.

A fish jumped beside her, sending rippling cones across the water. She caught a glimpse of its silver body arcing into the air, heard the splash of it returning to the lake. And something in the sound it made, in the flash of light it created, jolted her from her numbed trance. She turned her head to the sky. A weak February sun had appeared among the clouds, sending pleats of pale light onto the surface of the lake, making it shimmer like raw silk.

She remembered Lorenzo's words about how beautiful and wonderful and godlike life was. Memories crowded in on her – the exploding pear blossom when she and Lorenzo first made love, the pungent leather of her father's riding whip as she pressed it to her face, the sapphire sweep of bluebells in Sherwood Forest, her children throwing green acorns from the branches of an oak tree. *I am not Anna Karenina. I will not be bullied into doing something so violent, so repellent. I want to live! And I will see my children again.*

When she got home with her wet skirts clinging to her and her body shuddering, Lorenzo glanced up from his easel and it seemed to her that his eyes were like two blue boats lost at sea. She rushed to him, knocking his easel over in her haste. And before he could protest, she had pulled off her wet coat and dress, torn the shirt from his back and pushed him roughly onto the couch. Quickly, she straddled him and they made love with such urgency neither of them noticed the coldness of her bones or the dampness of her skin. Later, as Lorenzo hung up her clothes in front of the fire, she told him she'd stumbled and fallen into the lake by mistake.

The following day, Lorenzo brought Frieda breakfast in bed and on her breakfast tray was a vase of olive branches. He went downstairs and she heard him scrubbing the floors and cleaning the windows and chopping the wood. When she got up, he stripped the bed and washed the sheets and pillowslips in the tin bath, then wrung them out and hung them before the fire.

'Now I'm going to wash your stockings,' he said, gesturing at the red stockings slung over the couch and stiff with mud. 'And then I'll darn them for you. They've holes at the heels. Now go and look in the larder, will you?'

Frieda went to the kitchen. All the copper pans gleamed. He must have polished them before she woke up. She pushed open the door of the larder and the smell of bitter oranges hit her. On the top shelf was an orderly line of jars. Marmalade! When had he made marmalade?

'While you slept, my Queen Bee,' he called. 'It's the best marmalade you'll ever taste, I promise. Now go to the parlour.'

She pushed open the door of the parlour. Huge, quivering chunks of light fell through the newly cleaned windows. On every surface stood vases and jugs, buckets and jars, each crammed with branches of almond blossom and myrtle and slender stems of wild cyclamen.

'It's my shrine to you. Now look at what the postboy brought.' He pointed to the table where an envelope lay, bearing Ernest's fastidious handwriting. It had been torn open and the end of a violet ribbon protruded from its ragged seal.

She frowned and looked enquiringly at Lorenzo. He was hopping round the table like a crow, watching her closely.

'It's your mad doctor's letters. Weekley's sent 'em back.' He stopped and gave a small skip, like a Morris dancer. 'And he's sent me this note from that old lover of yours, Dowson. He thinks I don't know about all your escapades. He thinks I'll send you home now. Bah! The fool has no understanding of love.'

The next day Lorenzo was back at work, writing so rabidly Frieda worried for his health. His normally pale skin had a pink hue, as though all the blood in his body had sprung to attention. He thrust a sheet of paper at her. 'Write down what you were telling me the other day, about the time your father jumped into a river with you on his shoulders and your head snapped right back. Don't miss anything out.' Then he ran the back of his hand quickly across his forehead. She tried to coax him away from his writing spot beneath the peach tree, but he shook his head, muttering 'Not yet, not yet. This potboiler will be the greatest book ever written.'

SIXTY-FIVE

Frieda

A week later, Frieda came up with a plan. She and Lorenzo were walking along the edge of Lake Garda after a long day of writing during which he had called out repeatedly to her: Did a mother feel differently about her sons? How did the kick of a foetus feel? How did it feel to give birth? How did it feel to spank your own progeny? On and on the questions went. Finally, Lorenzo flopped onto the couch beside her, coughing and shivering and insisting on an evening stroll to clear his head.

Outside, the damp air smelt of cypress trees and lemons. Above, the sky was pale and empty, the colour of dust. On the horizon, a cortege of dark clouds moved slowly towards them. I must speak quickly before the rain comes, thought Frieda. *Fräulein Winifred Inger* . . . the name rolled towards her like the clouds overhead, foreboding, unwelcome.

'I would like to go to London, Lorenzo.'

'Not yet, Queen Bee. My new novel is going so well. I'm facing the darkest corners of my soul, of *your* soul. I won't be able to work in that loathsome city.' He hesitated, narrowed his eyes. 'Is this about your children again?'

She reached towards him, gave his arm a mollifying squeeze. 'We're too much alone here.'

'Those children hang like a drawn sword between us.'

She pressed on, keeping her eyes fixed on a sailing boat that seemed to be spinning in circles out on the lake. 'There's something about me I've never told you. Never told anyone. It's in the very darkest corner of my soul.'

'Are you wanting to confess?'

'I thought you might like it for your new novel. The one about me and Elisabeth.'

'Why haven't you told me before? I thought we had no secrets?'

'I didn't want to think about it. It was too painful.' Her gaze strayed across the lake to the mountains, their peaks drowned in mist. 'But I'll tell you if you let me go to London.'

'Is it another lover? Some shameful thing you did with Otto Gross?' His top lip curled slightly although Frieda couldn't tell whether this was in scorn or in eager anticipation of more material for his 'potboiler'.

'You promise you'll let me go to London?'

'I'll come with you. But we shan't stay for long.'

She nodded. She knew he didn't trust her to return alone, that he was terrified she would return to Ernest, to her children. But she couldn't dwell on that now, not with the image of Fräulein Winifred Inger slipping in and out of the edges of her memory. She needed to find the right words to explain. Suddenly she felt as if Fräulein Inger was there, clinging to her like an old cobweb. Her spirit, her presence, seemed to have slipped over the misted mountains, slid across the water, snaked between the cypress trees that stood, like a line of sentinels, along the headland. Frieda batted at the air, pretending to flick away a fly. She would tell him quickly, get it over and done with. And then she could go to London and find her children. Before they forgot her entirely.

'We must keep travelling, Queen Bee. I need change, novelty – to shock me out of complacence. And I've got a mind to go south, towards Rome. So what is this secret you've kept from me?'

'When I was sixteen, I had a teacher called Fräulein Inger. She became a friend – Winifred.' With a great effort of will she kept her voice calm and steady. She was glad they were walking. She didn't want to see the expression on his face. 'I hated school. It was so regimented and stifling.'

'I know all that but you always said you didn't have any female friends,' he said, testily.

'She was more than a friend. We became very close. Only for a short time.' Frieda stopped, began phrasing her next sentence in her mind. Behind them the bells of the monastery started their ceaseless evening peal, the sound skimming across the lake, echoing off the mountains, until the whole valley seemed to vibrate with the ringing of bells.

'This is perfect for my potboiler. Carry on,' urged Lorenzo, suddenly moving as if he had beams of light under the soles of his feet. 'What did you do together?' His stride had lengthened, his fingers quivered at his sides. Frieda quickened her pace to keep up. She could feel the words queueing in her larynx, waiting to be released. 'I was desperate to please her, to be near her, to make her adore me. I thought she was the most perfect person in the world.' Frieda faltered. She could feel Lorenzo glistening beside her. With curiosity? Jealousy?

'Describe her.'

'She was a clergyman's daughter. Very athletic and proud, like a man. But tender and beautiful too. She took the swimming class and I wanted to be like her, swim like her, look like her.' Frieda paused and glanced at the darkening sky. Thunder was growling from beyond the mountains, and the coots and swans were gliding quickly to the shore of the lake. 'She held me in the water, in the swimming lesson, and I thought my heart would explode out of my body.'

'Then what happened?'

'She invited me to her house and we swam naked in a river.' Frieda shivered. How black and chill that river had been, how warm she'd felt in Fräulein Inger's arms, how she'd cleaved to her teacher in the dark surging water. Even now she could remember the hot insistence of Fräulein Inger's mouth as the icy water swirled round their knees. The way every ounce of her flesh had seemed to melt, like candle wax. The way Fräulein Inger's fingers had seemed to search into her flesh.

'Was that the end of it?' Lorenzo's voice sounded tight and restrained as though he wasn't sure how to respond. Suddenly Frieda didn't want to tell him any more. Winifred was hers, not his. She'd given him enough to get to London, surely?

'She went to Berlin. I wrote to her but she did not come back. I heard she got married.'

'But when you swam naked . . . what else happened?'

Frieda recognised the mulish set of his jaw, the determined glint of his eye. 'She kissed me in the river. That was it – just a schoolgirl crush.' But even as she said it, she could feel Fräulein Inger's tongue pushing her cold lips apart, edging into her mouth, slipping over her gums and her teeth, circling her tongue. She could feel Fräulein Inger's strong arms pulling her, the cut of Fräulein Inger's nails in the flesh of her upper arms, the marshy water churning and dragging between them. A few seconds later Fräulein Inger had released her, pulling back as if to catch her breath. And a current of desire and fear had torn through Frieda, so strong small whimpering sounds burst from her throat and her hands stretched involuntarily and desperately for her teacher.

'You love me, don't you?' Winifred had whispered, lowering her head to the surface of the river, licking at Frieda's neck, then running her tongue along each of her collarbones. Swilling with adulation and confusion, Frieda had whispered 'I love you, Fräulein Inger, I love you.' And Fräulein Inger had made her repeat the words, over and over. Refused to kiss her again until she'd said them fifty times.

'What sort of a kiss? And where did she touch you?' Lorenzo persisted, his face still tight but his eyes shifting, roused and restless.

'A full kiss on the lips. You can make the rest up, Lorenzo. Make it as titillating as you want.'

'Are you sure you haven't forgotten anything?'

Frieda shook her head and looked away. After her swim with Fräulein Inger, she'd had to wear long-sleeves to hide the rungs of damson-coloured ellipses that tattooed her arms. Later, she wondered if her fingers had done the same to Fräulein Inger, if Fräulein Inger's beautiful muscled body had carried the purple imprint of *her* fingertips.

Huge droplets of rain began falling from the sky. The cypress trees seethed and hissed beside them. Instead of walking more quickly, Frieda slowed down. There was something satisfying about the rain falling on her face, washing her clean of Winifred, absolving her in some curious way. She didn't want to think about it any more – all that pain, the way her young heart had wrenched in two. A week later, Winifred had disappeared abruptly, her absence unexplained by the other teachers. Night after night Frieda had written to her, begging her to come back. She left the letters at her teacher's cottage and cried herself to sleep each night, then woke violently, rushing downstairs to see if any post had come. After a month she heard, from another tear-stained girl at school, that Fräulein Inger had married a doctor and wasn't returning. Frieda's love had soured, slowly and bitterly. Other girls had come forward, claiming Fräulein Inger had written to them, sent them wedding photographs or pieces of wedding cake in ribboned boxes. One girl said Fräulein Inger had invited her to stay in her new Berlin home. Frieda said nothing. And when her love had hardened into something small and brittle, she wrapped it up and pushed it to a distant corner of her memory.

'I shall include it in my novel. It'll have a chapter all to itself,' said Lorenzo, nodding with approval. 'I shall call it "Disgrace". No I won't. I'll call it "Shame".'

'Shame?' repeated Frieda. 'Why? I am not ashamed.'

'Why haven't you told anyone then?'

'It hurts me to remember it. I am not ashamed,' she insisted. She recalled then that she had told someone. She'd told Otto, all those years ago. He'd seen it as another sign of her genius and her emancipation. Not something tinged with shame.

'And have you wanted to kiss other women since then?'

The memory of Lorenzo's hungry eye on the vine grafter's hips flashed before her – that split second of unmuzzled desire, of involuntary disclosure. Beyond the mountains a sudden streak of lightning lit up the sky, followed by a low snarl of thunder. 'No,' she said. 'A woman should be with a man. That is what nature intended.'

'Hurry up, Frieda! I need to get home and write this down.' Lorenzo had turned and was almost running, the legs of his trousers flapping in the wind, rain lashing at his back.

'I will catch you up.' She stood on the edge of the road and looked at the lake. Boats were rowing towards the shore, whitecaps frothed and bucked, the trees on the shoreline swayed and clutched at the darkening sky.

'London!' she shouted at his receding form. 'When can we go to London?' But the wind filled her throat, whipped her words away, tossed them into the rain. And Lorenzo was gone.

•

Villa Igea
Gargnano
Lake Garda
15 March 1913

Dearest Elisabeth

   Lorenzo has agreed that we can visit London. Thank God!
I have persuaded him that we are too much alone here and that I
must see my children. He likes having me trapped here, in the

mountains, with no one to entice me away. He likes the thought of us living like a pair of amorous outlaws. But even he now agrees that we are buried alive here and that such a very solitary life is not good for either of us.

He adores Italy, says it leaves the soul utterly free because it is so non-moral. But that is not the case for me. The Italians are so devoted to their children, so besotted and proud. If they knew I had left children in England they would chase me away with their pick axes and sickles! Lorenzo flies into a rage when I sink into sadness, so there is not a single person I can talk to. And every day some peasant woman shows me her child and I want to cry again.

There was one terrible morning, a few weeks ago, when I mentioned Monty. A sob erupted from my throat in the same breath. Lorenzo stormed out, threatening to move in with the monks at the monastery. I packed a bag, decided to go back to Ernest, left a note for Lorenzo and went to the jetty to catch the steamer. They said no steamer was coming because of the weather and they kept asking where my husband was. They laughed and shooed me away as if I was a lost dog. I stayed for two nights in a hotel, but then, defeated, I returned to our apartment and waited for Lorenzo.

I am glad of it now. If I returned to England alone, I would be entirely friendless. And penniless (I refuse to take any more of your money, dear Elisabeth). Ernest's family would make my life a living hell. And if Ernest had me back, it would be for show, for Cambridge, for his reputation. There is such bitterness in his heart. He would never trust me again. He (and all of petty, puritanical England) would think of me forever as a fallen woman, a loose woman. My misdemeanours would never be erased. No, that door is closed to me now.

Anyway, I must think of Lorenzo. Italy has turned him into a writing machine and when he writes to excess he becomes horribly ill and I must nurse him back to health. I know he will be a great writer, but this will only happen if I am with him. He tells me this repeatedly and I know it to be true. It is yet another thing that binds me to him. And I cannot destroy any more lives, can I?

So. I have perfected a mask for my grief. I keep it all to myself. My face is like alabaster, my eyes as dry as chalk. But all day I hatch a plan to see my children, to have them with me. Lorenzo and I quarrel and fight like cats, but I do not care. Because soon I will see my children!

Your loving sister
Frieda

PS He has agreed to get rid of that stupid title, Paul Morel, and use mine instead – Sons and Lovers. It is much better, don't you agree?

PART EIGHT

London 1913

'She hated herself, she wanted to
trample herself, destroy herself.
How could one become free?'

D.H. Lawrence, *The Rainbow*

SIXTY-SIX

Frieda

On her way to Hampstead, Frieda stopped at a sweet shop. Huge glass jars lined the wall behind the counter: butterscotch; lemon sherbets; toffees; liquorice laces; barley sugars; pear drops; mint humbugs; pineapple rock. She bought a bag of each, put them in her carpetbag, and walked, in a shimmer of nerves, up the hill towards Well Walk. The sun had thrown a generous sweep of gold across the Heath and the air was sweetly perfumed with mown grass. Frieda tried to calm herself by breathing in great lungfuls. For weeks she'd been mutely rehearsing her lines: *Hello, Granny Weekley. How are you? And how are Charles and Maude? May I just see my children please? How kind you are. Thank you, Granny Weekley.*

As she approached Well Walk, her heartbeat accelerated, her palms became clammy. Perspiration trickled from her armpits and her much-practised lines garbled in her throat. She had a peculiar sensation of all her previous incarnations collecting around her, willing her on. Tiny Fritzl, diving from rocks and swimming with frogs. Little Frieda, shinning up pear trees and squeezing into foxholes. Young Frieda, dreaming of adventure and love. Married Frieda. Adulterous Frieda. Queen Bee Frieda. The many Friedas seemed to crowd around her in an undisciplined scrabble.

She turned into Well Walk, pulled back her shoulders and walked with an attempted insouciance towards the Weekley house. She would ring the bell. Assertively. She wouldn't shake or tremble. She had nothing to fear. They were her children. She'd be polite but firm with Granny and Maude. She'd take her children in her arms and hold them for a very, very long time. Relish their gluey lips on hers. Stroke their hair, their cheeks, the downy napes of their necks. Then she'd take them on the Heath, and lie in the sun with them, feeding them sweets as if they were baby birds. She'd check their hair for lice. She'd pinch their ribs to make sure they were eating enough. She'd examine their teeth for rot and make sure their toenails were properly clipped. *And then I will smuggle them into my bag and run away* . . . her lips curved into a smile.

She could hear the thwack of a carpet beater. *Thwack*! *Thwack*! That would be Maude – cleaning as usual. Her smile spread. Maude would be easier to deal with than Granny. Perhaps Granny had gone out. Perhaps the children were alone with Maude – at their studies or helping their aunt with a spring clean. Frieda's stride lengthened. Her arms swung more loosely. Her bag with its bounteous contents felt as light as a leaf. The house was just ahead of her. *Thwack*! *Thwack*! She looked up, half-expecting to see Maude in the street, rug and beater zealously in hand.

But there was no Maude. As she got closer she saw the front door was closed and all the shutters drawn. She frowned. Adjusted her body. Moved with a rehearsed deference towards the front door. Raised her hand in the direction of the door knocker. Paused. The brass knocker was dim with tarnish. Dust slept along its bevel. Her eyes slid to the window. Weeds crept along the outer sill. Inside, dead moths and flies sprawled. The glass was dark with dust. Strands of cobweb clustered loosely in the corners. She lifted the knocker. Heard it echo through the hall, up the stairs, into the attic.

She stepped back and surveyed the house. Its curtained windows yawned. A skin of grime lay over the peeling paintwork. Purple thistles bristled from crevices in the stonework. She felt her heart fall through her body. Heard a sound like tearing paper in her throat.

She knelt down and opened her bag, her knees scraping on the damp, crusted stone. This is how it feels to kneel beside a grave, she thought. She took out all the bags of sweets and lined them up on the doorstep. *Such pitiful tokens of a mother's love.*

When all the sweets were arranged in a tidy mound, she went to the house next door and rang the bell. An upstairs window opened and a man's head appeared.

'Where have the Weekleys gone?' Frieda pulled down the brim of her hat so he wouldn't see her pink-edged eyes.

'I don't know.' His moustache moved in indolent circles as he spoke.

'When did they go?'

'September last. Left no address.' He withdrew his head and raised his arms as if to push the window closed.

'Wait! Please. You must have some idea where they've gone? Please?' She put a pleading, steadying hand against her chest.

'The boy said he was going to a school called St Paul's. Could be in Timbuktu for all I know.'

She heard the rattle of the sash and a flat thud as the window closed. As she turned back to the street, a surge of anger shoved aside her pain and disappointment. How dare Ernest do this! How dare he!

SIXTY-SEVEN

Ernest

From his new study in West London, Ernest could smell the River Thames. It was particularly odorous today: fishy with an undertone of sewage. He didn't have the energy to close the window. All this travelling up and down from Nottingham was exhausting him. He sat at his desk, nodding his head in a gesture of respect at a first edition of Trollope's *Lady Anna*. He caressed its tan leather spine and ran a finger gently over its brittle pages. Its bindings gleamed. Its embossed title had an effulgent certainty that warmed and comforted him. He'd purchased the book in an act of now-unusual extravagance, while visiting Mr Wells, the firearms dealer, last week. Mr Wells, it had turned out, dealt not only in pistols but in first editions of well-known novelists.

He opened the book and sniffed. Even the smell comforted him – ecclesiastical, hallowed, dusty. He pressed the pages to his nose, letting the scent distract him from the blare of his mother's voice. He could hear her now, telling someone – the children? – that if they resisted the devil, Satan would flee. He looked down at the page in front of him. Words, words, words. His whole life had been built on words. Translating them, dissecting them, understanding them, tracking their provenance. And yet they had failed him. He had been unable to keep his wife happy, unable to understand her, to talk to her.

He looked up, suddenly aware of Monty standing awkwardly in the doorway. His eyes flickered to his desk drawer. He breathed out, relieved he'd remembered to lock the drawer after oiling his new Lancaster pistol.

'Yes, Monty?' His voice came out more sharply than he'd intended. Why did that always happen to him? He moved his jaw from side to side in an attempt to loosen it. Perhaps that would soften his words.

'I f-found this.' Monty held out an ivory-handled clothes brush, the von Richthofen crest just visible beneath his fingers.

Ernest's jaw locked. Why did the boy keep finding these wretched things, presenting them as though he'd panned for gold and found an ingot?

'I've treated myself to a new first edition for my collection, Monty. Indulgent, I know. Would you like to hold it?' Ernest nodded at the book in his hands.

'W-won't Mutti need this? Won't she be needing her things?' Monty tightened his fingers round the brush.

Ernest put his book on the desk and opened his hand. 'Give the brush to me. I'll put it somewhere safe.'

Monty drew back, his fingers gripping its ivory handle.

'Can I keep it, Papa?'

Ernest felt a deep sympathy for his son. He wanted to reach out to Monty, to hold him. Perhaps share the ache of betrayal with him. How comforting it would be to take his son in his arms. He sensed his own yearning, wrestling with an inner resistance. Why could he not simply reach out and touch Monty? Damn it all, I will, he thought. Slowly, his arm crept out again. His fingers beckoned, tentatively, to his son. But to his dismay, Monty recoiled into the hall. Ernest quickly withdrew his hand and placed it squarely on the cover of his new first edition.

'Th-the boys at school,' said Monty, slipping the clothes brush behind his back.

'Yes?'

'They talk about their mothers.' Monty paused, rocking on his heels.

'And what do they say?'

'Archibald's mother is a suffragette. And George's mother has five pugs that she dresses in knitted boots and vests. And William's mother has hair that goes to her knees and she lets him brush it when he gets full marks in Greek. And Leonard's m-mother . . .' Monty's chin wavered and he began blinking rapidly. Ernest turned away, feeling his throat close tight.

'What does Leonard's mother do?'

'P-p-pillow fights.'

Sharp lines shot up between Ernest's eyes, into his receding hairline. 'Pillow fights?'

'Like M-Mutti used to have. With us.' Monty's voice quavered and cracked.

Ernest fixed his eyes on his new book again. He was aware of a thin wind coming up through the floorboards, snapping round the sharp corners of his stacked books, and he wished it would carry him away. Far far away.

'What should I say about Mutti, Papa? What do I tell them?'

'Do all your friends have mothers?'

'Yes. Except Harold. His mother is dead.' Monty shifted uncertainly from foot to foot.

'There's your answer, Monty. You say she is dead.' Ernest's eyes slid to his desk drawer. Then back to his son. Monty was staring at him, pale, motionless, horrified.

'D-dead?'

Ernest gave a forced laugh. 'So Harold doesn't feel left out.' Monty was still staring at him with glassy eyes and a stupefied expression, so he added, 'I've explained this before. We must think of her as dead.'

'How do I hon-honour her?' Monty swallowed and looked at the floor, as if he couldn't bear to look at his father any more. 'At school and church they say honour thy father *and* thy mother.'

Ernest coughed and tried to think of a response. How could he explain that she was unworthy of their honour? That her sin had brought disgrace upon them? That she had broken his heart? His fingers moved over the cover of his book in anxious whorls as he tried to formulate an answer.

'Barby and Elsa think she's coming home. When Granny says Mutti doesn't love us any more, they think it's because she has an illness. Like amnesia. Where you forget who you are.' Monty's voice tailed off.

'We must not tell them anything, Monty. It's not proper that young ladies should hear such – such immoral things.' Ernest gulped. He could hear his mother in the kitchen, calling on the Good Lord. He wished Monty would go. And leave him alone with his first edition, and his pistol. Real, solid things with certainty and weight. He pressed his fingers against his eyes. All this thinking. All this questioning. How barbarous it all was.

When he opened his eyes, Monty had gone, and his mother's voice was floating down the hall . . . 'She was made by Satan himself – Satan himself!'

SIXTY-EIGHT

Frieda

It was a bright June day when Frieda made her first visit to St Paul's School. She took the son of Lorenzo's editor, Bunny Garnett, who was keen to help. Lorenzo insisted on accompanying them, prowling up and down Hammersmith Road while she and Bunny conducted a thorough reconnaissance of the area, checking the exits and entrances and trying to guess which door Monty would come out of. Whenever she saw a uniformed boy flitting across the lawn or lurking on the steps, she hurried forward straining to see if it was Monty. After a week of lurking round the school grounds with Lorenzo and Bunny in tow – and still no sight of Monty – she decided to enlist the help of her new friend, Katherine Mansfield. Katherine was a writer from New Zealand who, like Frieda, was living in sin. Together they walked up and down in front of the school, day after day, waiting for a glimpse of Monty, and sharing the burden of their respective predicaments. Lorenzo traipsed glumly behind or watched them from the omnibus stop on the opposite side of the road.

'He does not trust me,' whispered Frieda to Katherine. 'He thinks Monty will take me from him.'

'Why would he think that?' Katherine turned and looked curiously at Lorenzo skulking under a tree with a vinegary expression on his face.

'Because he knows the power of a mother's love. He has been a victim of it.' Frieda looped her arm through Katherine's and swivelled her round, back towards the school gates. It was midday – the hour when the boys broke for lunch. She knew the timetable exactly now: morning break, lunch break, tea break, home time. She knew which buildings they came out of and which buildings they streamed back into.

'I do think your old husband is an ogre,' said Katherine sympathetically. 'To not let you see them at all.'

'He loved me absolutely and so now he hates me absolutely. And I know they all blame me.' Frieda scoured the knots of boys walking out of the classrooms in their grey trousers and blue blazers. Why didn't Monty come out? Where was he?

'But weren't you aware of the law when you ran away with Mr Lawrence? You must have known you would lose the children.' Katherine prodded impatiently at the ground with the tip of her silk parasol.

'I didn't run away with him. I was just going to my father's party and he was going to his relatives and we thought we'd have a few days in Germany together. But then he wrote to Ernest and everything blew up. Anyway, I'm their mother!'

'You're also an adulterous, deserting wife. Didn't you know that there's a special punishment reserved for mothers? Anyway, the laws here are archaic.' Katherine's gaze followed Frieda's across the playing field to a herd of small grey boys pushing and jostling. 'I hope Mr Lawrence has been worth it. Is he a terrific fuck?'

Frieda snorted but kept her eyes fixed on the boys, squinting from one to another. She would have liked to confide in Katherine. But something in her friend's eyes – something a little tart and sharp-rimmed – stopped her. She didn't fully trust Katherine, not enough to tell her how she sometimes thought of other men when she lay with Lorenzo, that she suspected Lorenzo thought of men when he took her so enthusiastically from behind. And how could

319

she articulate the feelings Lorenzo inspired in her? The way he made her feel grateful for being alive . . . The way he seemed to need her with the whole of his being. No one, not Ernest, nor Otto, not even her children now, needed her like Lorenzo did.

'It always seems to me that he sucks at your health and vitality like some sort of vampire.' Katherine patted lightly at her hair with her fingertips. 'And how you bear all that buggery I've no idea. He's told John all about it.'

'It helps him. It's my gift to him,' Frieda retorted, keeping her voice off-hand. Katherine's words perturbed her, made her feel a vulnerability she didn't want exposed. She suspected her *gift* was merely a means of keeping Lorenzo close, a pathetic unconscious attempt to prevent his lusty eye straying to other men.

'Haven't you given him enough already?'

'And what about everything he has given me? He has helped me see beauty in everything. He has loved me for who I am. He has let me be part of his life – every bit of it, not just the homey bit preserved for wives. He has given me a life broader and richer and deeper than I would have with any other person.' She heard herself gushing but she didn't care. She didn't want anyone's pity and certainly not Katherine's.

'I'm merely saying that forfeiting three children is a high price,' said Katherine waspishly.

Frieda ignored her. More and more boys were streaming from the school and she didn't want to miss Monty. And then she saw him. A cry leapt into her throat. 'Oh Katherine – it's him!' She pointed at a boy walking from the building with two other boys, all of them clutching satchels and looking at the ground. 'How tall he is!'

'Are you sure it's him?' Katherine asked, shading her eyes with her hand and squinting at the boy with the fair hair and the scooped-out cheeks. 'The tall one? He can't possibly be thirteen. He looks like a fully-grown man.'

'Oh, it's him! It's Monty!' Frieda gripped Katherine's arm. 'I can't go. You go! Go and get him for me. Bring him to me! Hurry – he's nearly at the refectory.' Frieda gave Katherine a little push and then ran her hands over her hair and down the bodice of her new dress. Her shaking fingers adjusted the rose in her lapel and she ran her tongue quickly over her lips. How nervous and overwrought she was. What if he didn't want to see her? What if he didn't recognise her? What if he'd forgotten her?

She watched Katherine approach Monty. He looked up, startled. And then he was walking hurriedly in her direction, his overlong arms swinging like broken branches at his side.

'You? Is it you?' he stammered. His eyes slid over her shoulder to Lorenzo skulking at the school gates.

'Oh Monty! It's me! How tall you are. Oh Monty!' Frieda's eyes filled with tears. How different he looked, taller and thinner as though he'd been stretched on a rack. His face was angular and sculpted now. He'd lost all his puppy fat. Or weren't they feeding him properly? 'Are you eating well, *mein Liebling*?' She leaned towards him, desperate to hold him, but he moved back and his eyes flickered sideways to the boys swarming into the refectory.

'Can you come out and have cake with me? Katherine, won't you take Lorenzo away so Monty and I can have tea together?'

'I'm not allowed to leave the grounds alone.' Monty shifted from one foot to the other while Katherine sloped away.

'Go and tell your teacher that an old aunt has arrived to take you for lunch. Go on, Monty! Tell them I'm your Aunt Maude.'

Monty loped off and reappeared a few minutes later, smiling sheepishly. 'I can come out for a bit.'

'We shall eat strawberries and cream.' She sighed and folded Monty's hand into the crook of her arm. And as she felt his hand, she noticed how the bones jutted, how depleted his hand felt despite its long tapering fingers. Tears sprang to her eyes again. 'They are

not feeding you properly, Monty! Your hands were so fat before . . .
Oh my dear!'

Monty nodded in agreement. 'Granny's puddings are inexcusable.'

Frieda gave a choking laugh. 'Oh you funny boy! What a peculiar
word for a pudding, inexcusable.'

She took him to a café she'd earmarked on an earlier trip. But as
soon as she sat down at the little table with its sprigged tablecloth,
she began crying. She gulped, bit her lips, clenched her teeth, but she
couldn't bring her weeping under control. The tears dripped from
her nose onto the linen. Every time she thought her tear ducts must
be empty, she turned her watery gaze to Monty and started crying
again. A waitress placed two bowls of strawberries and a large jug
of cream in front of them. Frieda wept into the strawberries. And
then into the cream.

'Here Mutti, take this.' Monty passed her a handkerchief that
looked as though he'd cleaned his shoes with it. She pressed it to
her face, breathed in its smell and wiped it over her eyes.

'Don't cry. Tell me what you're living off, what you're doing.'
Monty bit into a large strawberry, squirting red juice over Frieda
which made her give another juddery laugh.

'I wrote a novel,' she replied between little sobs. She was glad
Lorenzo wasn't there to dispute this. She didn't want Monty to
think of her as a mere muse.

'Oh, there's no money in writing.' Monty took another strawberry
in his long, thin hand and dipped it carefully into the cream jug.

'You sound just like your father.' Frieda wiped her eyes again
and pushed Monty's handkerchief into her bag. It would be her
keepsake, a reminder of him. 'Monty, will you draw me a picture?
Something I can put on the wall of my bedroom?'

'What shall I draw?' Monty frowned but Frieda had come
prepared and was already pushing paper and coloured pencils across
the table.

'Whatever you like. A self-portrait?'

'Oh no! I couldn't do that. I'm a hopeless artist.' Monty eyed the coloured pencils warily.

'Draw your school so I can always remember where I saw you.' Frieda sniffed, trying to stop the wave of tears building inside her again. 'Can you meet me tomorrow?'

'Where?' Monty kept his eyes on the picture he'd started, using first one pencil and then another, and making small, hard strokes that Frieda was sure would mark the tablecloth.

'Turnham Green, near the station. Can you bring Elsa and Barby too?' She saw Monty's top lip wobble and felt another ripple of remorse run through her. 'You know I could not stand Nottingham and the life any more. It was killing me.'

She saw Monty push his pencil so hard the paper tore beneath the lead. 'It was nothing to do with you. I know you can't understand now, but you will later on. I want to be able to see you, Monty.'

'Shall I ask Papa?' Monty's words came out like a small tremble and tears began welling in his eyes and then spilling down his peaky face and dropping off the bony ridge of his nose onto his drawing.

'No, just bring the girls and meet me at Turnham Green. Come – I must take you back.' Reluctantly she fished his handkerchief out of her bag and offered it back to him.

He wiped his eyes and sniffed into it. 'Would you like a tour of the grounds before you go?'

'I would like that very much, *mein Liebling*.' She offered him her arm and together they walked back to his school. Out of the corner of her eye she glimpsed Lorenzo loitering in a doorway, a stiff black shadow. She wondered if he'd been watching her through the café window, making sure she didn't abscond with Monty. She tossed her head disdainfully. What did she care anyway. She had her boy now, her beautiful boy!

After Monty had shown her round the school and pointed out where he'd scored a try last season and where he'd got five runs the previous week, she pressed half a crown and a letter into his hand. She'd written and rewritten the letter so many times, its exact words were cut into her head.

'Don't tell anyone you've seen me. It must be our secret, Monty.' Tears rose in her eyes again. Behind her, Lorenzo prowled, bristling and suspicious. She felt a flush of guilt and regret. All this pain and sadness she'd caused. But then she thought of the following day, imagined holding, kissing, smelling all her children. And the prospect brought such joy, her sadness softened, diffusing into the pale afternoon air.

•

Monty, mein Liebling

I have written this letter so many times and still I cannot get it right. But I want you to know I love you and I love your sisters – more than you can imagine, more than you will ever know. It was your father I left, not you. I know the Weekley family will not tell you this. But it is true.

I did not mean to go in the way I did. I truly thought I would return. But Mr Lawrence made a return impossible and your father, with his anger and jealousy, did not help.

All of this has broken my heart. But my destiny is now with Mr Lawrence. And I hope you will meet him very soon and like him as much as I do. He is an extraordinary man – a genius – with an important future ahead of him. I cannot leave him for he depends on me utterly. But I hope he will be like a second father to you, when Ernest calms down. Do not be hard on your father – it is only that he loved me very much indeed. I am trying to find it in me to forgive him and you must do the same.

Now destroy this letter, mein Liebling. And never forget that I am . . .

Your own dear Mutti

324

SIXTY-NINE

Monty

Monty didn't want to destroy his mother's letter. It was all he had of her now. He put it in the pocket of his trousers and kept it clasped between his fingers as he walked home. He could feel his lip trembling. Lugubrious drops of sniffle kept falling from his nose onto the pavement or onto his tie. He was glad none of the St Paul's boys were around to see him.

He'd wanted to move his mother to the far edges of his memory, where she couldn't hurt him any more. But how could he do this now he'd seen her? She said she loved him but how could he be sure? Other mothers didn't leave their children.

For twelve months he'd said nothing about her, not once mentioned her name, except for the dismal conversation with his father. But tomorrow he would take his sisters to meet her, and then he'd be able to say her name again. If he wanted to. Would he want to? Monty frowned and wiped his dripping nose with the back of his hand. He didn't know what to think. But he knew someone was lying. And he knew it was wrong to lie. His father said she didn't love them. And so did Granny Weekley and Aunt Maude. But she said she did love them. If she loved them, why had she left? And why did she want Hungry Fox to be his second father? He already had a father. He felt a spike of something sour rise up in his throat and then something corkscrewed sharply in his stomach.

He took a big breath. It was how he'd taught himself to ease the cramps that appeared sporadically in his abdomen. 'Tomorrow we'll see her. And we'll make her come home! Barby and Elsa will make her come home!' He said the words out loud. They sounded more hopeful, fatter with possibility than if he said them in his head. 'She will see that she loves us best.' And his fingers closed protectively round her letter.

SEVENTY

Barby

'Where are we going? Why aren't you going to school?'
Barby and Elsa skipped behind Monty who was smiling
secretively and trying to be all grown-up and important.

He grinned and pointed ahead. 'We're going there, to the Green.
Just to sit for a bit. And then you can go to school.'

'But we'll be late,' Elsa protested, gripping her satchel a little
tighter. 'We'll get in trouble.'

'Who cares about a bit of trouble. This is an adventure! Will
there be sweets?' Barby gave a small jump of delight.

'You'll be late, Monty. You're already late. This is silly. Why
won't you tell us?' Elsa sniffed and tilted her chin a little higher.

When they got to the Green, Monty stopped and looked around.
Bowler-hatted men in dark suits marched across the grass towards
the station, a couple of uniformed nannies pushed perambulators
towards the church, a clutch of school children in matching straw
hats strolled in the direction of the High Road. And then a woman
came running towards them, one hand clutching her hat and the
other outstretched in the air, her face split by a huge smile.

'It's Mutti!' Elsa ran towards her and Barby followed, shouting,
'Mutti's back! Mutti's back!'

She scooped them up and held them to her, one under each arm, and her eyes were all silvery like minnows. When she released them, they started dancing round her, skipping and jumping and calling, 'Mutti's back! Mutti's come home!'

'Come, let's sit on this bench. Oh my dears!' She couldn't stop touching them – stroking their hair, kissing their cheeks, nuzzling their necks, patting their knees.

'Are you going to the house now? Where's your luggage? Does Papa know you're coming home today?' Barby bounced up and down with excitement. She had waited for a year, a very long year, and now Mutti was home.

Frieda exchanged a look with Monty. 'Do they not know?' she whispered.

'No,' he mumbled, looking at his feet.

'Are you better now? Has your memory come back? Have you got any sweets for us?' Barby loosened a coil of hair from Frieda's head and twisted it round and round her finger. She suddenly felt as light as ribbon, so light she could fly away on a gust of wind. What a lovely feeling it was! Like a kite when its strings had been let go. For a minute she forgot the grip of her too-small navy wool jacket, and the tightness of her outgrown belt.

'I can't come back. You must come to me.' Frieda rubbed her eyes with the heels of her hand and Barby could see they were full of tears. 'But I am hoping to see you – often. It is up to your father now. You must tell him you want to come and stay with me.'

'If you're better, why aren't you coming home?' The colour had drained from Elsa's face as she stared at Frieda, her smile frozen on her lips.

'I am marrying another man soon. But I still love you all, very much.' She swallowed loudly and a tear rolled down the side of her face and into her ear.

'Why don't you come and visit us then?' Barby slid onto her mother's knee and wound her arms round her mother's neck. 'Please stay, Mutti! Please stay with us. Granny is always grumpy and doesn't give us nice food. And Aunt Maude is always cross and we have to call her Mama when she's not our mama.' Barby tightened her grip, pressing her face into her mother's warm neck.

'I don't understand,' Elsa said, stiffening and moving away. 'We thought you were ill . . . with amnesia. Or in a lunatic asylum. Why has no one told us this?'

'Your father won't let me write to you. I have no address for you. I am so sorry, Elsa.'

'So everyone at home knows you're marrying someone else – and no one told us?'

Frieda nodded miserably and pressed her nose into Barby's hair.

'We thought you were ill!' Elsa stood up and turned angrily to Monty. 'You knew, didn't you?'

'Don't spoil this little moment, *mein Liebling*,' Frieda begged. She patted the bench. 'Come and sit beside me again. I have to go soon and you have to go to school.'

'Who are you marrying?' Elsa perched on the end of the bench and glared at her mother.

'Mr Lawrence. Do you remember him?'

Elsa looked disbelievingly at her. 'Papa's creepy student with the red moustache?'

'Oh, Elsa, he is a genius! He is unlike any other man I have ever met. He will be a great man one day. His books will change the world! I want him to be your second father.'

'But Papa's book is out now. It's been reprinted several times. He's a great man too.' Elsa's voice rose. 'And I don't want a second father!'

'I cannot come back. But I want to see you all. I must see you all! You are *my* children.' She reached out for Elsa's hand and squeezed it, but Elsa shook her off.

'I love you, Mutti,' Barby said, planting a wet kiss on her mother's cheek. 'I'll ask Papa to let us see you. He's a kind man.'

'Ask him, yes! But do not say you have seen me. He will be very angry if he knows I have met you like this.'

Across the Green, the church bells started their mournful tolling and a train rattled past. Thick white clouds had rolled in and blotted out the sun. Frieda looked at the clock on the church. 'Oh my dears! You must go to school now or we will all be in trouble. You won't forget me, will you?' And she pulled each child into her, pressing kisses on their heads.

That evening, Monty was unable to eat and pushed away his plate of mutton stew with a look of undisguised revulsion. Barby forked the paltry chunks of grey meat round her plate, carefully separating them from the coins of soggy carrot and the cubes of boiled potato. Elsa ate with her usual meticulousness but paused her chewing at regular intervals and stared out of the window, as if she was expecting a visitor.

'Your food is getting cold,' snapped Aunt Maude. 'Stop playing with it, Barby. Monty, what's wrong? Is it your stomach again?' She gave a long weary sigh.

Monty nodded and stared at the mottled leaves of poison ivy twined round the rim of his plate.

'When will Mutti be well enough to come home?' Barby turned to Aunt Maude and looked straight into her darkly-circled eyes. It seemed to her that Aunt Maude had changed since moving to Chiswick. She had become brittle and unyielding. There was something severe about her now, as though she had hardened like a piece of bread left out too long.

All the children turned their gaze on Aunt Maude, waiting to see how she would respond, waiting to see if she would lie to them again.

'She's been ill for more than a year now,' added Barby, mashing a lump of potato with the prongs of her fork. 'Perhaps she's better now.'

Monty reached hastily for the water jug. It wavered perilously in the air, as though it was too heavy for him. And when he poured, he missed his glass and water streamed across the crotcheted tablecloth.

'Oh Monty! How can you be so clumsy?' Aunt Maude sprang up from her chair and snatched the jug from him. 'Run to the kitchen and get a cloth. Hurry!'

'It's the devil's work.' Granny appeared in the dining room, her arms crossed on her stout bosom. 'There is something devilish in these children today, Maude. Idle hands are the devil's own workshop. Can you take them to church?'

'No!' Barby's voice erupted from her throat. 'I won't go to church! I won't! I want Mutti!'

Granny's eyes narrowed to black slits. She looked at each child in turn. Monty hurried out of the dining room, his hands cradling his belly. Aunt Maude busied herself pushing back the tablecloth and dabbing at the pool of water with her napkin. Elsa stared fixedly at her plate.

'That woman has brought shame and disgrace on this family. She left you. She didn't love you. Now go to your room, Barby.' Granny moved towards Barby's chair and pulled it away from the table with such force Barby lost her balance and fell to the floor.

'You are the devil's own child! Now get up and go to your room and when you've calmed down, your mama will take you to church.'

'*Sie ist nicht meine* mama! *Sie ist nicht! Sie ist nicht!*' Barby pulled herself up and lurched towards the door.

'One more word of German and your grandfather will take his belt to you!' Granny bellowed.

'She is not my mama either.' Elsa shoved back her chair and ran after Barby, slamming the door behind her so that the crockery rattled and chinked and the window panes shook in their frames.

As the two girls sat in their room, wiping at their tears with the hems of their dresses, Elsa turned to Barby and said, 'I still love Mutti but I hate her too. Sometimes I really hate her. I didn't know you could love and hate someone at the same time. Is that wrong?'

'You can confess to God when we go to church,' sniffed Barby. 'You can't love and hate someone at the same time.'

'I didn't hate her before this morning. I just loved her. But now I love her and hate her and I don't know which feeling is coming next.'

'She's our mutti! You must always love her.' Barby pulled her bear from the end of her bed and rocked him against her chest.

'But she left us! She left us.'

Barby stared at Elsa. Her sister's voice frightened her. It was so cold, so hard. So definite. She put her lips to her bear's torn ear and began to sing a lullaby, *Schlafe, mein Kindlein, schlaf ein*. Their mother had sung it to them as children and in her head she heard Mutti's crooning voice.

'No!' shouted Elsa. 'You must never sing that song again! Never! Do you hear me?'

Barby gripped her bear, pressing his soft head against her neck. 'What shall I sing to him then?'

But Elsa said nothing, just shook her head and stared at the crucifix on the wall.

SEVENTY-ONE

Frieda

'I found this on the lawn, Frieda. I think it's for you.' Edward Garnett shuffled towards the dining table, where Frieda sat glumly consuming slice after slice of cold toast with honey. It was four days after her meeting with the children and she and Lorenzo were staying in Kent at the home of his editor, Edward Garnett.

'It would appear the sender felt unable to use the letterbox. It's a bit dewy.' He wiped the letter half-heartedly on his dressing gown. 'They must have deposited it in the middle of the night. Most peculiar.'

She looked at the envelope, hoping it might be from the children. The handwriting was vaguely familiar. Efficient loops and fluent flourishes, but with a hurriedness and panic that made the letters cant drunkenly across the envelope's face. Not from her children. Disappointed, she swallowed down her mouthful of sticky toast crumbs and reached for a cigarette.

'Not bad news I trust?' Edward had already turned to leave and Frieda heard his pace quicken.

'I think it's from the wife of Ernest's friend, Professor Kipping.' She clamped a cigarette between her lips then slipped her finger into the mouth of the envelope, cutting herself in her haste. She ignored the blood smudging on the paper as her eyes skittered across the single page.

'Lorenzo! Come quickly!' She ran from the dining room to the back garden and began turning in agitated circles, her bare feet scuffing the grass. 'Ernest is on his way to kill us . . . to shoot me!' She shook her head in disbelief. But Professor Kipping's wife was the sanest and most sensible woman in Nottingham. How could she possibly disbelieve Mrs Lily Kipping?

'Lorenzo? Where are you? Hurry! We have to leave. Ernest has bought a pistol!' She could hear the seconds and minutes snapping at her ankles, like the jaws of a vicious dog. Where was Lorenzo? He'd got up early, saying he wanted to write beneath the apple blossom, to feel the fluttering petals fall, coy and blushing, on his bare shoulders. Where was he?

'Ernest has really gone mad,' she shouted. 'He knows I met the children and now he is determined to shoot me!' She turned back to the letter. So this was it. Or had she misread it, misunderstood something?

She read it again . . . just to be sure.

Dear Frieda

I write for your own safety. The Weekley family found out about your meetings with the children. Apparently the children were so out of sorts they guessed something was amiss. Mrs Weekley interrogated poor Monty. Then they found your letter to Monty, which the poor boy dropped on the stairs, in his distress. Oh how my heart bleeds for the poor mites!

Mrs and Miss Weekley waited for Professor Weekley to come home on Friday evening and then presented him with your letter to Monty and the news of your clandestine meetings.

As you can imagine, Professor Weekley exploded. He threatened to shoot you. Yes – to shoot and kill you! Apparently he'd already bought himself a pistol.

His sister, Miss Maude Weekley, wrote directly to me as she has no address for you. I have tracked you down using every brain cell I possess, finally guessing that you were with Mr Lawrence's editor. I am begging you, Frieda, not to attempt any more meetings with your children. I could not forgive myself if he was to shoot you. Then he would surely be hanged and the children would be left as orphans.

This letter is too important for me to entrust to the postal service. I am delivering it by hand so I can be sure of getting it to you. By the time you receive it, I will be on a train back to Nottingham.

My dear husband has remained a staunch friend to poor Professor Weekley throughout this sorry episode, but I must tell you that we have never seen an angrier or more bitter man. Rest assured he's still kind and gentle with the children and he has tried hard to protect them, but Professor Kipping has found him to be most intractable on the subject of yourself. For this reason I urge you to take precautions for your personal safety.

Yours
Mrs Lily Kipping

Lorenzo appeared on the front lawn, scowling. 'What? Not another letter!'

Frieda passed it to him and drew anxiously on her cigarette while he read. His face flushed with anger as he held the sheet of paper in front of her and theatrically tore it in half. 'What rot! This is the final straw, Frieda. I can't take any more of this ridiculous drama.' He ripped the half sheets, again and again, then scattered the torn pieces over the grass. 'Now pick 'em up! I won't have you littering Edward's lawn.'

Frieda felt tears springing to her eyes. She knelt down on the grass and began scooping up the fragments of paper, squeezing them into a ball. Her cigarette hung from the corner of her mouth. She knew Edward Garnett was watching from the window of his study and she felt belittled, ashamed.

Lorenzo began circling her, moving with more and more speed. 'Put your legs together! Why are your legs always apart? Even when you're kneeling down! Close them! Close them! Everyone can see!' His thin voice grew louder and higher. 'And take that cigarette out of your mouth! Why can't you be without a cigarette for five minutes!'

Frieda could feel him closing in on her. His feet thudded as he orbited her. His circles became tighter and tighter until his shadow covered her entirely. When she had picked up all the pieces of Mrs Kipping's letter, she pushed them into her pocket, plunged her cigarette butt into the lawn and put her fingers in her ears.

'You're too fat now! Why d'you eat so much all the time? If Weekley came with a pistol, d'you really think I'd care?' Lorenzo jeered, pointing at her. 'I hope he brings his pistol and shoots you. And he can shoot me while he's at it!'

Frieda said nothing. Her eyes flickered round the front garden. On the edge of the terrace, beneath a straggling rhododendron, she saw a small terracotta pot. She took her fingers from her ears and spread her legs so that she was sitting comfortably on the cool grass. Lorenzo began dancing with rage, still circling her, his arms and legs jerking up and down. 'Stop looking at me like that! Get back on your knees and close your legs! Pick up that cigarette butt – now! Women have no souls! No souls!' He collapsed onto the grass, eyes closed, breathing hoarsely as if the effort of his anger had exhausted him.

As quick as a flash, Frieda jumped up and lunged for the terracotta pot. She resumed her position on the grass and put the flowerpot under her skirt. The sun was warm now and the dew had evaporated leaving the grass dry and scratchy against the soles of her feet. She had forgotten Ernest and his pistol. Forgotten the children. Forgotten everything except the pot beneath her skirt. She could feel its rough rim between her knees, pressing into her skin. Abrasive. Reassuring. Patient. Lorenzo started humming one of the Hebridean folk songs he'd been teaching her. His hands picked absently at the lawn as he hummed and his white feet beat out the rhythm.

'Come and lie beside me, my Queen Bee,' he murmured. 'Come and sing with me.'

Frieda slid across the grass until she was beside him. Silently, she removed the terracotta pot from beneath her skirt and held it behind her back. He reached out a hand in her direction. His eyes were still closed and the sun gave his face a golden hue, so that the red hairs in his beard glinted like threads of polished copper.

She lifted the pot above his head and then brought it down on his skull with all the force she could muster.

Lorenzo's head whipped round, his face blind with anger and shock. Shards of broken terracotta had snared themselves in his hair, his beard, his moustache. Larger fragments lay scattered over the grass. Blood trailed from his scalp, down the side of his face, down his neck and into his collar.

Frieda was just leaning over to inspect the wound when he started laughing. He grabbed her hand and pulled her back. 'Lie down and sing with me, Queen Bee. Let's see if we can rouse Garnett from his work with our dulcet tones.'

Her gaze strayed to Edward Garnett's window. He was standing there, framed by a pair of vermilion curtains, a look of bewildered dismay on his face. And later, much later, when he asked her how she bore Lorenzo's abuse, she paused, blinked and said, 'If you have lived with an artist, other men are just so boring.'

SEVENTY-TWO

Ernest

Ernest sat with his head in his hands. Everyone was asleep and the house was so quiet he could hear the wooden joists creaking as they expanded in the summer heat. Moths flung themselves against the dark window, making small slapping sounds. Outside, a solitary cart rumbled past. When Ernest finally lifted his head, he caught sight of himself reflected in the window. How old and weary he looked. Beneath his eyes were large pouches as commodious as travel bags. At the corners of his eyes and at the sides of his mouth were deep lines of loneliness. The skin of his neck seemed to hang in sorry folds. His fair hair was so thin and lacklustre he could barely see it. Did he have any hair left? He put a hand to his head, smoothed the remaining strands over his pate, and turned back to the half-written letter on his desk.

This was to be his final letter to Frieda. Then he would pass everything to his solicitor. A court order would follow, preventing her from seeing the children, ensuring he had sole custody forever. All this sneaking around Monty's school – it had to stop. Last week, Monty had told him about a lady with bobbed hair and a mysterious smile (Monty's words, not his) who kept popping out from behind trees with money and little notes. All from Frieda. According to Monty, the woman then chased him round the school insisting he take these 'gifts from your mother'. Monty politely explained that he wasn't allowed to accept gifts from strangers, but she continued pursuing him. Eventually Monty had complained to the headmaster, and the woman – some amoral, divorced New Zealander – had been escorted from the school. Whatever was Frieda thinking? Did she have no idea how absurd she was being? How improper and inappropriate her behaviour was?

Ernest picked up his pen and dipped it in the inkwell. And then he began writing . . .

You are no longer just dead to the children, but, as far as we are all concerned, a decomposed corpse.

He wouldn't put her name on it and nor would he sign it. He had no address for her so he would have to send it care of her mother, the Baroness. He folded the sheet and put it in an envelope. Anger rolled through him, as it did whenever he thought of her now. Sometimes he thought vitriol had replaced blood in his veins. An image of his body, cut open by a surgeon, came to him. His heart like a small prune. Dying embers where his lungs should be. Intestines full of grey ash. Testicles half-full of curdled milk. And his penis – like one of those flailing worms after he'd sliced through it with his spade.

The image of the worm pulled his thoughts back to his old garden, with its potatoes and tomatoes and orderly rows of beans and carrots. No energy for gardening now . . . the weekly commute, the long hours trying to keep his job, the miserable room he lodged in during the week. And then the weekends trying to be both mother and father to his children, placating Maude and his parents, marking his students' work, preparing the next book his publishers were pleading for. He glanced at the pistol lying in the open drawer of his desk. And for some reason, it soothed him. Such a small, neat thing with its carved handle. Such a purposeful object, he thought. He pushed the drawer closed, turned the key in its lock and then put the key in the palm of his hand. He scrutinised it and as he did so, images of Frieda swept through his head. Those green eyes with flecks of gold. Her rounded hips. The swell of her breasts. Her glorious thighs, like rolls of butter.

He felt his lips stretch and lift at the corners. How odd the movement felt . . . When had he last smiled? And he thought of her smile and her big boisterous laugh. The way she used to throw back her head and laugh with such abandon her fair hair came loose from her bun and fell around her face in wild tendrils. He felt the stiff muscles of his face ease. His smile stretched a little further. And then, quite suddenly, he remembered the one time he'd come home early from work. Pushing open the door of her bedroom. Seeing her naked body as pale as a church candle. Turning. Spinning. Her cushioned hips swivelling. The sun staring greedily through the window. His wife weaving round the room, a fringed silk shawl trailing from one gracious hand. Half toreador. Half Isadora Duncan. He'd been too embarrassed to speak, so he'd watched her with confused, mortified delight for a silent second. Then slunk away and never mentioned it. How free and beautiful she'd looked that day. His facial muscles yielded a little more. Perhaps he shouldn't have moved to a separate bedroom. Perhaps he should have paid her more attention. Not worked so hard. Perhaps. Perhaps. And he saw her again, her breasts bouncing as she leapt naked from the bed waving her fringed shawl and shimmying across the floor. And from somewhere deep inside him, he felt the early rumblings of laughter. It rose within him, caught in his throat and then spluttered forth – a small choking laugh.

He unlocked his desk and carefully lifted out the revolver. He turned it over slowly in his hand. He would throw it in the River Thames tomorrow. At first light. What on earth had possessed him to buy a revolver? What had sparked such madness in his brain? He looked at the letter. It wasn't kind, he knew that. To call her a decomposing corpse . . . they were not the words of a gentleman.

But he'd post the letter. At first light. It was to be his last letter and she must know the depths of his feelings. She must know that all this slinking around behind his back, accosting the children at school, sending strangers in pursuit of them – she must know that such behaviour was unacceptable.

Unacceptable. He repeated the word, rolled it around in his mouth, felt its syllables roll against his teeth, his tongue, let the word flop into his throat then bounce into the roof of his mouth. Unacceptable. From the Old French *acceptable*, he thought. And before that from the Latin *acceptabilis*, and before that undoubtedly from *acceptare*, meaning to take or receive willingly. He had taken Frieda willingly, accepted her for what she was. She had taken him willingly, received him into her welcoming arms. And now things had changed – but he must accept that. He must close that chapter of his life, accept and remember the good bits, let her go.

Acceptable. He said the word aloud. He liked the sound of it, the movement of his lips around the vowels and consonants. Every English word and every English name has travelled through a multitude of permutations, he thought. And in each one lies buried a rich seam of history, a well of myths, stories, geography, fact. To think of so much richness lying undiscovered in such ubiquity. He felt the hairs rising on his neck, was surprised to see goosebumps running down his forearms. It was time to turn his thoughts to his new book, an etymological guide to names. He would call it *The Romance of Names*. He nodded, gratified. Yes, it was a good title and would sit well alongside *The Romance of Words*.

When he looked back at the window he no longer saw his reflection. Instead he saw the first pale flush of sunrise. A blackbird sang from a branch immediately outside his room and its persistent melody cheered him. He took the pistol from his desk and put it in his pocket. He would take it to Hammersmith Bridge and hurl it into the dirty swirling waters of the Thames. Then he would come home and start work on *The Romance of Names*. As he slipped out of the front door, he thought about the origins of the word 'Thames'. The Romans had called it the *Tamesis* river. And before that it probably derived from the Celtic word *tamesas*, meaning dark. He smiled – for the first time in a year – and it felt good.

SEVENTY-THREE

Frieda

That same night, in Edward Garnett's garden, Frieda and Lorenzo lay entwined in a bed of green ferns. Moonlight cast a white glow over the grass and the glittering trunks of the silver birch trees. Behind them foxgloves and columbines thrust into the sky and tiny midges swarmed in clouds. A pair of owls hooted overhead.

'I want to write a novel about you and me.' Lorenzo stroked Frieda's hair as he gazed up at the moon. 'About love and sex and class and the desire for children. I want to write about the things that people think and want but dare not speak of. And about how man is destroying nature, destroying all this.' He swept his arm up to indicate the moon, the stars, the leaves that trembled above them.

'No one has your honesty or courage, Lorenzo.' Frieda curled her head into the hollow beneath his collarbone. She could hear the thud of his heart in her ear, feel the hard poles of his ribs beneath her throat.

'It'll be about two folk of very different classes who liberate each other, like we have. Through tenderness and passion.' He paused and pulled her closer into him. The cool air, heavy with the scent of moss and bracken, nestled round their naked bodies. 'I want it to be the most honest book ever written. Truthful and honest and pure.'

'Perhaps you could write about someone else, not me.' Frieda opened her eyes, surprised at her words. It wasn't that she didn't want to be another of his fictional characters, but more that she was beginning to feel like a dissected rabbit, that she had given him everything she had.

'No. It'll be you all right. But I'll soften you, make you less belligerent.'

She sighed, but it was a sigh replete with contentment. So the battle between them would go on, she thought. But he would take it to the pages of his books and there he would dominate her, have her surrender to him. She smiled to herself. She could live with that. She knew the truth. As did he. The truth was this book would never happen without her.

'I need you to force me to go deeper into the bowels of my soul.' He took a lock of her hair and curled it round his finger. 'And then I shall change the prissy English attitude to sex.'

'If only everyone could cast off the shackles of repression, as we have,' murmured Frieda, thinking suddenly of her old lover, Otto. She owed her new life to Otto. It was he who had brought her from the margins of life, liberated her, enabled her to liberate Lorenzo. Where was he now, she wondered.

'We must be married though, Frieda. The sanctity of marriage is important and I want you to be my wife.'

'Maybe,' she murmured. The owls had ceased their hooting and the silence seemed to yawn, full and black, around them in their ferny nest. She shivered. The air was cooling now and she could feel the raised hairs on Lorenzo's arms.

'We must be married,' he repeated, his voice a little harder, a little more brittle. 'I want the intimacy and nakedness of marriage.'

She closed her eyes and breathed in the smell of him. She'd seen spots of bright red blood on his handkerchief again this morning and noticed the faint smell of sickness on his breath. But she didn't want to think about that now. She wanted to think only of how she could help him achieve the great things he was destined for, before . . . before . . . No, she couldn't and wouldn't think about it.

'I can't write it without you, my empress. None of this is possible without you. I need you always beside me, Frieda. Always.'

Lines from one of his poems swam into her head . . . *Do not leave me, or I shall break . . . And God, that she is necessary . . . Necessary, and I have no choice. Do not leave me . . .*

'Hush, Lorenzo. I will never leave you. I promise.' She turned her face to his, felt the energy of him vibrating against her skin. This is my life now, she thought. Not my children, not my sorrow, not my sisters with their superior wealth and possessions, not the comforts of a nice home with a tidy garden.

'We'll be penniless, but we'll have enough. And we'll be truly alive – most vividly, most perfectly alive!' Lorenzo craned his head, tilting his ear towards the sky. 'It's a nightingale. Can you hear it?'

The song of the nightingale cut through the air, rising and falling in waves. And to Frieda its notes mirrored the landscape of her soul – persistent, resolute, strong. She would share her life with Lorenzo. She would give him everything except her soul. She would keep her own soul. And one day she would see her children again. And they would understand.

Epilogue

'It is one's self that matters,' she said.

'Whether one is being one's own self

and serving one's own God.'

D.H. Lawrence, *The Shades of Spring*

1927

His long pale fingers tugged at her sleeve. His chest – almost concave now – heaved and jerked. But his eyes were bird-bright, and seemed to leap in their sockets. As they always had done.

'I want to read you my new chapter, Frieda.' He gave a long rattling cough, then flopped back against the pillows.

'I am listening, my dear.' She settled herself beside him, cheerfully and calmly so that he wouldn't notice her disquiet. He'd left the house at eight, as he'd done every morning since he started writing his new novel. Or rather the third version of his new novel. From her bedroom window she had watched him lope slowly into the chestnut woods, a notebook under one arm, a paisley cushion under the other, an inkpot bulging from his torn jacket pocket. He always worked outside now, propped against the trunk of a tree or lying on a grassy bank. After he'd written three or four thousand words, he'd come home and crawl into bed, his pale emaciated arms shaking with exhaustion.

Then he'd start calling for her, in his high plaintive voice. Wanting to read his latest chapter to her, wanting her opinion. As he was doing now, in a voice that had lost none of its petulance or eagerness. Often he clutched at the air with his thin fingers, bent and rigid where he had gripped his pen too vigorously. She would put his fingers between hers, rub them loose and kiss their blunt roughened tips. Then she'd fatten his cushions, and smooth the damp hair from his face.

'Stop fiddling with me! Just listen.'

The room fell quiet but for the thumping of the typewriter in the kitchen below. He had hired a local typist to start the laborious job of turning his handwritten pages into a publishable manuscript and their afternoons were now accompanied by the punching of typewriter keys and the sharp whirr of the cartridge being flung back. Frieda liked the sound, in the same way she liked the boisterous flute-playing from next door and the raucous braying of mules from the track below. To her, they were the sounds of life, a constant reminder of its richness and promise.

She closed her eyes. 'I am ready, my dear.'

'This chapter is a love letter to you, Queen Bee. The whole damn book is a paean to you, but this chapter . . . well, you'll understand when you hear it.' He cleared his throat and started to read, slowly and steadily.

Frieda stiffened. Her eyes flew open. Her brows rose into her hairline. She turned and stared at him, her eyes growing wider and wider until her sockets hurt. He carried on reading in his slow steady voice, as if he hadn't noticed her reaction.

'Stop!' The word flung itself from her gaping mouth. 'You cannot say that, Lorenzo!'

He looked up from his notebook, his expression glazed and unfocused. As if he was no longer there, as if he'd left the little square room with its green shutters and its green bedhead painted with yellow roses, and was somewhere else entirely.

'No one who is sane will publish this,' she said, raising her voice a fraction.

He reached for her hand, his eyes half-closed. 'Do you remember the beech woods in Germany? Do you remember, my Queen Bee?'

Her face softened, she squeezed his hand and closed her eyes. Above her fluttered the raw green canopy of beech trees, beyond shone a pearly wedge of moon. She felt the damp pressed leaves, thick and pulpy, beneath her feet, beneath her spine. Smelled, again, the sap and bark of the forest. She smiled. 'How can I forget?'

There was a soft thud as his head fell back against the bolster. 'That was the happiest time of my life. I have fed – no, I have feasted – from that week for so long now. We called it our honeymoon, d'you remember?'

She nodded, running her fingers delicately through his hair. 'There will be more good times,' she murmured.

He said nothing, but she could hear his breath coming, hoarse and dry, and the soft gurgling in his lungs. After a few seconds his breathing settled and he whispered 'Why, oh why, did we quarrel so much?'

'How could we help it? We had been made violent creatures by all that was done to us.'

He nodded and gave another long grating cough, as if grit was dragging through his lungs.

'Rest a bit, then you can finish reading to me.' Her mind drifted back to the beech woods, and after a few seconds she started to laugh. Muffled and quiet at first, but then the laughter seemed to swell inside her so that it burst from her mouth in great gulps and snorts.

'Why are you laughing?' He lifted his head weakly from the bolster and opened one suspicious eye.

Her whole body was shaking. She was laughing so hard she could barely speak. Her words spluttered from her. 'Your skinny w-white buttocks flashing through the trees . . . And the bed full of leaves and mud . . . Were we mad?' She fell back against the bolsters, her hands clutching at her sides.

'We were mad with love.' A grin stretched slowly across his face. And then his mouth dropped open and he started to laugh. A thin reedy laugh that came from high in his chest. His legs curled up and his frail body rocked with mirth. Tears began to stream from his eyes and he beat his thin hands feebly against the mattress. Frieda rolled to and fro on the bed, her hands hugging her ribs, tears streaking down her cheeks. 'Oh so many good times!' she gasped. 'But your little white bottom . . . that was funny . . .'

After a few seconds, their laughter subsided and he began to cough. 'Enough!' she commanded. 'All this laughing is not good for you. I will make some tea.' She stood up, shook out her embroidered skirt, pulled up her long red socks and pushed her hair carelessly from her face. As she did so, she noticed how quiet it was. At first she could not work it out. It was uncannily quiet. Then she realised the typing had stopped. Perhaps the typist was making herself some tea.

'Who is coming up here, Queen Bee? I don't want to see anyone,' Lorenzo croaked, waving his arm vaguely at the door.

She heard the hurried hectic tread of someone on the stairs. She frowned. Had she invited someone to tea and forgotten?

The door burst open. It was the typist, her pink umbrella jabbing furiously at the air, her arms darting up and down at her sides. She hopped to and fro in the doorframe, the ends of her mouth dragging and twisting. As if she had a throat full of words but could not arrange them.

Frieda moved swiftly towards her. 'My dear girl, what is the matter?'

'Never, never can I type something so – so disgusting!' Her face blazed, her upper lip drew back in an outraged snarl. 'You – you insult me with this filth!' She turned on her heel and they heard the angry joust of her shoes on the wooden stairs.

He raised himself on one elbow and called out, weakly, 'It's a warm-hearted love story!'

The front door slammed and the glass panes rattled in the window frames.

Frieda glanced uncertainly at him. 'Who will type it now, my dear?'

He looked, beseechingly, at her.

'Oh no! You promised. All those years ago. I said I would never type any of your work and you said you would never ask me.'

'I haven't asked you,' he replied. 'But it's a bit of a bomb, a bit of a revolution.'

'So. No one will type it. And no one will publish it. And we have run out of money.'

He laughed gleefully, his eyes shining and his hands stirring feverishly on the quilt. 'I'm going to publish it myself. I'm going to fling it in the face of the world. We'll evade the censor morons, you'll see.'

'If that is what you want, then we must do it.' She thought back to his earlier book that had been banned and burnt, a thousand and eleven copies set alight by a public hangman in London. The news had been crushing, embittering. But time was running out now. She had an odd prescient feeling this might be his last work, his last great novel.

'I don't give a fig for the censors! Let those damn puritans smite me down. I hope it makes 'em howl. But for God's sake, don't let your mother see it.'

'She will never see it, I promise.'

'I'll have it bound in mulberry-coloured paper. And I shall draw a phoenix for the cover, a black phoenix.' He pulled himself upright, his eyes flickering a bright peacock blue. 'Let's drop a little bomb in the world's crinoline of hypocrisy, shall we?'

'If we cannot find someone to type it, how will we find someone to print it?'

'There's a printer in Florence. None of 'em can read, let alone understand English. And then I shall sell it myself!' He sounded so certain, so defiant, she caught his mood and clapped her hands with excitement, so that her silver bangles ran dazzlingly up and down her arms. But then he fell back against the headboard, a choking cough wracking his body, his bony hands slapping limply at his chest.

'Tea,' she said, decisively. 'And then you can read your new chapter of *Lady C* to me. And we shall remember all the good times we had, so many good times.'

As she laid out a tray with the red enamelled teapot and two chipped cups with their cracked saucers, she heard voices and laughter from outside and her heart leapt. She craned to look. Yes, it was Barby and Elsa returning from their trip to Florence, brown paper parcels clamped beneath their arms, yellow ribbons trailing from their new hats.

She reached to the top shelf where she kept her best porcelain, the teacups painted with honeysuckle and rimmed with gold leaf. She took down two cups and saucers and added them to the tray. She looked at the cluster of cups, chipped, cracked, opalescent, gold-leafed, and, for the first time, felt a profound contentment. It seemed to her as if each cup was an aspect of herself. A self that had been scattered and wounded for as long as she could remember. And yet a self that had, in spite of this, caught the light, shone like gold, twined and blossomed like a wildflower.

Her entire past, she reflected, had been a long arduous struggle to become herself. She had left Metz to find herself. Only to become Mrs Weekley, Ernest's snowflower. With Otto she had reclaimed herself. But only to forfeit it as Mrs Lawrence, as a multitude of fictional characters, palimpsests of herself, dredged from Lorenzo's imagination. And only to find that, without her children, she had been robbed of a vital piece of herself. For what was herself?

Her *self* had eluded her. She'd believed it was all that mattered. She'd believed that it took courage to find oneself, that its discovery would bring freedom. And yet her *self* had slipped, so often, through her fingers, throwing up other versions of herself. As if she'd lived all her life in a hall of mirrors. But now – with the company of her daughters and letters from Monty, with Lorenzo absorbed in his most daring novel and his rages subdued, with the Italian sun romping over the walls – now she felt a supreme gleaming triumph of infinity.

She put a small jar of wild rosemary on the tray, admiring its tiny purple flowers and breathing in its rich woody perfume. All these little insignificant things – laying a tray, listening to Lorenzo read, taking pleasure in the return of her girls – this was the vast marvel of life. This was herself.

She pushed open the window. Outside, the sun was a rose-pink circle, fading and falling slowly, drowsily, over the edge of the earth.

She waved at her daughters and they waved back, their parcels held aloft like trophies.

'Come and show me what you bought in Florence! Isn't it the most glorious city ever?'

Historical note

Frieda never accepted the loss of her children. She pursued them – in spite of Ernest's court order forbidding her access – until each came of age. At the age of twenty-one, Monty, Elsa and Barby were legally free to renew relations with her. All three chose to see her again.

Frieda's life with Lawrence has been well documented by her and by many others. After marrying in 1914, they travelled restlessly from country to country (a self-imposed exile that Lawrence termed his 'savage pilgrimage'), always in search of the sun and clean air necessary for Lawrence's health. They argued constantly, violently and publicly. Her readiness to fight back, according to Lawrence, enabled him to produce the huge volume of work for which he's now known.

Throughout many of Lawrence's works, a particular female character appears. Frieda was the model for this character, which includes Johanna Keighley in *Mr Noon*, Ursula Brangwen in *The Rainbow* and *Women in Love*, Tanny Lilly in *Aaron's Rod*, Harriet Somers in *Kangaroo*, Kate Leslie in *The Plumed Serpent* and Lady Chatterley in *Lady Chatterley's Lover* (a novel considered by many to be a love letter to Frieda). According to her first biographer, Robert Lucas, 'Possibly never before nor since has a great writer been so intensely and so permanently influenced by one woman as Lawrence was by Frieda von Richthofen . . . And certainly never before has one single woman, as interpreted by a poet, so radically changed the moral climate of her time.' Frieda also played an important role in the writing, editing and titling of Lawrence's most acclaimed novels (*Sons and Lovers*, *The Rainbow* and *Women in Love*) and his most infamous novel (*Lady Chatterley's Lover*).

Lawrence was neither Frieda's last husband nor her last lover. She embarked on an affair with their landlord, an Italian married father-of-three and soldier (twelve years her junior) called Angelo Ravagli, shortly before Lawrence died of tuberculosis. In a situation reminiscent of the Mr Dowson affair, she was godmother to Ravagli's third son. However, the first Mrs Ravagli seemed quite happy to relinquish Angelo in return for the financial security Frieda provided. Ravagli became Frieda's third, last and least faithful husband.

Frieda died from a stroke on her seventy-seventh birthday, in 1956. She was buried in Taos, New Mexico, beside the memorial chapel she had built in Lawrence's name and from cement supposedly mixed with Lawrence's ashes. Here, she finally reclaimed her own name: her husband had the von Richthofen coat of arms carved into her tombstone, after she chose it as the frontispiece of her autobiography, *Not I, But the Wind*.

ERNEST WEEKLEY

Ernest Weekley never remarried. He never saw or spoke of Frieda again. Nor was her name ever mentioned in his presence. Barby later said of Frieda's departure, 'It was a mortal blow to my father: he never recovered.' He later described this period of his life as his 'ten days of insanity'. But at the very end of his life, when Barby made a disparaging comment about the von Richthofen family, he suddenly said, 'Ah, but she was the best wasn't she?' After he died, a photograph of Frieda taken during her first pregnancy was found in his desk.

He left no written account of this period in his life. Instead, he was vilified through Lawrence's fictionalisation of him in works such as *Lady Chatterley's Lover* and *The Virgin and the Gypsy*. According to Victoria Manthorpe, 'In a covert but far more powerful way Lawrence destroyed him.'

And yet Professor Ernest Weekley was an exceptional man. Initially self-educated through night schools and correspondence courses, he was an eminent linguist and etymologist. His popular books on language (including *The Romance of Words* and *The Romance of Names*) made him a household name. He spent his entire career at Nottingham University (previously University College Nottingham), never making it to Cambridge after the scandal of his wife's departure. Out of respect to Professor Weekley, Nottingham University refused to add Lawrence's novels to the curriculum until he retired. During his lifetime he wrote many pioneering books on etymology, grammar and linguistics, most of which have never been out of print and can still be bought today.

ELISABETH JAFFÉ-RICHTHOFEN

Elisabeth was known throughout her life as Else but I have used her full name to avoid confusion with Frieda's daughter, Elsa. Although her marriage to Edgar Jaffé fell apart, her affairs with both Alfred and Max Weber continued until their deaths. Indeed both she and Max's wife, Marianne Weber, nursed Max Weber through his final illness and were with him when he died. Elisabeth's affair with Max Weber remained secret until her death when she had stipulated that her love letters to and from him could be made public. Despite the many years that had passed, Germany was shocked to discover that one of its most distinguished philosophers and the founding father of sociology had led such a complicated double life.

JOHANNA (NUSCH) VON SCHREIBERSHOFEN NEE VON RICHTHOFEN

Nusch's first marriage, like that of both her sisters, crumbled as her husband began gambling and womanising in the pattern of the Baron von Richthofen. She married again, but lived out her final days in poverty, relieved only by contributions from Frieda whose old age was made financially secure by the endless royalties from Lawrence's estate.

EDGAR JAFFÉ

Edgar Jaffé continued his illustrious political and economic career, eventually becoming a minister in the 1918–19 Bavaria Soviet Republic. A nervous breakdown – from which he never recovered – then ended his political career. He died in 1921 and is now considered one of the key players in the erotic movement that unfolded in Munich and Ascona at the beginning of the twentieth century.

DOCTOR OTTO GROSS

The relationship between Doctor Otto Gross and Frieda has been described by Lawrence biographer Brenda Maddox as 'an important event in the history of the erotic movement', because of its consequences for literature and censorship. Otto Gross, who is thought to have coined the term 'sexual revolution' and who featured as a character in the 2011 film *A Dangerous Method*, was considered one of the most intelligent and creative psychoanalysts of his time. Both Freud and Jung considered him a protégé, perhaps the most obvious person to forward and develop their ideas. However, his commitment to anarchism, his linking of psychoanalysis with radical politics, and his extensive drug use eventually made him a liability and both Jung and Freud washed their hands of him, deleting his name from publications and, according to Gross's biographer, 'writing him out of history'. After stints in various hospitals (both as a patient and a doctor), Gross was found on the streets of Berlin in 1920, near-starved and freezing. He died of pneumonia shortly after, although his grave has never been found.

Gross was an extraordinary man – 'a catalyst for radical change, who played a pivotal role in the birth of modernism,' according to Gross scholar, Dr Gottfried Heuer. He was the first person to develop a theory of personality types (which he allegedly worked on with Frieda), later adopted by Jung as 'his famous introvert-extrovert classification' (Martin Green, *The von Richthofen Sisters*). Gross deserves to be remembered.

DAVID HERBERT LAWRENCE

Lawrence (Lorenzo as Frieda called him) died of tuberculosis in 1930 at the age of forty-four. In his short life he wrote more prolifically than almost any other writer – poems, plays, travel books, essays, literary criticism, short stories, novels (many of which were made into films) and thousands of letters. He also painted.

More has been written about Lawrence than perhaps any other writer (over one thousand books at the last count), with many hailing him as a genius, some hailing him as a sexual revolutionary, and others as an outdated misogynist. Many of his novels showcased Frieda's life and sexual liberation to generations of readers, in particular *The Rainbow, Women in Love* and *Lady Chatterley's Lover*. But the works that best document his early experiences with Frieda are *Mr Noon* (a novel not published in its entirety until 1984), the play *A Fight for Barbara*, and the volume of poems he titled *Look! We Have Come Through!*

Of Lawrence's suspected homosexuality, Frieda wrote, 'I think [it] was a short phase – I fought him and won.' The debate about his sexuality continues.

Lawrence was an extremely complicated man. Accounts of his life make enthralling – and sometimes barely believable – reading and I urge you to read more.

MONTAGUE WEEKLEY

Monty Weekley set up and ran the V&A Museum of Childhood in Bethnal Green, London. He remained there for the rest of his working life. He married and had two children but spoke rarely of his childhood or his mother, although he and Frieda corresponded regularly in later life. More recently, his son (Frieda's grandson) was reported in a national newspaper article tellingly entitled 'The Loveless Legacy of Frieda Lawrence', as saying Monty 'took it very badly . . . it left a lasting fear of ever forming a relationship.'

BARBARA WEEKLEY

Barby Weekley became a translator, had a family and lived in Italy. Of all three children, she was the one most like Frieda. As a teenager she was expelled from St Paul's Girls' School in London for drawing naked men in her maths book. She was the only Weekley child to fully renew relations with her mother and to forge any relationship with Lawrence. Her subsequent nervous breakdown and depression were noted in private letters, including those of Lawrence.

ELSA WEEKLEY

Elsa married a naval officer and had a family. She remained steadfastly loyal to Ernest, looking after him in her London home until his death. She rarely wrote to her mother and visited her only once in Italy.

FANNY ZU REVENTLOW

The Countess Franziska zu Reventlow is now recognised as one of the more radical voices in the early European women's movement as it unfolded at the turn of the twentieth century. She believed that the suffragette movement, with its emphasis on political freedom, was doing a disservice to women. The abolition of marriage and sexual freedom, were, she argued, the key to female liberation. Known as the Bohemian Countess of Schwabing, she was a single mother, writer, artist and translator who wrote several novels based on her Schwabing experiences, spent considerable time in Ascona, kept her own name when she married, and lived in a ménage-à-trois later immortalised in the Roché novel and Truffaut film, *Jules et Jim*. It was Fanny who, according to Elisabeth, 'inspired Frieda to follow her path toward erotic freedom' (Martin Green, *The von Richthofen Sisters*).

MAX WEBER

Max Weber was a sociologist, economist, historian, philosopher, scholar, jurist and writer, now considered one of Germany's greatest historic thinkers and the founding father of sociology.

NOTTINGHAM, MUNICH AND ASCONA

At the time of the events related here, Nottingham, Munich and Ascona were, to varying degrees, very different from the places they are today. Nottingham was a heavily industrial town in the heart of an area renowned for its collieries and pits, a landscape brilliantly portrayed in much of Lawrence's writing.

Munich ranked second only to Paris, as an avant-garde city, with its suburb of Schwabing attracting writers, artists and 'free thinkers' from all over Europe. Many of these bohemians travelled regularly between Munich and Ascona in Switzerland, where an area known as Monte Veritá ('mountain of truth') was established as a colony for those wanting to explore new ways of living. The colony embraced vegetarianism, nudism and cooperative living. Conventional politics, religion and institutions were rejected, including marriage. Many well-known names are thought to have spent time here, including Max Weber, Herman Hesse, Carl Jung, Isadora Duncan, Rudolf Steiner and Paul Klee. Daphne du Maurier famously fictionalised Monte Veritá in her short story of the same name.

THE BANNING OF LAWRENCE'S BOOKS

D.H. Lawrence is sometimes known as the patron saint of banned books – and for good reason.

In 1915, *The Rainbow* was banned for eleven years. Described as a 'mass of obscenity', it was the Frieda-inspired lesbian scene that most outraged the censors.

In 1928, *Lady Chatterley's Lover* was banned for over thirty years. It wasn't until 1960 when Penguin won a landmark case that the full, unexpurgated text of *Lady Chatterley's Lover* could be read in the UK (in Australia the ban continued until 1965). The book sold more than thirty million copies in the three months following the trial – a trial in which the Crown Prosecutor famously asked, 'Is it a book you would wish your wife or your servant to read?'

In 1929, a typescript of Lawrence's poetry collection, *Pansies*, was seized and destroyed by the English postal authorities for being 'indecent'.

In the summer of 1929, a London exhibition of Lawrence's paintings was forced to close because the paintings showed pubic hair. The books accompanying the exhibition were destroyed. More insidiously, many of his novels and poems were effectively censored when publishers – fearing government intervention or censorship by public lending libraries – asked for edits, cuts and revisions. For example, ten thousand words were removed from *Sons and Lovers*, mostly to do with perceived 'decency'. Meanwhile many of his war poems were censored for political reasons, and only published in their unexpurgated entirety one hundred years after he wrote them.

Author's note

After writing my first biographical novel, *The Joyce Girl*, which ends with the protagonist never achieving the freedom she so longed for, I wanted to explore a true story with a very different outcome. Like many, I knew of Frieda as 'the woman who left her children to run away with Lawrence'. And yet as I became more and more immersed in the early lives of Frieda and Lawrence, this appeared to be fallacious. The myth of Frieda and Lawrence's elopement is indeed compelling. But the truth (as I interpreted it) was very different. This is my story of Frieda as a mother.

The British child custody laws of the time were draconian. A woman found guilty of adultery and divorced by her husband could be entirely deprived of access to her children. In many cases, women divorced by their husbands and identified as the 'guilty' party had the same legal status as children and 'lunatics'. When Ernest saw how determined Frieda was to see her children, he obtained a court order forbidding her from seeing them. She was not, therefore, a woman 'leaving her children'. She was a woman who believed in her right to choose her own life and, as a result, was denied access to her children.

How did she end up in this situation? Because her hand had been forced by the letter of confession Lawrence sent to Ernest, without her agreement. It seems Lawrence was fully aware of the effect his letter would have in bringing events to a head. In a letter to Frieda at this time, he wrote, chillingly, 'I got your letter and Ernest's this morning. In Ernest's, as in mine, see the men combining in their freemasonry against you.'

While initially sympathetic, Lawrence became increasingly enraged at Frieda's devastation over the loss of her children. Meanwhile, Ernest played his part by using the full force of the law to punish his errant wife.

Throughout my research I was struck by the depth of feeling Frieda inspired in the significant men of her life. Ernest's refusal to marry again, Gross's letters to her (which moved me to tears), Lawrence's poems about her, were all testament to her personality. Her courage, resilience and fearlessness seemed to be quite remarkable, particularly so in the historical context in which they must be seen.

Although *Frieda* is a novel of the imagination, melding fact and fiction (often inspired by Lawrence's own writings), I have broadly followed the biographical outline of Frieda's life during this period. However, I have taken two major liberties, mainly to aid narrative flow. Firstly, her affair with William Dowson took place *before* she met Otto, but to emphasise the impact of Otto Gross on her life and to better show the arc of her journey of sexual liberation I decided to place it after her undisputedly significant sexual awakening with Gross in Munich in 1907.

Secondly, Frieda also had a short affair with Swiss anarchist and artist, Ernst Frick, in 1911, eight months before she met Lawrence. There are very few facts known about this affair and while that makes it ripe for a novelist, I wanted to show the way in which Gross's ideas fed (via Frieda) directly into Lawrence's work. I felt including the Frick affair would have impeded the pace of the novel and diluted the Gross-Lawrence connection. Frieda is also thought to have had two sexual encounters with other men during the early days of her relationship with Lawrence. While included in earlier drafts of *Frieda*, I subsequently removed them. Mainly to keep the plot tight. Partly (sadly) for other reasons. While women's freedom has made huge strides in the last hundred years, the sexual freedom of mothers has advanced less rapidly.

For readers wanting to fully unpick fact from fiction, there exists a huge wealth of Lawrence-Frieda information. Like all writers of biographical fiction I am hugely indebted to the painstaking work undertaken by the writers, scholars and biographers who came before me (of which there are many). I read many, many works but relied most heavily on the following and have no hesitation in recommending any of them:

Not I, But the Wind – Frieda Lawrence

Frieda Lawrence: The Memoirs and Correspondence – ed. E.W. Tedlock

A Genius for Living: A Biography of Frieda Lawrence – Janet Byrne

Frieda Lawrence – Robert Lucas

Living at the Edge: A Biography of D.H. Lawrence & Frieda von Richthofen – Michael Squires and Lynn K. Talbot

D.H. Lawrence and Frieda: A Portrait of Love and Loyalty – Michael Squires

The von Richthofen Sisters: The Triumphant and the Tragic Modes of Love – Martin Green

Mountain of Truth – Martin Green

Frieda Lawrence – Rosie Jackon

Lawrence's Women – Elaine Feinstein

D.H. Lawrence: The Story of a Marriage – Brenda Maddox

D.H. Lawrence: The Life of an Outsider – John Worthen

Triumph to Exile 1912–1922 – Mark Kinkead-Weekes

Frieda Lawrence and her Circle: Letters to, from and about Frieda – Harry T. Moore & Dale Montagu

Experiments: Lectures on Lawrence – John Worthen

D.H. Lawrence: A Composite Biography – Edward Nehls

Freud's 'Outstanding' Colleague – Gottfried M. Heuer

Selected Works 1901–1920 – Otto Gross

The Romance of Words – Ernest Weekley

The Romance of Names – Ernest Weekley

Munich: Its Golden Age of Art and Culture 1890–1920 – Reiner Metzger

The Era of German Expressionism – Paul Raabe

Ernest Weekley, Biography with Intent – Victoria Manthorpe (unpublished MA dissertation, UEA, 2003)

Lawrence's own work was, of course, critical to my understanding of both him and Frieda. In particular:

Sons and Lovers

The Rainbow

Women in Love

The Lost Girl

Mr Noon

The Fight for Barbara

Lady Chatterley's Lover

The Virgin and the Gypsy

Twilight in Italy

The Complete Poems of D.H. Lawrence (particularly the volume Look! We have Come Through!)

Collected Letters of D.H. Lawrence

Love Among the Haystacks and Other Pieces

Fantasia of the Unconscious

The Collected Short Stories

Where relevant I have inserted quotes (or entire letters in some cases) from the letters and writings of Gross, Lawrence, Weekley and the von Richthofen sisters into the novel's text.

Acknowledgements

I would like to thank the following biographers and scholars who generously gave their time answering my questions: Dr Gottfried Heuer, Professor John Worthen, Victoria Manthorpe, Dr Rosie Jackson, Dr Julia Launhard and Dr Howard Bailes.

I would also like to thank my early readers, agents and professional editors for their invaluable feedback: Barbara Abbs, Claire Baldwin, Thomasin Chinnery, Alex Craig, Lisa Dart, Sharon Galant, Annie Harris, Celine Kelly, Kate Lowe, Nina Oden, Benython Oldfield, Clare Stevenson-Hamilton, John Worthen.

Thanks are due also to the following libraries: the British Library; the Manuscript and Special Collections at the University of Nottingham; and Gladstone's Library where I completed the final edit of this novel. Thanks, too, to the generous strangers who let me look around the homes that Lawrence, Frieda and the Weekleys inhabited during this time, most of which are still standing.

I would like to express my huge gratitude to everyone at Hachette Australia, particularly Rebecca Saunders and Karen Ward, who worked tirelessly to make this happen. In the UK, I would like to thank everyone at Two Roads – Lisa Highton, Rachael Duncan and Emma Petfield – for their unwavering enthusiasm and support, and special thanks to Becky Glibbery for the beautiful cover design.

'The one duty we owe to history is to rewrite it.'

Oscar Wilde 1891

Also by Annabel Abbs

The Joyce Girl

Paris, 1928.

Avant-garde Paris is buzzing with the latest ideas in art, music, dance and literature. Lucia, the talented and ambitious daughter of James Joyce, is making her name as a dancer, training with some of the world's most gifted performers. When Samuel Beckett starts working for her father Lucia falls deeply in love, believing her destiny is marriage. But when her beloved brother is enticed away, the hidden threads of the Joyces' lives begin to unravel, destroying Lucia's dreams and foiling her attempts to escape the shadow of her genius father.

1934.

Her life in tatters, Lucia is sent to pioneering psychoanalyst Carl Jung. For years she has kept quiet. Now she decides to speak.

'A hugely impressive debut. Annabel Abbs has brought to life an extraordinary cast of characters – Joyce, Beckett et. al – and painted their rackety, bohemian world in vivid technicolour.'

Observer

About the Author

Annabel Abbs lives in London with her husband and four children. Her bestselling debut novel, *The Joyce Girl*, won the Impress Prize for New Writers and was longlisted for the Bath Novel Award, the Waverley Good Read Award and the Caledonia Novel Award.